THE FRONTIER OF VENGEANCE:
THE COMPLETE NORTHWOODS
STORIES OF FREDERICK NEBEL,
VOLUME 2

FREDERICK NEBEL

THE FRONTIER OF VENGEANCE: THE COMPLETE

NORTHWOODS

STORIES OF
FREDERICK NEBEL

INTRODUCTION BY
ROB PRESTON

PRIMARY ILLUSTRATOR
GEORGE H. WERT

COVER ILLUSTRATOR
H.C MURPHY

ALTUS
PRESS

2022

© 2022 Altus Press, an imprint of Steeger Properties, LLC • First Edition—2022

SERIES EDITOR
Rob Preston

PUBLISHING HISTORY

"Introduction" appears here for the first time. Copyright © 2022 Rob Preston. All rights reserved.

"The Frontier of Vengeance" originally appeared in the December 8, 1926–January 22, 1927, issues of *North•West Stories*.

"Trail Tales of the North: The Lovable Tramp" originally appeared in the December 22, 1926 issue of *North•West Stories*.

"Courage of the Strong" originally appeared in the March 22, 1927 issue of *North•West Stories*.

"A Man Must Fight" originally appeared in the April 22, 1927 issue of *North•West Stories*.

"Return of the Exile" originally appeared in the July 8, 1927 issue of *North•West Stories*.

"The Raw White Edge" originally appeared in the October 8, 1927 issue of *North•West Stories*.

"It Takes a Man" originally appeared in the October 22, 1927 issue of *North•West Stories*.

THE FRONTIER OF VENGEANCE:
THE COMPLETE

NORTHWOODS

STORIES OF
FREDERICK NEBEL

INTRODUCTION BY
ROB PRESTON

PRIMARY ILLUSTRATOR
GEORGE H. WERT

COVER ILLUSTRATOR
H.C MURPHY

2022

SERIES EDITOR

Rob Preston

PUBLISHING HISTORY

"Introduction" appears here for the first time. Copyright © 2022 Rob Preston. All rights reserved.

"The Frontier of Vengeance" originally appeared in the December 8, 1926–January 22, 1927, issues of *North•West Stories*.

"Trail Tales of the North: The Lovable Tramp" originally appeared in the December 22, 1926 issue of *North•West Stories*.

"Courage of the Strong" originally appeared in the March 22, 1927 issue of *North•West Stories*.

"A Man Must Fight" originally appeared in the April 22, 1927 issue of *North•West Stories*.

"Return of the Exile" originally appeared in the July 8, 1927 issue of *North•West Stories*.

"The Raw White Edge" originally appeared in the October 8, 1927 issue of *North•West Stories*.

"It Takes a Man" originally appeared in the October 22, 1927 issue of *North•West Stories*.

TABLE OF CONTENTS

INTRODUCTION BY ROB PRESTON

THIS IS a book of Frederick Nebel firsts: his first published story, his first series character, his first long novelettes (in a career filled with many of this length), and the first volume of his collected Northwestern yarns.

He broke into the rough paper fiction writing field with "Trade Law" in the July 1925 issue of *North•West Stories*. Nebel wrote in the September 10, 1928, issue of *Short Stories:*

> At sixteen or so I went off on a spree into the Canadian Northwest. It was in the springtime. I came home late in the fall and fell back on the railroads to make a living. Then I wandered off into the South for a spell. Back-trailed and struck west, getting as far a Tejon, Colorado. Then east again and then north again, up through Ontario and on up through Manitoba. Back to Montreal with a ticket to New York and a quarter to squander on three meals. Another job to jack up the battered bankroll that never was. Threw up that and bought a Corona and wrote steadily, for four months, almost day and night, gathering the most sweetly worded rejections slips on record.

Time has erased all knowledge of who these rejection slips were received from, but certainly some of them were from Fiction House. The hard work paid off and his first sale would lead to just over a hundred story sales—long and short—to Fiction House over the next six years.

At the start of his writing days he was published as Lewis Nebel, but within a few months the yarns begin to appear under his full name. It isn't for a few years that he finally dropped his middle name, or in many cases just shortened it to an "L."

Northwestern yarns were obviously a genre that Nebel held an affinity for, as every one of these stories has strong plotting and a rapid fire—though not frantic—pace along with excellent dialogue that many fledgling writers struggle with. A signature writing style that would come to the forefront with his well-known series characters for the detective pulps was already here at the beginning, just in a slightly rawer form. More importantly these tales were a vehicle to showcase rough, elemental, action-oriented men. These sort of characters continued to appear throughout his entire career writing for the pulps.

Can you hear the blizzard blowing in? Can you see the pulse of the northern lights? In your mind, put on your *capote*, strap on the snowshoes, get your mitts on. It is time to get on the trail and face the coming storm. There is an enemy to be faced, a girl to be saved, a vendetta to be settled. There is not a better place to do it than from the comfort of your easy chair reading this groundbreaking collection.

THE FRONTIER OF VENGEANCE

A NEW, POWERFUL, GRIPPING NOVEL OF THE GREAT NORTH WOODS—OF MERCILESS, THUNDERING NATURE IN THE RAW—OF A WHITE MAN'S NERVE WHEN ALL THE CARDS ARE STACKED AGAINST HIM—AND AN ALLURING GIRL

THE OIL lamp, suspended from a rafter, shone on the faces of two men seated in the snug living-room of the little house adjoining the trade-store on Windy Creek. They faced each other across a table covered with a cloth of picturesque Indian design. One was patently a man of the wilderness. The other was not. Pellets of wind-driven snow clattered against the window panes; the wind itself sang in a wild, high key, throaty as a trumpet, shrill as a fife.

The man of the wilderness was saying, "Well, Mr. Devlin, it will mean a trade-war, it will."

"Well... and what of it?"

"They're kind of nasty things to start, I mean."

"Yes," nodded the man Devlin, "if left unfinished. But anything I start, my dear Mr. Pitney, I likewise finish. Lankford must be driven out! I've talked terms to him, offered him a fair price, but he is as stubborn as a jackass. Fort Surprise is, I tell you, a serious drain on the very life blood of the Bay West Company. It has been for years, but none of my predecessors had the initiative or the ability to concentrate on it. Why, you yourself should have taken steps toward that end. A dozen years you have been with the Company on Windy Creek and, I understand, eighteen years altogether in its employ. And believe me, a mighty comfortable station you have. But mark me! If your trade keeps dropping the way it has been for the past three years you may find yourself out of a job."

Inspector Devlin punctuated this by taking a flat-handed crack at the table.

"Sure," replied Sam Pitney, "the Company wouldn't go an' kick out a man that's served 'em so long; a man that's laid trails, kept peace 'tween the Injuns an' the Company—"

"The Company," cut in Devlin, tapping his chest, "will discharge any man I have a mind to indicate. What's more, I am very much in favor of young blood at out stations. But never mind that. We deviate from the issue. Do not think that because I am on my first tour of the posts that I haven't business acumen. I have made, let me insert, a thorough, analytical study of the fur business, and I know precisely what I am talking about. With Fort Surprise in our hands, or at least out of the hands of anyone else, the business at your post will increase, say, five hundred per cent. In the event that it does, it is likely that I will recommend to headquarters a bonus in your favor and possibly a cozy increase in salary. But at present, my dear Mr. Pitney, your footing with the Company is very precarious—very shaky. A little move—and out you go—out, quite out, you understand."

Devlin sat back with an important frown, inserted a cigarette between his teeth, rolled the ends of his small, blond mustache. He was slim, neat, straight-backed, good-looking in a sleek, highly-polished way, and officious—very, very officious. He knew the fur business from A to Z—according to his own fine estimate. In a warm, well-appointed apartment in Winnipeg he had read about it. His uncle had advised him along that line.

His uncle, you ought to know, was a big man in the Company whose dictum, backed by his money, went a long way. In most things he was a man foursquare, but he also had his faults, and one of them was an inclination to dote on Devlin, to treat him as a spoiled son, himself being a bachelor. Hence Devlin had spent six months in the Winnipeg office, when his old uncle had granted him his request to go into the North as a post inspector, hoping this would enable his nephew to get close to the fur game in the rough so that he would be in line for a dignified office with the Company in later years.

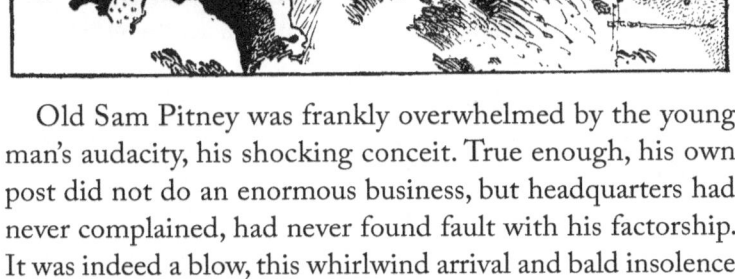

Old Sam Pitney was frankly overwhelmed by the young man's audacity, his shocking conceit. True enough, his own post did not do an enormous business, but headquarters had never complained, had never found fault with his factorship. It was indeed a blow, this whirlwind arrival and bald insolence of Devlin.

He had always considered his future with the Company secure. He had never had cause to believe otherwise. But this new, sudden turn in events caused vague, unpleasant pictures to loom up in his mind's eye. He could not afford to be thrown, in his advanced, somewhat palsied years, upon the cold mercy of the merciless wilds. He couldn't. Oh, there were reasons— plenty of them.

His old heart thumped irregularly. His head pained a bit. He wished he were ten years younger. He was only fifty-five, but he felt older, looked older. He was a small wisp of a man, with faded blue eyes and snowy hair, gnarled and bent and twisted by an arduous existence. He had to limp around with the aid of a stick. During his first year at Windy Creek he had been caught in an avalanche, and his leg, broken, had not repaired favorably. The manhood in him rebelled at Devlin's words, but caution, the product of age, held him in check, made him look ahead. For he had to look ahead. There were reasons—reasons....

"Well," he sighed vaguely, and then sucked on his pipe in silence.

Devlin said, "We will make things damned uncomfortable for this man Lankford. I have a number of ideas. To begin with, as an experiment, you will begin to pay more for pelts. You will send men out to the traplines to circulate this news and have them close the deals right on the spot, wherever possible. Draw freely on your reserve stock of trade-goods, and make offers that will indebt your white and Indian trappers for one or two years to come. Another thing: make it a point to send your men to those trappers who have made it a practice to trade in at Fort Surprise. We can afford to pay higher prices than Lankford, as he is merely an independent trader with no great financial backing to speak of. By God, we will break the man, crush him, grind him down and out, one way or the other!"

Old Pitney listened with his eyes glued vacantly on the table-cover. Somehow Devlin's words came to him as if from afar. He could not seem to realize clearly the portent of the insidious plan into which, through the cruel force of circumstances, he was being drawn. Here was a young man striving for glory; a cock-sure, ruthless, unscrupulous young man ready to break the law, ready to exert force against a rival post, ready to shed blood—for surely it would come to that in the end.

He found himself saying, absently, "The law...."

And Devlin snapped, "The law be damned!"

Outside, at this moment, the sharp yelps of sledge-dogs commingled with the tumult of wind and snow.

"Who's that?" asked Devlin.

"It's—wait'll I see."

The factor, gripping his cane, rose laboriously and limped to the door. He pulled it open, and a cloud of snow was whipped in by the vicious wind. Then a girl, muffled in furs, appeared out of the mottled gloom, assisted by an Indian. Pitney took her from the Indian, and the latter, grinning, muttered a greeting in dialect, backed out and closed the door with the same movement.

Devlin stood up, took a drag at his cigarette and snapped it into the wood-box by the stove. Pitney was helping the girl remove her furs.

"You're kind of late, Judy," he drawled, kindly.

"The storm, dad, held us up a bit. I didn't mean to be."

"That's all right. Expected it would."

He hung her furs on a peg in the wall, while she stood where he had left her, just inside the door, rubbing her hands and staring fixedly across the room.

"'Spect you'll be hungry," Pitney ventured as he came back and took her arm. "I'll have Annie rustle some grub, if you'll just sit down by the stove here an' warm your feet an' all. I'll take off your moccasins and fetch out your slippers. Oh… here." He looked at Devlin. "Shake hands with Mr. Devlin, Judy. He's the new inspector. This is my daughter, Mr. Devlin."

Judy held out her hand but did not move, and stared straight ahead. Pitney caught Devlin's eye and touched a finger to his own eyes. Devlin made a round "O" of astonishment with his mouth and took a step forward, grasping the girl's outstretched hand.

"I can't see you, Mr. Devlin, but—"

"I understand the situation perfectly, Miss Pitney," put in the inspector gracefully. "I am mighty glad to meet you. Your father did not tell me he had such a pretty daughter."

She smiled at this, a delicious, white-toothed smile.

"I've been to the mission doctor. He's twenty miles away, and when he cannot come here I have to go there. He's trying his best to bring back my sight, but"—there was a slight catch in her throat—"I doubt if he'll ever succeed."

"Unfortunate—most unfortunate," Devlin hurried on. "You have always been this way?"

"Not always—no. It came about a year ago. I came back from school in the 'Peg, and my eyes were very weak, then, and gave me a great deal of pain—probably from too much studying and reading. I was warned I might go blind. Then one day I was out when the snow-glare was awful, and that really completed my loss of sight."

"Oh, I see! Well, let us hope for the best. Let us hope the doctor will give the use of your eyes to you again. There is nothing like hope. It has conquered worlds. Without hope one becomes desolate and resigned to one's fate. Believe that you will see again. It is half the game."

"I am trying hard," she said.

Pitney hobbled into the kitchen, roused Annie, the Indian cook, and came back into the sitting-room cramming fresh tobacco into his pipe. Devlin had assisted Judy into a rocking-chair by the stove. There was a smouldering light in his eyes—subdued, but there nevertheless. He was bending and removing her moccasins. He was very solicitous, and a carefully regulated gentleness had crept into his voice.

Pitney, perplexed at the swift change in the man's manner, stood for a moment scratching his snowy head and then went off to get Judy's slippers. In the next room, bending to pick them up, he remained on one knee in a thoughtful attitude. He wondered if Judy would ever be able to see again. At thought of her being forever blind he shuddered.

In his simple, undemonstrative way he loved his daughter. Last summer he had sent her south to a doctor, paid staggering doctor bills, and she had returned hopeless, unable to see. He was willing to pay more bills, willing to put himself in pawn if by so doing he could help to bring back her sight. Even now his supply of cash was low. And here was Devlin hunting glory, telling him he might be discharged!

He would have to bow to the inspector's demands. He couldn't do otherwise. He was old, half-crippled, unable to stand the rigor of the trail. If he should be discharged he would become penniless in short time. And what would become of Judy?

With a sigh he returned to the sitting-room. Devlin took the slippers from his hands and put them on Judy's' feet.

Annie, so fat she could hardly move, oozed out of the kitchen and placed a steaming meal on the table. Devlin drew up a chair and guided Judy toward it with great gentleness. Then he dropped into the rocking-chair she had vacated by the stove and was able to see her face in profile. He studied her through a screen of smoke from his cigarette. His eyes dreamed. She was exquisitely beautiful, a rare Northland flower, clean and fresh and pure as virgin snow.

She said to her father, "We met two men at the forks, dad. They were bound for Fort Surprise, and they said they had two black fox skins. One I knew. You know him too. Jean Cyriac."

"Cyriac? Yes, Judy—sure I know Jean. He trades in at Surprise regular. Other one a stranger, huh?"

"Yes. He didn't speak much. He was having some trouble with the lead-dog. His voice was low and rather deep, and I was trying my best to place it when Jean said, 'This is M'sieur Burr—Jeem Burr.'"

"Burr?" This from Devlin, in a quick tone that made Judy turn her face in his direction instinctively.

"Yes. I'm sure that was it—Jim Burr," she repeated. "You know him?"

"N-no. Thought you said something else. Pardon my interrupting."

Pitney had looked at him, too, and he saw color rising to the man's cheeks—saw a somewhat agitated, baffled expression in his eyes. But the old trader said nothing. He leaned back in his chair and blew a stream of smoke ceilingward—and gazed after the smoke with meditative eyes.

CHAPTER II

TWO MEN FROM THE BARRENS

FAR FROM their birthplace on the frozen roof of the world the vagabond winds, slashing across the naked ice-fields and barren tundra of the arctic wastes, at last found stubborn resistance in the mighty forests of Prince Rupert's land. Here they boomed like thunder among the sturdy spruces, roared bull-throated through the wooded valleys, screamed madly over the hoary, crenelated ridges, and sought to beat down the grim battalions of the earth that had withstood their devastating onslaughts for centuries. It was their last mass attack of the long white winter, and all the fury, all the unearthly malevolence of the wilds, were in that fight.

The two travelers, realizing the nearness of a warm shelter, had not stopped to make a camp at nightfall. No shelter they might have constructed could withstand the wind and snow of that gale, and it was far better to keep in motion than to crouch and freeze, perhaps, with inactivity.

"Wan more hour, Jeem, an' we be dere," said one close by the other's ear, when they stopped to disentangle a dog from the traces.

"Good enough, Jean."

Their parkas were coated with ice and snow. The stubble on their faces was ice-caked, and the salt-rheum froze as it ran from their red-rimmed eyes. They spoke through dark, frost-cracked lips.

They did not stop for long. The trace adjusted, the four dogs bent to the task of drawing the toboggan through the snow. The man called Jean swung ahead of the lead-dog on broad snowshoes. The other trudged beside the toboggan, his head bent down against his chest, a thirty-foot caribou-gut whip gripped in one mittened hand. He eased the toboggan over any irregularities in the trail, watched that it did not turn over on sharp inclines, and occasionally snapped the whip over the dogs, more from force of habit than anything else. All about him the great trees, their tops hidden by the clouds of snow, reeled and strained, fought stubbornly against the legions of wind and snow.

The outfit began to descend a slight grade. A little later the man in the lead led the way on to a flat surface that was a frozen waterway. For a moment he paused, holding up his hand, trying to peer through the wild chaos of the night, while the wind tore at him, rattled his ice-caked furs, spun the snow about him in whistling spirals. Then he clapped his mittens together, lowered his head and cut diagonally across the frozen river.

Hard at his heels pulled the shaggy lead-dog, its breath spouting out in vapory clouds that fell back against its matted hair and congealed there.

Against the white surface of the waterway there soon appeared a solid wall of darkness that was the forest on the farther shore. The man in the lead strode toward this with steady, regular strides. In a few minutes he plowed through the low shore bushes, emerged upon what appeared to be a wide clearing, and then saw through the murk a pale halo of light. The wind carried his lusty cry of cheer back to the man who toiled behind the sledge.

Squat shapes loomed up indistinctly—the forms of closely bunched cabins, three of them in all, with one considerably larger than the others. The man stopped in front of this. The dogs stopped. The other man rocked forward and joined his companion. They clapped each other on the back. The man called Jean pushed open the door, and they entered the trade-room of Fort Surprise.

In the center of the large room a big box-stove glowed red. Half a dozen Indians and as many white men lounged about in rough split-log chairs near its drowsy warmth. Two hard-bitten old souls lay sprawled on one of the counters, snoring mightily. Most of the men waved greetings. Another man came yawning and stretching through a curtained doorway behind the rear counter—there were counters breasting all walls except the front—and, at first squinting, suddenly exploded with—

"Well, now, look who's here! Well, of all— Well, I'll be damned!" he concluded, chuckling, beaming, rushing forward with outstretched hands.

"*Mon ami!*" boomed the more picturesque of the arrivals, gripping those hands.

"Jean Cyriac! The first man out of the Barrens this year! Darn your hide, Jean, you're a glutton for speed, damme now if you ain't!"

Cyriac's great, deep-throated laugh rang through the cabin. He stopped in mid-career, and with a grand flourish nodded to his companion of the trail, who was leaning against the door and removing his mittens, mildly amused.

"Ah-ha, m'sieur, you forget dat I have de partner now! Jeem, dis is ma long tam frien' M'sieur Luke Lankford. An', Luke, dis is M'sieur Jee-ames Burr."

Jim Burr took one easy stride and extended his hand.

"Glad to make your acquaintance, Mr. Lankford," he said briefly, in a low, subdued voice.

"An' me, you, friend. Only call me, Luke, won't you? Takes less time, an' when a man says Mr. Lankford to me I sometimes kinder forget, it bein' unfamiliar."

Jim Burr chuckled.

Cyriac said, "Me, I'm put away de dogs, Luke, if you geeve me somet'ing to feed de poor brutes."

While Cyriac went out to feed the dogs and drive them under a lean-to in the rear, Burr and Lankford strolled into the back room. A young Indian was sitting there. At a word from Lankford he got up quietly and began busying himself with pots and pans on the stove.

Soon Cyriac joined them, white teeth flashing below his black mustache, his spirits buoyant despite the fact that he was greatly fatigued. He threw off his white-fox capote, hung it up, sat down, and began unlacing his moccasins. Burr, on another chair, was doing likewise. Cyriac remarked, meanwhile:

"*Parbleu!* What a trail! Luke, we have two *mar*-velous blackies besides mooch odder pelts. *Oui!* Jeem he was in de Barrens wit' me. I'm meet heem at Waskayowaka on de way down to de Barrens. I'm seek unto de death, an' Jeem he tak' care of me, nurse me back to de life. Jeem he is ver' wise wit' de medicine. He is somet'ing of de doctaire. We mak' de partners den. I am trap all ma life, an' I'm teach Jeem 'bout de traps. Jeem he teach me 'bout de curing of de ills. M'sieur, I am not seek wance all de tam in de Barrens—not wance. An' Jeem he mak' dam' fine trapper. He learn queek lak hell. An' attend! He catch wan of de blackies!"

"No!" said Lankford, sitting up straight.

"*Oui!*" retorted Cyriac, hanging up his duffel on a line over the stove.

Burr put in, "Rotten country, the Barrens."

"Yeah," Lankford nodded. "Spent a winter up there. Years ago. Say you're a doctor, Jim—doctor?"

"I know a little about the business."

"Doing government work, I suppose, among the Injuns?"

Burr had by this time removed his last pair of socks and was feeling his feet.

"No," he replied briefly, and there was something in the way he said it that did not invite continuation of the subject.

"Oh-o," drawled Lankford understandingly; then to the Indian, "Shake it up, Joe. My friends must be hungry as hell."

Cyriac, inspecting his own feet, remarked, "Oh, Luke! We meet de poor Pitney girl at de forks. *Mon Dieu!* I'm wonder if ever she weel see again."

"Damn shame, ain't it?" sympathized Lankford.

Burr looked across at his partner. "Blind, Jean?"

"I did not tell you?"

"Don't remember. Just introduced us."

"Blind—*oui!* More dan wan year now. Blind complete. 'Tis pity. She is so beauti-*ful*—so sweet an' gentle, an' so mooch de perfect ma'mselle. You, Jeem, aire know mooch 'bout de medicine. Perhaps you could mebbe-so help her."

Jim Burr did not reply immediately. He stood staring at his roughened hands with moody, vacant eyes. A cloud suddenly passed across those eyes, and he shrugged away the mood.

By this time the meal was on the table. Cyriac sat down and Burr sat opposite him. He was a big man, this Jim Burr, bulky in the shoulders, a trifle bull-necked, with a fine flat sweep of jaw and level gray eyes. Unlike the gay, laughter-loving Cyriac, he was silent, rather economic with words, yet not taciturn. He emanated power—mental as well as physical force. The evidence of rugged, brute strength that at first impressed you paled somewhat when you looked into the intelligent eyes, noting the hints of fine character that were mixed with his ruggedness, the subdued timbre of his unhurried voice.

Lankford, sitting next to the stove on a box and whittling himself a chew, said, "Reminds me, you speaking about the Pitney girl, Jean. What you think? Inspector for the Bay West paid me a visit yesterday. Yeah! Was on his way to Pitney's post. New man—cocky as hell—traveling with two dog-teams an' six Injuns. Wanted to buy me out for the Bay West. Yeah! He'd probably heard about the good business I do, an' maybe Pitney's reports ain't been so good. Ought to heard him! Be Gad, I never met a man could talk so much. An' so highfalutin! Lord! Of course, I turned him down flat. Yeah. I'm not selling out. Seems to me he's out to make a record. I don't think he knows a hell of a lot about the fur game except maybe what he's read. Think he's going to make enemies for the Company if he keeps on shooting off his mouth the way he was here."

"You do well here, eh?" Burr remarked casually.

"Say, Jim, there's no post within a hundred miles does better. But I've worked pretty hard, even if I have to say it myself. I've been here fifteen years. I've made friends for miles about. I pay fair prices. If a man's down-an'-out I'll stake him for the season. Most men are on the square. I send my assistants out in winter with loads of provisions and have 'em barter on the trail. If they find a man that's got nothing, but hopes to get something, why it's my orders to help the chum out with grub an' things."

"*Oui*, Jeem; Luke is mighty on de square," Jean put in.

Talk dwindled until Burr, lighting his pipe, ventured, "This Miss Pitney. Any idea what caused her blindness?"

Cyriac offered, "She was great reader—study mooch in de 'Peg. Mak' de eyes strain. Den las' wintaire she be on de trail when de sun he is bright lak hell. Her eyes dey are already ver' mooch seek, an' de sun shining on de snow mak' terrible glare an'—so—no more she can see. 'Tis pity! *Mon Dieu*, 'tis pity!"

"I see," nodded Burr. "Maybe we'll drop in there sometime after we've disposed of our pelts. Far from here?"

"About ten miles," offered Lankford. "Her dad's Sam Pitney, factor of Windy Creek House."

Burr rose. "Well, we'll do that then, Jean, sometime. Now I think I'd better go out and look at our leader's feet. Noticed they got cut up pretty badly coming through that muskeg south of the forks. Be right back."

He put on dry socks and moccasins, got into his furs, and went out.

When he had gone Jean said to the trader, "A great man, dat Jeem Burr—a great man!"

"Looks mighty good to me, Jean. Quiet sort. Notice those hands and those shoulders, though? Bad man to cross, I reckon. How old is he?"

"'Bout t'irty. An' such good care he tak' of de dogs! Such care he tak' of heemself! He be dead tired now, but know our leader is in wan dam' bad way, so he go feex."

"Kinder strange, a man like him up here trapping," mused Lankford. "Burr... Burr. Where'd I hear that name before? Seems I read it in a paper long time ago. Doctor Burr. Yep, I did. Let's see. A Doctor Burr was charged with performing an operation in some lumber camp while drunk or something. I think it was—"

"Dat is wan dam' lie!"

Cyriac was on his feet, his hands clenched, his wide chest heaving, dark fires in his midnight eyes.

"Luke, you nevaire read dat a-tall!" he ripped out, advancing.

Luke stood up, and the two men faced each other, eye to eye, unwavering. For a full minute they poised, neither batting an eye, until Lankford finally laid a hand on Cyriac's shoulder.

"You are right, Jean," he said, simply. "I never did read anything like that at all."

CHAPTER III

LANKFORD CROSSES RAAB

BEFORE MORNING the storm had blown itself out. Old-timers arriving at Fort Surprise prophesied an early spring, said there would be no more snowfalls in the land of Keewatin that season. The last attack of the long winter had come and gone. At any rate, that morning dawned clear, and later the sun climbed above the timbered ridges in a riot of color and seemed to put life into scenes that otherwise would have been stark and desolate and cold.

There were big drifts about the post-buildings, and a couple of Lankford's Indians were out bright and early to shovel pathways. A number of trappers joined in willingly, without being asked, and one threw a snowball that caught another in the ear. Before very long the snow-shoveling business was discarded for a free-for-all fight, in which others joined heartily. Snow flew in lumps of various sizes, men yelled lustily and gleefully, others swore dark blue streaks, and a good time was being had by all.

Lankford, opening the door to see what the rumpus was about, had the misfortune to get his face in the way of a healthy missile. He snorted, coughed, cursed, and finally, having no more words in his extensive vocabulary, decided to grin.

"My mistake, boys. I shouldn't have hit the snowball with my face at all. But, say, would you all mind moving off a bit so's my boys can shovel those paths?"

That ended the carnival. Some men drifted away, others rejoined the Indians in clearing away the snow. Lankford still stood in the doorway, smiling to himself, pleased with life, genial and good-humored. Presently he espied a three-dog team plugging out of the timber to his clearing, led by a huge, burly man with another, a much smaller man, at the gee-bar of the sledge. Lankford made a slight grimace of displeasure and unleashed a swift shot of tobacco-juice out of the corner of his mouth.

As the outfit drew up there issued no usual greeting from the men shoveling snow. Here and there you might have noticed a scowl. The big man slowed down as he drew abreast of the tradehouse, and bared stained teeth in a twisted leer.

" 'Lo, Lankford," he flung out.

"Hello, Raab," briefly.

With a deft, casual movement of the wrist Raab coiled his long dog-whip around his mittened hand.

"I got some fine pelts here. I'm out o' provisions an' want to sell."

"Windy Creek House is ten miles west," said Lankford, his arms akimbo. "You could make it easy before sundown."

"Yeah, but I got an idea I want to sell here."

"Me, I've got ideas to the contrary somehow."

"Meanin' just what, huh?"

"Meaning," drawled Lankford, as he leaned forward and spat carefully, "that I'm not buying your pelts. That plain?"

Raab closed one eye and narrowed the other. "You don't say!"

"I do say, an' I can't make it any plainer."

"You refuse me grub, huh? You turn me away when my grub-sack's clean empty?" His fists clenched.

"I'll give you a day's grub, an' you can feed your dogs," explained Lankford. "But, Raab, you couldn't sell me the tail of a skunk. What's more, it ain't exactly polite on my part, but I ain't inviting you to camp around here either."

Raab spread his legs and jammed his hands against his hips. His massive jaw jutted out.

"You an' your charity grub can go to hell! I wouldn't take it. But I got a mind to just pick you up an' wrap you around the nearest tree. Gettin' mighty partic'lar about who sells to you, ain't you? Camp here? I'll camp here if I like, an' I'd like to see the man that'd stop me."

"You always was a lot of noise, Raab," returned Lankford. "Now don't go gassing so much. I don't aim to hold a confab here with you. I'm just telling you what's what. I'll give you enough grub to reach Windy Creek House, but I'll be damned if I'll buy your furs. You know why without me telling you."

"I got a mind—" Raab began with a snarl.

But his little companion was at his elbow now. "S'y, Buck, let's tyke the bloomin' grub 'e offers an' get goin'. We c'n myke Windy Creek terd'y an' sell the pelts there. 'E's just tryin' ter myke yer mad, Buck. I s'y, now, don't let 'im, y' know."

"You clamp your jaw, Pinky," snapped Raab.

"Aw, s'y, that's no w'y ter talk ter a bloke as means good by yer. Let's mush, I s'y, now, Buck."

Raab scowled at his partner, undecided whether to take his counsel or to take him by the neck and wring it. By this time the door slammed. Lankford, having declared himself, had retired.

"We'll squat here f'r a while," Raab rumbled.

"Aw, Buck, s'y, what's the bloody use—"

"Will you shut up? Cripes, I'll f'rget meself some fine day an' paste you in the mouth. Shut up!"

"No harm meant, ol' top. I—"

"*Shut up!*"

Pinky gulped and shut up. Raab dropped to his sledge and loaded his pipe, scowling darkly.

Inside the trade-house, Lankford, having slammed the door, strode across the room and paused by the stove where Burr and Cyriac were mending their rackets.

Cyriac ventured, "De argument all done, Luke?"

"Don't know, Jean," grumbled the trader. "That chum's got gall all right. Buy his pelts? Not till they make snow-balls in hell! Huh! He never got them pelts honest. He ain't never turned an honest penny in his life. Two years back he robbed the traps of one of my best friends. He's so crooked he could hide behind a corkscrew!"

"*Oui*, I know," nodded Cyriac. "Las' year dey drive heem off de Albany."

"Bad one, eh?" put in Burr casually.

"They don't come worse, Jim,"—from Lankford. "An' a big bully too. He's licked most men in these parts, But then he ought to, him being so big an' so used to dirty work. He'll meet his match some day, though."

Burr laid aside his racket and strolled over to the window. When he came back, after a moment, he said, "He looks as if he might be able to handle himself. Who's the little fellow?"

"Pinky Smith. Hangs to Raab like a lost dog. Dangerous little runt."

At this juncture there was a frantic yelping outside. Lankford swiveled about.

"That sounds like Susie. How'd she get out?"

He strode for the door and yanked it open. Susie, one of his pet dogs, limped toward him, her face gashed open and bloody.

"Who hit that dog?" he roared in swift anger.

"I did," clipped Raab. "Keep your mutt inside."

"Susie's expecting pups, you skunk!" shouted Lankford as he cleared the doorway and made for Raab.

Raab chuckled dryly, doubled a fist, and let Lankford have it square between the eyes. The trader was carried from his feet and hit the snow on the back of his neck. The trappers who stood about muttered. One said:

"Go easy there, Raab."

Raab, snarling, lunged after the fallen trader and drove a foot into his ribs. At this moment Burr had reached the door. When he saw this he leaped out. An instant later he was standing over Lankford.

"This is no argument of mine," he told Raab quietly, "but I don't like to see a man kicked when he's down."

Raab glowered. "An' who the hell are you?"

"Never mind. Luke's a lot smaller than you are and a lot older. Be fair."

With that he bent down, swung the senseless trader over his shoulder, and strode back into the trade-room. Raab stood for a moment in perplexed indecision. Then he started after Burr with clenched fists. At the door he walked into the muzzle of a rifle behind which stood Jean Cyriac.

"Dat weel be far enough, m'sieur," smiled Cyriac.

The other trappers were edging nearer, now, some with rifles. Raab looked around, scowled, muttered deep in his throat. He glanced over his shoulder and saw Pinky standing by the sledge and motioning for him to come back. With a clipped oath he swung about and rocked toward his companion, cracking his whip savagely over the dogs.

"I'd like to meet that guy alone some day," he snarled. "I mean the big stiff. I'd bat hell out of him."

"Sure yer would, Buck, ol' top," agreed Pinky, as they reached the waterway. "No bloke better 'an yer, Buck."

Thus they crossed the waterway, bound for Windy Creek House.

CHAPTER IV

DEVLIN HIRES RAAB

THE ROADS to glory are many. The means are of two kinds: fair and unfair. Sometimes there is a little of one and much of the other. It all depends on the man. There are two kinds of men that venture into the wilderness: one disregards its traditions, the work of ages; the other accepts them and all other things of the wilds as something vast, cosmic, inevitable.

Roger Devlin was not of the latter. On the contrary, he believed himself to be inevitable. Power in a man of his type is dangerous. He was ambitious without the finer instincts of ambition. He was not a builder, as were the pioneers, who thought not of themselves but of generations to come. Devlin thought only of Devlin. He liked to do things with a flare, attain his ends in one great sweep. He was impatient, unwilling to progress step by step. He wanted seven-league boots.

He had by this time been ten days at Windy Creek House. He had taken things in hand, ignoring the counsel and the very existence of old Sam Pitney. He gave Pitney orders to send more men to draw the trappers' trade, and Pitney, resigned to his fate, carried those orders out. He didn't like the way Pitney had his trade-goods stocked, so Jerry Sand, the hard young apprentice, had to make changes. Devlin altered the whole scheme and schedule of things, operated the post on a plan that was nothing short of fantastic, and he considered this plan the best in the world. He had been given a certain degree of authority by head-quarters and he was drunk with it, going far beyond its limits.

Old Pitney saw this, realized it full well. He saw chaos, ruin ahead, but somehow or other he dared not raise his hands. He only hoped that in some way Devlin would be thwarted in his mad plan. He knew that if he revolted against the young man's wishes, the young man, who was very persuasive, could no doubt get him discharged. The quality of courage is sometimes difficult to define. You could not say flatly that Pitney was afraid for himself. He was an old man, very old, very sluggish of mind, with a blind daughter to take care of. He was cornered, groping for light, half-rebellious against Devlin, but only mutely so. Another man might have taken the matter up with headquarters right off the bat, but old Pitney was slow to act, slow to come to a conclusion.

To Judy he told nothing. She knew nothing of what was going on. With her Devlin was soft-spoken, attentive, entertaining. He took her for rides in his cariole, talked much of interesting things, helped in a way to remove some of the drabness from her sightless wilderness life. Old Pitney saw that she enjoyed this, and he could not spoil her present happiness by telling her of his own troubles. He was one of those men who bear their agony alone.

When Buck Raab and Pinky Smith had arrived, a week before, he had hesitated in buying their pelts, for he knew Raab's reputation. He had explained the case to Devlin.

"Business is business," replied the inspector. "Don't let a thing like that worry you. Buy the man's pelts. Buy them, I say."

And now Buck Raab and Roger Devlin sat in a little nondescript trapping-shack about a mile north of Windy Creek. Raab was a whale of a man, built to gorilla proportions, with a massive iron jaw and little ears. His nose was flat, his eyes opaque. He had muscle-lumps between thumb and forefinger as large as golf-balls.

"Listen, mister," he remarked to Devlin, "talk cold turkey. You want t' know if I'm willin' to be your silent partner sorta in some little game you got up your sleeve."

"Not partner—"

"All right. I'm a plain-spoken guy. You want a hired man, then. That's what you want, ain't it?"

"Well, yes."

"That's the stuff. Say, you ain't talkin' t' no high-toned guy. Talk plain an' straight, so I can understand you. Yes, I'll hire out t' any man that's got the money. That's my special little hobby. Me, I make no bones about it."

"It's this way," Devlin finally said. "I've struck a little difficulty. Windy Creek House hasn't been doing the business I should like to see it do. I am working solely in the interests of the Company, and I am quite sure that a little exploit engineered by me toward that end will not be amiss. As you well know, I have caused the rate of exchange of a 'made beaver' to be raised, and already this has drawn a number of trappers who have never traded at Windy Creek before. The plan is working out swimmingly as it is, but I want to prepare for another stroke if it does not continue working as I think it ought. I want to have a man upon whom I can rely to carry out any orders which, in my present position, would be impossible for me to consummate personally. In a word, as you say, I want a hired man. I am endeavoring to cripple the business of Fort Surprise, and one way or another I am going to do it and do it thoroughly—thoroughly—*quite* thoroughly."

Raab narrowed one eye and said, "Pay me price an' Lankford'll be out of the way by this time t'morrow."

"You mean…"

"I mean… What the hell you think I mean? I mean I'll drill Lankford—pot him when he sticks his knob outside his door. That's my business."

Devlin paled a trifle at this blunt statement. He had never before stacked up against a man quite like this Buck Raab.

"No, nothing so crude," he argued, grimacing. "You are much too hasty, my dear fellow—quite savage, in fact."

Raab leaned back, rapped the table with the palm of his hand.

"Savage is it? What's that t' you? When you hire a man t' do your dirty work, mister, you don't want t' be so partic'lar. All right, I'm a savage. I know it, most folks know it, an' I ain't denyin' it. I ain't afraid o' no man livin'—an' there's a guy over at Lankford's now I'd like to meet—I ain't afraid o' no man livin', I says, your lobster-back Mounties included, an' there ain't no job so big it scares me. I'm bad? Sure, bad through. I got no use f'r these here now midway guys—not good enough t' be good an' not bad enough t' be bad. When you do a thing, do it good; that's my motto. All good, or all bad."

"That may be all very well," replied Devlin. "But since I am to pay you for such services as I may desire, hire you, in short, I don't want you to let that philosophy carry you away. This is not a partnership, as I have given you to understand before. I intend paying you."

"I ain't good enough f'r a partner, huh?"

"You are absurd! How can there be any talk of a partnership when I am working solely in the interests of the Company?"

Raab laughed. "Ye-es, you are. Ho! Ho! You're workin' in the interests o' nobody but Mr. Roger Devlin. Go on, don't tell me! I wasn't borned yesterday."

Devlin stood up, tactfully ignoring the last remark.

"Then I can rely on you?"

"Rely on me? Why, sure. I'll be here. Don't know who owns the shack, but it's mine now an' I'd like to see the guy that'd put me out."

"Very well. And by the way, we must not be seen together around Windy Creek House."

"Uh-uh." Raab stood up, stretched his great arms, broke into a crooked leer. "Still ridin' around wit' the factor's daughter? Pretty, ain't she? Blind… but a woman. Ho! Ho!"

Devlin tilted up his chin. "A very charming young lady. Er— well, I'll see you again shortly."

He turned on his heel, pulled open the door, and strode out as Pinky Smith, his arms loaded with wood, came out of the timber.

" 'Lo, inspector," called the scrawny little fellow. "S'y, d'yer t'ink we'll 'ave an early spring?"

"It is possible," clipped Devlin, and strode on.

Pinky stared after him with his misshapen mouth agape, his button eyes wide. Then he twitched his nose and giggled.

"S'y, 'e's a cheery bloke, now, aren't 'e? Strik' me pink!" he chortled, as he pushed into the cabin, dropped the wood down by the rusty stove and rubbed his hands gingerly. "See the bloomin' inspector dropped in to 'ave tea wit' yer, Bucky, eh?" he ventured.

"Yeah," grunted Raab. "We're workin' f'r him now, Pinky. Listen."

He explained what had passed between himself and Devlin. Pinky clucked and grinned with Satanic mirth.

"Ow, hit looks like somethin' soft, Bucky, doan't it, though, what? But, Bucky, s'y—pst! Doan't let the bloody toff put anything over on yer. Yer can't trust hoomanity these d'ys, yer can't."

"You just leave it t' me, Pinky."

"Sure, ol' cabbage—"

"Don't call me 'old cabbage'!"

"Sure, Bucky, ye're all there, I s'y, but yer need a bloke like me at times ter warn yer, I s'y. A big, strong man like you gits reckless now an' then. But I'll see 'e doan't flimflam yer, Bucky. Leave it ter li'l Pinky 'ere. Let's 'ave a drink."

On that they drank.

CHAPTER V

THE WILDERNESS SINGER

AT A leisurely pace Devlin headed back for Windy Creek House. Usually it was his custom to travel in state, bundled in his private cariole drawn by six well-kept dogs, with half-a-dozen Indians at his command. But this was different. He wished to keep his visits to Raab as secret as possible, and secrecy would have been entirely out of the question if he wished to travel in state.

The air was crisp, cool, exhilarating, a trifle above freezing. The sun shone brightly on the snow, and against this menace he wore colored glasses. It was a world of clean, white silence, of mighty forests that tumbled away in all directions, of half-forgotten waterways and remote lakes that gleamed like lost jewels. It was the wilderness, the breeder of great hatreds, great loves, the moulder of courage and the Nemesis of cowardice, the playground of the devil and the cathedral of God.

Here Devlin had come to flaunt his insolence in the face of traditions which a century had fashioned, to defy a code that Time had etched in the hearts of these simple men more indelibly than figures on a copper plate.

When he arrived at the post he went directly into the trade-room and espied old Pitney, bent over a ledger on the rear counter.

"Well, what news, my dear Mr. Pitney—what news?" he clipped, lighting a cigarette.

"Um. Well, Louie just drove in," replied the old factor slowly. "Says he's got the trade of six trappers, all of 'em bein' used to tradin' in at Fort Surprise."

"Ah-ha! What did I tell you? What did I tell you? You just leave it to me, old man, old man. I will show you how to run a trading post. I will show you how to drum up trade. I will show you many things. You are behind the times, my dear old man—sadly behind the times. What we need is new ideas, new life-blood. Efficiency! That's it. We need efficiency. The trouble with a lot of you old fellows lies in the fact that you still use the dog-eared methods employed by the first traders that came over from the Old Country on Prince Rupert's expedition, with a charter from Charles the Second that is today even the greatest of its kind, much to the gratification of the estimable H.B.C."

"Um," grunted Pitney, studying the ledger before him. "But we can't keep on payin' these prices we are, Mr. Devlin. We—"

"Who says we cannot? Who? I? No! Indeed not. Please do not refer to that item again. I know quite well what I am doing, let me assure you. I am working solely in the interests of the honorable Company. Another thing. I don't fancy having your trapper friends using the counters to lie upon as if they were bunks. Print a sign to that effect and hang it in a conspicuous place."

Following this harangue the inspector passed into a room in the rear, which he had taken over as an office and sleeping quarters.

Jerry Sand, who had been idling nearby, drifted over to Pitney and remarked, "Cripes, ain't he ever goin' to let up on them long-winded lectures? I wish somebody'd take a poke at him. There's been some wire-pullin' at headquarters for him to get a job like he's got. An' it's my bet he don't last long. He talks too much. I'd like to haul off myself an' clout—"

"Let's hope for the best, Jerry," Pitney cut in. "Somethin's bound to break sooner or later."

Half an hour later Devlin reappeared, passed through the trade-room and went outside. He called one of his Indian dog-drivers and ordered him to get the cariole ready. Then he stalked across to the little cabin, entered briskly, and found Judy sitting in a rocker by the window.

"I used to sit here when I had my sight," she explained, "and a habit seems hard to break."

"It certainly is," he replied. "Now I've got into the habit of taking you out in my cariole frequently, and I cannot break it."

"Which is all very pleasant," she laughed.

"Indeed—indeed. Well, are you ready?"

"Oh, in a moment, if…"

"Yes, I'll get your furs and help you on with them. Just sit here. I know where they are."

Once outside, he led her to the waiting cariole and helped her in. The Indian driver got his whip ready, but Devlin took it from him.

"You men need not come," he said. "I'll drive the dogs myself."

He cracked the whip sharply and the team started off, passed quickly out of sight of the post buildings, and struck the creek, along which it proceeded eastward. Here he slowed the dogs down to a walk, and at the end of an hour drew up in the shelter of a clump of willows and sat down on the edge of the cariole.

"Just to spell the dogs," he explained, taking a cigarette. "The day is wonderfully clear."

He removed his sun-glasses. Judy wore glasses also. Though blind, her sightless eyes were still sensitive to strong light unless properly shielded.

"I can feel how clear the air is," she agreed, clasping her hands. "The sun feels warm too, and the awful bite has gone from the cold. Soon we'll have spring. I hope it will be an early spring."

Wisps of raven hair escaped from her scarlet toque and clung to her healthy pink cheeks. Against the pearly whiteness of her even teeth her red lips were fresh and soft and tempting as ripe, luscious cherries. Sitting there, his hands clasped about one knee, Devlin studied her through squinted lids, puffing languidly on his cigarette.

"Have you ever wondered what I look like?" he asked after a moment.

"I was just going to suggest that you tell me," she said. "I'll tell you why. You see, I've been building an image of you, as I do of everybody I meet, and I want to see how right or wrong I am."

Devlin chuckled. "The inspector is of medium height, rather slim but fairly well-proportioned, and has been told that he carries himself with military stiffness. He weighs about one-hundred-and-fifty, has blond hair and a thin mustache, a small mouth, the nose acquiline, the eyes blue, and the face inclined to be long and thin with prominent cheek-bones."

"I am almost right," Judy declared. "Annie would only tell me that you were good-looking."

"Thanks to Annie!" he said. "And you—you are beautiful… Judy."

"Oh, Mr. Devlin, you make me laugh!"

"I mean it. And why not call me Roger, Judy? You are beautiful—exquisitely beautiful."

He leaned over and put an arm about her shoulders, tried to draw her closer to him.

"Mr. Devlin, please—don't!" she cried, removing his arm.

"I love you," he said, taking her hand.

"Don't. Please don't. I've considered this merely a little friendship. I—I couldn't consider it more. Really."

"You could learn to love me too."

"No. I'm sure I couldn't. I couldn't. Just a friendship. Please don't speak of it again… Mr. Devlin. Forget it. Don't you think we'd better drive on?"

The lead-dog, who'd been sniffing the wind, suddenly let out a sharp yelp. Other yelps, muffled by distance, came down the wind.

Devlin got up, muttering under his breath, and took a few quick strides toward the leader. The dog saw him, and its hair bristled; in defiance, it bared sharp fangs and barked again and again. Devlin changed his mind and backed away. He was not a favorite with the dog.

Snatches of a human voice raised in song reached him commingled with more dog cries. He became a trifle annoyed. He squinted eastward through the tangle of willows and scrub spruce that bordered the muskeg on his right. The clear, resonant voice of the singer was drawing closer, ringing through the forest.

Judy said, suddenly, "Oh, I know that voice! That's Jean Cyriac, the gayest man in all the North. I told you I met him and a man named Burr on my last trip from the doctor's. Remember?"

"Yes."

Judy, being blind, did not see the way the inspector paled. He looked about hurriedly, biting his nether lip. Then suddenly he cracked the whip, lunged up ahead of the dogs, and started off.

"We'll go to meet them," he yelled back to Judy.

Judy, being blind, could not see that Devlin was heading the team west—not east, toward the singer.

After a while she said, "I don't hear Jean any more."

"Must have stopped, I guess," shot back Devlin, and Judy was surprised at the sudden rasp in his voice.

He drove the dogs to their utmost, cracking his whip continuously, tearing over bumps and through brush with a recklessness that made Judy grip the sides of the cariole and hold her breath.

"Guess we've missed them," he said at length.

But he did not stop. Steadily he drove on toward Windy Creek House, sparing not a minute, driving, driving, driving.

CHAPTER VI

BIG BARRENS

"JEEM," SAID Cyriac, "you t'ink mebbe-so you mak' ma'mselle Pitney see again?"

They were sitting on their ten-foot toboggan, spelling the dogs and enjoying a smoke.

"Don't know," replied Burr, shrugging his shoulders. "I can at least take a look at her, if she'll let me. If she doesn't, well, I shan't have the opportunity, and I may be kicked out into the bargain."

After a moment Cyriac asked, "Weel you nevaire go back?"

"Back?" Burr chuckled grimly. "It would be hard, Jean. I'm an outcast in my profession. But, by God, I'm innocent!"

"*Oui*, I know, m'sieur."

"You know? How do you know, except what I've told you myself?"

Cyriac sighed. "Jus' know—dat's all. Lak' I'm know dere is *le bon Dieu,* above."

They smoked for a moment in silence. Then Burr said: "Those dogs we heard, I suppose that was an outfit from Windy Creek?"

"Mebbe-so. Mooch trappers weel be arrive now. Let us *marche*, Jeem."

They got up and Cyriac, speaking to the leader, started off. They moved through shady isles of dark spruces, from which a great deal of the snow had been removed by a recent high wind. Here and there twisted deadfalls offered mute evidence of the strength of that wind. Presently they emerged upon a field of ragged muskeg, where reeds and willows were frozen in the hummocky ice. Crossing this, they again attained solid land, and Cyriac pointed to fresh tracks.

"Dese were made by de dogs we heard, Jeem," he observed. "Also dere was somewan on rackets. Come dis far an' den mak' a turn back."

They did not pause, and after a while Cyriac, swinging jauntily ahead of the outfit, broke into one of his favorite *voyageur* songs. It was an hour later when he led the way onto Windy Creek, followed its frozen course for a short distance, and, rounding an abrupt curve, came into sight of the post buildings.

In the trade-house, he presented Burr to old Sam Pitney with his customary buoyancy.

"Jeem Burr, ma partner," he announced, his dark face beaming.

"My daughter told me about meetin' you an' Jean, here, up at the forks short time ago," remarked Pitney.

"Yes. Jean and I've come up out of the Barrens. Spent most of the winter there."

"Ma'mselle, she is in de house now?" asked Cyriac.

Pitney shook his head. "No. Her an' the Company inspector went out for a ride in his cariole. He's been here almost two weeks now."

"*Oui,*" nodded Cyriac. "He mak' a stop at Luke Lankford's on de way over."

"Yeah," Pitney drawled, absently scratching his head. "Yeah. Guess he did. First trip in. New feller. Name o' Devlin."

Burr had turned away a trifle to knock the ashes from his pipe into the wood-box by the stove. At mention of Devlin's name his jaw muscles hardened, his calm gray eyes narrowed, his hand closed tightly over his pipe, and the stem cracked in two. His back was turned to the two men, hence neither saw this sudden display of passion. When he swung to join them again, he said in his usual subdued tone:

"Wonder if you've got a stem to fit this, Mr. Pitney. Just broke it."

"Uhuh. Guess I have," replied the factor, and reached down a box full of pipes and stems.

Cyriac said, "Ma frien' Jeem, here, is somet'ing of de doctaire. I'm tell heem 'bout Ma'mselle's poor eyes, an' he would lak to tak' a look. Mebbe-so he can feex; mebbe-so not."

Pitney's faded eyes grew round.

"You think you could bring back her sight, Mr. Burr?" he exclaimed eagerly.

"I don't know, frankly, Mr. Pitney. Just thought it would do no harm to take a look."

"You're a doctor?"

"I… was a doctor. A surgeon of sorts."

"As soon as she gets back!" Pitney exclaimed. "Me, God, I'm beginnin' to give up hope! Judy don't complain, but sometimes I can see how she feels, too. If you could only help her, make her see a little, I'd give anything I got. Only it wouldn't be much, I s'pose, what I have, me bein' a poor man an' all."

The sledge-dogs outside began a wild snarling, and Cyriac flung out to quell them, leaving Burr with the factor. As soon as he reached the door he saw the cause of the disturbance. Another dog-team was drawn up outside the factor's dwelling, and both teams were yelping at each other. He also saw a man helping Judy Pitney from a cariole. He flung up a hand.

"*Bon jour*, ma'mselle."

"Hello, Jean," answered Judy, pausing. "I recognize your voice."

She introduced the two men. Devlin was nervous, impatient.

"Let us go in," he plied, pulling at her arm with gentle firmness.

Before she quite realized it she was inside, and Cyriac, very much abashed and hurt, found himself staring at the outside of the closed door.

"By dam'!" he managed to clip between his teeth, and swung back to his dogs.

Burr was just coming out of the store with the factor, but by this time Cyriac had managed to subdue his sudden attack of hot indignation. He stayed with the dogs while Pitney led Burr to his cabin, almost stumbling in his eagerness. Once inside, they found Judy alone.

"Mr. Devlin go?" Pitney asked.

"Yes, dad. He was in a hurry."

"Left the dogs outside, too. H'm."

Burr had not yet uttered a single word, but Judy must have sensed the presence of someone besides her father, and she remarked it. Old Pitney explained.

"Yes, I remember your voice," she told Burr after he had spoken a few words.

Pitney put in, "An', Judy, he's a doctor—or used to be one, an' he would like to look at your eyes."

"Doctor?" from Judy, surprised.

"I specialized in diseases of the eye," Burr said.

For almost half an hour he asked her questions in his slow, low voice. With a powerful glass he studied her eyes, peering straight into them, observing them from an angle. Then he sat down, lit his pipe, and smoked in silence for five minutes, staring vacantly into space. Old Pitney could not restrain his anxiety.

"Well, doc?"

"I may be able—" Burr began.

"You—" gulped Pitney.

"You—" gulped Judy.

"I may be able to bring back your sight," said Burr. "Your trouble must have begun with iritis—inflammation of the iris—due to excessive eye-strain, possibly—reading, no doubt. I don't think your trouble is retinal. There's a film or growth across your pupil, the result of the inflamed iris. This film grew together slowly at first, giving you some pain and hazy vision at times, and finally it grew together entirely. This last no doubt was caused by a strong glare of some kind—say, the sun shining on the snow. It will mean a bit of an operation."

"I'm willing to try anything," cried Judy.

"Just so," Burr nodded, thoughtfully. "But it might interest you to know that I'm an outcast in my profession. I was accused and convicted of operating on a man in a Temiskaming lumber camp. Against the charge that outlawed me, I can only say I was innocent. I was not drunk, only tricked."

"Tricked?" Judy echoed.

"Yes, tricked. The only man who's heard the story from my own lips in the north is Jean Cyriac. No one else. I'm not a talkative man, and I'm not hunting pity. But, seeing that I may operate on you, Miss Pitney, you ought to know."

"I'd like to, doctor," she offered, wistfully.

"Thank you for that," he replied, a little touched at the "doctor." He went on, "I'll be brief. Five years ago I was engaged by a group of lumber companies down Temiskaming way to render medical attention to such of their men as might be injured while at work. This appointment automatically discharged a doctor who had been suspected of malpractice. There was no proof, but he had a bad name elsewhere, so they got rid of him. But he still hung around the camps, gambling and making things unpleasant for me.

"It happened that he met a young chap who was knocking around at the loose end of things—an educated fellow, but seemingly unscrupulous. I'd gone to school with him, and there was something of a grudge between us. He had a well-to-do uncle, but it seemed he had been temporarily cut off from the bank-roll. He met the doctor and they lived together.

"One day this young fellow came over to me and asked me for a job—said we ought to forget the old school-day grudge. He wanted to work, show he was made of the right stuff, and so on. I didn't need a man, but I put him in my little office to take care of the phone and things that didn't require my personal attention.

"It was winter, then, and pretty cold. We got along fairly well. I rather liked him. He still chummed with the discharged doctor, but that was none of my business. I don't think I've ever been thoroughly drunk in my life. I've always touched a drop of liquor here and there, and it's the truth that on cold days, if I had a tough job ahead of me, I'd take a bracer—never any more than three fingers. In fact, I always carried a flask in my bag.

"One night there was a man shot in a bad brawl. A wild night, cold as I've ever seen it, and I had to plow a mile or more to reach the scene. When I got him back to my little makeshift hospital I found I'd have to operate to get the bullet. I was chilled to the bone, and just before I operated I asked this young fellow to pour me a tot of whisky. He did and I drank it. When I got half-way through the operation my head began to spin, my legs wobbled, and I collapsed.

"That tot of whisky had been drugged! And by the man I'd given a job! While I was out, unconscious, the discharged doctor appeared as if by magic, and finished the operation, for which he got the credit and his old job back. But here. The young chap swore that before I started the operation I drank a whole flask of whisky. He tricked me! He was paid by the other doctor to trick me.

"What could I do? The evidence was against me. I could only give my word. And what is that?" he ended ironically.

"A lot," came Judy's soft voice. "A lot, doctor. I believe you—I believe."

"Thanks. Thanks," he murmured. "It's kind of you."

"Me, I believe you, too, doc," offered old Pitney. "I know it's hard to make the law believe, but, me, yes, I believe you."

"Thanks to both of you. But don't tell the story around. It might bring pity from others—and I hate pity. I hate it. I'm sure I can perform the operation on your eyes successfully, Miss Pitney. I'm sure I can admit light to the retina of your eye. I'll have to send south for my instruments. They're all packed away in storage, but I can have them shipped here."

"Whatever happened to the man as did you in, doc?" Pitney asked.

"He disappeared for a long time," replied Burr. "He has a good position now, and I've learned of his whereabouts recently—in fact, *quite* recently."

"Um. Why don't you give him what he deserves?"

"I probably will," Burr drawled.

"Oh, I wouldn't kill him, doctor," ventured Judy. "It would make things worse."

"Vengeance is gratifying, Miss Pitney. Killing is not the only kind of vengeance. But if I met him face to face I don't know what I'd do."

Some place a door thumped shut. Pitney looked around, then took his cane and limped into the kitchen. He paused, glanced at the back door, then continued toward it, eased it open, and peered out. He saw Inspector Devlin running away through the scrub spruce.

"Now, what the devil!" he exclaimed under his breath, and closed the door softly. When he returned to the sitting-room he said, "Annie must have left it open, the door, an' the wind must have banged it shut."

Burr was standing now, his massive hands hooked in his wide belt, his furs thrown back.

"I'll be going, then, for a while," he said. "Jean and I will camp nearby. When does the next courier pass on the way south?"

"Expect one day after tomorrow, doc," Pitney replied. "Sorry I ain't got room to put you up, but—"

"Perfectly all right. We have a tent of sorts. Well, so long, Miss Pitney. I hope you will have faith in me though I don't know why I should expect you to, with the bad record I have. However—"

"I have faith in you now, doctor," she said.

He could only say, "Good-bye," in a rather low whisper.

CHAPTER VII

THE CLUTCH OF FEAR

DEVLIN HAD not left the cabin when Judy thought he had. He had said goodbye, opened the front door a crack and kicked it shut, then had tiptoed into the kitchen, where he remained.

He heard Burr and Pitney come in, heard Burr's analysis of Judy's ailment, heard his statement that he could cure her. Inwardly he cursed. Then a sly look came into his eyes; he sneered.

He waited until Burr was ready to leave, crept across the room, opened the rear door, and in his haste shut it too quickly, making a noise.

He ran across the clearing, plunged into the scrub spruce, and did not look back once. Nor did he stop once he had attained its shelter. There he slowed down to a brisk walk, and circled until he was heading north. Wearing no snowshoes, he advanced with some difficulty, and where the snow was exceptionally soft wallowed miserably. Once he stopped, half turned to go back, but changed his mind, and with a string of impotent curses plowed ahead.

Finally he emerged out of the deeper timber, wound his way through some scrub willows, and came upon the trapping shack where but a short time back he had spoken with Buck Raab. He shoved at the door. It was barred. He rapped. There was a stir within, movements, a yawn, and then a thick voice asking, "Who's there?"

"Devlin. Open up."

The door opened. Devlin swung in. Raab closed the door behind him, and dropped down the cross-bar that secured it.

"Well, what's up?" he droned with an amused leer.

Devlin was lighting a cigarette. He sat down, opening his furs, mopping his sweaty neck with a handkerchief. Raab, cocking an eye, produced a bottle of whisky and set it on the table. He scaled a tin cup across to Devlin.

"Take a drink, mister. Tighten you up."

"I hurried," Devlin explained, accepting the offer.

"S' I see."

"There is a man at Windy Creek House who may interfere with my plans," Devlin went on, after a pause. "I want you to get him out of this particular part of the country."

"Sure," Raab droned, licking his lips.

Devlin put up his hand. "Now, there's to be no killing. You just waylay him and take him off. Catch him when he's not with his partner, a chap named Cyriac, and pretty husky. The man you'll waylay is husky, too, so don't think he's easy. They'll camp near the creek. You'll take him off into the woods and keep him there. Do it tonight."

"Pinky ain't around," Raab said. "Pinky figured we ought to have more men, so he's gone out t' hunt some up—some guys we know we can depend on."

"Well, do it alone. Get him and be sure you keep him. Don't let him try any tricks or goad you into a fight."

"I'll bring him right here. Hold him here till you say. How about a little cash?"

"Here is fifty. I'll give you more when you have this fellow in hand. Now, mind you, get the right one. Don't waylay Cyriac by mistake."

"Just leave it t' me," grinned Raab. "I know the guy you want."

"When do you expect this—er—Pinky fellow back?"

"Dunno. He'll be back, though, wit' some good men. S'pose you got a grudge against this guy I'm gonna waylay, huh?"

"I am working," said Devlin, "solely in the interests of the company."

"Oh, yeah?"

"Quite so," replied the inspector, rising. "Well, I must be going. If I should wish to speak with you while the prisoner is here, I will signal by flashing a mirror from the bushes. You will see the flashes on the walls. If there is no sun, I'll fire three quick shots. Understood?"

"I got you, inspector," Raab nodded.

Devlin's return to Windy Creek was very cautious. He did not go by the usual route, but followed in a general way the trail he had made on the way to Raab's shack. He approached the post buildings from the rear, passed behind them, and wound his way warily through the stunted growth that bordered the creek.

Twilight was settling. Soon he saw smoke, then the glow of a campfire, a small tent, and beside this Cyriac and Burr. He crouched there motionless for a long minute, his eyes glued on Burr. The Frenchman was cooking and singing.

Satisfied, Devlin, retraced his steps and entered the little cabin, affecting a lively mood.

"Well, I'm back, Judy," he said, rubbing his hands together. "Little business."

On that day he had begun to eliminate the "Miss."

"You seemed in such a hurry," Judy remarked.

"Business. My interests in the welfare of the company is so great that at times, perhaps, I become blunt. If I was unseemly, I apologize."

"Oh, that's all right," she replied.

She told him of Burr's visit, of his offer, of her willingness to have him operate on her eyes. Devlin listened in silence, biting his nether lip, frowning.

When she had finished he said, "No doubt Mr. Burr is in earnest. I must walk down to his camp and say hello. But I think you are unwise in letting a man of that sort experiment on your eyes. Of course, I can understand your eagerness. You, being young and beautiful and very much alive, are willing to try anything. But I'd advise you consider more carefully what you are doing. A really expert surgeon doesn't go to trapping for a livelihood. Remember that."

"I know, but…" She had not told Devlin about Burr being outlawed from his profession. She was prompted to, but some inner sense warned her. "Oh, I think he can help me!" she finished, hopefully.

"But logically—" he began.

"I have faith in him… somehow," she persisted gently, with a soft smile.

She remembered the low, calm timbre of Burr's voice. Involuntarily she found herself comparing it with Devlin's. The blind learn to tell much by the sound of a voice.

Devlin, a trifle impatient, argued. "Absurd, my dear, on the face of it!"

The door opened and old Pitney came in. Devlin turned to him. "You are going to permit this—this—um—a vagabond *doctor* to operate on your daughter's eyes?"

Pitney limped to the wood-box by the stove, got rid of a wad of chew tobacco, and said. "Why, yes, I figure to, Mr. Devlin."

"So. Um. I don't appreciate your discretion—or lack of it."

Pitney was an easy-going old soul. He stood leaning on his cane, one hand against his hip.

"I kinder figure the doc is better 'an what most folks think. I kinder like the doc."

"One may form a kind of liking for a casually met Indian, and yet not trust him five minutes alone with his trail outfit."

"Thet so? Oh, well, I figure the doc can't be classed that way."

"I don't know," Devlin mused; then, shrugging his shoulders, "Well, if you think so little of your daughter—"

"Now don't go sayin' anything like that, Mr. Devlin," Pitney rolled at him. "I'd do anything in the world for Judy, I would."

Judy put in, "Oh, don't argue. Anyway, I'm of age and my eyes are my own."

"If you feel that way about it, my dear…" purred Devlin, his vanity struck to the quick.

With a petulant gesture he took his fur cap and went out.

"I can't understand him at all," Judy told her father.

"Oh, gosh, gal, they ain't no understandin' most folks anyhow," said Pitney.

"No? But isn't it peculiar? I've really spoken to Mr. Burr only once, and yet I feel I understand him thoroughly. He seems to say such a lot in so few words. Even when I met him that day at the forks, and he merely said hello, I felt I'd known him a long time. It's strange, isn't it, dad?"

"Well," dragged out old Pitney, "they's folks an' folks." And he let it go at that.

The factor himself knew that something was in the wind. Devlin was making too many quick moves, acting too peculiarly. He couldn't quite make it out. What little he did surmise, which even to himself was rather vague, he did not circulate. He was far from brilliant, the factor. He thought slowly, ponderously, and took long to come to a conclusion. He did not tell Judy that he had seen Devlin running away from the cabin while Burr had been there that afternoon.

He told Judy nothing.

CHAPTER VIII

THE NIGHT ATTACK

BURR AND Cyriac rested in their camp in the lee of some spruce scrub. Burr was lying on his robes, propped against his blanket-roll, his hands behind his head and his pipe between his teeth. Cyriac sat opposite, with the fire between them. Overhead arched a canopy of stars; about them tumbled the shadowy wilderness, through which the south wind murmured with a soft cadence.

"You wrote de letter?" Cyriac asked.

"Yes, Jean. I think the instruments should reach here within a month."

"An' by dat tam, Jeem, spring she weel be in de air, in de woods, all about us lak a song. Dere is no spring lak de spring in de lan' of Keewatin, where de air she is lak rich ol' wine."

"Jean, you have the soul of a poet. But I'm a little happy, too."

"Eh? *Parbleu!* So long you have been sad."

"But I'm a little happy now," said Burr. "The faith of you wilderness people is working a spell over me. Old Pitney believed in me right away. His daughter is willing to let her fate rest in my hands. I told them I am an outcast. This faith of the wilderness—I can't quite understand it myself. But I suppose that's because I wasn't born under its spell."

"Jeem, mebbe-so it is de faith of a woman," ventured Cyriac, his eyes shining.

"Eh?"

"Jeem, ma frien', when you come from de talk wit' ma'mselle, a great sadness is gone from your face. Ma'mselle she has fait' in you, Jeem. I know—ah, I know!"

Burr didn't answer. He puffed on his pipe for a while in silence, then knocked out the ashes and sat up.

"I'm going to turn in."

Cyriac followed this move a little later. The campfire died from flames of life to dull embers that glowed in the shrouded darkness like a lone red eye. Just beyond the fringe of willows lay the post buildings, yet the camp seemed isolated, remote. But for the low murmur of the light winds and the occasional snapping of the ice nearby, the silence was complete.

After a time, a shadow rose from the thickets—a shadow that rose and remained motionless for a long minute. Presently it moved, took a step, and paused again. Buck Raab had come to fulfill his pledge. He stood there, a massive hulk in shaggy furs, squinting at the white tent.

For an hour he had crouched in the bushes, watched the men turn in. Now he advanced, crouched, cautious, deadly.

He reached the tent, listened intently, gripped his revolver tighter. His great shoulders passed in. His arm went up. It came down swiftly, surely. The gun-butt solidly struck Burr's head. Burr scarcely groaned. His hands, clenching, started to crawl upward, but fell back.

Cyriac moved a trifle. Again Raab's arm rose, and slashed down murderously. The Frenchman, sighing, turned over as if in sleep and lay very still. Blood flowed down his cheek.

Raab hauled Burr out of the tent. Though the latter weighed something like a hundred and eighty, Raab lifted him on his shoulder and trudged off into the thickets with no great diffi-culty. He traveled this way for about half a mile, when he came upon a sledge and three dogs. He dropped the unconscious man on the sledge, untied the piece of babiche that had secured the dogs to a sapling, and started off.

Through the night, on a dim trail, he drove at a fast pace. He struck a waterway where the crust was hard, and where what little trail he left was mixed with the marks of other outfits that recently had come out of the north with their winter's catch.

When Raab reached his cabin Burr was slowly regaining his senses, yet not so much that Raab could not drag him inside with ease, and drop him on a pile of dirty blankets in one corner. He then struck a match, lit a candle on the bare table, then went outside and drove his dogs into the little makeshift kennel in the rear.

When he returned Burr was rubbing his head, muttering to himself, still on his back. Raab sat down by the table, laid his revolver on it, and stuffed tobacco into his pipe.

When Burr finally rose to one elbow, and his eyes began to distinguish things clearly, he saw Raab sitting there. He saw the massive, granite-like face, the ape-like jaw, the little, evil eyes, the coarse, leering lips. At first he was bewildered. Sharp daggers of pain shot through his head. Gingerly he rubbed the lump caused by his attacker's blow.

At last he asked, "Well, what's the idea? What have I ever done to you—besides preventing you from kicking Lankford when he was down?"

Raab chuckled. "Not a damn thing, mister."

"Oh... I see. Just banged me to pass the time away, I suppose?"

"Yeah—thassall."

"Just what I thought," Burr nodded; then, "Mind if I stand up?"

Raab tapped the revolver on the table with his fingers.

"Sure. Stand up all you want."

"Thanks." Burr rose, flexed his muscles, and resumed, "That was a dirty crack. Say, time must hang heavy on your hands, if you've got to slug a man while he's sleeping to pass it away. You look big enough for any man while he's awake."

"Ho-ho! I guess I am. They don't come better 'an me."

"No?"

Raab evidently didn't like the way Burr said that. He scowled and licked his lips.

"Why, no," he dragged out, cocking one eye.

"Then why didn't you come around when I was awake?" Burr plied, eyeing him frankly.

Raab removed the pipe from his mouth and leaned forward.

"Hell, you don't think it would have done you any good, do you?"

"I don't know," Burr calmly replied. "You've only got about fifteen pounds on me. I think—yes, I think inside of ten minutes I could lay you flat. Maybe less. It all depends on how you can take a beating."

Raab's eyes opened wide. He was shocked. He was so shocked that words failed him for a full minute. The unperturbed, matter-of-fact way in which Burr had said it appalled him. He stared at the man, who now leaned against the wall with one hand in his pocket. He noted the breadth and thickness of that man's shoulders, the bulge of the chest, the flat stomach, the leonine neck, the sturdy legs and big, muscled hands—and the calm, gray eyes, so calm and level they were baffling. For once in his life Raab had a vague idea that he was facing a man who would be a tough proposition to knock over.

This annoyed him, rattled the great opinion he held of himself as a fighter. But what annoyed him most of all was that simple, casual, unheated manner in which Burr had stated himself.

Finally he sank back in his chair and half-laughed, half-snarled.

"You're off your head, mister! That bump, maybe. Why, hell, I could—I could break your neck in one twist, I could."

"Just a matter of opinion," Burr drawled. "I think you would have to twist twice. You would have to, but on the other hand I don't think you would be physically able. I'd break your own before you got that far."

"My Gawd A'mighty, you ain't stuck on yourself at all, are you?" Raab roared. "What are you, anyhow, one of these here perfessional boxfighters?"

"No. I am—or used to be—a doctor."

"A doctor! Hell an' damn! You get funnier every minute."

"I hope you find my comedy amusing."

"Aw, shut your trap! You give me a pain! Another one o' these high-soundin' guys like—like— Well, what you lookin' at?"

"Go ahead. Like?"

"None of your lousy bizness!" Raab gripped his revolver. "Sit down an' shut up! I ain't s'posed to kill you, but this here gun might go off accidental. Sit down!"

Burr sat down. "How long do you intend keeping me here?"

"Maybe a day, a week, or maybe a month."

"Uhuh. Well, if you get a longing to pass the time away again, tell me about it. Between us we may be able to do something."

Raab half rose, his nostrils quivering. But he dropped back with a throaty snarl and poured himself a shot of whisky.

CHAPTER IX

FAITH THAT IS STRONG

CYRIAC HAD received a nasty blow at the hands of Raab—a blow far more destructive than the one dealt Burr. He bled a long while before he could move. The gun-butt, striking him just below the left temple, had ripped open his cheek.

The first words he uttered were, *"Mon Dieu…Jeem!"*

He groped in the darkness of the tent. In a vague way he realized that Burr was not there. He dragged himself into the open, peering through a semi-conscious fog. He struggled to his feet, reeled, tottered, plunged to the snow again.

On hands and knees he crawled through the willows, struggled for one of the cabins.

Finally he reached the living quarters of the factor. His head was spinning. He felt weary, weak, as if all his strength had been sapped from him, but he managed to pound a few times on the door, then lay huddled there, panting.

After minutes that seemed to him like hours, the door opened, and old Pitney, clad in a thick robe, looked out. He saw Cyriac's upturned face—saw the pain there, the blood.

"God!" he gasped.

Cyriac, raising one hand, muttered, "Jeem…Jeem…"

Old Pitney bent down, dropping his stick, and little by little hauled Cyriac in, grunting with the effort, for Cyriac was no little man.

"Judy—Judy!" he called.

An answering voice, then Judy felt her way from her room, her glorious black hair hanging about her face like velvet clouds.

"What—what, dad?"

"Jean Cyriac—he's all but murdered!" exclaimed the factor, closing the door. "His head—face—bashed in."

"Oh!" she gasped, clutching at her bosom. "And Mr. Burr—Dr. Burr?"

"Dunno. Jean's unconscious now. Last words I heard him say were, 'Jim—Jim.'"

Judy stifled a cry that sprang involuntarily to her lips.

Old Pitney rumbled, "I wonder what he meant?"

"Oh… I don't know!"

"Guess I'd better rouse the others."

He opened the door and called across to the trade-store. He was trying to bathe Cyriac's wound when Devlin and Jerry Sand rushed in.

"You call?" Devlin flung at him.

"Yes. Look here."

Devlin stiffened at what he saw. Inwardly he cursed Raab's clumsiness.

He asked, "How'd it happen?"

"Dunno," said Pitney. "Jean just about made the door, I guess, an' knocked. He said, 'Jim—Jim,' an' then fainted. He tried to say more, but couldn't."

Devlin thought for a moment. "That's his partner's name—Jim—isn't it? Where is this Jim Burr?"

"Dunno," the factor answered; then to his assistant, "Say, Jerry, take a run down to their camp an' look around."

When Jerry returned he reported, "No one there. Their dogs are in the kennel, though."

"Burr gone, eh?" Devlin clipped. He was thinking fast now. "Say, do you suppose this—um—doctor could have clubbed him?"

"Oh, that's absurd!" Judy exclaimed, a little breathless.

"I don't think so," was Devlin's quick rejoinder. "The evidence is against him. He is not about. He has disappeared. Could you suggest someone else?"

Old Pitney shot the inspector an oblique glance, but said nothing. Devlin bent over Cyriac, then looked up.

"Why, this man needs a doctor. His face is badly gashed. He will need at least six stitches in that wound. Where's the nearest doctor?"

"If we could be sure Doctor Burr—" Judy began.

"*Mister* Burr evidently has flown," interjected Devlin.

Pitney remarked, "There's Doc Saunders, twenty miles to the north'ard."

"Then get this man to him," Devlin said. "And quick. My God, what a blow that must have been! Better have no delay. It may mean the loss of his life. And it is the policy of the company to be humane. Why, if I knew the way, I'd drive there myself."

"I'll take him," offered Jerry Sand. "We've got eight dogs here that can outmush any team in these parts. I'll take him. Wrap him up warm, so the cold can't get at his wound. I'll drive them dogs for all their worth."

"Maybe, if we waited until he regained consciousness, he might be able to tell us something about Doctor Burr," ventured Judy.

"Perhaps if he told what he knew all of you would be shocked," Devlin retaliated. "There's no one more anxious than I am to hear. But a life is in danger. We cannot wait. All right, Sand. Get your outfit ready."

Jerry Sand nodded and swung out. Pitney and Devlin bundled the senseless Frenchman in robes and blankets. Judy sat down in a rocker. She could not bring herself to believe that Burr had committed this cowardly act, but his disappearance gave her vague misgivings. Indeed, from the way Devlin had stated it, the evidence was against him. Two men had retired to their camp. One came crawling for aid in the middle of the night with a mutilated face. The other was missing. This hint of foul play could not be disregarded entirely.

But some inner instinct had on their first meeting prompted her to hold great faith in the man who was now under suspicion. Such a faith once born in a woman—and particularly a woman of the wilderness—is infinitely hard to crush. So she clung to a slim thread of hope—clung to the hope that Burr would turn up and explain himself.

It was no more than ten minutes later that Jerry Sand, driving the post's prize huskies, swept off into the gloom of the forest with the unconscious man bundled on his sledge. Pitney, watching until the outfit disappeared, observed:

"He'll make it, Jerry will. He practic'ly raised them there dogs. An' them dogs can mush!"

"It is always the policy of the Company to do everything within its power to save a man's life," remarked Devlin, who had been with the Company not quite a year, and only four months in the north.

Sam Pitney, who had been with the Company for eighteen years, and all his life in the north, merely spat and muttered, "Yeah." After a moment he added, "Soon as dawn breaks we'll scout around."

"To be sure," agreed Devlin emphatically. "I will personally conduct the search. It will be necessary for you, of course, to remain at the store."

"I can—"

"Your chief assistant is away temporarily, hence it will be necessary, as I said, for you to remain here. Depend upon me to conduct a thorough search."

Pitney started to say something, but merely cleared his throat, scratched the back of his neck, and went inside. He closed the door behind him, stood there fumbling meditatively with the latch for a long moment, and finally turned away.

"Better get back to bed, Judy," he suggested. "Mr. Devlin and the rest have turned in again."

"Dad," she said suddenly, "do you think Doctor Burr is guilty of mauling Jean that way?"

"Gal," he answered, "I been tryin' to make myself say he's guilty for the past hour, but I can't do it. I can't forget the doc's handshake, an' the level, open way he looks at a man. An' I can't forget the way he up an' said right out that he was an outcast in his trade. No big defense—no long, sad story."

"Then you believe he's innocent?"

"Judy, I'm a slow-thinkin' man, slow to make a final statement, but I kinder think—yes, me, I kinder think the doc's been fouled."

"You don't believe he had anything to do with Jean's trouble?"

"No, I don't. The doc'll turn up, an' when he does…" Pitney stopped.

"Yes, dad?"

"Well, when he turns up he'll—he'll explain," finished the factor, weakly.

Judy caught the irresolute note in her father's voice. She gripped the arms of the chair.

"Dad," she cried, "you mean to say something else! You know something!"

"I don't know nothin'!"

"Then you suspect something."

"Gal, everybody has suspicions of some kind nor other 'bout things an' folks. Suspicions is bad things to air. Now me, bein' a awful slow-thinkin', man, I got to be careful 'bout lettin' 'em loose. I'm the kind o' fool that never knows for sure what he knows. In the mornin' Mr. Devlin'll conduct a search. Better turn in now, Judy, like I said."

"But, dad, if you know something—"

"Like I said, Judy, I don't know nothin'. G'night."

And Pitney shut up like a clam.

BRIGHT AND early next morning Devlin was astir. He took with him three Indians who had been hanging about the post for the past few days.

One of the Indians picked up a snowshoe trail near the place where Burr and Cyriac had camped, and started off, with Devlin at his heels. Presently they reached the point where the marks of a sled and a dog-team began.

"He must have bought another team on the sly," Devlin said. "There's only one pair of snowshoe tracks from his camp."

They went on, following the trail easily. When it led them upon a narrow waterway they became confused, traveled slowly, trying to pick the prints they sought from the confusion of other prints, for this apparently was a trail much used. Finally a trail branched off, and one of the Indians said it was the same trail as the one they had picked up at the camp.

Devlin, a little fidgety at first, argued. Then, seeing a way out, he remarked, "All right. I'll follow this one. Two of you keep on following the stream for a way. You, boy, stay here with the dogs. I'll be right back."

Once started, Devlin smiled to himself at the cleverness with which he had handled the annoying situation. It did not take him long to come within sight of Raab's cabin. The sun was pretty well up by now, so he could employ one of the several means he and Raab had invented to focus the attention of the latter. From a pocket he took a little mirror, got the sun against it, and flashed it against the shack's single window. This flash, he knew, would penetrate the room and be reflected on the walls.

Five minutes later the door opened and Raab came out, paused, and squinted to determine the location of the signal. He came rocking down toward the bush where Devlin was concealed.

"Well, I did it," he grinned.

"So I see," Devlin snapped. "But why did you have to bash in the Frenchman's head? A devil of a lot of thinking I've had to do. Cyriac was unconscious, and I sent a man off to a doctor with him before he woke up. He mentioned Burr's name, but no more, and I've been trying to cast suspicion on Burr at the post. Lucky if Cyriac doesn't die."

"I had to bash him an' bash him quick," growled Raab. "He was just about to wake up."

"How's your prisoner?"

"Able to walk around an' talk too damn much."

"About what?"

"Nothin' much. Just thinks he c'n fight—thassall."

"Not loose now, is he?"

"No. Got him handcuffed t' the bunk post while I'm out an' when I'm tired. Keep him that way most o' the time. Pair a hand-cuffs I swiped from a Mounty once. Pinky's still away t' look up some old friends."

"H-m-m. Keep him there. The longer you keep him the more you get. I'll be over this way every so often and you watch out for signals. I'd better get back now. You, too."

When Devlin joined the Indians he said, "This can't be the trail. I followed it to an old trapper's camp and talked with him. Let's go on."

"This is the trail," persisted the Indian who had first discovered it.

"It can't be," Devlin clipped. "I've followed it, spoken with the old-timer that made it. Get a move on."

Devlin stayed out most of the day, and when he returned to Windy Creek House said they had found no trace of Burr.

"He's probably cleared out of the country," was his verdict. "They were partners. Possibly argued over the division of the season's catch. Burr bashed him while he slept and ran away. And that, my dear Miss Pitney, is the type of man you would let perform a serious operation on your eyes."

Judy made no reply. Neither did the old factor.

The days, passing, turned into weeks. Jerry Sand's return from the doctor had not enlightened the case. Cyriac, he said, had been delirious all the way, unable to answer questions.

"The doc said maybe there was something the matter with his brain, from the blow. I waited a day, hopin' Jean would be able to speak, but he got worse. Doc didn't expect him to live. So I came back."

Two more weeks slipped by. Spring came early that year. Broken ice and unleashed waters foamed in the rivers, and in places the earth appeared through the snow. Trappers came out of the deeper wilderness by the score, some packing their pelts overland, others braving the dangerous waterways in frail canoes.

Gay songs rang through the wilderness, thrown out from the throats of rugged men whose simple hearts responded to the magic of the first hints of spring—men who for more than half a year had been imprisoned in the frozen-hearted wilds. Up out of the north they came, bearded and dirty but happy as children, swapping yarns by their nightly campfires, telling tales of the winter's vigil on the white frontier, laughing at hardships gone and hardships yet to come. They spun tales of trap-thieves, tales of precious foxes yet to be caught, of starvation on snow-blocked trails, of low temperatures and winds that cut like a knife. Men from the Barrens there were, men from Baker Lake, men from the frozen, wind-bitten inlets of Hudson's Bay. All trails pointed south.

Still no word of Burr sifted to Windy Creek House. But many trappers came, trappers who had never come before, for Devlin's scouts had traveled far and fast with word of fancy prices. Windy Creek House got the first spring trade, but the news spread suddenly, and Fort Surprise was not deaf. Nor was Luke Lankford the one to sit back and take his medicine without a stroke of his own. He promptly jacked up his own prices, placed them even a trifle above the ones set by Devlin. And heavy trade came his way, too.

When Pitney heard of this he said to Devlin. "Think you picked on the wrong man when you riled this here Luke Lankford."

"Never mind. We'll go him one better," Devlin snapped.

"But, my God, headquarters won't stand for such prices!"

"Just now you're taking orders from me. Prices go up. I'll show Lankford a thing or two!"

To himself Pitney said, "There's ruin ahead—*ruin!*"

CHAPTER X

THE TEST OF BRAWN

THE WEEKS of imprisonment had changed Burr from a clean-shaven, presentable young man to a bearded, shaggy giant, whose gift of silence irritated his unkempt captor.

Only once a day had Burr talked at length since the beginning of his forced sojourn in the filthy cabin. Each day he had told Raab he could beat him to a pulp. And each day, for some strange reason, Raab had restrained himself.

Burr sat on the edge of the bunk, his right hand manacled to the post. Pinky Smith had not returned yet, and the business of guarding Burr was becoming nerve-wracking to Buck Raab. Raab had grown vile. He refused Burr water at times. He refused him the solace of a smoke. For hours at a time he sat slumped by the table and stared malevolently at his prisoner.

Raab hated Burr—hated him with all the venom of a half-savage soul. He hated him because Burr had told him time and again he could beat him. He hated him because deep in his heart there was a vague fear that Burr could do it, battling with an equally strong conviction that he could not. Between these two fires, Raab, the man, was being torn to ribbons. He was a man who could not bear to lose—not even the thought of it.

Burr asked, "How much longer do you think you can hold me here?"

"As long as I damn please!" Raab growled.

"No you can't."

"Can't I, though?"

"No."

"An' why not, hey?"

"Because before very long you're going to fight me. I'm going to pound your head off, break a few of your ribs, blacken your eyes, and mess you up generally."

Raab's fists knotted, but he did not move.

"Take a better man than you."

"On the contrary I think a poorer man could do just as well."

"You clamp your trap, d'you hear?"

"The trouble is, Raab, you're afraid. You're scared stiff. You may be big but you've got no fighting heart. I know a man where I come from, a little fellow, only half your size, who I bet could knock daylight into you. Why, hell, man, you're easy… easy!"

Raab's nostrils quivered. "Shut up or I'll knock your teeth down your throat!"

"Why, give me, say, ten minutes, and I could lay you flat," pursued Burr calmly.

"Like hell you could!"

"I'm used to fighting with certain holds barred, but if you've got any nasty tricks of your own invention, I'd be willing to let you try them out and have you find how rotten they are. In other words, Raab, I could handle you like a baby."

"My God, you don't think nothin' of yourself!"

"Just facts. Now, see here. Do you know why you won't fight me? Do you know why you won't take away these handcuffs? I'll tell you why, Raab. It's because you're yellow. There's a streak of it up your back a mile long and a yard wide!"

"By—"

Raab could say no more. He lunged from his seat at the table and struck out. Burr warded off the blow with his one free arm.

"With the manacles on?" asked Burr.

"No, by cripes! You'll need both hands an' both feet!"

"I can do it with my hands, Raab."

Outside the sun shone with a new warmth, bringing forth the perfumes of the earth. The poplar buds grew fat, the grasses thrust up fresh shoots, the dogtooth violets sought the benevolent sunlight. The air was laden with the exhilarating aroma of jackpine and spruce, the strangely sweet smell of lily roots, in the thawing muskeg. All the awakening world seemed clean and beautiful and restless.

None of this virginal beauty permeated through the cabin. For three weeks these two men had lived together under a tremendous strain—the strain of one mentality pitted against another—the slow, gruelling process of one mentality trying to wear down the other. Such a conflict is infinitely terrible to a man whose brawn completely overshadows his brain. Thus with Raab. He had reached the breaking point. He felt he could not stand his captive's jibes and taunts for another minute. He could not. He would burst. That is just the way he felt.

Burr had waited three weeks for this—not only waited, but worked. He had played constantly on Raab's vanity, belittled the man's brute strength, goaded him on and on, bragged of his own prowess. Not that Burr was a braggart; it was simply his method of wearing down his man. Burr knew that Raab was no easy mark. He knew that he would have to fight as he had never fought before, if he wished to hold his own. But he had the heart of a fighter, and in that heart he believed he could beat the man.

Raab flung the table against the wall. For a brief moment, then, they faced each other.

Burr carried the fight to Raab, whipped a one-two punch to wind and jaw, got under the man's guard, and pounded his ribs with short, jolting stabs. Raab clinched, awed at the sudden fury of that attack, snarled, and tried to use his knee.

Burr twisted aside, broke loose, and flung away, but he was right back with another fast, devastating attack. His blows were straight, accurate, and his fighting poise was expert.

An overhand punch caught Raab on the left cheek. Two left crosses rapped the point of his jaw and made his teeth rattle.

Another right that carried a world of steam behind it landed on the same point. Raab reeled back and stopped with a jolt against the wall.

He could not seem to get started, somehow. He had not figured on Burr taking the offensive. He was awed, shocked, dumfounded. His head, banging against the wall, made him groan, and within his being a Niagara of fury was suddenly unleashed.

He rebounded from the wall, charging head-down. Burr side-stepped, let him pass, and he brought up against the opposite wall. When he turned Burr was ready for him, and pounded his head mercilessly so that Raab hugged it with his arms. His stomach and ribs took those blows until he again resorted to the use of his knees and feet. Burr stepped back then.

For a moment they faced each other again. Burr laughed tauntingly.

"You're easy, Raab—easy," he jibed.

Raab only licked his bloody lips. Then he charged headlong, caught Burr with his shoulder, and knocked him down. Burr landed on the side of his face in an awkward position, and was heaving up when Raab caught him on the chin with a hard-driven boot. Burr fell back again, gritting his teeth, groaning deep in his throat. He felt Raab's boots against his ribs, realized that if he didn't get on his feet now he probably never would.

He rolled over quickly, bounded up, and caught another boot in the ribs before he finally stood erect. His head spun. He saw the leer on Raab's face, saw Raab coming at him.

Instead of stepping away he ducked under two wild swings, and brought his own fist up under Raab's iron jaw. Again and again he brought up lefts and rights, until Raab, shaking his head, snorting, fell away. Burr kept right after him with a continuous rain of blows, broke through his guard, landed squarely on his jaw, his mouth, his nose, drove him about the room, back and forth, never letting up, every blow clean and most of them landing solidly.

Again Raab used his knees and feet. Burr buckled under a vicious, utterly foul kick that brought a groan through his clenched teeth and doubled him up on the floor. He lurched away across the floor in this position, trying to dodge the kicks that Raab dealt as he reeled after him, sweat streaming from him with the intense pain.

He caught one of Raab's flying boots with an outstretched hand and yanked the man off his balance, brought him toppling to the floor amid a fusillade of vile oaths.

Locked in each other's arms, they rolled back and forth, their heads and heels rapping the hard floor, their great muscles bulging like pine knots through their tattered shirts, their shaggy beards matted with blood and sweat.

Burr knew that very soon the fight must end, either one way or the other. The blood pounded in his head, his heart thumped, the muscles of his stomach ached from the terrible exertion. Raab's battered face was very near his own, his breath came in quick, hot gasps, his huge hands struggled for a throathold.

Burr, flat on his back, held those hands away with a strength that even he himself never knew he possessed.

Little by little Raab was working up his right knee, striving to plant it in Burr's stomach. Finally he succeeded. That stomach of Burr's was strong and padded with muscles of steel, but he knew he could not withstand that brutal pressure for very long.

In a desperate effort he tried the scissors hold—swung his legs up about Raab's ribs, locked his feet together and pressed. Meanwhile, Raab's hands were nearing his throat.

The scissors was telling; it was working, pressing Raab's sides together, interfering with his wind, causing him intense pain. First of all it made him relax the pressure of his knee on Burr's stomach and concentrate all his power to reach his opponent's throat.

Raab's eyes glazed, his breath grated. Suddenly he realized that his struggle for Burr's throat was not gaining; instead, it was losing. Little by little Burr was thrusting him away, and all the while the scissors was pressing tighter on his sides, until he thought his ribs must snap.

Worst of all, he began to realize, with a sense of horror, that he was losing. He had exerted every ounce of strength in his great body. He was not weakening, but Burr was getting stronger in a last superhuman effort, at that critical time when clean-living and stamina carry a man through.

Burr turned him over, flattened him out, and caught him by the throat.

Gradually Raab's vision clouded, his breath rattled in his throat, his stomach heaved. Suddenly he relaxed, fell limp, expired.

Burr released his hold, fell away to one side, lay down with his face in one arm, struggling for breath. He had gone the full limit of endurance. His body had stood the awful strain only a minute longer than Raab's, but that single minute had won the fight for him.

He crawled across the room for a drink of water, dragged himself to a stool, and sat there, staring vacantly at the man he had beaten senseless.

"If I've done this to Raab," he mused, "God knows what I'll do to Devlin."

And he took another drink.

CHAPTER XI

FUR COUNTRY

THINGS IN general were not working out as Devlin had hoped they would. Indeed, he had underrated the redoubtable Luke Lankford.

In the midst of his feverish exertions to kill the trade of Fort Surprise Devlin had brief moments of clear reasoning, but the insufferable egotism of the man prevented the wisdom of these short interludes from directing his thoughts in rational channels. There was a certain wild, unreasonable tenacity in his make-up that would not give in. He had boasted that he would crush the trade of Fort Surprise. He had been sure his idea of raising the prices would turn the trick. But Luke Lankford went him one better each time, and Devlin began to think up another plan.

He was desperate now, willing to try anything. He would have to show something at headquarters for all the expense he had cost the company.

He left Windy Creek one bright afternoon and headed along the trail that led to Raab's cabin. His nerves were on edge. The twittering of the rock-sparrows irritated him. A gorgeously colored Canada jay, bursting forth with its shrill note just over his head, caused him to start and catch his breath, then swear between his teeth. Shortly after this he heard crunching sounds up ahead. He paused, listened intently, then suddenly dodged to one side and crouched hidden in the thickets.

He saw a man rock by not ten feet away. The man was big, bearded. There were bruises on his face and a grim, resolute look in his eyes.

In a moment the man was out of sight. Devlin gasped.

"My God! Burr!"

He leaped up and hurried on with frantic haste. He reached Raab's cabin, saw the door swinging open, and rushed in. He stopped just inside the door, groaned deep in his throat with mixed agony and rage.

Raab was trying to get up. He was on one elbow, shaking his head, grunting. Both his eyes were black, one ear was puffed up, his lips were swollen, and his beard was caked with blood. His head and torso were wet, and there was a puddle of water on the floor, for Burr apparently had thrown a bucket of water over him.

Devlin stood with his hands on his hips, whispering oaths, quivering with suppressed rage. Raab cocked one ludicrous eye at him and tried to grin.

" 'Lo, Devlin," he said, weakly.

"What the hell happened to you?"

"Say, will you hand us a drink o' water?"

Devlin crossed the room, filled a tin dipper, and held it to Raab's lips. He said:

"Didn't I tell you not to fight with him? Didn't I tell you to let him talk his head off? Oh, you plagued fool! A fine mess you are!"

"Yeah, but you should see Burr."

"See him? I did see him making tracks for Windy Creek, and I didn't see anything the matter with him, either."

Raab was wobbly. "Oh… you seen him, huh? Ugh! Kinder help me onto that stool, will you? Be all right in a li'l while."

"My God, what a mess!"

Raab flopped down on the stool and held his head in his hands.

"Guess I wasn't feelin' so good when we started," he complained. "I was sick—kinder dizzy an' all."

"Oh, don't think I'll swallow that!"

Devlin went about bathing Raab's wounds, and finally the latter was able to sit up and see things clearly.

Then Devlin said, "We've got to drive Lankford out, one way or the other. I don't care to jack up the company's prices any more."

"Yeah?" droned Raab, once more himself. "I'll go right over that way tomorrow and bump Lankford off, but first you got to show me more money."

"No, you're not going to shoot him," protested Devlin. "And you'll get your money later. Don't worry."

"I want to see money before I start, mister. There's no tellin' when Burr might run across you, an' if he does he'll break you in two. He suspects that you hired me."

"You told him?"

"No. He told me. So if I'm goin' to keep on doin' your dirty work I want to see money first. I'm not workin' for you because I like you. I'm workin' for money. So get that straight. An' say, what the hell you got against Burr, anyhow?"

"His being here merely interferes with my plans."

"In other words, he's got a grudge against you, an' if he meets up with you there'll be hell to pay."

"Don't let that angle of it interest you," clipped Devlin. "We were talking about driving Lankford out."

"An' we was also talkin' about money, if your mem'ry ain't bad."

With an impatient gesture Devlin reached into his pocket and flung a roll of bills at Raab.

"Almost a hundred there. That's all I've got on me. You make me sick."

"Not half as sick as you make me," dragged out Raab, counting the money. "You don't know what the hell you want to do. You think up high-soundin', intricate ideas an' they go smash. Me, I still say there's no better way to get Lankford out of the way than by squattin' in the bush an' clippin' him neat when he comes out."

"No, you idiot!" Devlin cried. "You'd get caught and most likely you'd squeal. Listen. If this hot sun keeps up for a week the bush and grasses around Fort Surprise will be rotten dry. You could go over that way and start a blaze with the wind in the right direction. Light it a couple of miles away, so it will get a good lively start. It will sweep the post buildings clean. But don't let anyone see you over there. It would be like you to bungle things, just as you did here."

"Aw, shut your face about that," muttered Raab. "You ain't bungled nothin', have you? Oh, no!"

"Now, let's not argue. You'd better clear out of here as soon as possible. Get over in the Fort Surprise country and lay low. Cyriac hasn't been heard from yet. I'll go back to the house."

"Look out for Burr!"

"He can't prove anything. I'll bluff my way through. Take a chance, anyhow. It's my last card. I've got to stay around the house."

So Devlin retraced his steps toward Windy Creek. It was the only thing to do. He had tried everything in his power to avoid meeting Burr, but now there was no way out. He would have to bluster his way through.

When he arrived he went into the trade-store and found the place packed with newly-arrived trappers. Jerry Sand was behind the counter.

"Where's Pitney?" Devlin flung at him.

"Next door with Jim Burr. Burr just blew in from God knows where, all banged up."

Devlin went outside, and paused to light a cigarette. Then he threw back his shoulders, set his jaw, and strode across to the little cabin. Without a moment's hesitation he pushed open the door and stepped in. Pitney was the only one in the room. He was stuffing tobacco into his pipe.

"Pretty busy next door," Devlin said. "Better go over. Oh, by the way, I hear that Burr chap turned up?"

Pitney said, "In the kitchen with Judy an' Annie. Annie's bathin' his wounds. I tol' you he'd turn up. He was waylaid by Buck Raab, a bad man in these parts, an' him an' Raab fought it out. Guess the doc was the better man, 'cause he got away an' come back here, though he ain't said yet who won, him or Raab. But I guess the doc won all right, him bein' here an' all. Want to speak to him?"

"No, I've got a lot of reports to write up. I'm going into my office in the trade-store, and I don't care to be disturbed this afternoon."

With that Devlin turned on his heel and went out. Perspiration pimpled his forehead in beads. At the last moment he had paled at the thought of meeting Burr face to face. He would wait a little while longer....

CHAPTER XII

SUSPENSE

WHEN BURR came out of the kitchen into the living-room some time later his beard was gone, his hair was combed, and he looked clean. But his face was patched here and there with strips of white plaster, and on one cheek was a black and purple lump where Raab's boot had connected. His right hand, that had punished Raab unmercifully, was also patched with plaster over the knuckles. He had not come out of that raw brawl unscathed by any means.

Judy was radiant. She had not given up hope for Burr. Her faith in his goodness had been external. And her happiness knew no bounds when that faith was vindicated.

"Dad and I—we knew you would come back," she said, when Burr led her to a chair.

"Yes, I guess it looked as if I had done Jean in, the way I dropped out of sight," he replied, enjoying his first pipe in many days. "There is something mysterious behind it. You've had no word from him since he was taken to the doctor's?"

"Not a word," said Pitney.

"I must get in touch with him, if he's alive. If he's dead, God help the man that dealt the blow!" Burr struck his knee, then settled back. "So my instruments have arrived, and the medicines? Are you still willing to trust your eyes to me, Miss Pitney?"

"Yes. Oh, I wish it was over!"

"I'll begin tomorrow," Burr said. "I should have an assistant, or a nurse, but—let me see—I'll ask Mr. Devlin to substitute."

Old Pitney shot him an oblique, quizzical look.

Burr added, "Is Mr. Devlin around?"

"In his office, doc—back o' the traderoom," Pitney offered. "Tol' me would be busy this afternoon, though. Doesn't want to be disturbed."

Burr got up. "I'll go over and speak with him about it, anyhow."

He strode out, and the factor stood in the center of the room, in perplexed indecision. Burr entered the trade-store and waved to Jerry Sand.

"Mr. Devlin in?" he asked.

"Yeah, he's in. But he left word that I shouldn't let anybody near him. He's busy, he said."

"That's all right, Jerry. I'll walk right in. This the door?"

"Yeah, but—"

Burr passed him, pushed open the door, and closed it quickly in Jerry Sand's face. In the little room Burr stood with his thumbs hooked in his wide belt. He looked down on Devlin, who sat in a chair with his feet perched on a table. For a full minute no word passed between them. They just stared at each other. Then Burr offered:

"Thought you wouldn't be busy."

Still Devlin did not speak. Burr strode forward and sat down opposite him, planted his elbows on the edge of the desk.

"Well," he drawled in his low, subdued voice, "we meet at last. And of all places, at Windy Creek House. And you an inspector for the Bay West Company. You are scared dumb, aren't you? No, I'm not going to twist your head off. If you were as big as the man you hired to keep me out of your way, I might do it. *You* would be too easy—too easy. But you'll pay for the blot you put on my good name, Roger Devlin.

"I'm not the one to stage a show, else I would make a spectacle of you here at the post. But, dear man, you are going to write a confession. You are going to tell about the scurvy trick you played me down Temiskaming way. What's more, besides the written confession, you are going to appear before the medical board and clear me of my disgrace with your own spoken words."

"You can't—" flared Devlin suddenly, his lips quivering, his feet flying down from the desk. With a sudden movement Burr reached across and caught him by the throat.

"I can't what? I can't make you? But I can wring your neck! I can do that!"

"You're twice my size—"

"Thank God for that! And I will make good use of it if you don't come clean. You need tell nothing but the bald truth. That's all I want. Take that pen in your hand!"

He released Devlin's throat and sat down. The inspector rubbed his neck and coughed. His eyes watered.

"Take it!" Burr commanded.

Reluctantly Devlin picked up the pen, biting his lips, shooting furtive glances at Burr. His left hand pulled open the drawer, apparently to pluck out a sheet of paper. Instead it leaped out with a short, stubby revolver, and there was a terrific explosion.

Burr had ducked and shoved over the desk when he caught the significance of the move. The bullet grazed the top of his head as he tumbled to the floor. Devlin, leaping clear of the chair, dashed for the door and bounded into the traderoom.

"Hold that door!" he snapped at Jerry Sand. "That man is off his head! Hold it or I'll shoot him dead in his tracks!"

Jerry and a number of other trappers rushed to block the door while Devlin sped outside. Already Burr was trying to drive his shoulder through the stout boards. Failing in this, he picked up a log stool and hurled it with all his strength.

"Open that door!" he roared, and attacked it again.

"Listen. Take it easy!" cried Jerry Sand.

Again and again Burr drove the heavy stool against the door, until finally the boards gave way. He crashed through like a charging bull and carried two men with him. Jerry Sand, a rifle in his hands, blocked his way.

"Damn you, Jerry, clear out!" snarled Burr.

"The inspector says—"

"I don't care a rap what the inspector says!"

Burr drove into Jerry, tore the rifle from his hands, and plowed into another mass of men. They held him back on general principles, because they had heard Devlin's cry, and had seen Burr overpower Jerry. Through that knot of men he could not move, and, seeing that they probably had an altogether different slant on the situation, he subsided.

"All right, men," he said quietly. "Call it quits. I have no argument with you."

"Nor us with you, doc," ventured Jerry, rubbing his shoulder. "We just wanted to stop what looked like the beginnin' of murder. You almost wrenched out my arm that time, doc."

"I'm sorry, Jerry," Burr apologized. "By this time your estimable inspector is somewhere in the woods and on the prod."

"Who fired that shot?"

"I guess the inspector's gun went off accidentally," Burr replied, and went out. Outside he met Pitney, limping excitedly from his cabin.

"Who was shootin'?" Pitney asked.

"Mr. Devlin got nervous," Burr explained, "and his gun went off. Perhaps Jerry can help me in the operation now. The inspector left suddenly. I don't know for where. Let's go into the cabin."

Inside the two men were alone. Pitney sat down opposite Burr and looked at him for a long minute in silent contemplation.

Finally he said, "I ain't ever pried into no man's affairs, doc, but they's somethin' tells me that the inspector just tried to kill you."

"Yes, he did," admitted Burr frankly. "He tried to kill me. But this is not the end."

Pitney bowed his head. "An' now he's tryin to kill me, doc."

"Kill you?"

"Well, sort of. He's runnin' things here like a madman. He'll ruin the company's name. He'll ruin me!"

Pitney told Burr of Devlin's actions since his arrival at Windy Creek House.

"And you stand for that?" asked Burr, when the factor had finished.

"I had to give in, doc. I'm gettin' old, an' there's Judy to take care of, her havin' no sight. He threatened to get me discharged if I didn't do what he said. An' what could I do if I got discharged? What would Judy do? It sounds like I'm a weak sort of man, doc, an' maybe I am a little, but I can't help it. I ain't as young an' anxious to fight as I used to be. Me, I like peace, doc. An' I got to think of Judy."

"I won't say whether you've done right or wrong, Mr. Pitney," Burr remarked. "I have a score of my own to settle with Devlin. When I get through with him he'll wish he never was born. But first I am going to attend to your daughter's eyes. Tomorrow I'll operate."

BURR OPERATED at ten the following morning, with Jerry in the room to jump at his commands. Outside the cabin waited a score of trappers, solemn and speechless. Among them was old Pitney, leaning on his cane, one hand on his hip, his eyes moist with the light of hope. Near him stood an old-timer, one hand resting on the factor's shoulder, as if to give him courage.

All was silence. Even the gentle southwind seemed to brush its way noiselessly through the forest.

Finally the door of the cabin opened, and Jerry Sand stood there rubbing his hands on a towel. Pitney started forward. The old-timer by his side patted his shoulder. Somewhere a man heaved a vast sigh.

"The doc says I should tell you the operation is over," Jerry stated, "an' Judy is restin' right comfortable."

"Thank God!" exclaimed Pitney.

The men relaxed, spoke freely amongst themselves and crowded forward. Jerry raised his hand.

"Better not come in, boys. Only you, Sam. Judy's eyes is bandaged an' she needs quiet."

Inside Pitney gripped Burr's hand.

"D'you think she'll see, doc?"

"I think so, Mr. Pitney. I'm quite sure. But we'll have to wait for about ten days, until your daughter takes off the bandages. Now no noise, please."

"Oh, doc, God bless you!" cried the old man.

CHAPTER XIII

JEAN CYRIAC, VOYAGEUR

THREE DAYS after the operation Burr came and sat down by Judy.

"How do you feel now?" he asked.

"All right. There's a little pain, but not much. Oh, I hope it's successful!"

"I have every reason to believe it will be," he replied. "Now I'm going on a little trip. I've engaged an Indian to show me the way to the doctor's where Jean Cyriac was taken. I must see about Jean. I can't wait any longer. There is nothing for you to do now but wait until the time comes to remove the bandages. I'll get back as quickly as possible. But I must see about poor old Jean."

Up until the time he left with the Indian guide there had been no sign of Devlin. The inspector had disappeared completely.

Burr left bright and early on the morning following his talk with Judy. Both he and the guide carried a light pack. The last patches of snow were disappearing rapidly under the strong sun. Only in the deep, dark valleys, where the drifts had piled high, did the sun fail to melt it. But on the ridge tops and the level stretches of the wilderness the earth and trees were bare, and the first spring birds filled the air with melody.

The going was arduous all day. At nightfall they camped five miles from their destination, making a balsam shelter near a noisy waterfall.

They were up and off with the sun next morning, winding through a forest of great trees where the air was cool and sweet with the smell of fresh earth. Somewhere ahead of them the silvery song of a black-throated thrush came down the wind. When this died away Burr stopped short and put a hand to his ear, listening intently. Another song was coming down the wind—a gay, lilting song that *voyageurs* sing in the spring.

Burr rapped palm to thigh and started off, shouting:

"Oh, Jean! Oh, Jean!"

The song stopped. Burr rocked on, with the Indian tagging at his heels. He tore over a ridge, ran down the other side, and came face to face with Cyriac. Cyriac's arms went up in a grand gesture.

"Jeem, *mon ami!*" he cried, and threw his arms about Burr.

"I was on my way to find you," said Burr, gripping his arms. "Man alive, you're a ghost!"

Cyriac was very pale, and a deep scar fully three inches long ran down his left cheek.

" 'Twas a nasty blow, Jeem," he explained. "For ten days I'm out of ma head. An' dis scar! *Mon Dieu,* what happened? Who did it?"

Burr told of his own capture, his imprisonment, and his fight for freedom.

"You must have begun to wake up when Raab hit me," he added, "so he cracked you, too. But Raab was hired to do it, and by the very man who caused my professional disgrace."

"Eh?"

"Yes. You met him."

"I?"

"That Inspector Devlin."

"You knew all de while, an' nevaire tol' me?"

"I had to think. I didn't want to stage a show."

Cyriac was the only man in the North who had received Burr's confidence, who had been told by Burr the story of his medical downfall.

"And he is still alive?" Cyriac asked.

"He got away. Probably joined up with Raab, and the two of them beat it. By the way, I operated on the factor's daughter. Think she'll be able to see again."

"Ah, dat is news!" Cyriac cried. "Let us *marche.*"

Cyriac was still weak, and they had to travel slowly, with many halts. He said he had started south against the doctor's advice, with no news from Windy Creek, with no word of Burr, he had become impatient and anxious for his partner. As they headed south now, his breathing spells became more frequent. He began to totter and stumble.

"Jean," said Burr at last, "you should not have started out. You're still a sick man. We'll travel no more today."

"I start, Jeem, because I'm not hear from you," he replied weakly, dropping upon a fallen tree.

The Indian gathered balsam boughs and they made a bed for Cyriac in the warm sunlight. He rested for the remainder of the day and slept well during the night. In the morning he insisted on taking up the trail again. Burr argued, but Cyriac was adamant. They started off, setting a slow pace, making frequent stops. Cyriac lasted until two that afternoon, when his legs wobbled and he stumbled. He cursed his weakness, and cried with the rage of a strong man, whose strength has been sapped, leaving him weak as a child. Burr urged him to be quiet.

They camped there for the rest of the day, having covered only four miles since sun-up. Then Burr suggested making a litter, but the Frenchman swore he'd crawl on hands and knees before he'd allow anyone to carry him.

The spirit of him would not accept defeat. Next morning he took the trail again, with the aid of a stick. They were two hours along, just toiling over a steep ridge, when the Indian paused, and, shading his eyes with a hand, gazed across the wilderness to the eastward. He called to Burr and pointed toward a mass of dark clouds that rolled sluggishly above the distant roof of the forest.

"Fire," he stated.

Burr nodded, feeling the wind. "East wind, too."

Cyriac said, "De sun she's been hot for more 'an a week. Dere is mooch dead wood in de forest here, mooch grass an' bush. Below us are de forks in de trail. Over dot way by de fire is Luke Lankford's place."

"We'd better get along," announced Burr a little grimly.

They started down the grade, while the smoke clouds rolled skyward and half-blotted out the sun. Burr took Cyriac by one arm while the Indian led the way. The Frenchman labored. His breath came hard. He stumbled, but Burr held him up.

The wind grew, rolling the thick smoke clouds before it, bringing to the men's nostrils faintly the tang of burning wood. Flocks of birds passed overhead, winging into the west, away from the advancing menace. The smell of wood smoke became more pungent. The faint, distant roar of the inferno reached the travelers. Lurid streaks of flame could be seen shooting through the gray clouds. There was a far-away crackling like the rifle-fire of armies in conflict.

"T'ree miles more an' dere is a lake, Jeem," Cyriac panted.

"Keep strong, Jean."

"*Oui.*"

CHAPTER XIV

THE RED FURY

THE FIRE rolled on, gaining headway, sweeping viciously over fields of dry-rot, crackling through dead brush, leaping on to the twisted deadfalls, creeping slowly through the greenwoods, and sending up great clouds of dark smoke where the dampness offered resistance.

Partridges beat about in panic, rabbits darted along with lightning swiftness. Burning splinters sizzled through the air.

Raab reeled through this chaos—this inferno, that was of his own making. He had started it not quite two miles north of Fort Surprise, when a good wind was working out of the northeast. He had watched it gather way, then had started west himself to get clear of the country. But winds are peculiar; they have a habit of changing suddenly, without much warning. And so the wind had swung around from northeast to almost southeast, sweeping wide of Fort Surprise, and the fire ran to catch up with the man who had started it.

Nor was Raab, by this time, far ahead of the flames. The smoke rolled over him, choked him, blinded him, so that many times he fell or ran headlong into a tree. He lost all sense of direction for a while, floundering about until the wind parted the smoke and showed him a mass of roaring flames.

With a horrified groan he turned in the other direction and plunged onward in mad haste, regardless of the briars that ripped away his shirt and coat and slashed open his skin.

Suddenly he stumbled headlong and fell over something that lay in his path, and clawed at the earth as he struck with full force on his face. He clambered to his feet. Something tugged at his legs. He whirled about and saw Devlin lying on the ground, his clothes in rags, his face a study in pain and horror.

"My leg, Raab! I can't stand on it—twisted it! Oh, God!"

Raab looked back, saw the flames leaping at him, the smoke billowing in low-banked masses, the hot sparks swirling about. He kicked himself free, started to run off, then cursed, stepped back and swung Devlin over his shoulder.

Devlin screamed with pain at the rough handling, but Raab made no amends. He lumbered along, his eyes burning, his throat baked dry, falling sparks singeing his beard. He did not ask Devlin how he came to be there. He did not care. Some instinct, buried far down in his dark soul, had sprung to life, and prevented him from leaving Devlin to a fiery death.

He clung to his burden grimly, crashing through briars, leaping over fallen trees. Devlin cried out again and again at the agony of his sprained leg. Raab did not stop, nor could he afford to take the time to handle Devlin with care.

He took another headlong fall. Devlin went flying over his head, to land with his mouth dripping curses and prayers.

Raab was on his feet in a flash. He caught a new hold of Devlin, swung him up like a bag of meal, and reeled on. The flames were behind him, and their heat blistered the back of his neck. Sparks rained about his face, and patches of fire started up ahead, ignited by the flying splinters.

He caught a fleeting glimpse of water through the trees. He tried to roar out the delight, the thankfulness in his heart, but his throat was parched dry and no sound came. He put every last ounce of energy into his legs, and the water, sparkling cool, beckoned him on to safety.

The red tongues were beginning to lick his back when he finally reached the shore, and plunged straight into the water, still hanging to Devlin. He waded out on the sandy bottom. The incline was gradual, and enabled him to put sufficient distance between himself and the shore by the time the water was level with his shoulders. It was cool. The sudden immersion proved quite a shock to his heated body, but he stood there, Devlin still on his back, though seeming quite oblivious of the inspector's presence until he heard him groan. This brought him back to his immaculate surroundings.

He said, "Aw, shut up! You ain't dead."

"But, damn it, you handled me like a dead rat! Oh, my leg!"

"Lucky I handled you at all, mister. Me, I was so close to hell back there that for a minute I felt religious, an' I understand it ain't religious to let a man burn to death if you can help it. That's the only reason I can figure for pickin' you up. An' what the hell was you doin' up here anyway?"

"Looking for you. I'd changed my mind about that fire business, and wanted to tell you."

"Changed your mind! Gawdamighty, what a bloke you are! What made you change your mind, huh? Burr, maybe?"

"Never mind that. You bungled the job as it is."

"Could I help it if the wind changed, you blasted fool? Don't tell me I bungled the job. You been doin' more bunglin' 'an I ever done in all my borned days. Now shut up, or I might drop you here in the lake!"

The fire swept around the lake, sweeping on with devastating fury, leaving the country behind it charred black, with here and there a tree burning like a giant torch. Embers still sputtered and crackled in the red wrath's wake. When Raab waded back toward the ravaged land his body was numb with cold from the long immersion. He reached shore and laid Devlin down, swept his gaze across the water, and watched the clouds of smoke billow toward the west, shot through here and there with the red blades of flames.

"An' that," said he, "is what one little match can do. Ho! Ho!"

"This leg of mine!"

"Aw, shut up! You an' your leg. You're like a woman, you wit' your sprained ankle! Let's see it."

Raab bent down, unlaced Devlin's boot none too gently, and massaged his ankle. Devlin groaned, squirmed, cursed and prayed, while Raab stretched, jerked, rubbed and twisted in the name of a massage.

"There," he said finally. "Try it now."

Devlin got up painfully and tried to walk.

"Not so bad. I can only limp, but that will be all right. It seems you have twisted it back in shape again. Well, here we are. I wish you had used better judgment in setting that fire. I'll wager it didn't come within a mile of Fort Surprise."

"Did so. Was about half-a-mile."

"At any rate, Fort Surprise still stands."

"Now, I ask you, how the hell can I help it if the wind changes?"

"Oh, let us drop it—let us drop it."

"An' by the way, mister," Raab said suddenly, "you know you ain't been comin' across wit' money lately?"

"You'll get money. Don't worry about that, my dear fellow."

"I will, hey? All right. I wan't' see it, though, before I pull another job. I— Sh! Hear voices."

He drew Devlin into the thickets, and they crouched motionless.

For a minute or so they heard no sound but the movement of feet crunching through thickets. Then somebody swore, and another voice chuckled. Followed another voice—

"Now, s'y, I'm f'r mykin' a bloomin' fire an' dryin' these 'ere duds o' mine."

"So 'm I."

"Me too."

Raab stood up as Pinky Smith, leading six men, came trudging into view. Pinky stopped short, his crooked little mouth puckered up and his eyes popped.

"Why, Bucky, ol' cab—ol' man!" he exclaimed. "S'y, it's pleased ter meet yer I am, Bucky."

Raab strode out of the thickets. "Oh, you are, hey? Where the hell you been f'r the last six weeks?"

"Bucky, ol' sport, it's a bloomin' long story. Me an' the b'ys 'ere got kinder mixed up wit' the Mounties. Yer know 'ow it is, Bucky. We 'ad ter keep bleedin' low f'r a while. The b'ys are good stuff, though. Yer know 'em all 'cept this un, Bucky. This is Bub all."

Raab nodded to the gang with an important scowl, and they drew near him. It was a tough-looking crowd. Three were white. The other three were crossbreeds, lean, rangy fellows who had run with Raab many times before. Not one in all the gang could have looked a policeman straight in the face. They had no respect for the law, and very little for any man the three 'breeds especially; they were insolent, deadly, swaggering, and they were having a little joke amongst themselves on the bedraggled appearance of Devlin.

Raab spoke: "Well, let's make a fire so we can dry up."

One of the 'breeds chuckled liquidly. "Fire, m'sieur. *Sacre!* Has it not been enough of de fire?"

"You tryin' t' be wise, Paul? Clamp your jaw!" snarled Raab.

A fire was made.

Pinky drew Raab aside and said, "S'y, 'as 'e been tryin' t' flim-flam yer, Bucky? I mean, 'as 'e been comin' acrost? Y' know, I tol' the b'ys 'ere'd be pretty pickin's."

"I spoke t' him about that just before you came," Raab replied. "Yeah, he'll come across all right. You just leave that t' me."

"Don't let 'im 'oodwink yer, Bucky. S'y, we'll bleed 'im f'r all 'e's got, what!"

"Well, Pinky, I ain't doin' his dirty work f'r nothin', that's a sure thing. Guess we'd better get started soon, huh?"

Devlin was not in any too buoyant a frame of mind. He didn't like the way those 'breeds eyed him, and talked among themselves with many little chuckles and sly winks. Their actions hurt his super-sensitive vanity. And he didn't like little Pinky Smith.

Pinky had a nasty, malicious way of grinning at him. For that matter, he had no use for Raab either. But there was nothing secretive about Raab, he knew. He could almost anticipate every word that the big man was going to say.

He feared Pinky because he knew that inside that misshapen little head was a crooked, wily mind, and he noticed that quite often Pinky drew Raab to one side and spoke to him in low whispers. He didn't like this business at all. And he didn't quite fancy the way these vagabonds considered themselves his equal. Their disrespectful attitude made him seethe deep in his soul. But he realized, vaguely, that he was enmeshed in a net from which, for him, there was no escape.

He would go the limit now in a last effort to carry through his original designs. Oddly enough, he still believed himself to be invincible. He could not afford to lose. He could not bear to lose. He had started something that must be finished at all costs. He was a victim of his own vanity.

CHAPTER XV

EYES

WHEN BURR and Cyriac arrived at Windy Creek House they found everybody there in a state of anxiety.

"We saw the clouds o' smoke," explained old Pitney, "an' we knew you'd be in that part o' the country. Jerry, here, was gettin' ready to start north to see if you were all right."

"We made a lake before the fire reached us," Burr said.

"An' I'm weak like de baby," put in Cyriac.

Jerry remarked, "That must have been some crack you got, old-timer. Hell, what a scar it left. Come on, Jean. I'll fix up the bed the inspector used to sleep in, so's you can lay down an' take it easy."

"Inspector Devlin hasn't showed up yet, eh?" asked Burr, quietly.

"Not yet," Pitney answered. "I sent some men out t' look for him, but they ain't found no signs. I was thinkin' maybe I oughter send a courier out with a message t' headquarters."

They were entering the trade-house. Burr, at the factor's elbow, ventured, "How is your daughter now?"

"Feelin' all right. Little pain, like you said. She can't wait till the day when she can take off the bandage. An', by the way, doc, 'tween me an' you, why did the inspector fire that shot, huh?"

Burr looked at the factor, but did not offer a reply.

"I think I know why, doc," Pitney said after a moment. "I been puttin' two an' two t' gether, watchin' things, like. Me, I'm a pretty slow-thinkin' man, doc, an' it's took me a long time to put this here now two an' two t'gether. But now, lookin' back, an' rememberin' certain incidents, I kinder think I know what's 'tween the inspector an' you. But I ain't told a soul, doc."

Burr patted him on the shoulder.

"I guess you know, all right, Mr. Pitney. Now I think I'll go next door and see your daughter."

He found Judy eagerly awaiting him.

"I thought you'd forgotten all about coming in," she said, with a little laugh.

"Not a bit. You see, Jean is pretty weak, and I wanted to get him safely placed. He told me he was out of his mind for a long time, and the doctor thought he would never come around. But he's all right now, except, of course, his weakness. He has a terrible scar, too, the result of that blow."

"You weren't even singed by the forest fire?"

"No. We reached water in time. But about you now? Feeling all right?"

"A little pain now and then, but otherwise I'm first rate."

"Good. In about three days we'll take off the bandage."

"Oh, I can't wait! But of course I must. I feel that I will see. I am sure I will see. Oh, and I will be so thankful to you! I am now, for what you've done."

"Your faith in my ability is worth more than you can imagine. I have found so much evidence of good faith among you wilderness people."

She was silent for a moment. Then—

"Do you think Mr. Devlin will show up again?"

"I—don't—know."

"Would you want him to?"

Burr looked at her searchingly. "Why do you ask that?"

"Oh!" She laughed lightly. "My eyes may be blind, but I'm not blind otherwise. Mr. Devlin had been acting strangely for some time. Dad, too. I tried to get something out of dad, but no chance. I'm pretty certain, doctor, that Mr. Devlin is the man that tricked you five years ago."

"Eh?"

"Well, isn't he?"

Burr stroked his jaw. "Oh, well, I've tried to hide it long enough."

"I thought so. You hated to make a scene, didn't you? You held off. You didn't know whether to kill Devlin or make a show of him. Doctor, you're a very strange man."

"Guess I am," he mumbled, rising. "I'll be going. Ought to look after Jean."

"That's only an excuse," she told him banteringly. "Won't you sit with me a while, and just talk about—well, about anything. I like to hear you talk. I like your voice. Please stay, doctor."

He sat down again, mopping his moist forehead, and talked— well, about anything.

Three days later the word went around that Burr would remove Judy's bandages that evening a little past sundown. Jean was up and about by this time, looking a little wan, but cheerful and buoyant as of old, with a laugh that still rang lustily in the trade-room. His mustache was neatly clipped, and his dark eyes sparkled with the gay fire of his *voyageur's* soul. Something of his old devil-may-care swagger came back. He spoke with a flourish, and a grand air at times melodramatic. He seemed like a character from an old world romance. He claimed that Gascon blood ran red in his veins, and that his forefathers had fought the Spanish at the siege of Arras.

He was sitting in the little cabin, relating graphically Burr's exploits in the Barren Grounds. He spoke to an audience of one, and that one was Judy. She listened enthralled, for Cyriac was a vivid, dynamic talker, even though at times he became so excited that he broke into French and almost choked.

He was hitting it off in great style when there came a knock on the door. An instant later Burr entered.

"Jean was telling me of your trip to the Barrens," Judy said.

"Oh… that. Yes, that's a favorite topic of Jean's," chuckled Burr. "And every time he tells it, you know, he adds a little more."

"Jeem, you go shut up!" grinned Cyriac.

At this juncture old Pitney entered with Jerry Sand.

"Ready, doc?" he asked.

"Yes." Burr took Judy's arm.

"Oh… now?" she breathed.

"Now," he said, gently.

As he led her into the other room he turned and smiled comfortingly at the factor. Then he closed the door. No one spoke. No one moved. Pitney stared at the closed door like a man in a trance, his old jaw clamped hard, his hand gripping the cane till the knuckles were snow white. Beside him stood Cyriac, his mouth twitching nervously, his hand resting on the factor's shoulder. Behind them stood Jerry Sand, staring fixedly at the floor. The silence was tomb-like.

Abruptly it was shattered—this silence. A wild cry shattered it, a cry that was half chaotic laughter, bearing a note of happiness that pained. Cyriac sucked in a breath through clenched teeth. Jerry Sand retreated a step. Old Pitney started for the door, his eyes wide, his lips quivering. The door flew open and Judy ran into his arms.

"Oh, dad, I can see! *I can see!*" she cried.

"*Le bon Dieu* be praised!" shouted Cyriac, flinging a hand aloft.

Burr stood in the doorway, smiling faintly, a strange, ecstatic light in his eyes. In the midst of his happiness he was serene, unruffled.

Jerry Sand had pulled open the door and bawled the good news to the men outside. Cheers echoed. Hats were tossed up into the air. The men grabbed one another and waltzed about.

Pitney had Burr by the hand now.

"I—I can't ever repay you for this, doc! God, it's great! Thank God! Judy can see. An' me—there's a burden off my shoulders, a ton weight that was killin' me."

Cyriac had Judy by the arm. They ran outside, and Judy stopped short, looking about excitedly, half-sobbing, half-laughing.

"Oh, Jean, isn't it wonderful!" she exclaimed. "I can see again! I can see again! Aren't the spruces wonderful—beautiful? Look how radiant the sky is across those hills, where the sun has just disappeared. Look at all the men, Hello, Joe! Hello, Tim! Oh, how beautiful the world is when you can see!"

Burr was leaning in the doorway, stuffing tobacco into his pipe absently, regarding Judy with thoughtful eyes. Turning, she saw him and came rushing up.

"Didn't I tell you I would see?" she cried. "I was sure I would. Somehow I held great faith in you. I knew you couldn't fail. Oh, I am so happy!"

Burr felt uneasy. "I—I'm happy—you're happy," he managed to say.

She swayed. He caught her before she fell, drew her gently inside, and looked for a moment at her flushed, lovely face, framed in the wealth of raven hair. Her eyes flickered.

"I—I am all right," she murmured. "Just a little dizzy from the—the excitement."

She regained her balance, and Burr led her to the rocking-chair. Old Pitney was already limping in from the kitchen with a drink of water.

"Better rest a while," Burr suggested, with a slow smile.

She smiled back at him, a warm glow that came from her heart.

CHAPTER XVI

LANKFORD ARRIVES

ON THE afternoon of the following day a canoe bearing an Indian and a short, stocky white man came up Windy Creek from the eastward, and grounded on the sandy beach below the post buildings.

The white man wore a set expression on his chubby face. As soon as he cleared the canoe, he jammed a wad of tobacco into his mouth and strode resolutely up the pathway for the trade-house. This man was Luke Lankford, owner of Fort Surprise, and his demeanor suggested that he was on a mission of importance.

He banged into the trade-room, and strode straight across it until he was face to face with old Pitney, who stood behind the counter. The two men eyed each other fixedly. Then Lankford said:

"I just come over, Sam, to find out what the hell's the big idea."

"What idea, Luke?"

"Why, this here idea of up an' paying damn near double for your pelts. There's no other Bay West post doing it. What's the idea? Are you trying to put me out of the running?"

"Now, Luke, wait a minute!"

"It looks pretty rotten to me, Sam. I ain't never done nothing to you. You got me down to my bottom dollar. My pelts are all baled, ready to go south soon as my boys finish repairing my bateau. But I'll be lucky if I clear expenses."

"Luke, listen now, will you?" Pitney pleaded. "They got a new inspector, an' it was his idea. I couldn't raise a hand. I might have lost my job. An', listen, Luke, I had Judy to look after. He went right over my head, an' he sure did put things in an awful mess."

"Where is he?" Lankford growled.

"Dunno, Luke. You see, he dropped out of sight more'n a week ago."

"Wish t' hell he'd fall in a nice, deep lake an' stay there."

"Yeah. Well, he ain't turned up yet. Last night I began runnin' the post my own way again. There's no more big prices, Luke."

"Huh! Why didn't you do that long ago?"

"Well, Luke, I just couldn't. Judy was blind an' all—"

"Where's Judy now—away?"

"No. Judy's around, an', Luke, *she can see!*"

"Go 'way!"

"Yup. She can see. Young doctor came in some time ago with Jean Cyriac, an' he fixed her eyes."

"Jim Burr, eh?"

"The same. You know him?"

"Little bit. Good man." Lankford rubbed his ear. "Well, Sam, I'm glad to hear it wasn't you as tried to break me. Of course, maybe you had to do it like he said, Judy being blind an' depending on you an' all. I can understand, Sam. But now that Judy's able to see, an' take care of herself, you ought to stand up for your rights."

"If the inspector comes back an' starts any of his old tricks, Luke, I'm going to make a kick," Pitney declared. "If it comes to the worst, Judy'll have to go teachin', an' me, well, I'll get out of here an' take my chances."

Lankford reached over and gripped Pitney's hand.

"That's talking, an' any time I can help you, Sam, I'm always ready."

"You always was a good sort, Luke. Stay for the night."

Cyriac came in a little later. He was so overjoyed to see his friend that he grabbed him around the neck and danced around the room with him.

"Here, now, Jean, cut that out!" Lankford grumbled, trying to suppress a grin.

"Ah-ha, Luke, what you do over dis way?"

"Business," clipped Lankford; then, under his voice, "Do you think there's any chance of this here new inspector falling in a lake an' never comin' up?"

"Let us hope for de best," sighed Cyriac. "Mebbe-so Burr would lak dat he come back."

"Yeah? Why?"

Cyriac laughed, patted Lankford on the shoulder, and sauntered out.

"See you later, Luke, ma frien'," he called back.

Lankford grinned a moment, then turned back to Pitney.

"Suppose you know about the fire, Sam? Saw the smoke, didn't you? Gosh, for a while there I thought my post was doomed. Lucky the wind changed. That early spell of hot weather we had simply made dry-rot of the bush, an' it burned like hell."

"Started by itself, huh, Luke?"

Lankford and Pitney looked at one another in significant silence.

"I—was—wondering—about—that," Lankford drawled. "You know, Buck Raab's in these parts, an' he's got no use for me." He suddenly stood erect, snapping his fingers. "Say, put two an' two together. Maybe your inspector hired Raab— By God, I wonder! Maybe that's where the inspector is now; with Raab!"

Pitney dropped his hand on Lankford's arm.

"Luke, I'm loyal to my company, but I don't think it's wrong for me to say I guess you're part right. I don't say he's with Raab now, but he's been meetin' Raab before. For certain reasons he hired Raab to capture Doc Burr. Devlin'll ruin the company. I been holdin' off long enough, me bein' a slow-thinkin' man, but now I'm goin' to send a courier with a letter to headquarters."

CHAPTER XVII

THE WOLVES GROWL

S OMETIMES A man may do a lot of evil, and get away with it for a long time. The righteous don't always reap the rewards. On the other hand, the seed of evil is sometimes liable to grow into a boomerang, and a boomerang has a peculiar habit of coming back to the man who threw it.

Three miles north and east of Windy Creek House was the camp of Buck Raab and his men. Their shelter was a huge cave, near the summit of a rugged hogback that afforded a view of the country for miles about. There was a flat ledge directly in front of this cave upon which a camp-fire burned. Sprawled about this were the six ruffians that Pinky Smith had recruited. To one side, away from the others, sat Roger Devlin, his shirt dirty and torn, his face unshaven. He stared steadily in the direction of Windy Creek.

Within the cave sat Raab and Pinky Smith, their heads close together. Raab was listening intently, his eyes glued on the balsam floor. Pinky was talking in a hoarse whisper.

"Lookit, Bucky. Myke the bloke come acrost! Wot's the bleedin' use o' 'angin' onter 'im if there's no money in it? 'E's tryin' ter flimflam yer, Bucky—tryin' ter flimflam us all. The b'ys are gettin' restless, an' I tol' 'em there'd be pretty pickins'. Don't be a fool, Bucky! 'E's in our 'ands now. We oughta use 'im."

"M-m-m. I'll talk t' him first. Call him in."

When Devlin came in he looked from Raab to Pinky quizzically, distrustfully.

Raab said, "Well, I want t' know what you're goin' t' do, inspector. You talked a lot about me gettin' money, but I ain't seen any in a hell of a long while."

Devlin scowled at Pinky. He sensed that the little fellow had been urging Raab to action.

"You've bungled twice already," he said to Raab. "You let Burr get away, and you failed to wipe out Fort Surprise. As things stand, I can't do anything while Burr is at Windy Creek. I haven't any money on me, and it would be useless to go back to the House while Burr is there. What is more, my dear fellow, I didn't tell you to scour the woods for an army of cut-throats. I'm paying you, not an army."

"Never mind that, mister," Raab rumbled. "I want t' see money, or you're goin' t' regret it."

"What will you do?" Devlin tilted up his chin.

"What'll I do?" Raab leaned forward and leered. "I'll carry you down an' hand you over t' Burr."

Devlin blanched. Burr was a thorn in his side. Burr had caused his plans to crumple. How he hated the very name of Burr! The man was his Nemesis. And in his malicious way he hated old Pitney because the factor had seemed to hold faith in Burr. And Judy too. He had thought her easy to fascinate, thought he had stirred her deeper emotions with his honeyed words. And, after all that, she had told him that he merely interested her. Devlin almost pitied himself. His soul cried that everybody was against him. But he still concealed his emotions behind that pompous demeanor of which he was master.

"You would get no money by doing that," he replied crisply.

"But a hell of a lot of satisfaction."

"Oh, you are absurd! I would pay you if it were possible, but under the present circumstances how can I?"

"S'y, listen," chirped Pinky. "There's a safe at the 'ouse where they keeps money. I seen it y' know. Seems ter me yer oughta 'ave the combination."

"You are absurd, too," snapped Devlin.

" 'Ow, yer don't s'y now!"

"Shut up, Pinky," Raab put in, then to Devlin, "You got the combination t' that safe?"

"Well, suppose I have?"

Raab looked at Pinky. "Suppose he has, Pinky?"

"Why, I'll go pinch the bloomin' thing."

"But see here," cut in Devlin, "that will not get Burr away."

Raab smacked hand to thigh. "We got to see money before we make another move. If there's plenty o' that we'll go the limit. Why, say, we may even get the woman f'r you, inspector. Blind… but a woman. Ho! Ho!"

Being cheechakos, they couldn't stand his hands together in front of his crooked little face. Devlin frowned studiously but said nothing. He revolved the thought in his brain for an instant, then stowed it carefully away.

Raab said, "Well, the combination, inspector?"

Devlin gave in. It was the only thing he could do. He had no money of his own. He was at the mercy of a gang that would think nothing of cutting his heart out. Secretly he condemned Pinky Smith—loathed the little fellow. He might have been able to handle Raab alone. But not with Pinky around. That satanic imp was full of ideas, and those ideas he very cleverly transferred to Raab's sluggish intellect.

Having given over the combination to the safe, Devlin went outside and sat alone. After a while he found himself recalling Raab's words, "Blind… but a woman." Perhaps by this time she was not blind! Perhaps Burr had been successful, if he had operated. But she was still a woman, and desirable. Perhaps, if Burr were removed….

Pinky Smith left that afternoon, with two others, for Windy Creek House. They trudged down into the valley below, Pinky strutting cockily in the lead, his two dark, rangy companions swinging behind easily. Overhead the sky was almost cloudless. The sun was high and gleamed on the green wilderness, glittered on the narrow river that bubbled noisily through the valley.

They came within sight of Windy Creek House as the sun dropped behind the distant, shaggy hills, and the first shadows crept over the wilderness. Pinky called a halt.

"We camp 'ere till it's late," said he. They were not stopped for very long when one of the breeds saw through a rift in the bush a girl passing along a beaten footpath not thirty yards distant.

"Judy Pitney 'erself!" Pinky whispered, "An', s'y, she c'n *see!*"

" 'Twould be ver' easy," murmured one of the breeds, "to make a sneak behind her an'—"

Pinky gripped his arm. "Yer blarsted fool, we're a'ter money now! D'yer t'ink it'd be youse'd get 'er? Guess not! It'd be Bucky… an' me!" Pinky licked his lips. "But not now. We're on bizness, an' bizness an' women don't mix—not this 'ere kind o' bizness any how."

Judy passed out of sight and the men relaxed.

The hours dragged by, bringing restlessness. At last Pinky straightened, stretched his limbs, and with a muttered word started off. The other two slid along behind him, silent as ghosts among the dark shadows. When they reached the clearing before the post buildings, Pinky raised his hand and they crouched down, listening. No lights shone. The only sound was the faint rustling of the trees, and the subdued murmur of the creek that coursed near by.

"Guess it's all right," Pinky whispered. "The safe's in the back room. S'y, I guess we oughter creep 'round ter the back."

Cautiously, silently, they slipped through the bush until they were behind the trade-house, where they paused again.

"The clerk gen'rally sleeps in there," Pinky said. "You blokes go knock on the door. When he opens it stick yer guns in 'is fyce, an' myke 'im put 'is mug ter the wall while I pinch the money."

The 'breeds stood up and strode from the bush. One of them rapped on the door. The other stood a little to one side, with his rifle ready. There was a movement within, and a tired voice asked, "Huh?"

"Open queek, m'sieur!" pleaded one of the men.

"Oh, that you, Jean?"

The 'breeds looked at one another. They grinned evilly. Then one said, *"Oui."*

A moment later the door swung wide, Jerry Sand stood there yawning. A split-second later he found a rifle jammed against his stomach. His hands went up.

"Why, you dirty, lousy—"

"Shot up! Back in! Turn de face to de wall or by *le diable…*"

Jerry was backed to the wall and turned roughly about. The rifle was pressed to his back.

"Wan word…" warned the 'breed ominously, while the other signaled Pinky that the road was clear.

Pinky slid in, grinned, and knelt before the safe with a bit of paper in his hand, which he glanced at from time to time as he spun the dial. A moment later he thrust the paper into his pocket and pulled open the heavy door. In a small bag he had brought along he piled the loot.

When there was no more to be had, he rose, drawing the bag shut. For a brief moment he stood scratching his chin, as though some new thought had presented itself to him. Then he grinned maliciously. His eyes popped. His lips smacked softly. He motioned to one of the 'breeds, and drew him aside.

"Listen," he whispered. "Cripes, it's great the w'y ideas strike a bloke! Go tie 'is 'and be'ind 'is back an' blindfold 'im. We'll tyke 'im along an' plug 'im someplace. Get me, d'yer?" He poked the 'breed in the ribs. "They'll t'ink 'at it were Jerry as robbed the safe! Aren't I the clever bloke, now, aren't I?"

Five minutes later they were filing through the dark aisles of the forest. Jerry Sand, gagged and blindfolded, his hands tied behind his back, stumbled along, while a man behind him kept jabbing him with a rifle.

CHAPTER XVIII

NORTH WOODS

MORNING YAWNED over Windy Creek. The mists hung in layers over the water and over the marsh grass beyond, obscuring the lower trunks of the trees so that their crests seemed to float on the white vapor. The trappers camped on the beach began to stir in ones and twos, and here and there a fire began to glow. Someone was whistling. Someone was grumbling at the damp chill.

Sam Pitney came out of his cabin, limped across to the trade-house, and was surprised to find the door still barred. He knocked. Then, thinking that perhaps Jerry was still sleeping, he went around to the rear. He tried the rear door and it opened easily. He entered. The sun had not risen yet and the room was dim.

"Hi, Jerry!" he called.

No answer. Not a sound. He knitted his brows perplexedly and went into the trade-room. This, too, was deserted. He stood leaning against the counter for a moment, stroking his jaw. Then he returned to the back room and, his eyes having become accustomed to the gloom, could discern objects more clearly. The gaping safe was the first thing he saw. He gasped. He lurched across the room, dropped to his knees, and ran his hands inside the safe. He groaned. It had been swept clean. For a long moment he remained on his knees, looking around the room, staring at the empty cot on which Jerry had slept.

"Jerry!" he murmured desolately.

Jerry, his trusted apprentice, who had been with him for six years! The safe robbed. Jerry gone. He braced his cane against the floor and pulled himself to his feet. With a sigh he eased the safe door shut. He was not angry. That might come later. Just now he was sad, unutterably sad and heart-sore, for he had trusted Jerry, held great faith in him. This was a blow.

He shuffled into the trade-room and opened the front door. Burr was swinging up from the creek, and waved a hand to the factor as he approached. When he saw the expression of anguish on Pitney's face he exclaimed:

"What's the matter!"

"We've been robbed," announced Pitney in a dull voice.

"Robbed?"

"Safe opened. All valuables gone. Come in."

He led Burr into the rear and showed him the rifled safe.

"But it hasn't been broken," Burr said. "Someone had the combination."

"Yeah," sighed Pitney. "Jerry's gone."

"Jerry Sand, you mean?"

"The same. When I come over this mornin' the front door was still locked. I come around the back an' this door was open. I come in an' find no Jerry. It hurts, doc, me havin' liked Jerry so much an' trusted him more'n any man."

"I know how you feel," Burr nodded reflectively.

By the time the sun was above the horizon and flinging its dazzling banners across the tawny wilderness, everyone at Windy Creek knew of the robbery, and the trade room was packed. Burr had advised Pitney to keep them out of the back room, however, and to leave everything just as he had found it.

"I got to report it to the police," Pitney said gloomily. "It's mine an' the Company's money. Maybe if it was mine alone I wouldn't. But it's my duty to the Company."

He called a post Indian and despatched him with a message to the nearest Mounted Police detachment post, a hundred

miles distant. Following this he and Burr again returned to the scene of the robbery.

"Damme, it don't seem like Jerry would do it," Pitney said for the dozenth time.

There was plenty of light in the room now. Burr leaned in one corner, smoking his first after-breakfast pipe, and turned his eyes about the room slowly. Looking at the floor, he frowned quizzically, but said nothing. His gaze then ran across the room and settled on the rumpled cot. After a moment he moved over to it, picked up a corner of the blanket and dropped it again. Then he went back to studying the floor. Presently he sat down and looked at Pitney.

"You know, Mr. Pitney," he said, "perhaps Jerry didn't rob you."

"Huh? What's that? Didn't rob me? But..."

"That blanket over there," went on Burr, "has been torn. Some of it has been torn off. And there are footmarks on the floor that are neither yours nor mine. There are three distinct pairs of footprints besides Jerry's and yours and mine. Take a look and you will see. They were made by moccasins that had traveled through mud before reaching here. The ground is moist, and you can see mine among them; also yours. The man who opened your safe had the smallest feet of all. In fact, as I see a pair of Jerry's moccasins by the bed, I'm sure he was not near the safe at all. Anyhow, as his moccasins were dry, I don't see any prints at all that look as though they might be his. Three men were in here last night—three men who had come over wet ground, else we'd not be able to see their prints on the floor."

Pitney was inspecting the floor, handling the blanket on the cot.

"Yes, doc. This blanket has been ripped," he agreed.

"Sure thing. They probably tore some strips off to bind and gag your apprentice."

"By God, doc! I'll bet you're right!" exclaimed the factor. "Oh, I hope it's so, too! I can't believe Jerry'd do a thing like that."

They went out through the rear door, and followed tracks that led to the bush a dozen yards away, where they lost them.

"See," said Burr, pointing to the ground. "Now there are four pairs of prints. The three that came took Jerry with them to give the impression that by his absence you would suspect him."

"Poor Jerry," groaned the factor. "I wonder what'll happen to him. They most likely threatened to blow off his head if he didn't tell the combination. I'll bet it's Buck Raab behind this. I can't think of nobody else. Buck Raab an' that devil Pinky Smith."

When they went back into the trade-room Luke Lankford was getting ready to return to Fort Surprise. Pitney told him of his new-found suspicions.

"Wouldn't be surprised, Sam," growled Lankford. "I better get back before he decides to take a crack at my post. He's starting his deviltry again, and the country won't be safe till he gets bumped off. He's probably ganged together a lot of bums, and fur brigades going south had better look out for him. They ran him off the Albany for trying to hold up six flatboats last year. Too bad they didn't shoot him. Well, I figure my place'll be a lot safer if I'm there, so I got to get along, Sam. If you ever need me, friend, just send the word."

"An' if you ever need me, Luke, do the same."

The fare-ye-wells went around and Lankford left with his one Indian for Fort Surprise. Judy and Burr lingered at the creek's edge after Lankford's canoe had disappeared around a curve. Judy sat down on a convenient stump while Burr absently pitched pebbles into the water.

"You know," Judy said after a moment, "I have a keen suspicion that Inspector Devlin is behind this robbery."

Burr made a stone skip across the surface of the creek and said, "Oh, I don't know," in a half-hearted way.

"And I'll bet you had the suspicion before I spoke," she went on. "But you're not malicious, doctor. I don't think Jerry would have given up the combination. He's stubborn. He'd let them shoot him first. But Inspector Devlin knows the combination. Either he gave in to Raab's demand for it or he himself planned the thing."

Burr turned and faced her; smiled his slow smile. "Perhaps you're right. Yes, I'll confess that I had a similar idea from the first. The man must be mad! If, as your father remarked to me, Raab has recruited the scum of the woods, Devlin will regret he ever saw Raab. For I don't think Devlin's the man to swing a gang with him. Raab is, and Devlin will be at his mercy. I hope Raab doesn't do away with him."

"Forgetting your vengeance, doctor?"

"Not a bit of it. That's why I want Devlin to live. I want a written confession out of him explaining the way he tricked me five years ago. After that, well, I don't care what happens to him. But he's got to erase the blot from my name!"

"And then you'll leave us—go out of the wilderness?"

Burr shot her an oblique glance. She had spoken wistfully. Now she scrawled aimlessly on the ground with a piece of wood. Her face, in shadow, was wistful too, he thought. Her black hair, parted in the middle and drawn down over the ears to a simple knot on her neck, seemed soft as velvet. For a moment he wondered how that hair would feel under his big, ungainly hands—how the soft, pink cheeks would feel. With an effort he shook off the mood, and for want of something else to do crammed fresh tobacco into his pipe.

"This afternoon," he ventured after a while, "I'd like to take a canoe and paddle up the creek, just to look around. Want to come along and show me the way?"

"I'd love to!" she cried, looking up into his face with big, round eyes.

"Er—good," said he, and almost flushed.

CHAPTER XIX

TRICKERY

PINKY AND his men had traveled through the night. At sunup they arrived within sight of their lofty retreat. Raab spotted them as they toiled up the trail and, seeing there were four, came down to meet them and investigate. When he saw Jerry Sand bound and blindfolded he grunted, "What the hell?"

Pinky's gimlet eyes popped and he tapped his meager chest.

"My idea, Bucky, old cab—old man," he said, drawing his chief aside. "Did it so they'd put the blime on 'im. Aren't I a clever bloke, Bucky?"

"Uhuh," Raab mumbled, without conviction. "What are we goin' t' do wit' him, though?"

"I was goin' ter plug 'im, Bucky, an' drop 'im in the creek, but maybe yer got ideas o' yer own."

"Yeah, H-m-m. Well, bring him up, but keep the rag over his eyes. Got the goods, I suppose."

Pinky tapped the bag he carried and grinned.

At the ledge they met Devlin, who frowned and swore silently. Pinky, passing him, chuckled devilishly and poked the inspector in the ribs. Devlin fairly hissed at him. Pinky slapped his thigh, as though the joke were on the inspector. They stowed Jerry in the depths of the cave. The rest of the band followed, eager to share in the loot. Devlin remained outside, coldly aloof. A little later Raab appeared.

"Some haul!" he chuckled.

Devlin cut in with, "Why did that fool Smith bring Sand along?"

Raab explained.

"Oh, I see," said Devlin. "Where's the money?"

"I gave all the boys a bit, an' I'm holdin' on to the rest."

"I think I'm the one to hold it, Raab."

"Oh-ho! You do? Now ain't that funny! No, mister, I'll hold it. Before you get through you'll owe us a hell of a lot more, so I'll keep it an' pay the boys now an' then."

Devlin shook with suppressed rage. "Dammit all, you are double-crossing me, right and left!" he ripped out.

Raab laid a ponderous hand on his shoulder. "Take it easy, mister. Listen. Pinky saw Pitney's gal. An' what you think? She's got her sight back!"

Devlin scowled. Raab came a little closer, leering.

"Say, you kinder like her, don't you? Say, would you like to have her up here in the wilderness?"

Devlin brought his eyes to meet Raab's slowly. The two men looked at one another.

"Sure you would," chuckled the big man. "Ain't she worth all the money we're holdin' on you? Say, she's some gal!"

Devlin turned half away, rubbing his chin thoughtfully.

"There's Burr…" he said at length.

"If we get the gal, Burr an' the whole dam' lot'll come huntin' f'r her. Then it'll be easy to pick him off. They got nothin' against us. They won't know who's got her. They might suspect, but what's that? An' wit' Burr out o' the way your road'll be clear. All the time now they'll be thinkin' Jerry Sand run off wit' the money. Burr'll be out o' the way, you c'n make up a story about bein' lost, an' then there'll be Fort Surprise."

"You never thought of this," Devlin shot at him. "That Smith fellow's idea, I'll wager."

"Well, Pinky, he—"

"Yes, so I divined," nodded Devlin, and Pinky's idea gave birth to an idea in the inspector's head which he very cleverly kept there, for the time being. "Understand," he said, "that Sand fellow must not know I'm here. Keep him bound and blindfolded, and see to it that your men never mention my name in his presence."

Raab swung back into the cave and Devlin smiled to himself. There was still hope. He had a plan, and if that plan worked out he would be able to laugh at them all. Damn the ruffians! He'd show them if they could treat him as their equal. Equal! Why, of late, they'd been acting as if they considered him as dust under their feet. Well, he'd show them! Yes, there was a ray of hope, and Roger Devlin still thought himself unconquerable.

But Pinky Smith, that little offspring of the devil, also had ideas. In fact, his head was full of ideas, and Raab in his sluggish brain often wondered where Pinky got so many. The crooked little fellow had an idea to fit every occasion. He and Raab were sitting in one corner of the cave, far enough away from Jerry so that the latter could not hear their low-spoken words.

Pinky announced, " 'Ere's the idea, Bucky. We all gang t'gether an' myke straight f'r Windy Creek. This 'ere is our chancet ter myke a bit of a fortune. But we got ter act before Pitney's fur brigade goes sout'. We'll sweep the country clean. An' wot's our object, Bucky?" He leaned over and rubbed Raab's arm gently. "Blackies, Bucky. 'E'll 'ave 'is black fox skins in one bale, an' that won't be big. We'll pinch 'em, tyke a couple canoes, an' head east on the creek."

"East?"

"Sure. Don't yer get me? Lankford's plyce. We'll raid 'is dump an' 'it out f'r the Bay. Yer got a score ter settle wit' 'at bloke, any'ow, Bucky. But wait a minute. I'm gettin' too far ahead. First, o' course, we pinch the woman."

"Yeah. She's some gal, Pinky. I figure she might learn t' love me."

Pinky snapped his fingers. "But we doan't 'ang on ter her, Bucky!"

"What's that?" Raab growled.

"Doan't be a bleedin' fool, Bucky! Wit' the blackies we'll pinch at Windy Creek an' Fort Surprise, an' sell ter a bloke near the Bay as don't ask questions, there'll be plenty o' women'll look up ter us. Now talk sense. I'd like ter 'ave her too, but never let a woman stand in the w'y o' bizness. Look 'ere. We pinch the woman, an' that'll draw most o' the blokes at Windy Creek ter lookin' f'r 'er. Then we plant 'er on the inspector an' leave 'im an' 'er, givin' 'im directions 'at'll tyke 'im aw'y from us. They'll foller 'im, an' wit' most o' the blokes aw'y from Windy Creek 'untin' 'im, things'll be easy. There's no bloody use o' 'angin' wit' Devlin no more. We got all outer 'im we c'n get. An' we ain't never goin' ter get another chance like this."

Raab leaned back and rubbed his jaw. "I hate t' give up the woman, Pinky, but your plan's a bird, an' I guess I'll have to. Ain't you got an idea, so's we could hang on t' the woman too?"

"No, Bucky. We can't do it. We got ter plant 'er on Devlin ter tyke the Windy Creek blokes a'ter 'im instead o' us. An' Devlin'll get plugged on sight, I'll bet. 'E won't be able ter talk an' tell wot 'e knows."

"Well, Pinky, I got t' hand t' you," grinned Raab, finally. "You got ideas. We'll make a clean sweep."

"Just leave hit ter li'le Pinky, Bucky, ol' cab—old man. Leave it ter Pinky Smith, an' yer won't go wrong."

CHAPTER XX

THE BITTER QUEST

IT WAS the day after Burr had taken Judy in a canoe down the wilderness creek that he came to his decision regarding his vengeance. He was sitting on a bench in front of the trade-house with Cyriac.

"You know, Jean," he remarked, "I'm going to pack up and scour the country between here and the forks for Devlin."

Cyriac sat erect, and his teeth flashed. "So-o! When do we mak' de start?"

"I'm going alone, Jean."

"*Non,* m'sieur. I'm go too."

Burr shook his head. "No, Jean. I'm going alone. I've waited here long enough. I'm going out to find him—alone." There was finality in his tone.

Cyriac shrugged. "Ver' well, Jeem."

Burr left his companion sitting there, and went over to the cabin. Yesterday, in a quiet, shady nook on Windy Creek he had told Judy he loved her. He had kissed her, and she had clung to him after a passive moment. He had felt her glorious hair and the soft, clinging warmth of her red lips. His was a rugged, strong, deep-rooted love. Judy's was the rich, passionate love of the wilderness woman.

He was grave now when he entered the cabin, took Judy's hands, and pressed them in his own.

"Judy," he said, "I'm going away for a little while. Since you told me you loved me I am restless. Now or never I am going to settle this thing between Devlin and me. He must be in the woods some place between here and the forks. I'm going to find him."

"But they'll kill you!" she cried, gripping his hands. "Oh, forget all about Devlin. I love you, Jim. I believe your story. I believed it the very day you told it. I know you were tricked. Don't go, Jim. I love you too much to lose you now."

"God knows I love you, too, Judy," he said, gently. "But you wouldn't want me to go through life with that cloud over my name, would you? Some men may be able to forget their vengeance easily, but I am not so fortunate, Judy. I've got to settle this thing."

It was inevitable that he should go. When the seed of vengeance has grown in a man's soul for five long years it's not easy to snuff it out in a day.

He left at sunrise next morning. He carried a rifle, and on his back a light rucksack. He shook hands with Cyriac and old Pitney. Judy walked with him a little way into the timber. He kissed her and told her he would be back before very long. She stood smiling as he strode off, but her eyes were moist. He kept waving back to her until the foliage shut her from view.

His trail led north and east into a country heavily timbered, where tawny-backed ridges rose from secluded lakes, and rapids foamed white and sudsy in narrow watercourses. Spring was flourishing on this northern frontier. Wild life teemed in the bush. The white sunlight was like tonic, and the air was rich like wine.

Burr went down into a luxuriant valley, moving through spruce that rose like cathedral spires under the pale blue dome of the cloudless sky. He forded a narrow, gurgling stream littered with rocks, strode through a grove of slim poplars, and struck a dim trail that ran parallel with the stream. After a while this trail petered out. He was in a wild, tangled country where bush was plentiful and vines and briers rambled and coiled about aimlessly. He found the going hard and painfully slow. When he made a camp that night he was torn and scratched in a dozen places, and glad to lounge on his blanket and relax over his pipe.

Next day he began to zigzag through the country, watching for campfire smokes or for isolated cabins. He toiled up a ridge, and from its summit studied the wilderness beyond. Not the faintest wisp of smoke did he see. No sign of human life besides his own was in evidence. Far, far to the northward he noted a stretch of charred country, and remembered the forest fire that had almost caught up with Jean and himself. All about him was the wilderness, vast and immeasurable, beautiful and awesome and mysterious, stretching it's rugged miles to the walls of the visible universe.

He crossed a chain of low hills, and late that afternoon toiled up a slope that was steep in places he had to grasp bushes to keep from slipping. Finally he neared the summit, stopped for a breathing spell on a broad ledge cluttered with camp refuse, and wondered vaguely if at some time this had been the retreat of an outlaw gang. A cave yawned at him from the side of the slope. He thought he heard a movement of some kind within. He waited a moment, and heard the faint rubbing noise again.

His finger curled around the trigger of his rifle. He crept cautiously up to the mouth of the cave at an angle; an animal of some sort might be in there. For a moment he paused, debating whether he should investigate or leave the cave alone and go his way. He had no grievance with the wild life of the frontier, and it was not a habit of his to go about shooting any animal he might come upon. But the peculiar rubbing sound he had at first heard was now supplemented by a low, muffled groan that he was sure did not emanate from an animal.

He edged closer, and peered into the gloom of the cave. Again he heard the groan, this time with a kind of insistence in it. He crept in by inches, trying to accustom his eyes to the semi-darkness, and presently saw a form moving—writhing—in the back of the cave. He made it out as the form of a man, bound hand and foot, and also gagged.

He did not hesitate any longer. A moment later he was bending over Jerry Sand.

"Jerry!" he exclaimed softly.

With his knife he cut away the man's bonds. When he was free Jerry relaxed and sighed.

"Are you hurt?" Burr asked.

"No, doc—just played out from tryin' to break these damn ropes."

"Anybody else around here?"

"Don't think so. They pulled out yesterday mornin' an' left me to die, I guess. Say, doc, will you get me a drink, please?"

"Right here," replied Burr, and gave Jerry his canteen. Jerry drank deep.

"Lucky you found me, doc," he chuckled grimly. "I would have died sure as hell."

"Suppose they took you from the house so Mr. Pitney would believe you robbed the safe," Burr remarked.

"Guess that was it. It's Raab an' a gang he's got. But Raab didn't pull the job. Pinky Smith an' two others."

"Is Devlin with them?"

"Don't know. I didn't hear him speak, an' I didn't hear his name mentioned. What gets me, though, is how the hell they got the combination to the safe. I'll bet Sam thought they got it from me. Well, they didn't."

"Sam believes in you," Burr said. "He doesn't think you're guilty."

"Good old Sam! But listen. I got an idea Raab an' his gang left on a raid. I didn't hear much, but once or twice I heard Fort Surprise mentioned, an' once I heard Pinky say Lankford's name. I wonder if they're goin' to raid Luke's place? Now I like Luke, an' I'm goin' to hotfoot it for Fort Surprise. I know a short-cut. Is there a party with you?"

"No. I'm out looking for my friend Devlin."

"Oh, I see. Your friend. That's a good one, doc! Well, I'll beat it for Luke's alone, then."

"No, I'll go with you, if you think Luke is in danger."

"Good. We'll have to travel like blazes, though, an' by night. Can't afford to wait till tomorrow."

They made a fire on the ledge and cooked a hasty meal. Jerry ate ravenously, for he had had no food since the morning before. They left the ledge as the red sun tumbled down in a glory of color behind the shaggy wilderness, and lavender shadows began to creep through the valley.

Thus Burr's quest of vengeance was again temporarily suspended. For Raab and his raiders were loose and hungry for spoils, and a wilderness post was in danger.

CHAPTER XXI

DEVLIN TURNS

THE RAIDERS lay camped not half-a-mile from Windy Creek House. Now and then a pair of them crept nearer to the post buildings, watching for Judy to stray away from her cabin. The men were becoming impatient. They had been held in check too long, and their wild natures craved action.

Devlin, as usual, sat by himself. He was thinking hard, turning his plan over and over, looking for flaws. He realized that these outlaws were far beyond his control. He knew, too, that they would not hesitate to do away with him in the swiftest way possible. He realized that mentally he was their superior, yet he held some reservations on that score for Pinky Smith. He sensed their rough, unrestrained passions, and he was not so blind that he failed to estimate the possibility of their taking Judy for themselves. Raab was a raw, elemental man, and by certain speeches he had hinted at a desire to possess Judy. Against Raab's desire Devlin knew that he himself would be impotent.

Devlin was coldly analytical. It was his idea to let these outlaws capture Judy, then rescue her from them. He would take them by surprise. They would not expect such a move. He had a revolver, and he would take a chance. He would tell Judy he had been held prisoner by Raab, invent a fantastic story of hardship, brutal treatment, and so try to win her sympathy and support when he returned to Fort Surprise. Had he known of the insidious plan Pinky Smith had formulated, he might have arranged a different course of action. But he did not know the outlaws were going to attack the post after they had captured

Judy. He was ignorant of it all. He thought they were merely after the woman, and that Fort Surprise would be another issue.

Two men returned from a fruitless morning, and there was a deal of grumbling as the gang ate. Afterward Raab and Pinky, after a short conversation, decided to look around themselves. As they left, Raab winked at Devlin, and Pinky chuckled in his satanic way. They crept cautiously through the tangle of brush and approached the post buildings from the rear. For a while they crouched here, then moved about and took up another position.

An hour passed, and another. Raab grumbled.

"Don't she ever come out?"

"Tyke yer time, Bucky."

The words were scarcely out of Pinky's mouth when they saw Judy walk across the clearing.

"Ain't she a beauty?" muttered Raab, his eyes staring wide.

"Think o' the blackies we'd get, Bucky!" Pinky exclaimed.

Judy crossed the clearing and strolled into the timber. She was dressed entirely in white. She strolled aimlessly, pausing here and there to pluck a flower, or to listen to the note of a bird.

Little by little she drew farther away from the post-buildings.

"Now's our chance," Raab whispered.

They bent low, and circled through the timber until they reached a point some distance ahead of Judy. Here they crouched near a footpath along which Judy was approaching.

"I'll grab her," Raab told his companion.

She passed within ten feet of them, stopped, and bent down to add another flower to her bouquet. Raab stood up. He took two quick strides, and had his huge paw clapped across her mouth before she could utter a sound. He lifted her easily in his gorilla arms and bore her away into the forest, with Pinky tagging gleefully at his heels.

Judy fought like a wildcat. She kicked and clawed. The more she struggled the more Raab was pleased, for she was powerless against his brute strength, and he gloried in her ferocity, her wild struggles. He ran with her, leaped over fallen trees, laughed at her.

When he rocked into camp he held her up and said to his men, "Ain't she a beauty?"

One of the 'breeds blew a kiss from his fingers.

Raab set her down, still holding her by one wrist. She was flushed, panting, and her black hair cascaded over her trembling shoulders. Her eyes blazed.

"You—you—"

"Aw, take it easy, sister," Raab chuckled. "You're goin' t' like me a lot."

She flew at him, and clawed his face with her one free hand. As the blood tickled down his cheeks Raab jerked his head and shook with laughter.

Then he threw his arms around her and crushed her to him. His leering lips reached for hers. She struggled, grimaced with horror and loathing, then collapsed. He let her drop at his feet, gazed down at her loveliness with heavy eyes and the ghost of an evil grin.

"I like em when they fight," he droned, and wiped the blood from his face.

All through this Devlin had sat half-hidden by a bush. He knew she had not seen him. He smiled to himself, and did not move.

Pinky had Raab by the arm. "S'y, Bucky, wot the 'ell yer trying' ter do? F'r Gawd's syke doan't let a woman turn yer 'ead!"

"Ain't she a beauty, though? Pinky, ain't there a way we could hang onto her?"

"Doan't be a fool, Bucky! D'yer want ter spoil our plans?" He lowered his voice. "Now let's be gettin' along. We wanter put some distance between 'ere before dark, so's we c'n turn 'er an' 'im loose wit' bum directions, an' get back 'ere ter raid the post ternight when the blokes are 'untin' f'r 'er."

Raab stroked his chin moodily. "I like her. She's worth all the pelts on Windy Creek."

"Bucky, yer mad! Wot did we come 'ere f'r? Yer can't flimflam us 'at w'y, Bucky!"

"Tell you what, Pinky. I'll take her an' start headin' east now. You an' the boys pull the raid tonight. We'll meet, an' then take a crack at Fort Surprise."

Pinky groaned. "Bucky, listen ter yer ol' friend, will yer? Yer goin ter smash all our plans. Listen ter reason, f'r the love o' Gawd!"

Judy's eyes opened and she looked forlornly about her. Another wave of rebellion swept through her and she jumped to her feet.

"Buck Raab, you let me go! Don't you dare touch me again!" she cried. "You'll die for this. You'll be hunted down like a wolf."

"Better not tyke 'er, Bucky," oozed Pinky's voice.

Raab leered and reached a hand for the girl. She ducked away.

Suddenly Devlin stood up from the bush in which he had been half concealed. In his hand was a revolver.

"The first man who moves I shall shoot down," he said. "Miss Pitney, you had better get behind me for protection."

Judy looked at him, bearded, unkempt, his clothes torn. Unable to comprehend this new situation, she edged away from Raab and stood beside Devlin.

Raab was dumfounded. He stood with mouth and eyes agape. Pinky held his breath and his little eyes popped. The rest of the gang muttered.

"Not a move, you villains," Devlin ordered in his old, pomp-ous manner. "And you, Raab, are indeed made of base material. You have tried to kill me, tortured me beyond dreams, but you shan't soil this lady."

Judy was bewildered. Roger Devlin, of all men! Devlin making a heroic gesture, shielding her from the worst cut-throats on the frontier! It didn't seem real, yet it was. There was some-thing noble and pathetic about the way he stood there, his chin upthrust, his gun unwavering. She did not know that Devlin had prepared carefully for this. She did not know that he was acting a part, striving to impress her, so that she would stand by him later at the post.

Raab at last overcame his surprise. "Well, if this don't beat all! Put down that gun, you bum!" he snarled. "At him, boys!"

"Move and I shoot!" clipped Devlin.

Raab moved, and one of his gang spun up with a gun. Devlin, not very expert in the business of gun-fighting, hesitated, unable to decide in that split-second whether to shoot at Raab or the man who was trying to swing his rifle into play. He fired instinctively as his gun wavered, and the shot went wild.

The 'breed fired. Devlin grimaced, tottered, and twisted down to his knees. But he played his part even as he sank.

"I tried, Miss Pitney," said he.

The next moment Raab had his arms around her.

"I've got her now, an' I keep her!" he yelled. "Let's f'rget Windy Creek, boys. There's Fort Surprise. The woman is my share. The pelts at Fort Surprise'll be your'n. Let's get away."

Pinky groaned. "Wot's the bleedin' use o' 'avin' ideas when a bloke goes daft over a woman? Blarst me bloomin' blinkers!"

"Quick!" ripped out Raab. "They might investigate them shots."

Still bemoaning Raab's weakness for women. Pinky started off with a word to the others. Raab, with Judy in his arms, brought up the rear.

"Now f'r Fort Surprise, boys!" he yelled.

CHAPTER XXII

"DRIVE, BOYS, DRIVE!"

WHEN SAM Pitney, crossing from the trade-house to his cabin, heard two shots echo down the wind, he paused for a moment in thought.

"Them shots," he mused, "were fired by two different guns. Wonder who's shootin'."

When he entered the cabin Annie told him that Judy had gone out for a walk about an hour before.

The afternoon passed. Twilight began to shadow the land. When the factor sat down to eat, the chair opposite him was empty. Judy had not returned. He began eating listlessly, and after a few moments gave it up entirely. Judy should have been in long before this.

He pushed back his chair, reached for his cane, and was about to get up when the door burst open and Jean Cyriac cried, "M'sieur Devlin is jus' arrive on hand an' knees. Ver' mooch seek from wound. He lak to speak wit' you, Sam."

In the trade house Pitney found a limp, dirty, bearded man. He had to look twice before he was sure the man was Inspector Devlin.

"Your daughter, my dear Mr. Pitney," Devlin gasped, "is the captive of Buck Raab and his fellows. I tried to save her, having stood the fellows off with my revolver, but somehow or other I was slow in shooting, and one of the fellows drilled me in the right thigh. I have been at their mercy ever since I disappeared from here. I have been a captive in their hands."

"Judy—Judy!" Pitney choked. "Where—where—"

"Raab has her, and I heard him remark they were going to attack Fort Surprise."

"Are you tellin' the truth?" Pitney cried, his face white.

"Quite the truth. Perhaps, my dear Mr. Pitney, I have done one or two indiscreet things in my time, but what I have told you is quite the truth. I had the better of them, and was about to bring your daughter here when the fellow shot."

Pitney said to Cyriac, "Jean, call all the men, an' tell 'em to bring their guns!"

"*Oui!*" said Cyriac, his eyes flashing.

Devlin faced a new Sam Pitney now. The factor was white and grim. There was life in his faded eyes. A note of command had entered his voice.

"An' it was you started all this," he scored the inspector.

"I? Why, my dear man—"

"You, it was, mister—yes, you, with your high-toned ideas about how to run a tradin' post! If you hadn't made me buy Raab's pelts, he would have drifted on to some other post. But, no; you invited him to stay. You sure got things in an awful tangle."

"Sir, I am an inspector for the Company, and as such I am due a certain degree of respect."

"Respect, after what you done? You won't be inspector long! An' most likely you'll go south with a Mounty."

"You don't seem to appreciate my attempt to save your daughter."

"I don't know whether you made any," Pitney said. "It's gettin' so I don't know when you're lyin' an' when you're tellin' the truth. Don't talk too much. I'm factor here, an' your bein' inspector don't count any more. I moved like you said once, but that's over, 'cause my poor Judy can see!"

Indeed a new man faced Devlin now. He was awed beyond words.

"My wound—oh!" he winced suddenly.

"Annie'll wash it 'till we get a doctor, if we can get one. God, I wish Jim Burr was here!"

"Where is he?" Devlin asked.

Pitney glared at him. "Where is he? He's gone lookin' for you, for a reason all his own."

Cyriac came in with a dozen men. "We mak' a start now!"

"Right," affirmed Pitney, limping quickly across the room to get his rifle.

"Sam, mooch bettaire you stay here," ventured Cyriac.

"Jean, I'm goin' too. Annie'll take care o' him. God save Judy!" he groaned suddenly.

The band, led by Cyriac, trooped out, with Pitney hopping along to keep up. They all piled into three large canoes, and the men at the paddles drove lustily. The first pale stars were winking, and broad shadows lay on the water.

"Drive, boys, drive!" urged Pitney.

"For de fairest of de fair, Ma'mselle Judy!" cried Cyriac.

"For the queen of the North!" rumbled the men in the first canoe.

The brigade raced on, all three canoes striving for the lead, driven by shaggy men with arms of iron and hearts of gold. A big, yellow moon was just topping the dark wall of the forest, and its mellow rays painted the water and outlined the grim, bronzed faces of the toiling men. Their paddles gleamed, their bodies swayed rhythmically, the bows of their canoes threw off little white wavelets.

At the end of three hours they reached a bit of sandy beach and pulled their canoes ashore. Ahead of them lay a dark tangle of wilderness, and a three-mile portage. There was not a moment's pause. They shouldered their dripping canoes, and Jean, who knew the trail well, took the lead. Three miles beyond they would strike a broad, turbulent river against whose current they would paddle the remaining miles to Fort Surprise.

CHAPTER XXIII

BATTLE!

BURR AND Jerry Sand, traveling light and fast, blew into Fort Surprise two hours before the dawn, and did not hesitate to rouse Lankford by banging on the door with Burr's rifle butt. Lankford came out with a gun and a lot of grumbling, but when he saw who his visitors were he clamped his jaw and looked surprised.

"Something tells me—" Lankford began.

Jerry pushed him inside and Burr kicked the door shut with his heel. Lankford made a light and they sat down.

"Raab pass here yet?" Jerry asked.

"Raab? No."

"Well, listen. Me an' the doc has an idea he's goin' to pay you a visit—not friendly, either."

"A raid, you mean?"

"About that," nodded Jerry, and related briefly his capture, imprisonment, and what he had heard at the cave. "The doc here found me, an' lucky he did. I thought we'd be late in reachin' you."

Lankford smacked the table. "I'll bet Raab's on the war-path again. Yep. Between him and Pinky Smith I don't know which is the worst. Well, thanks, boys, for warning me. I'm ready for him. He robbed Windy Creek, eh? Tried to put the blame on you, eh, Jerry? Well, let him come here—just let him! He'll get a hot reception. My pelts go out tomorrow, an' I'd like to see the man who's going to stop them. They're all baled in the cabin next door. Hang around, friends, till I put my pants on."

He strode into the rear room, a stocky, sturdy chunk of a man in a wrinkled old robe.

"Raab should at least be in the vicinity," Burr remarked to Jerry.

"Yeah—sure. I kinder thought we'd be late, or just in time to see him moppin' up."

Lankford returned in a few minutes, pulling on his shirt.

"Got a rifle or revolver you can lend me?" Jerry asked.

"Sure. Take that .305 on the wall. Bullets in the drawer under the back counter. She's a baby, that gun, but me, I can't seem to get away from my old .38-.55."

Jerry went to get the rifle and Lankford said to Burr, "There's a number of places I can think of that might be a lot more healthier than Fort Surprise for a peace-loving man. There's no use in you getting mixed up, Jim. I figure we can hold our own, so why not sneak?"

"No, Luke. I'll wait for Jerry." Burr patted his rifle. "That is, if you don't mind."

"Oh, hell, it ain't that! I just didn't want you to go taking chances in our little private arguments that spring up now an' then."

"I tell you, Luke," said Burr. "A universal good would be done if Raab were in jail and permanently out of these woods."

"Right you are, Jim. He is two dozen skunks put in a heap, that guy is. An' I for one—"

Bang!

Burr flung back his chair so hard it crashed against the wall behind him. Lankford was diving for his rifle before the echo of the shot died away. Jerry Sand vaulted over the counter neatly, and crossed the trade-room in less time than it takes to tell it.

Burr yanked the door open. Lankford, having snatched up his rifle, slid for the door while he crammed a chew into his mouth. The three of them got jammed in the doorway as each tried to be the first out. Luke bent down, untangled his legs, and hit the ground head first. Jerry Sand leaped over him. Burr paused long enough to grab Luke by the back of the neck and haul him to his feet.

"Thanks, Jim. There they are, trying to bust into the cabin for my pelts!"

A knot of men, scarce discernible in the pre-dawn darkness, were bunched at the door of the storehouse. One of them evidently had tried to blow off the lock with his gun.

"There's three locks on that door," grunted Lankford as he clapped his rifle to his side and let rip with a shot that brought a howl of pain from one of the raiders.

The rest of the gang was stationed in the bushes at the end of the clearing. Daggers of flame slashed through the gloom as they opened fire.

Burr clipped, "Let's close with that bunch at the door. The others won't fire for fear of hitting their own men."

He led the rush. The three men at the storehouse turned tail and made a bee-line for their companions in the thickets. Lankford fired low and knocked one of them off his feet. The other two scrambled for safety.

"Behind the cabin," warned Lankford, "else they'll cut us down."

As they ducked behind the storehouse four men with rifles strode past the trade-store.

"Friends o' mine from the river camps," Lankford remarked.

The raiders in the thickets opened fire on these new arrivals. One of the men spun down with a choked cry. Burr and Jerry sent a string of shots into the thickets, and the three remaining trappers came bounding over to join them.

"What's up, Luke?" one asked.

"Raab's at it again, boys. Lay low."

For a while the firing ceased. Gun smoke drifted lazily on the night air. The raider whom Lankford had knocked down with a pretty shot was crawling inch by inch for the thickets.

One of Lankford's trappers said, "Might as well finish that guy, Luke. You know, the huntin' code says it ain't noways humane to let a bad wounded animal t' the mercy o' the woods. It don't specify sech, but I figure thet word 'animal' likewise includes skunks. Here goes, Luke!"

"It don't say two-legged skunks, Ben," clipped Luke, as he knocked down the man's rifle; then he added, "but it ought to."

Burr put in, "I think they're spreading out."

"I—" Jerry began, but clipped it short and fired almost without aiming.

"I got that guy," he said after a moment. "He was just gettin' set to pot one of us."

"They're spreading all right," came Luke's voice. "Pretty soon we'll have to shift. Listen. Let's all make a dive for the trade-house. I mean, for the back. I got a key to the back door, an' we can get in before they get at us. From the front window, then, we can pot any man who tries to monkey around the storehouse door. Ready?"

"Sure," Jerry answered. "Get set. One… two… *three!*"

Luke led the way with the key in his hand. An angry yell rose from the raiders. A shot barked. But in short order Lankford had the door open, and those behind him piled in. He slammed it shut and locked it from the inside."

"Guess they're sore as hell now," he chuckled, as he strode into the trade-room and looked through the front window.

Jerry threw down the bar on the front door.

One of the trappers said, "Poor Joe didn't have time to fight. They got him clean through the heart. Died before he hit the ground."

An hour passed with no action on the part of either side. Gray patches of light were growing in the east. A bird began to sing. Burr, who was watching by the window, raised his ear.

"Sounds as if they're chopping a tree or something," he remarked.

The others crowded near him. Soon they heard a splintering of wood, and then a swishing sound followed by a light thud.

"They're chopping down saplings—poplar poles," Lankford said. "Now I wonder why."

The men listened intently. There was more chopping. More poplar poles swished to earth. The men looked at one another quizzically. The chopping went on for half an hour. Then followed another half-hour of silence, of expectancy, while the men became restless.

"They're up to something," was Lankford's remarks. "We'll just wait for their next move."

The dawn grew, and now a pink flush was spreading up in the eastern sky. The wilderness river rustled by, murmuring its ancient song beneath the morning mists.

Lankford was at the window when the raiders made their next move. He gripped his rifle and his jaw went hard.

"Look!" said he. "That's what the chopping was. They've lashed a lot of poplar poles together for a shield, the beggars!"

The men looked. They saw a shield about six feet square, made of cut poplar poles that were lashed together with three cross-pieces to hold them rigid, moving across the clearing toward the storehouse.

"There's only one man could have thought of that," clipped Lankford, "an' that's Pinky Smith, the rat-faced devil! An' there's no less than four men walking behind that contraption."

He shoved his rifle through the window and emptied it savagely.

"No use," said Burr. "They're safe behind that."

By this time one edge of the big shield was flush against the storehouse, and one of the men was firing apparently in an effort to blow off the locks. Lankford's face reddened with rage.

"I'm going out an' settle this here thing one way or the other."

"Take it easy, Luke," Jerry threw at him.

"Take hell easy! Lemme go, Jerry. I say… damn… lemme go!"

Burr grabbed the trader's arm. "Listen. Out the back way. Come on. If we go out the front way the men in the thickets'll have easy targets. The back way. We'll run around the off side of the storehouse."

"Good!" Jerry cried.

"Let's go," growled Lankford, and rolled for the rear door.

He led the way out with Burr at his heels, and Jerry and the others bunched close behind. Shots rang out as they raced across the short space between the two cabins, but none took effect.

CHAPTER XXIV

REWARD OF COURAGE

"**NOW**," **SAID** Lankford, pausing for a moment behind the cabin.

"Me first," urged Jerry, crowding him.

"No you don't!" And Lankford thrust him back.

The trader held his rifle close by his hip and swung around the corner of the cabin. A shot staggered him, but he rushed on. Another shot brought him to his knees just as he reached the front corner. He tried to get up, but keeled over sideways, firing his own rifle blindly. Burr and Jerry passed him, and Jerry got a slug through his left leg that almost turned him around.

Burr was the first to reach the men at the door. There were four of them, two holding up the shield. The other two had just broken open the door as Burr crashed into them. He caught one fellow behind the ear with his clubbed rifle and rushed the second bodily into the cabin. The others dropped the shield as the three trappers behind Burr leaped on them and went to it in a business-like manner.

The man Burr rushed was no easy mark. He was lean and rangy, and quick as a cat on his feet. There was no room to spare in that cabin, with the baled pelts awaiting shipment, and the raider's clever footwork did him little good. Burr was on him like a whirlwind, and the two of them went crashing over a bale of furs. Their rifles clattered away. Burr smashed his man flush between the eyes while they were falling, and hit him again as they landed.

The man doubled his knees, caught his feet against Burr's stomach, and hurled him off. Burr rebounded like a rubber ball, and drove out with a terrific right, but he was off balance, and his arm wrapped around the outlaw's neck like a rope.

They spun around in the small space. By this time Burr's opponent had his knife out and was trying to use it. Burr caught his wrist and rushed him against the wall far from gently, bringing up a short jab to his jaw that snapped back his head viciously. The fellow groaned, and blinked his eyes. Before his head could clear Burr picked him up bodily and flung him through the doorway, knocking Pinky Smith flat.

Recovering his rifle, Burr looked out and saw that Buck Raab and three more men were rushing from the thickets to aid their hard-pressed companions. Lankford lay dead or unconscious at the corner of the cabin. One of the trappers was sprawled flat on his face. Jerry Sand was hopping around on one leg. Burr appraised the situation in a glance. It looked as if the raiders were going to mop up.

He grappled with Raab, tussling with the man he had beaten to a frazzle not so long ago. They locked in each other's arms. There were no blows. They tried to break each other; one attempted by sheer brute strength to bend the other to the ground. The blood of superhuman exertion surged to their necks and faces; their muscles bulged till they were as taut as steel cables. They rocked, swayed, scarce moving at all from the spot where they had first closed.

There were shouts of dismay, followed by a sudden lull in the general conflict. Someone shouted, "Windy Creek men, by cripes!"

A 'breed called, "Bucky, mak' a sneak!" and hit Burr a glancing blow with his rifle.

Burr went a bit dizzy. Raab, startled, threw him away and looked about. A dozen men or more, led by Jean Cyriac, with Sam Pitney limping among them, were surging up from the river.

"Let's duck!" Raab snarled.

Only two of his followers were able to run with him.

"Pitney, eh?" he snarled again. "Well, his daughter'll pay f'r this!"

Cyriac yelled for them to stop. Raab flung a curse at him. The Windy Creek men's rifles went up as Cyriac shouted a second time. Raab kept going. The rifles blazed, and Raab's last two men stopped running and crouched with upraised hands. But Raab flew on, crashed into the thickets, and was lost to sight.

Burr toiled to his feet, rubbing his head. Cyriac ran up to him, and threw his arms about him.

"*Mon Dieu,* Jeem, you aire hurt bad?"

"Not a bit, old scout. Good you came."

"Ma'mselle Judy is safe?"

"Judy!"

"*Oui.* Raab have keednap ma'mselle—"

"My God!" Burr groaned. "So that's why you're over this way! I haven't seen her. After Raab, Jean! Oh, Judy!" he ended passionately, as he started off.

He passed old Sam Pitney without seeing him. He was already into the timber by the time Cyriac and half-a-dozen Windy Creek men tore after him. Red passion, a thing that in Jim Burr was difficult to stir, now coursed through his veins like a violent flame. The thought of Raab touching Judy, of his even looking at her, filled him with loathing. Judy—*his* Judy—in the filthy hands of that coarse chunk of humanity! He would kill Raab for this! He would choke the life out of him!

Wrath boiled within the ordinarily complacent soul of Jim Burr. He tore through the forest in great bounds, his eyes two orbs of fury whipped white-hot. He brought up suddenly on the river's bank, saw Raab half-way across in a canoe, with Judy lying between the thwarts, bound hand and foot, disheveled, struggling. He looked back for the men who were rushing to his aid. He heard them, but they were not in sight yet. In desperation he dived into the swift river, struck out with powerful strokes, fighting across the strong current. Raab paddled madly.

Jean Cyriac was the first to reach the shore. He saw Burr swimming, saw Raab paddling for the opposite bank. He raised his rifle, took a firm stance, gazing down the sights, and pulled the trigger.

"So!" he murmured.

Raab fell forward in the canoe, tried to rise, toppled and pitched sidewise into the river. He sank, and once or twice his body was seen near the surface. But he never came up.

The canoe, with Judy in it, was spun about by the current and started downstream. Burr saw this and let the current take him down while he swam a diagonal course, in an attempt to head it off before it should smash into the ragged boulders at a sharp bend not half-a-mile below. The race was close, for now the canoe was running parallel with the current at a swift rate of speed. He put all his strength, all his heart, into that gigantic effort, swimming as he never before had believed he could swim. Back on shore he heard faintly the voices of men shouting encouragement.

It was a fight against time, against minutes, seconds. The waters swirled about him, tugged against him, foamed in his face and blurred his vision. But he kept on, plowing along with every ounce of strength that was in his strong body. He drew nearer, nearer, yet it seemed to him that he would miss the canoe by a fraction.

He drove with his feet, dug hard with his hands, and saw the bow of the canoe shoot by mockingly. Its gleaming side slid smoothly by.

With a choked groan he exerted a last, enormous effort, raised his right hand, and clutched desperately at the passing stern. His fingers gripped it, and tightened savagely. He relaxed his body, letting it drag momentarily to check the speed of the canoe. The bow swung broadside to the current, and by this time he had both hands on the gunwale. He resumed his efforts, steering it laboriously across current, losing three feet for every one gained.

He swept by within a foot of the jagged boulders, and gave a cry of thanks. The river turned sharply. Burr and the canoe with its precious freight were swept upon the sandy beach below Fort Surprise. He pushed it farther ashore, leaned over, and lifted Judy in his dripping arms. Standing knee-deep in the water he held her tightly, kissed her, and murmured husky words of endearment.

"My Judy!"

"Jim… oh, Jim!" she whispered passionately, and clung to him.

He carried her up across the beach. "Did—did Raab harm—"

"No, Jim—no. He was too busy—traveled all night. But he would have. Oh, thank God you came! He—I saw him fall over. Did he—"

"He never came up again. He drowned."

Cyriac and a crowd of men ran down to meet them.

"Jeem! Jeem!"

"Everything's all right, Jean. But why didn't you let me get my hands on Raab?"

"Jeem, I'm know dat if he reach de shore he shoot you while you sweem. Ah, ma'mselle, *le bon Dieu* be praised! You aire safe!"

Pitney was limping down excitedly, as Cyriac slashed away Judy's bonds while Burr held her. Once on her feet, she ran to meet her father, who clasped her in his arms.

"My poor Judy! My poor Judy!" was all the old man could say, over and over. Over her shoulder he gulped to Burr, "Doc, I owe you more an' more every day."

CHAPTER XXV

VENGEANCE

WHEN THEY all returned to the post buildings Burr had a job on his hands. Luke Lankford was alive but sorely wounded. Jerry Sand had a bullet in his leg. Two of the raiders were wounded; one was dead. One of Lankford's men was dead and another had a scalp wound. Most of the others were cut up and needed slight medical attention. Pinky Smith had lost three teeth, but outside of that was little damaged.

All the raiders who could walk about were under heavy guard. Burr looked over the wounded men quickly but expertly and considered the situation.

"We can't take them to Windy Creek," he explained. "Luke especially cannot be moved. Somebody will have to make a fast trip to the house and get my instruments."

Cyriac stepped forward. Two others followed.

Pitney put in, "By the way, doc, the inspector is wounded too. I left him in Annie's care. He says he tried to save Judy from Raab, but one of the gang shot him."

"Yes," said Judy, "he tried to save me. He stood up against the men but one of them shot him and he fell."

"He did that?" asked Burr, thoughtfully. Then he turned to Cyriac. "Bring out Pinky Smith," he said.

Pinky Smith came warily at the point of a gun.

"Did Mr. Devlin try to save Miss Pitney from you fellows?" Burr put to him.

"Why, Jim, don't you believe me?" came Judy's voice.

"I do, Judy, but I want to find out something else."

Pinky replied, " 'E tried ter. But, s' 'elp me, I can't figure out the bloke yet. Y' see it was 'im was ter get the leddy."

"What!" Burr seized Pinky by the throat.

"S' 'elp, mister! Raab—Gawd rest 'is soul—put it up ter Devlin, an' Devlin says all right, all right. Doan't go blimin' everything on us poor blokes. Devlin 'ired us, an' Devlin gave us the combination ter the safe. Devlin wanted ter wipe out Surprise, but 'e got cold feet or sumpin' an', I dunno, everything went 'round the wrong w'y."

Burr flung him away.

"You're a liar!" he bit off.

"S' 'elp me—"

"Take, him back and lock him up, Jean," Burr said. "Then you and I will make a dash for Windy Creek."

Judy gripped his arm. "Jim you're not going to kill Mr. Devlin?"

"No, Judy," he assured her, taking her hand. "I understand he is wounded. If I don't look after him he may die. And he mus'n't die. That would cheat me of my vengeance."

"You have not forgotten your vengeance yet, Jim?"

"That is something I could never forget," he replied gently, and strode off into the trade-house.

He left with Cyriac in a canoe. Jean promised they would be back that evening. He guided the canoe deftly down the swift river. Once they had to make a short portage around a waterfall. Otherwise travel was swift, and they left the river for the three mile portage to Windy Creek before noon.

When they finally reached the post not a soul was in sight. A pall of abandonment hung over the place. They beached the canoe, went into the trade-house, and paused there to listen. The door into the rear room opened. Annie looked out, then waddled forward.

"Where's Mr. Devlin?" Burr asked.

She pointed to the rear room. Burr went in. He paused just inside the door, leaned against the frame and gazed at the man on the bed. Devlin stared back at him with a quizzical frown. No words passed between them. Still unshaven, bruised, unkempt, Devlin seemed like a ghost of the once dapper, debonair young inspector for the Bay West Company.

Burr quirked his foot around the leg of a stool and slid it over beside the bed. He sat down, without a word, and examined Devlin's wound. He thought for a moment, got up, went out and reentered in a few minutes with his instruments. With him came Cyriac, to help. Burr looked at Devlin steadily.

"Not bad, your wound. Merely laid your leg open. The bullet passed on. A few stitches will do the trick. Annie bandaged it well, though. By the way, Devlin, before we begin. Some news. May interest you. Raab is dead. Pinky Smith and the rest have been captured and are under guard."

"I—I told them here about the proposed raid on Fort Surprise," said Devlin. "Is Miss Pitney safe?"

"Yes. You made a pretty fizzle of the whole thing. You are really the cause of it all. You hired that crowd. Pinky is alive, and Pinky knows a lot about you. We know you gave the gang the combination to the safe. And Pinky said you agreed to have them come down and kidnap the factor's daughter."

"I saved her from them!" Devlin cried. "Ask her. I defied them, but one of them shot me."

Burr laughed. "Devlin, I've known you since we were kids. I can read right through you. I know your own mind better than you do. You had to get back to Windy Creek somehow. The gang was getting the better of you. You never could sway a crowd, Devlin. You're not made of the right stuff. It strikes me that you tried to save the factor's daughter to put yourself in right. It was your last straw. You were beaten in every other way. In other words, to serve your own ends, you double-crossed your hired cutthroats. It was not to save the girl, Devlin. It was, indirectly, an attempt to save yourself. You're a natural born double-crosser. Remember how you double-crossed me?"

Devlin looked away, covering his face with his hands.

"Well," Burr resumed after a minute, "despite all that I'm going to fix up your leg. After that you are going to write a confession about that night five years ago in the Temiskaming lumber camp."

Devlin turned on him. "Is that your price for attending my wound?"

"No. I'll dress your wound free of charge. The confession is the price of five broken years you've caused me. There will be witnesses to sign, as testimony that you did not write it under coercion. Lie quiet now. I'm going to patch you up."

An hour later Devlin was resting easily, so far as his wound was concerned. Cyriac carried Burr's equipment down to the canoe. Burr stood beside Devlin. He had placed pen and paper on a chair, and pulled the chair beside the bed.

He announced, "Now I am going back to Fort Surprise, where I have plenty of sewing, cutting, and other things to do. You'll have plenty of time to write the confession. It will help you pass the time away. When I return here I hope you'll have it finished. I've instructed Annie to take care of you. Keep your leg as still as possible and under no circumstances try to take it off the bed. That's all. Good-bye."

On the way out Burr cautioned Annie, "Take care of him. See that he stays in bed. He may be foolish enough to try to skip out. Don't let him. Keep your rifle handy."

Annie grinned and nodded.

Burr and Cyriac left for Fort Surprise. They arrived a little after sundown and Burr went right to work. For three hours he toiled over Lankford, and at the end of that time predicted that the trader would pull through. Next he took Jerry Sand, then another casualty. When dawn came he fell asleep in his chair. Judy found him there later. She did not rouse him. She ran her hand across his shoulder, patted it, and slipped away again noise-lessly with a little sigh.

Two days later Burr found he could leave Lankford long enough for a trip back to Windy Creek.

"I'm feeling pretty good, doc," the trader declared. "Thanks for everything."

"I'll be back in a day or so. I've left instructions with Ben, one of your trappers."

Pitney was ready to go also. Cyriac had the prisoners tied in single file to a long rope. He and two others led them down to the canoes. The party left in five canoes, two of which had been borrowed from Fort Surprise. Even as they departed several men were bringing Lankford's pelts from the storehouse and prepar-ing to go downriver with them. Another had set out earlier for an Indian camp a few miles to the eastward, to secure freighters for the brigade.

"Them pelts have got to move," Lankford doggedly announced.

CHAPTER XXVI

WILDERNESS PEACE

THE CANOE, bearing among others Pitney and Burr, was the first to slide onto the beach below Windy Creek House. Another canoe was there, clear of the water. Apparently it had been beached shortly before, for it still was wet.

"That," said Pitney, "is the canoe my Injun used who went off for the police."

Burr stepped ashore, looked up, and saw a red-coated figure leaning idly in the doorway of the trade-house, puffing a cigarette. The policeman moved presently, flipped away his cigarette and came strolling down in no great hurry. He was tall and lanky, and didn't seem to have a care in the world.

"I'm Clark," he drawled and jerked his head toward the approaching canoes. "What's this, a parade?"

"Some fellows for you," Burr said. "It's a long story."

"For me, eh? Oh, well, I suppose I'll have to take 'em. Say, who's Burr around here?"

"You're talking to him."

"Oh, that so? Well, here."

He handed Burr two sheets of closely written script. Burr needed only a glance at it to know it was Devlin's confession in full.

The constable explained, "I just blew in a little while ago. I found this man Devlin in the back room. He had a gun in one hand and that letter in the other. Killed himself—sure. Must have been afraid to face the music. Well, say, these prisoners look pretty hard-boiled!" He drifted down to the water's edge and eyed them levelly as they came ashore. "Well," he remarked to himself, presently, "I've seen tougher ones."

Burr was reading the letter again when Judy touched his arm.

"Devlin," he said gently, "has committed suicide."

"Oh!"

"It was, I suppose, the easiest way out. Twenty years in prison is the least he would have got, with all the counts against him. He was decent enough to write and explain all before he shot himself. He might have done worse."

"Let's not be too harsh with his memory. He tried his best to save me from Raab."

Burr had ideas of his own about that, but he thought it better to let Devlin's memory rest with his soul; if Judy persisted in believing that Devlin had tried to save her, why, it would do no great harm to let her keep that belief. It was the woman in her who pitied Devlin. Burr himself could find no pity for the man. He was not given to maudlin sentiment. For his own part he could not really see why he *should* pity Devlin. The confession was a natural thing, for the vilest of men finds a desire to bare his soul before the dark plunge into eternity. But Burr kept all this to himself, leaving Judy with her own beliefs.

Constable Clark was an easygoing, casual man. He told Pitney that the story concerning the prisoners and safe robbery would wait a while until the party rested after the trip. Having locked the prisoners in one of the post cabins, he sat on the bench in front of the trade-store sunning himself and smoking cigarettes.

A Company courier arrived at sundown with a message from The Pas. It was a reply to Pitney's letter explaining the state of things at Windy Creek House following Inspector Devlin's arrival. In it the superintendent advised Pitney to disregard further orders from Devlin and use his own discretion until another inspector should arrive.

Another letter was addressed to Devlin. The contents of it struck an ironic note. It was a brief, clipped order recalling Devlin to The Pas to await his discharge from headquarters. It was now superfluous, for by his own hand Devlin had discharged himself from all worldly duties.

In the evening the constable remarked that, if it were all right with everybody else, he wouldn't mind hearing the reasons for all the rumpus. He sat behind one of the counters in the trade-room, with pencil and paper; and a lazy, genial smile. Jerry told his own story of the robbery, swearing that Pinky Smith had been one of three who had robbed the safe. Pinky, under cross-examination, swore Devlin had given them the combination and agreed to the robbery, because he had no money and his hired men were demanding pay. He also swore that Devlin wanted to wipe out Fort Surprise. Then Pinky started off to enumerate his own virtues.

"Enough, Mr. Smith," drawled the constable. "I just wanted a brief outline. The court will hear anything else you have to say."

Clark heard each witness with mild, courteous interest, making his notes rapidly, demanding brevity. When the brief inquest was over the prisoners were marched back into their cabin.

"That's all I want," Clark told Pitney. "Just a few details, to know where I stand, and get a general idea of the case I'm reporting. From the scant testimony, it seems to me that Mr. Devlin has evaded a long prison term. Too bad. His own story might have been interesting."

Pitney left the trade-house a little later and found Judy alone in their little cabin. He took her in his arms.

"Well, Judy, these have been awful times. Your old dad ain't acted none too heroic, I guess."

"Oh, Dad, I understood all the time!" she told him. "It was my being blind that made you take all those blows silently. But I saw that you'd changed as soon as I was able to see again. You were wonderful, Dad."

"I'm glad you feel that way, Judy. But—but I s'pose I'm goin' to lose you soon, little gal."

"Lose me?"

"Jim… Well, I'd be happy, Judy. I'm mighty proud o' Jim."

"Oh, Dad!"

A little later Judy found herself in a canoe on the creek. Jim Burr was drawing the paddle through the water slowly. The pale radiance of the moon and the stars shone on the creek like a silver mist, and the soft night wind blew perfumed with balsam.

Burr steered the canoe for a patch of secluded beach, grounded it and stepped ashore. Judy leaped after him. He caught her hand, held it, and drew her to him with gentle firmness.

"This," he said, "is the place where I first told you I loved you, Judy."

"Oh, do you think I would forget? I remember it. I always will remember this spot, Jim."

"I want to marry you soon, Judy. With you I'll rebuild my life. I'll work hard to win back my name."

"We'll both work hard, Jim."

He held her face between his hands, and kissed her softly with restrained fervor.

They were startled, then, by the sound of a lusty singing voice that came down the wind raised in a gay song that *voyageurs* lift to the stars on wilderness nights. They stood silently, secure in the shadows.

The voice drew nearer. Soon a canoe glided slowly past. The paddler did not see them. His dark face shone like bronze. His white teeth flashed as he sang. The tassel on his scarlet toque bobbed jauntily as he swung his head to the rhythm of his song. They did not stop him, and he glided out of sight.

"It's Jean," said Burr, "out for his evening ride."

"Jean, the happiest man in all the North," Judy added.

Burr shook his head and smiled.

"No, my Judy. I am the happiest man in all the North—in all the world!"

TRAIL TALES OF THE NORTH: THE LOVABLE TRAMP

ARCTIC—YES, AMIABLE VAGRANTS SOMETIMES FIND THEIR WAY EVEN INTO THE DESOLATE WASTES OF THE FAR NORTH.

BEING A tramp has its good and bad points.

     I said this aloud, by the way, and Jim, with an eye on the moon rising across the lake, remarked:

"Yeah. Like everything else in life. For every good point, if you look far enough, there will be a bad one. And, speaking of tramps, now, I'll never forget the one I ran across way over on the River du Rocher, many years ago.

"There was a crowd of us in the trade-room, all fresh from the trail with pelts and stories of bad weather, bum traps and thieving wolves. A big snow had just kicked over, and most of the trails were blocked. We didn't expect anybody else till the crust froze, but the tramp I'm telling you about blew in, sure enough, and someone of us started to cheer on general principles, and the whole crowd joined in.

"The tramp was pretty well done in from trail breaking, and, to boot, this poor chum was in tatters, his feet wrapped in all kinds of rags and an old undershirt tied some way or other around his neck and head, and socks pulled over his torn mittens. A sorry sight, I'll tell you, all the more pitiful because the poor old soul took our cheering so to heart. His frost-bitten old face smiled tender as a woman's, and his eyes were half crying and half laughing, and he stumbled about shaking hands with everybody, he was so blooming happy.

"He was a kind of sawed-off, hammered-down chunk of a man, with a mop of gray hair that hung almost to his shoulders.

He had a bad cough, and we gave him a shot of good brandy, and MacMasters, the factor, piled him full of food. He said he hadn't a cent to his name, but insisted that some return be made for the food, and from his rag of a pack he pulled a battered old flute. And, sir, he could play that flute.

"Bud Moore, the factor's clerk, passed the hat around and we all chipped in and gave him a couple of dollars. Bud talked him into believing that he was only accepting money for services rendered. He looked us all over with wide, searching eyes as honest and free from guile as a baby's, mumbled something, took the money absently, and sat in a corner communing with himself for a whole hour. He gave us no name, so we called him Old Fluty among ourselves and Mr. Fluty to his face, and this pleased him as much as a new rattle pleases a baby. I say baby a lot, because Old Fluty's reaction to any little favor was so child-ish and enthusiastic.

"He was in pretty bad shape physically, and we made him stay on at the post, and arranged for him to play two evenings a week, at which times everyone present contributed his little bit to the cause. The Indians enjoyed it immensely, and those who went on to their traplines told others, both Indians and whites, and Old Fluty not only made money but the business of the post was increased fifty per cent.

"His health returned a little, but he was not naturally a healthy man. However, he felt better, and he thanked us boys from his old heart for the way we'd treated him. He was such a gentle soul among us rough ones, and when his eyes rested on you at times, it was, well, it was like—like a benediction. You felt ashamed, at nothing in particular; you just felt ashamed of the things you might have done.

"He went out among the sick Indian children with his battered old flute, and he played for them, and they kind of worshipped him. Sometimes they got better, and the grown Indians regarded him with something akin to awe. No, I don't claim his music cured their illness, but illness is often a state of the mind, and, perhaps, it was his music, his soothing personality, his caressing eyes, that eased their minds. In any kind of weather you might see his hunched body with its raggedy clothing flapping in the wind as he scurried from lodge to lodge.

"The spring break-up came. The ice began to crash in the valleys, and we began to hear the pleasant sound of running water. The sun stayed up longer, and life began to move in the woods. Canoes came down the rivers heaped with pelts from the distant lakes and waterways, and the sound of Frenchmen singing as they paddled sure made you feel good.

"You know it yourself; there's nothing like the coming of spring in the woods. You seem to wake up then, take hold of life again, and when, after cursing the weather through a whole winter, you take a new slant on life cursing doesn't come so often. There's nothing makes me feel freer and more like living than seeing geese way up high on the wing and the foaming of the water on the rapids.

"I'm kind of stealing Old Fluty's thunder, because he said something like that. Fluty played to packed houses there that spring, and canoes came in every day or so. Everyone was singing. We all were happy, though there were some who had cause to be sad. And there was one fellow who was neither happy nor sad, but a plain up-and-down grouch. He came in on foot with a load of pelts, and right off the bat he had an argument with MacMasters over prices or something.

"MacMasters was one of those taciturn men who stare at you blankly while you talk your head off and then, by way of answer, lights a pipe and strolls off. Bud Moore took up the argument, and this trapper—name of Sorge—finally gave in, but did a lot of grumbling.

"That night was Old Fluty's night, and he came paddling in from some mission of mercy, eager to be on time. He seemed to have added to his clothing bit by bit. Now he wore a toque with a flaming red tassel and a pair of new moosehide moccasins.

"Most of us hung around to hear him play merely out of courtesy, for we kind of knew that if we drifted off this might hurt the poor old soul, and he was so kind, so gentle that none of us boys could bring ourselves to even do that.

"Understand, we did not consider Sorge one of us. He was an outcast, not because we made him that, but because it was his own fault. He was simply unbearable, a big, hard-boiled bully whom even the Indians and 'breeds shunned. Old Fluty took his place atop the table, brought out his flute, went through his usual preliminary motions, and started to play a merry little tune that set the voyageurs to humming and keeping time with their feet.

"All eyes were upon the old man, not mainly because of the music he played, but because of the sad, wistful figure he made. I don't know how it strikes you, m' friend, but when age tries to be young there is something sad about it—something that tugs at your heart and makes the eyes water. Anyhow, I noticed there were a lot of watery eyes there that night.

"And then Sorge broke out in a rotten laugh and told Old Fluty to lay off the tin-can music and give the owls a chance. It was not so much what he said; it was the sneering way he came out with it.

"Well, sir, poor Old Fluty stopped on a sighing note, removed the flute from his mouth with trembling hands and looked at Sorge. I can't tell you just how he looked. It was the kind of look you sometimes see in a mother's eyes when she is told a child of hers has died. My God, man, that look should have melted a heart of flint! It melted mine, I'll tell you frankly, and it kind of, well, turned my stomach around, if you know what I mean.

"But Sorge? Not a bit. He just threw back his head and roared his bull laugh, and afterward someone said that when he did that a tear rolled down Old Fluty's cheek. But I didn't see it. By that time I had turned to Sorge.

"I was the first to drive at him because I was nearest. But Bud Moore, as husky a young lad as you'd care to see, beat me to it. He let fly with a blow that caught Sorge smack between the eyes and sent him reeling across the room.

"Maybe it wasn't a fair fight, but, on the other hand, maybe it was. Anyhow, the place was a madhouse while the lot of us pounced on Sorge and beat the living hell out of him. We all were sore. I don't think any one of us would have been sorer if Sorge had called us a name which men of his kidney have a habit of doing sometimes. We simply wiped the floor up with him, slammed him around the place like a sack of meal, while old MacMasters stood behind the counter and smoked his pipe and looked on without batting an eye.

"When MacMasters didn't butt in, you can bet your bottom dollar he considered the fight fair, for he was not a man who ordinarily let you use his post for such purposes.

"Bud Moore had cracked him first, and Bud got the last crack too. He booted Sorge in the slats and sent him headfirst out through the door.

"But, wait, we hadn't counted on the Indians. Remember, those Indians revered Old Fluty, what with the things he'd done for them, the long nights he had sat up with their sick children. When Bud kicked Sorge out he kicked him right into their hands. Before we knew what it was all about they were running off with him.

"MacMasters came out and started after them, but half-a-dozen fellows who didn't care a rap for the law of the Ancient and Honorable Company, barred his way. MacMasters, true to form, stared at them blankly for a long minute, then lit his pipe and strolled back into the post. None of us moved to save Sorge. None of us gave a damn what the Indians did with him.

"But Old Fluty, his eyes still wet, shambled out and scampered off. We wondered even then why we didn't stop him. We knew, and even MacMasters himself knew, that he, MacMasters, couldn't have saved Sorge from the Indians. Only Old Fluty could do that, and, sure enough, a little later Old Fluty came hobbling back with Sorge behind him.

"Sorge asked no forgiveness. Sullen to the end, he took his pack and went his way. Old Fluty, watching him go, shook his ancient head and said:

" 'It's a shame that Mr. Sorge ain't got no ear for music.'

"That was all; no hate, no resentment. He was all peace and gentleness, and when his eyes rested on you, well, it was like—like a benediction.

"He left us a month later, to carry his tunes and his goodness along other trails, for he was a wanderer and could not stay long in one place. I heard that he traveled to the Pacific coast and was one of the first in the gold fields. And I heard, too, that he did not hunt gold, but played his old flute while other men became rich. He was one man in a thousand."

"In ten thousand," I said.

Jim went me one better by saying, "In a million."

COURAGE OF THE STRONG

FUR COUNTRY—SOME MEN ARE BORN TO SACRIFICE ALL THEY HOLD DEAR IN LIFE—FOR AN EMPTY DREAM.

THERE IS no gainsaying the fact that the North country breeds strong men. There is something in its rugged vastness that seeps into the soul of a man and toughens his moral as well as his physical fibre. Its long white winters, when all the wilderness lies throttled in a tomb of snow and merciless cold, make a man face eternity and struggle grimly and silently for his daily bread and even for life itself. There is no room for petty weaknesses.

Yet, on occasion, there are cases contrary to the fact.

Gabe Packard put down a dog-eared magazine and listened for a moment to the night wind that romped and frolicked about his split-log cabin. The yellow glow from the oil-lamp on the table shone on his weather-tanned face—a good face, with mild blue eyes, with jaw thews prominent and a mouth that was wide and straight but not harsh. Rounding thirty years, he had given most of those years to the wilderness, and in turn the wilderness had moulded him to its mood of silence, had built his body with solid bone and tough muscle, to withstand the rigors of those high latitudes.

His brows bent down in a frown now, as he regarded the clock on the shelf back of the sheet-iron stove. Arising, he jammed his big hands into his pockets and crossed the room to study the clock at closer range. Half-past ten. He went to the door, pulled it open and looked toward a cluster of lights in the valley below.

His mouth hardened a trifle and a hint of steel was apparent in his eyes.

He stepped back, closing the door thoughtfully, and stood in the center of the room staring at the floor and stroking his clean-shaven jaw. He sat down in an armchair by the stove, stuffed his pipe and smoked in silence for nearly a half-hour, raising his eyes every now and then toward the clock on the shelf. Finally he got to his feet, smacked fist to palm in a gesture of resolve, and reached for his mackinaw. On the way out he picked up a pair of snowshoes that stood near the door.

The night was clear. The sky was a girdle of stars buckled with a full moon. Underneath his rackets the snow crunched with a clean, crisp sound. Below and ahead of him were the lights of the settlement. Elsewhere, wherever he might choose to gaze, the shaggy, shadowy wilderness, sprawled its lean reaches to the visible rim of the universe. This infinity of space is a breeder of silence in strong men, and it humbles the weak.

Gabe swung down through the long lanes of pointed spruce, his snowshoes swishing rhythmically. The lights grew nearer, and presently he passed the first outlying cabin. Now a muffled din reached his ears, the sound of rough voices joined in song. This grew in volume as he went on, until finally its source could be placed in a large, low structure built half of logs and half of boards. "Rough-house" Haggerty's place: apparently a trading-post; actually, a shady dive where the riffraff of the trails congregated to drink rank rum, swap bawdy yarns, and dispose of furs procured under circumstances that would be difficult to explain to any self-respecting law officer.

Gabe stuck his snowshoes in the crust outside the door and entered deliberately, with his hands in his pockets. Smoke from many pipes hung in motionless layers under the ceiling. A huge stove roared defiance to the cold. Groups of men sat here and there, some in sodden slumber, others talking, while one group sang discordantly to the accompaniment of an accordion no less discordant. At a table half-a-dozen men were playing cards. In

the rear, behind a counter, Rough-house Haggerty a tawny slab of a man, leaned on his elbows and drowsed over a fresh cigar.

Gabe, his face serene and peaceful, moved to the table and stood behind a young man who at the moment was finishing a deal. He waited until the hand was played out, then placed a hand on the young man's shoulder. The latter looked around with a start, made a wry grimace, shrugged off the hand, and started fumbling with his small pile of chips. Gabe stroked his jaw thoughtfully, and another deal was under way. The young man caught three jacks and made one of the other players come three times before he finally called. He lost to three queens and swore a blue streak.

Gabe leaned down and said, "Better come along, Harry."

"You go to hell!" snapped Harry.

"Now, Harry, that's no way to talk. You promised you'd come home early. Come on."

"Let me go! Shut up! Think I can't take care of myself? I don't need any wet nursing."

One of the players, a lean, hawk-nosed spectre, cackled.

Gabe looked at the hawk-nosed man and asked, softly, "Did you say something, mister?"

There was no reply. Gabe caught Harry's arm and without any apparent effort lifted him to his feet. Harry, muttering incoherently, tried to break loose. Rough-house Haggerty jammed his cigar at a cocky angle and rolled over to the scene.

"'Smatter?" he grated through the side of his mouth.

"Nothing," replied Gabe. "Come on, Harry."

Haggerty took a hitch at his belt. "S' listen, you. Harry owes the house f'r three rounds o' drinks an' I'm just after stakin' him t' twenty dollars which he just lost."

Gabe grunted, "Humph!" Then he seemed buried in thought for a brief moment. Presently he looked at Harry who met the gaze obliquely, fear mixed with unreasonable revolt. "You owe the house for three rounds of drinks and twenty dollars besides, Harry?"

"That's my business! You stay the hell out of my affairs! I'm old enough to take care of myself. I—"

"Now, Harry," soothed Gabe gently; then to Haggerty, "I'll fix it up with you tomorrow. I'll give you an I.O.U., now."

"S' listen. I oughter get the money now."

"Isn't my word and my name on paper good?" asked Gabe, and the mildness of his tone and his level blue eyes was disarming.

"Well, all right," Haggerty agreed, pocketing the slip of paper.

Gabe took a firmer grip on his brother's arm and began propelling him toward the door. Somebody cackled. Gabe stopped, turned about and looked inquiringly at the hawk-nosed specter.

"Did you say something, mister?" he asked politely.

The man shuffled the cards and began dealing nervously. Gabe proceeded toward the door, opened it and passed out with his muttering brother. Harry was shaky on his pins and Gabe had to help him with his snowshoes. When they started off Gabe held his brother's arm, to steady him.

"Let go!" rasped Harry, thrusting him away. "I'm no kid. What do I look like? You make me sick. Got a mind to go back just for spite. By God, I will!" He stopped, swaying, and swung around.

Gabe stood in his path, his hands in his pockets, a serene, unruffled look on his face.

"You're going home with me, Harry," he said.

"Am I? Look here, Gabe, you want to stay out of my affairs. I'll pay my own bills, too. You needn't go butting in it at all. I'm twenty-five and my own boss. If I want to play a sociable game of cards and have a drink or two with my friends—"

"Your what, Harry?"

"I said my friends. Now move aside. I was just beginning to win when you nosed in. I'll win if— I say, get the devil out of my way!"

He lunged for Gabe, letting fly with a fist. Gabe dodged and retreated a step.

"Now, Harry, chum," said he, mildly.

"Don't you go interfering with me. Get out!" snapped Harry, reeling to one side.

Gabe reached out and caught him by the shoulder.

"Damn you!" Harry snarled, ripping up a short jab that landed on Gabe's cheek and left a red welt there.

A hint of steel came reluctantly to Gabe's eyes and his lips stiffened. Harry swung again and landed flush on his brother's jaw. Pain was now mixed with the steel in Gabe's eyes—not physical pain, but something deeper, a pain that wrenched at his heart.

"You're drunk, Harry, chum," he said thickly.

He parried the next blow, knocked off two more wild swings with his elbows, took the next two straight in the face and reeled back from the impact, groaning behind clenched teeth—groans that came from the depths of his heart.

"Harry, chum—"

The next blow crashed to the point of his chin. He reeled backward and went toppling down to the snow, his head spinning. He had not struck one blow, had scarcely tried to defend himself. He turned over on one side, while black spots danced before his eyes, and raised himself to one knee. Then he heard a voice—a woman's voice:

"What—what—"

Arms were about his neck and a warm, sweet breath was on his cheek.

"I'm—all right, Nan," he said slowly.

He toiled to his feet and stood swaying like a great tree in a storm. A bitterness that he could not suppress was stamped on his face.

"What—what happened?" cried the girl, pulling at his coat.

Harry was standing a few feet away, glowering sullenly, his fists clenched. The girl looked from, one to the other, gesturing aimlessly with her hands.

"My fault," Gabe was saying. "Harry was going to your place. I—I tried to argue with him. I shouldn't have said what I did."

"Oh, but you boys shouldn't fight like this!" Nan remonstrated. "I'm on the way home. That little MacVale girl is sick and she wanted me to keep her company for a while. Lucky I came along, else you two would— Oh, it isn't right! You shouldn't fight."

"Harry'll see you home, Nan," Gabe said, and strode off with lowered head, feeling very miserable.

The girl looked after him, started to follow, but stopped and turned to Harry. "Are you coming?"

"Sure, Nan. Be right with you. That big stiff of a brother of mine was butting in my affairs again and I showed him his place. Well, never mind about that. Come on."

They started off side by side, and a little later stopped before a snug cabin at the edge of the settlement.

"Now you'd better go right home," Nan advised Harry.

"Sure—sure thing, Nanny."

"You've been drinking again. I've asked you time and again to stop it—for my sake, Harry."

"And I've asked you to marry me time and again—for my sake," replied Harry, swaying on his feet.

"Good night, Harry," she said quickly, diving into the cabin.

"Hey—listen—wait a minute!" He started banging on the door. "Dammit!" he snapped.

There was no answer, and finally, muttering in his throat, he swung away.

GABE PACKARD loved his brother not wisely, perhaps, but too well. He considered himself his brother's keeper, and in a way, felt responsible for Harry's acts. The people of that wilderness valley either admired him for it or called him a fool. Rough-house Haggerty privately considered him a fool, but said nothing openly, for Gabe it was who settled most of Harry's debts, and Haggerty was not the one to bite the hand that fed him.

The two brothers were sitting at breakfast. Gabe was serene. Harry was fretful and shot black looks about the room. Suddenly he spat out:

"If you'd left me be last night I might have had my pockets full of money this morning."

"That's all right, Harry. Soon as I get some wood in I'll run down and fix it up with Haggerty."

"Give it to me. I'll run down."

"No, Harry. You have to run out that new trapline I staked last month—you know, the one that runs north through the muskeg to the lake."

"Oh, I don't feel like running traplines today. Devil take it!"

Gabe pointed a fork at his brother. "If you are expecting Nan to marry you, Harry, you'd better get busy on the traplines. And stay away from Haggerty's. Rum is all right. You know I always keep a bottle on hand. But why swill that bilge Haggerty sells?"

"How do I know Nan'll marry me?" retorted Harry. "She hasn't said so. If she promised, I would lay off Haggerty's, and I'd do more work on the traplines."

"Well, anyhow, you'll have to take care of that trapline today while I run down and pay Haggerty."

Gabe left the cabin an hour later and headed for the settlement in the valley. In his pocket was sufficient money to settle Harry's debt. He had not complained, had not in any way recalled to Harry last night's miserable clash. He was the soul of forgiveness and peace. Once, not so long ago, he had knocked a riverman unconscious for five hours with a single blow; that was last spring, at a camp near the mouth of the Albany, not far from Hudson's Bay. Yet last night a man had struck him half-a-dozen times and finally sent him sprawling, while he himself had not struck a single blow. But, then that man was his brother, and Gabe Packard was a strange manner of a man.

On the way to Haggerty's he stopped in at the cabin where Nan Shirley lived with an uncle and aunt. He fumbled with his beaver cap as he faced Nan in the cozy living room, and somehow or other his tongue got all twisted up for a time. He kept shifting from one foot to the other until Nan, chuckling, pushed him into a chair. Nan's rosy-cheeked face was framed in an aureole of soft brown hair, and her laughing lips were ruby-red against teeth that flashed clean and white.

"Well, Gabe, there is something on your mind," she said, sitting down. "I'm waiting to hear it. Ready! Go!"

"Y-yes. Ugh—um. I—I—um—fact is, Nan, I have something to say and darn me, I don't know how to say it. Funny. I had it all planned out, and now I can't seem to get a hold on my memory. Funny. Um. I—um—"

"I'll bet it's about Harry," she prompted, arching her brows.

"Y-yes; it's about Harry—about Harry. You—you see, Nan, Harry is a darn good boy, only he needs somebody to take care of him. He is a good boy, Harry is, even if he has got a few weak spots. We all have weak spots, Nan, and you can't hold that against a man. Well, what I wanted to say—what I want to ask—what—what—"

His tongue twisted again and he shifted uneasily, rubbed a hand across his moist forehead. He jammed his hands against his knees and squared his shoulders, inhaling deeply.

"It's this, Nan," he blurted finally. "Next time Harry asks you to marry him, won't you say yes? Won't you, Nan? It'll make a new man of him. He needs a woman like you to take care of him. You like him, Nan. He likes you. He's good, Harry is. I wish you would promise him, Nan—if you really love him."

Nan's smile had faded and now she stared at the floor with big brown eyes. Gabe rose and moved sidelong toward the door.

"Just think it over, Nan," he begged, and went out.

At Haggerty's place he settled Harry's debt and bought a cigar.

"Have a drink," urged Rough-house.

"No, thanks. I've got some good stuff up to the cabin."

Haggerty seemed in pain. "S' listen. Mean t' say my rum's no good, Gabe?"

"Sort of. Anyhow, don't give Harry any more. This is the last debt I'll pay, and if you give him credit you'll be the loser as far as I'm concerned."

"That so?" ripped out Haggerty, taking in a reef in his belt.

Gabe regarded him with level blue eyes. "Yes; that is so," he said softly.

Haggerty became uncomfortable and for want of something else to do, stuck a fresh cigar between ragged teeth.

"Just remember that," Gabe told him, and turned on his heel, stuffing his hands in his pockets.

Haggerty flung after him, "Then tell that lousy bum to stay the stinkin' hell outer here!"

Gabe stopped, turned, and marched back to the trade counter puffing placidly on his cigar. "You mean Harry?"

"Who the hell d'you think I mean?"

"I just wanted to make sure," Gabe replied.

With a quick movement he leaned over the counter and caught Haggerty by the shirt. He hauled the man across the counter, got a better grip on him, held him there for a moment, and then sent him reeling across the room. He started after him.

The hawk-nosed man rose like a flash from the table with a knife in his hand. Gabe, smiling serenely, caught the knife-hand as it slashed in an arc for his face. With a movement of his wrist he twisted the hawk-nosed specter to the floor, and the knife clattered away.

"Did you say something?" he asked politely.

The man fainted from the pain of his wrenched arm.

Gabe looked about the room with a mild, inquisitive gaze, his hands already in his pockets, the smoke from his cigar curling upward. He regarded one face after another, saw that Rough-house was sitting awkwardly among a pile of empty boxes, and that the hawk-nosed man was inert on the floor. Nodding contentedly to himself, he crossed the room and passed out without another word.

When he reached his cabin on the slope he found Harry lounging disconsolately in the big chair by the stove.

"Thought you were going out on the trapline," Gabe observed.

"Changed my mind," was the curt reply.

"H'm." Gabe stroked his jaw, staring into space. He had partly removed his mackinaw, but now he pulled it on again. "Well, then, I guess it is up to me to go. I'll probably be out late, so have a good meal ready when I get back. You ought to stock up on firewood, too. So long, Harry."

Harry grunted.

Gabe swung a string of traps over his shoulder and rolled out. He headed northeast through a gap in the hills where a narrow, frozen waterway wound crookedly through the shaggy land, and all the vast wilderness yawned into the blue of the Arctic sky. All day he prodded into the maw of the woods, setting his traps and gathering up a pelt here and there.

When he returned through the gap it was dark; the moon was already above the hoary roof of the wilderness, and the night wind was crisp and invigorating. His bag of pelts for the day was exceptionally good. He was in a pleasant frame of mind. But when he swung down the sloping trail that led to his cabin, his face clouded a bit. There was no light shining through the window. He felt, then, that he would find the stove cold and the cabin deserted.

This was precisely what he did find. Harry was not there, the fire was out, and there was no hot meal awaiting him. He lit the lamp and sat down on a stool, staring about dejectedly. Presently he stirred, opened the stove, and began building a fire. He moved about as if buried in thought, and prepared a meal. Harry might come home soon, so he set the table for two and made plenty of food. However, he ate alone and finished his after-supper pipe alone.

The night wore on. Finally, after much pacing, Gabe put on his mackinaw and started down the valley. He was a little grim now, though still retaining much of his innate serenity. He had no intention other than going to Haggerty's, finding Harry there, and bringing him away from the scum of the trail that hung out in that nook of iniquity. His responsibility was self-imposed. He believed that some men are born everlastingly to care for others. Believing thus, he accepted his lot as something inevitable. He was born to take care of Harry, to pay his debts, to get him out of scrapes, and to swallow unreasonable abuse as recompense for his own efforts.

When he entered Haggerty's place his gaze immediately fell on the table where he was used to finding Harry at poker, but Harry was not among those present. Gabe approached Haggerty.

"Seen Harry?" he asked.

"Ain't seen him since this afternoon, when I showed him the door."

"Thanks. You showed sense."

"Yeah? S' listen—"

"So long," Gabe cut in, and left Haggerty with mouth agape.

Getting on his rackets again, Gabe cut across to Nan's cabin. There was light at the window and he did not hesitate to knock.

"Oh, come in, Gabe," greeted Nan.

"No, thanks, Nan; not now, anyhow. Just wanted to ask you if you saw Harry?"

"Why, yes; that is, about four hours ago—"

"And you sent him away again without—"

She shook her head and dropped her eyes. "I promise, Gabe."

Gabe couldn't find the proper words to utter. There was a peculiar feeling in his heart—a kind of happiness mixed with a vague quality of remorse.

"Thanks, Nan," he managed to get out. "Where did he go from here, do you know?"

"I don't know, Gabe," she answered with a catch in her breath. "Isn't he at home?"

"No—no. But that's all right. I'll find him. Good night, Nan."

He turned away and hurried off. Somehow he had not dared to meet Nan's eyes. There had been a sudden awakening within him. Had Nan promised to marry Harry merely because he, Gabe, had asked her to? She had not seemed happy at the door. Something was wrong. Gabe drove himself on at a breath-killing pace, and then suddenly stopped and wondered where he was going.

"Now where the devil could Harry be?" he asked himself.

He hadn't the remotest idea where to look for his brother. He concluded, after a few moments, that Harry might be home now. He headed back for his cabin on the slope, hoping against hope that Harry would be there. Approaching the cabin later he saw a form in silhouette against the lighted window, and suddenly felt very much relieved. He quickened his pace and reached the door, kicking off his snowshoes and at the same time pulling at the latchstring. The door was barred from the inside.

"Who is it?" rasped a voice.

"Me, Harry; it's Gabe."

There was an interval of silence; then the bar went up and the door swung open. Gabe stepped in, a puzzled expression on his face. Harry was still fully clothed, and a revolver was gripped in his hand. A wild, hunted look was in his eyes, and his face was flushed beneath the tan. He pointed an unsteady finger at the door.

"Lock it—lock it!" he ordered in a muffled voice.

Gabe put down the latch, then leaned back against the door with his hands in his pockets.

"What's the matter, Harry?" he inquired gently.

" 'Hawk' Galtry!"

"What about him?"

Harry swayed and lunged for the big chair by the stove, dropping into it with a groan of despair.

"I killed him!" he choked.

Gabe said, "Oh, God!" very softly, as if to himself. A moment later he was gripping Harry by the shoulders. "Killed him, Harry? Killed him? You say you killed him?"

"Yes—yes. Haggerty kicked me out of his place. I went over to Nan's and she promised to marry me. Then, when I was on the way back here, I met Hawk and he suggested a game of cards. Told me to come over to his shack. He had some whisky there."

"But you didn't have any money," Gabe put in.

"I didn't then. I came up here to borrow some out of your box. I only borrowed it, Gabe. Then I went to Hawk's shack. I drank, and I lost. I told Hawk he was crooked and he flung a glass of rum in my face. I went after him—we mixed—I shoved a knife in his ribs."

"Anybody see you go there?"

"No. But—but, Gabe, I left the knife there. I was in a hurry to get away. I left it there, Gabe, *and it's your knife, the one with your initials on it!* You took mine by mistake when you went on the trapline today."

Gabe stood up, tall and straight, his fists clenched at his sides.

"There's one chance, Harry. We'll have to get that knife."

"But—but somebody might be there!"

"It's a chance. I'll go down and get it. You stay here and try to pull yourself together."

With that Gabe swung around, pulled on his mittens, and strode out. Now more than ever he was his brother's keeper, born to bear his brother's burden silently and without complaint. Swiftly he swung his rackets down through the moonlit aisles of spruce. Harry had broken faith with him, had broken faith with Nan, yet bitterness was slow to take root in Gabe's heart.

It took him half an hour to reach Hawk Galtry's shack in the poplar grove. He paused at the edge of the timber and listened intently for a few moments. Then he crossed the little clearing and softly pushed open the door. A light still burned on the table.

On the floor lay Hawk Galtry, a knife protruding just below his chest. Gabe shuddered, his mouth grim. He advanced a few steps. Dead, Hawk was—no doubt about that. He had hated Gabe while he lived. He it was who used to cackle whenever Gabe came to take Harry home. He would cackle no more.

Gabe bent over hesitantly, caught the knife-hilt, and with a grimace pulled out the blade, turning away with another shudder. Then his face froze and his muscles stiffened.

"Hello, Gabe," said Rough-house Haggerty from the doorway. He held a revolver in his hand.

A chill swept over Gabe. He took a step backward, drawing his frame to its full height and squaring his shoulders. He uttered not a word. Haggerty leered and came in, looked from the body of Hawk to Gabe and grunted.

"Never knew you was strong f'r a knife, Gabe," said he nasally. "Huh. 'S damn shame. Hawk owed me money too." He prodded the body with his foot. "This'll put me in good with the police. I'll just lock you up an' send a Injun off for the nearest Mounty. S' listen. Put that knife on the table."

Gabe dropped the knife and Haggerty picked it up.

"Bum bizness, Gabe, puttin' your initials on a knife," he said. "Well anyhow, it'll make a better case against you. You before me as we go out the door. Let's go."

Mute, like a man in a trance, Gabe went out. Haggerty followed him and they headed for the trade-store. On the northern rim of the wilderness the aurora was spinning fantastic banners across the stars. The moon was passing behind a troop of gauzy white clouds. The night breeze was plaintive in the spruce tops.

Gabe saw nothing, heard nothing. He was shocked to the depths of his being, numb at the realization of how he had been trapped. When they reached the store he saw the men's faces through a haze.

Haggerty said, "Well, boys, Hawk won't play t'night, or any other night. Gabe, here, stuck a knife in him. Yeah. I just walked in the shack when Gabe was pullin' out the knife."

"Let's swing him from a limb!" rolled out one man.

"Let's all put a shot in him!" rasped another.

They surged across the room threateningly. Rough-house waved his gun.

"S'listen. None o' that. We're goin' t' keep him till we c'n get a Mounty. I know what I'm doin'. We got t' stay on the right side o' the law. We'll get a good name f'r this haul."

The men stopped, muttering in their throats, glowering at one another. One had his gun drawn, another his knife. Gabe stood his ground, eying them all with steady, placid eyes.

"I know what I'm doin'," Haggerty repeated. "Back up, the whole lot of you, an' no damn argyments."

"Rough-house is got the right idea," grumbled one of the men.

They tied Gabe hand and foot and thrust him into a little cubbyhole packed with stores. He fell heavily. They closed the door and left him in the pitch blackness. He had not said one word in self-defense. He was ready to make the final sacrifice for his brother.

In the morning, when Haggerty brought him food, he asked if he might have a few words with Nan. Haggerty refused at first, but when Gabe handed him a few bills he changed his mind, remarking, "S' listen. No monkey bizness, now."

Nan came over a little later and Gabe spoke to her in low tones.

"Now that you've promised to marry Harry, I wish, Nan, you'd get it over with and take Harry away with you. The mission, you know, is twenty-five miles from here. You'd have to go there. Well, keep going. Tell Harry that, and tell him to take the money I've got hidden in the cabin—tell him to take it all."

"Gabe, you didn't do that," she declared, her eyes moist.

He nodded slowly. "Yes, Nan."

She gripped his arm. "You didn't—you didn't, Gabe!"

"Will you go to Harry and tell him what I've just told you?"

"Gabe, you are mad—*mad!*" she cried passionately, shaking him.

"Please, Nan, go away—go away—tell Harry. Harry is a good boy. You can make him better. Go far away, over to the God's Lake country. It's a good country; furs run big there. *Go away, Nan!*"

She flung out of the room with a sob in her throat. Gabe was thrust back into the cubby-hole. The day passed, and Harry did not come to see him. He had hoped Harry would come down at least to inquire. But night came, and no word from Harry. This was a blow to Gabe, a blow that would never heal.

The nightly crowd collected in the store. Rum flowed freely. There was some singing and much boisterous laughter. Two trappers blew in from the north with fresh tales. Despite the noise Gabe fell asleep, and when he awakened silence predominated except for the sound of the wind. He shivered with the cold. His arms and legs were sore and stiff under the tight bonds.

Vaguely he began to think of escaping. He would give them a merry chase—would lose them in the vast northern wilderness he knew so well. He would strike up along the coast toward the polar rim and hide with the Eskimos. Would he, though? Could he? Here he was bound hand and foot and locked in a black closet. He hated confinement. He would not let them take him out of the wilderness to rot in some jail. Somehow he must get away, at any cost, and lose them in the trackless wastes of the Barrens. He might die of the cold or perhaps of starvation, but he would die fighting against overwhelming odds, and that would satisfy him.

There was a stir in the trade-room, and he listened. Feet were moving across the floor. There was a yawn followed by a grunt. A moment or two of silence, then a door creaked on its hinge. A low, baffled snarl stopped short in mid-career. The door slammed shut. Feet dragged against the floor. A man snarled savagely. There was a low command, tense and brief.

"Open that closet!"

That—that was Nan's voice. Gabe caught his breath, instinctively wrenching at the thongs on his wrists. He heard the lock on the closet door rattle and then click. A moment later it swung open, and he saw Nan crouched with a rifle in her hands, and Haggerty with his hands in the air.

"Gabe, can you crawl out?" she called.

For answer he squirmed snake-fashion out of the closet and then sat up. Nan told Haggerty to back up and kept a watchful eye on him while she leaned down and slashed away the thongs that held Gabe's hands. Then Gabe took the knife and freed his feet.

"Come on, Gabe," Nan called, backing toward the door.

"S'listen," said Haggerty. "You're goin' t'regret this, miss. That man's a murderer. He killed Hawk Galtry, a good man. You just wait an' see, Gabe. You won't get far."

Gabe said nothing. With Nan he backed to the door, opened it and went out.

"Quick!" Nan cried.

She turned and ran for the timber, and Gabe lunged after her. In a spruce clump five dogs lounged in the traces and there was a nine-foot sledge loaded with provisions and trail equipage. Without a word Nan flung a pair of snowshoes to Gabe and began talking to the dogs. The brutes straightened. Nan took a caribou-gut whip from the sledge and snapped it deftly over the lead-dog. The team started off and Nan ran up ahead of it.

"Nan, what—"began Gabe, grasping the gee-bar and running behind.

"Never mind," she called back. "No time now. We've got to put some distance between ourselves and Haggerty. Mush, you huskies! Come on, Foro! That's the boy! Steady—steady, boy!"

Unable to comprehend it all, Gabe followed at the gee-bar, marveling at the swift pace of the girl who trotted ahead of the team. They left the settlement behind and struck a frozen lake. Here Nan increased her speed, running tirelessly, shouting encouragement to the dogs. Gabe plugged on, at times shouting for her to stop and explain about Harry. But she did not stop.

Hour after hour they pressed on, hugging the heavily timbered shore, reeling off the miles steadily. With the first wan streaks of dawn they were many miles from the valley.

When daylight broadened Nan slowed down, and finally stopped.

"The best team in the valley," she said, a little breathlessly, nodding toward the dogs. "We'll have a bite to eat now."

Gabe, a puzzled frown on his rugged, honest face, rolled up from the rear of the sledge to confront her.

"Nan, I can't understand this at all," he said. "Didn't you go to Harry and tell him what I asked you to?"

"Gabe will you for once forget that brother of yours?" she asked. "Yes I went up to your cabin and found him there. I told him you had been trapped in Hawk Galtry's cabin and that you as much admitted killing him. Harry was very nervous and said it was too bad. Oh, Gabe, I've tried so hard to make a man of him—for your sake, because you asked me. Can you imagine? He said it was too bad you killed Galtry—said he hoped you would get out of it somehow. I told him about the money, too. He jumped up and went after it like a mad man. He wanted me to run away with him right away. Right then, Gabe, I felt like shooting him. But I didn't. I held him up, though—took the money away from him—your money. It's in my pocket—here."

"But—but where is Harry?"

"God knows. You see, Gabe, you made the biggest sacrifice for him a man can make. You offered up your life, your freedom— everything. You didn't kill Galtry. *Harry killed him!* I was coming home from MacVale's when I heard a man scream, and then I saw Harry running from Galtry's shack. I looked in later and saw Galtry lying on the floor. I went home and said nothing."

"But—Harry?"

"Gone. When I took the money from him I told him what a coward he was, I told him that *he* had killed Galtry—that I'd seen him do it. I held a gun to his head and made him write a confession clearing you. I promised that I would hold it and use it only if *your* life was in danger. Then I advised him to clear out of the country. After that, Gabe, I don't see how you can regard him as a brother."

Gabe hung his head. "I don't see how I can, Nan, but I do. He's broken faith with me, with you, with God. But if ever I can help Harry, I will, because he is my brother after all."

Nan grasped his hand, her eyes shining. "Gabe, you are a wonderful man. There's nothing small and mean about you. You've got courage, Gabe—the courage of the strong."

"Oh, it's nothing," he said, taking both her hands and closing them in his. "You're wonderful, Nan. Could you go on with me? I don't feel right unless I've got somebody to take care of. Nan, the missioner is only ten miles beyond."

She pressed closer to him, and his big arm, the same arm that had knocked a riverman unconscious for five hours, went about the wilderness woman and held her with gentle firmness. The wind blew wisps of hair across her flushed, radiant face, and her eyes shone with a new happiness.

"To the ends of wilderness with you, Gabe," she murmured.

The rising sun sent streamers of dazzling sunlight across the shaggy, rugged land; rugged and strong like its men; clean and enduring like its women.

A MAN MUST FIGHT

**NORTH WOODS—THE FRIGID
SNOW GODS AND THE
GLITTERING SILVER STARS
BEHOLD AN AGE-OLD STRUGGLE
BETWEEN TWO STRONG MEN OF
THE WILDERNESS.**

CHAPTER I

NORTH WOODS

T. JEFFERY KIMBALL, acting chief of the wilderness railroad camp, lit a fresh cigar after the manner of a man who has all day in which to perform such an act, and blew out the match with a breath that was also a sigh of boredom.

"Oh, Tracy, don't bother me. I'm meditating. Go out and say I am busy—awfully busy, y' know."

Tracy, the old sandy-haired clerk, seemed reluctant. "But he said it was important, Mr. Kimball. In fact, he emphasized the word. I saw him approaching from my window. He was driving his team of dogs like the very devil. Hadn't you better—"

"Tracy!" snapped Kimball. "Am I to be told my business? Go out and inform Mr. Durand that if I am so disposed I may see him in—well, say, an hour. Yes, an hour, Tracy."

Tracy mumbled, "Yes, sir," and, wagging his old head sorrowfully, went out into his little office, closing the door softly.

Kimball leaned back in his swivel chair and propped his heels on the littered desk. He was a tall, lean man of the military type, sharp-featured, brusque, and not a little intolerant. Fair-haired, fair-skinned, tight-lipped, he looked his age to the year, which was his fortieth. In the absence of the original senior engineer, away to Winnipeg because of ill health, he was in command of the forces that were gnawing a path through the great northern wilderness with high and noble hopes of some day placing the end of steel at Port Nelson on Hudson's Bay. This vast undertaking was now holding the eye of all Canada. It was the greatest thing of the time, for the World War had not yet smothered a universe, and man was striving to create rather than destroy.

Kimball, sucking on his cigar, had just found a comfortable position in his chair when a sudden scuffling and a babble of words rushed in from the other room. He frowned his annoyance, started to remove his feet from the desk, then changed his mind and knocked the ash from his cigar with a petulant finger.

An instant later the door burst open and a big, husky young man surged in and stood spread-legged for a long minute without saying a word. His dark, fiery eyes cut Kimball like a razor; the set of his clean-clipped jaw was menacing. Suddenly he straightened up, booted the door shut with a heel and jammed rugged hands into the pockets of his red-blocked mackinaw.

"I told Tracy—" began Kimball, erect in his chair and white with indignation.

"You told him you were busy," bit off Durand.

"Yes, and by the Lord Harry, I am! What do you mean by smashing into my private office like a bull? I won't stand for such insubordination, Durand! I won't stand for it. Get out!"

"Busy, were you?" snarled Durand. "Busy, with your feet on the desk! Well, I'm busy, too!"

"I shan't listen—"

"Yes, you will!" Durand stepped forward and banged his fist on the desk. "Yes, you will! You'll listen to every word I have to say. You'll sit there and cock your ears and listen to why I came in from the sub-camp to talk to you."

"Durand, I am an engineer and a gentleman, and I insist—"

"I'm an engineer, too, but never mind about the gentleman part of it," cut in Durand. "You're my boss, but just now that doesn't mean a thing to me. I'm here in the interests of the men at my camp, and I'll see that their interests are served."

"Are you insinuating violence?"

"That's up to you. Violence, yes—if you don't come to your senses and realize you're in the wilderness, running the biggest job of its kind."

"Enough, Durand!" roared Kimball, trembling with rage. "Get out! Get out of my office!"

Durand stepped forward, his fists clenched, black scorn burning in his eyes. "Get out hell!" he rasped. "Keep your seat. Get up and I'll knock you down again. And listen!"

His voice went lower. "I came here in the interests of my men at the sub-camp. There's a hundred men there, Kimball, and they need rations to work on. We can't wait till that brigade gets in from The Pas. Old-timers around here say this last storm was the worst in years. The brigade is probably laid up some place and it can't get here in less than a week. The cooks are practically cleaned out and the meals that are being served are a disgrace to any decent outfit. Men can't work all day clearing away brush, bringing down trees and the like, on no meals. It breeds trouble!"

Kimball wet his lips. "Well, and what is your plan?" he asked with a sneer.

"You know as well as I do," Durand told him. "I've sent three different couriers here, and every time your reply was, 'I'll think about it.' Well, you've had plenty of time to think it over. Get down to brass tacks. Your camp is pretty well stocked; you made damned sure you wouldn't go short in the first place. And here's the idea: I want you to split it up and send sufficient rations to my camp till the brigade from The Pas arrives. That's what I came here for, and that's what my three couriers came here for, and you know it!"

"I have investigated matters here," droned Kimball, placing his finger-tips together. "I can't see my way clear. It would only mean taking rations away from my camp to give to yours. I have as many men as you, my dear Durand, and I am considering their interests also. You will have to get along the best way you can, living off the land—"

"Living off the land!" spat out Durand. "Why, the hunters have cleaned out what little game there was in the woods. We can't live off the land. We need tea and coffee and flour and a dozen other things, and you've got to split with us. The attitude you take would make a man think we were two rival camps instead of the same outfit. Man, you've just *got* to split with us!"

Kimball snapped to his feet, squaring his shoulders, pursing his thin lips. "I refuse!" he whipped out. "I can't do it!"

They stood eye to eye. Kimball's gaze was cold and harsh like ice; Durand's was hot, full of fire, full of the throb of life. And it was a level gaze, too, that bored deep into the other man, wrestled with Kimball's pale, agate eyes and threw them down in the end.

Kimball shook himself, glancing at some letters on his desk, fidgeting with his well-kept hands.

"Well, well," he snapped. "The interview is over. Please leave me to my work. Awfully busy. Hope the brigade will be in soon. Try keeping your men in good humor. Ahem! Good-day, Durand."

Durand breathed a noiseless oath, and his fists clenched and unclenched slowly, the knuckles showing white. "Kimball," he dragged out, "I think you're lying. I am going over to your storehouse and see just how much provisions you've got."

Kimball's head snapped up. "Don't you dare!" he clipped sharply.

"That's a dare, then, eh?" asked Durand, pulling on his mittens. "All right, I'll take the dare." He swiveled on his heel and made for the door.

"Stop!" shouted Kimball, springing forward.

Durand half turned. His eyes went blacker than ever. He sucked in a breath that hissed between strong teeth.

"Damn you, Kimball!"

Kimball stood poised in the center of the room, a heavy revolver in his hand. "Don't you try it," he warned. "I gave you my word, and I'll have no damned petty engineer doubting it. You think you can bull your way in this camp, eh? Well, I'm no lamb myself, Durand. You'll take orders from me, and if your gang of roughnecks won't work without food, let them lay off till it arrives."

"And they sent you out here to run a railroad camp!" chuckled Durand bitterly. "Don't get tough, Kimball. You're monkeying with the wrong man. You're in a God-forsaken pocket of God's country now, and the men working for you are not exactly boy scouts. Get that, mister. You've got the drop on me now. But if hell breaks loose in my camp, watch out for yourself—watch out!"

He shot Kimball a contemptuous look, yanked open the door and rolled out.

Kimball came out behind him, his gun still drawn. He followed Durand to the latter's sledge and dogs, where "Lank" Roper, Durand's labor boss, was pacing up and down. When he saw Kimball with a gun he immediately jumped for his rifle which was on the sledge.

"Never mind that, Lank," called Durand.

Lank rubbed his gaunt, grizzled jaw, and seemed disappointed. "What's up, chief?" he asked, taking a tobacco shot.

"Nothing much."

"D'you get the order f'r the grub?"

"No. This camp's cleaned out, too, Lank," replied Durand. "Get those dogs up. We want to make our camp before dark. That seven miles trip is no skylark."

"Hell!" swore Lank, picking up the whip.

The dogs lined out and Lank cracked his lash, starting off. Durand waited till he was out of earshot before speaking. Then he buckled on his rackets and turned to Kimball.

"Where do you carry your brains, Kimball? Coming out here with a gun! Lank Roper knows now there's something in the wind. You've started a job that's not going to be so easy to end. Think it over, Kimball—think it over. And watch out!"

Durand, swung off, broke into a trot and soon caught up with his outfit.

CHAPTER II

TROUBLE IS BREWED

THE NIGHT was cold and raw. The temperature had plummeted steadily following the three days storm that had swept down from the polar rim, locking the wilderness in its cold white arms. Somewhere in the trackless wastes between the camp and The Pas the grub brigade was stranded, probably waiting for the snow to harden and make travel possible.

In the sub-camp's headquarters, a sturdy, two-room cabin, Durand and Lank sat back over their after-supper pipes.

"I wisht," said Lank, regarding his pipe, "the old big chief was back. I don't like this guy a-tall, Steve. He ain't built f'r rough-house work like this here. Don't see why the blue-blazin' hell they didn't put you in his place."

Durand drew thoughtfully on his pipe. "Too young, Lank, I guess," he answered. "Only twenty-eight. Kimball's been with the outfit for years. Oh, he's a good engineer, Lank. He's built subways, lot of bridges, railroads and all that."

"Yeah, but I say he ain't used t' buckin' a real tough job like this."

"He'll get used to it. I've got nothing against him. I'll just plug along the best I know how."

Lank removed his pipe from his mouth and pointed the stem at Durand. "Say, Steve, I wasn't borned yesterday. You don't like Kimball and there's no use your tryin' t' make believe things is all right. They ain't! I don't know what happened in his cabin 'tween you an' him. He had a gun on you—"

"Something personal, Lang," put in Durand.

"I'd like t'believe you. You went there t'get rations f'r our men here. He turned you down. You threatened—oh, Steve Durand, I know you!—you threatened t'go an'take what you wanted an' then he yanked the gun. You might deny that, but I ain't believin' different. An', Steve, see here. Me, I'm with you t'the end. You're the best damned boss in the bizness, an'you c'n count on me in any pinch. I'm f'r my men, too, but in a showdown, Steve, I'm with you, s'help me."

"Thanks, old-timer," said Durand warmly. "I'll not forget that."

Lank was about to continue, when a sudden knocking at the door cut him short. He shoved back his chair, got up and crossed the room. With his hand on the latch-string, he turned to Durand: "I got an idea—"

"Open it," said the engineer.

Lank opened the door and a man rushed in, stopped short and fought for his breath.

"B-boss," he stammered, "them fellers in the mess-hall is raisin' holy hell."

"Who are you?" was Durand's shot.

"Dish-washer. Them bums 'll murder the cooks if—"

"I'll run over, Steve," cut in Lank, grabbing his mackinaw.

"Right with you, old-timer," said Durand, jumping for his own togs.

The two men went out together, with the dish-washer trailing behind, and ran for the mess-hall, a quarter of a mile away. Durand was thinking not of the rebellious men, but of Kimball, and his thoughts of the man were indeed bitter. Nothing but disaster would come if this man were in such a responsible position for very long. Kimball was a good engineer, but he was not a wilderness man. Durand was. Durand was born of the wilderness, and the four years at school had not robbed him of those qualities which the wilderness breeds in the hearts of its men.

The way led through a grove of poplars, and in the white gloom they could see the lights of the mushroom settlement. As they drew nearer they heard a muffled din, men's voices raised in anger, and a series of reverberating crashes. Not the gentlest, nor the noblest type of man labors in a railroad camp. Pretty tough birds, the most of them, and *all* big eaters. Swedes, Finns, Galicians, Germans, Poles. And they were hungry now! Indeed!

Lank Roper had not been made labor boss by accident or because he had a pull with the man higher up. When Lank entered that mess-hall it was with a bang and with the firm conviction that he could lick any ten men you'd care to mention. Durand was right at his heels, ordering him not to use a gun under any circumstances.

The long, low mess-hall, which in reality was three buildings strung together, reminded Durand at the moment of a madhouse. Imagine almost a hundred men—big, rough, tough fellows—imagine them surging about the low hall, pounding on the long boards that served for tables, swearing their heads off, flinging stools in the direction of the kitchen. Imagine the stuffy heat caused by three roaring stoves and the body-heat of all those men; think of the smells, the rank tobacco smoke, the din and clamor of half-a-dozen different languages from the red, lusty throats. Picture this, if you can, and then think of Durand and Lank Roper come to quiet this wild, untamed mob.

Lank plowed his way to one of the tables and leaped upon it. He cupped his hands to his mouth and bawled: "Lay off! Stop! Stop! Lay off!"

Durand elbowed his way among the men to the center of the hall and jumped upon another table. "Men! Men! Men!" he roared.

"Boss, we gonna turna deese camp whatcha call inside oudt!" piped a swarthy-faced man below him.

"Himmel!" shouted another. "Dot *verdammte schweinhund* hoff a cook—"

Somebody let fly a tin plate that rebounded off Durand's head.

"Men!" he roared. "Listen! Listen! Food tomorrow! Grub—grub—grub—*tomorrow!*"

"G' on, ye're a bloody liar!"

"I promise!" yelled Durand. "I promise fresh grub tomorrow!"

One of the laborers, a gang foreman, butted his way to the table and leaped up beside Durand. "You mean that, chief?" he asked huskily.

"I certainly do," replied Durand.

The gang foreman jumped down and went among the men commanding them to quiet down.

Lank Roper had been forced to knock six men sprawling in order to impress upon the others that he really meant what he said. He was no longer on the table, but down among the men now, his snowplow jaw thrust forward and his eyes popping. In his hand he held the leg of a stool. His left cheek bulged with a wad of tobacco the size of a golf ball.

"An' now you've heard," he boomed, "what the chief says. He says there'll be grub tomorrer. Next guy raises his mitt or tries t'ack intelligent, me, I'll brain him!" He shook the club menacingly.

Little by little the noise diminished. Men still grumbled here and there, but the majority were willing to compromise. The milling around stopped and they stood in groups, debating the situation. The older heads swayed the mob in favor of a compromise, for they knew Durand was a good man who invariably kept his word.

The gang foreman, Wolrab by name, a shaggy hulk of brawn, swaggered over to Durand as he was preparing to leave with Lank. "Chief, you'd better keep that promise o' yourn," he said.

"Are you the spokesman for these men?" asked Durand.

"Kind of," drawled Wolrab, rocking on his feet importantly.

"Food tomorrow, Wolrab," said Durand, and swung out with Lank at his elbow.

Back in the cabin again, Lank flung his cap across the room and cracked fist to palm. "Steve," he said, "you sure saved the night by promisin' them birds grub tomorrow. The thing is, where you goin' t' get the grub?"

Durand, unbuttoning his mackinaw, dropped to a chair and stared hard at the floor. He was in a pinch now. That was a wild crew to handle. He had promised grub by tomorrow, and if he failed them their anger would surmount even tonight's demonstration. Primitive men, the most of them, isolated now in a primitive country where raw instinct breaks through the brittle film of restraint on the least provocation.

"Lank, old boy," Durand spoke at last, and then paused. "Lank, I want you to hang around camp tomorrow and keep the boys on good terms. Let's see. We've got four sleds in this camp and about fifteen dogs. On your way back to your shack tonight, Lank, tell those eight Indian dog-drivers to be on their toes at daybreak."

Lank stroked his jaw and closed one eye. "Uhuh, Steve," he grunted. "Is that all? Don't you think I ought t' tag along, too?"

"No, Lank. You stay here. And watch out for Wolrab. I have an idea the men listen a lot to what he has to say. Wolrab strikes me as the type can cause a deal of trouble in a camp like this."

"You just leave Wolrab t' me, Steve. No use askin' what you're goin' f'r to-morrer?"

"You know, Lank," said Durand.

"Good luck, Steve!" Lank gripped Durand's shoulder warmly, then picked up his cap and went out.

Durand still stared at the floor.

"It's the only way," he mused. "I hate to do it, but Kimball has driven me till my back is to the wall."

CHAPTER III

DURAND STRIKES

AT BREAK of day Durand left the sub-camp at the head of four empty sledges and eight Indian drivers. The rest of the big camp had not stirred yet. Only Lank was there to shake hands with his chief and wish him Godspeed.

Seven miles lay between the sub-camp and Kimball's main outfit—seven miles of frozen swamps, dense bush and, toward the end, a ridge beyond which lay a valley of strong woods. In the southern nook of this valley lay Kimball's hastily constructed settlement.

The trail was rough and arduous, and it took Durand and his Indians three hours to reach the first outlying building. Farther up the valley he could hear a gang of men dynamiting stumps. Other gangs moved about the valley. Woodcutters were hard at work. Saws buzzed and axes rang. Giant trees toppled to earth with a roar, carrying smaller trees with them. Gang foremen bawled out orders and swore lustily. Somewhere a man was singing while he labored.

Durand, still at the head of his small brigade, told his head dog-driver to hang around the door, and entered.

The storekeeper was a little man who took his job seriously. He looked up from a ledger, adjusted his spectacles, and nodded: "Hello, Mr. Durand. Nice day isn't it?"

"Fine," clipped Durand. "I've got four sleds outside. They're all empty now, but I'm figuring on going back to my camp loaded down with flour, bacon, tea and other staples. What do you say?"

"Well, you see, Mr. Durand, you'll have to get a written order from Mr. Kimball."

"Let's just forget the written order. I'm in a hurry."

The storekeeper adjusted his spectacles again. "I'm sorry, Mr. Durand, but—"

"Listen!" Durand leveled a finger at him. "Did Mr. Kimball tell you anything since yesterday?"

"Well, no, nothing particular."

"How are your stores?"

"Very low, sir, very low. In fact—"

"Mr. Kimball told you to tell me that, didn't he?"

"N-no."

"Now look here, friend," went on Durand. "I'm going to see just how much stores you have. I am going to take half of what is on hand. My men need grub. They were short rationed to begin with. Step aside."

"B-but, without a written order, I can't let you—"

"Forget it. Just step aside. Your explanation to Mr. Kimball will be that I forced you to stand aside."

The storekeeper put up his hand, but Durand, dark and grim now, brushed the man aside and made for the big storeroom in the rear. He unbolted the door, lit a candle and entered. He found, just as he had surmised he would find, well-stocked shelves, barrels of flour, stacked boxes of tea and plenty of bacon.

With a bitter little chuckle he strode out and called in his Indians, leading them into the storeroom. In his hand he held a pad, and he marked down each item as it was removed from the room to the sledges. A slow anger was smouldering within him. There were more supplies here than he had suspected. And Kimball had told him that he could not spare him any. The memory of that hot interview made Durand's blood boil with righteous wrath. What could have been Kimball's motive for telling such a barefaced lie?

He was sending out the last package when a sudden barrage of warm oaths assailed his ears. Pocketing his pad, he left the storeroom and entered the storekeeper's office just as Kimball came in from outside. The senior's face was a study in cold white anger. His eyes were narrowed and hard as agate.

"Durand, what do you mean by this outrage?" he roared.

"Outrage?" Durand was a man with a hot temper. "Do you call it an outrage to take provisions to my camp and keep my men from breaking loose? I knew you were lying in the first place, and I've got as much right to these supplies as you have. If you don't think I have, then try to stop my brigade from pulling out. Last night my men almost tore down the mess-hall and came near to killing the cooks. That's a wild lot I've got, and they eat heavy. You've got plenty of grub here to go around, and there's no reason why you shouldn't give me an even break. You can't give me a reason!"

"Am I answerable to you for what action I choose to take?"

"Not at all. Neither am I to you, in a crisis like this!"

"Yes you are!" cried Kimball.

"The hell I am!" Durand shot back at him, his eyes blazing.

"I'll break you, Durand, so help me, I'll break you! You are an insolent young pup—"

Durand's fist whipped out and landed flush on Kimball's jaw. The senior reeled backward, struck a barrel and sprawled to the floor. Durand leaped to the door and yelled to his head dogdriver.

"Start for the sub-camp. Don't wait for me. Start and keep going till you get there!"

He slammed the door, whirled about and dived for Kimball as the latter was trying to pull his gun. He pinned the gun before it was half-drawn, tore away Kimball's hand and rushed him violently against the counter. Kimball's hands came up, groping, and Durand yanked away his gun and sprang back.

"As you are, Kimball! You've staged your act!" he bit off.

Kimball leaned back against the counter, gasping for breath, his hands working feverishly. His hair, usually sleek and carefully parted, now straggled over his forehead.

"Well, you got me that time, didn't you?" he snarled nasally.

"Right you are. I'm top dog, Kimball. You're getting kind of careless with that tongue of yours. Stay right where you are. You too, storekeeper. Not a move out of either of you. I'll just stay here and cover you till my brigade is beyond recall. My men will eat today and eat well!"

"Durand," grated the senior, unable to contain himself, "you will regret this—by Godfrey, you will! From now on it's war between us! Do you understand? *War!* By that I mean I will make things mighty damned uncomfortable for you. I cannot fire you without going through a deal of red tape and communication with headquarters. But I will drive you into such a tight corner that you will throw your job and run away!"

"Run away!" exclaimed Durand. "That's a challenge, Kimball. You nor any man living can make me run while I've got two legs to stand on. I'm not fast on my feet, Kimball. I'm not a runner. Get that? I'm not a runner! I was built for standing still under fire. Try to make me run, Kimball—just try. That's *my* challenge!"

"I accept your challenge!" Kimball snapped, tilting his chin.

"Then your war is on!"

Again the silent conflict of eyes, the cold, pale eyes of Kimball at grips with the hot, turbulent eyes of Durand. In Durand's gaze was all the fire of a strong heart, all the self-willed power of a nature born to tackle big obstacles. There was in that gaze a certain amount of stubbornness; a driving force in the whole chiseled ruggedness of his face, in the set of his heavy shoulders, in the deep, forceful way he spoke. Kimball was the cooler, the more calculating, capable of subtlety and not a little craft. He was not a driver like Durand, yet somehow you surmised he held a bag of tricks up his sleeve that was all his own.

"Suppose you put that gun away," Kimball ventured.

"Not for a while," replied Durand. "My brigade must be well out of reach before you move."

Kimball chuckled drily, looked away and put a fresh cigar between his teeth.

"Tell you what we'll do, though," went on Durand. "We'll go over to your office for a while. Come on."

Kimball moved toward the door. Durand eyed him closely, opened the door and indicated for the senior to go out first. When they were outside Durand touched Kimball's shoulder and said:

"Tell your storekeeper everything is all right. Tell him nobody need know what happened."

Kimball hesitated, eyeing Durand sidewise.

"Tell him now," prodded Durand.

Kimball bit off a muffled oath, turned and pushed open the door. "Just check up what was taken out, storekeeper," he called. "Give me the list later. Don't talk to anybody about this."

He banged the door shut and swung off toward his office with Durand at his heels.

"It's more private over there," explained Durand.

"Damned considerate of you!" spat out Kimball testily.

As they entered the outer office Tracy started to say something, but Kimball waved him to silence and strode on into his own office, with Durand right behind him. Then Kimball stopped short, caught his breath.

"Oh—hello—hello, Miss La Forge!" he jerked out.

"Greetings, m'sieur!" A young girl, with raven hair and midnight eyes and red, laughing lips, made a slight curtsy and extended a small white hand. "I just came in and the very dear M'sieur Tracy said I should make myself at home. So!" Her laugh was rich and silvery.

"Yes—yes. Glad you came," hurried on Kimball. "Ah—um—this is Mr. Durand, my assistant. Mr. Durand, Miss La Forge."

"How do you do, Miss La Forge," said Durand.

"I never have seen you, I don't think. *Oui?*"

"Guess not. I'm at the sub-camp mostly." He looked across at the senior. "If you've got an appointment here, Kimball, I'll step out and keep Tracy company for a while."

"Many thanks, Durand," Kimball returned with a bow.

Durand gave the girl a parting smile, turned and went out into the other office where the old clerk was typewriting. Durand took a seat and stuffed his pipe.

"Well, Mr. Tracy, how are you these days?" he asked casually.

"Oh, fair to middling, sir, except for a slight—very slight, you know—touch of liver."

"Don't say! By the way, you're not a wilderness man. Whatever possessed you to pack your baggage up this way?"

"Health, sir. I thought it might build me up. And it has, you know. Oh, yes, indeed, sir!"

Durand thought for a moment. Then: "This Miss La Forge whom I've just met. Is she to be added to the force, do you know?"

"Why, not that I know of. She—she is a frequent visitor. Just a friend of Mr. Kimball's, I take it. A very charming young lady. Her father, I believe, is dead. She lives with an aged mother not far distant from here. Miss Adrienne La Forge. A very charming name for a very charming young lady."

"Yes," said Durand. He put a match to his pipe.

CHAPTER IV

THE BITTER MUSKEG

THE OUTER door burst open at this instant and a short, bearded man entered in what appeared to be a state of excitement. "I wanter see Mr. Kimball," he shot at Tracy.

"Sorry, but he is busy just at present. Will you sit down?"

The man, fumbling with his cap, edged onto a chair, breathing heavily. He nodded to Durand, and then clamped his eyes eagerly on the door leading to Kimball's office. It was apparent that he was very much worked up over something, for he kept moving about on the chair, shuffling his feet, fumbling with his cap. After a few minutes he extended a hand toward Tracy.

"Listen, mister! Can't you tell him it's very important? Tell him Casey wants t' see him—Casey, the gang boss. Tell him there's trouble on the muskeg Job. Go ahead, won'tcha?"

Tracy sighed, got up and opened the door to the private office softly, shoving in his head. "Mr. Kimball, beg pardon, sir," he said. "Casey, the gang boss, has something important—very important, sir—to tell you about the—er—muskeg job."

"Tell him," came back Kimball's voice, "to see me later, I am very busy right now. And don't bother me again, Tracy."

Tracy closed the door and spread his hands palmwise. "I am sorry, Casey," he offered.

"But, f'r cripes sake, mister, this is—"

"What's up, Casey?" cut in Durand. "Tell me about it. I'll fix you up."

"Well, about that there muskeg job we're on," Casey explained. "The boss was warned not t' run his line so close t' it. It's where that ridge comes down t' the muskeg."

"Warned? What do you mean?"

"He got a letter signed just, 'The Trappers.' That muskeg is a great place f'r traps, an' we'll ruin all that by runnin' the bed along it. I don't care about that part of it. I'll run a bed any place I'm told. But me an' the boys is just been fired at. Some guy took a pot-shot at us an' hit one o' the Wops. I've called 'em off an' quit workin' f'r the time bein'."

"You did perfectly right, Casey," Durand told him.

"Well, that's what I wanted t' know,"

"And don't go near the place any more today. Keep your men away. About this man was shot. How is he now?"

"Not so bad. Just nicked on the arm. We fixed it up an' then Doc Fraser did the rest. Doc says it's all right. But I don't wanter go gettin' any more men shot."

"That's right," assented Durand. "You can go now. I'll speak with Mr. Kimball later."

"Thanks." Casey put on his cap and pulled open the door. "It's funny, Mr. Durand. I mean, ev'ry time I come t' see the boss he's always busy. S' long." He shuffled out with a broad grin.

"There was something in that I didn't get," said Durand.

Tracy threw a sidelong glance at the door, then leaned over and said, behind his hand: "It's known all over the camp that Mr. Kimball has been giving much of his time to mademoiselle. Just a little jest on Casey's part, I presume. You know the men!"

"Yes," was Durand's slow, meditative reply.

"Recently," went on Tracy, "Mr, Kimball has been giving very expansive dinners in one of the halls. Dr. Fraser was a guest; also Mr. Dennison, who handles the mail, Talbot, the superintendent, and a few others. In fact, there is to be another wilderness banquet tonight. But, of course, you have been invited."

Durand was on his feet, his fists knotted, his brows bent down in a savage, bitter scowl. Now he knew why Kimball had refused him rations, had refused food for those men in that lonely sub-camp. Kimball wanted it for his own personal parties, affairs that were unnecessary and nothing if not extravagant. Kimball wanted to put on a big front, to strut before this wilderness girl.

It was traitorous! It was vile! A hundred men in an isolated sub-camp deprived of grub because the chief wanted to throw a party. A hundred men battling with the wilderness, slashing and tearing through mighty forests in a noble endeavor, tricked by the man who was, in a way, their keeper.

A slow rage throbbed through Durand's hot blood. He thought of himself and good old Lank Roper trying their best to calm their men in the grim crisis. He felt as a man feels who has been basely betrayed. He had been betrayed! His men had been betrayed! Basely betrayed—no less! And it was plausible that Kimball would betray them again sometime, in another crisis perhaps more precarious than this.

Durand, his eyes blazing, took a savage step toward Kimball's door. But Tracy fairly leaped from his desk and grabbed the big man by the arm.

"Oh, sir, please don't!" he cried.

"Let me go, Mr, Tracy!"

"But, Mr. Durand, for my sake. I didn't think—I mean I thought you knew about these affairs. Mr. Kimball will discharge me. Perhaps I shouldn't have told you. For my sake, please, sir. I can't afford to lose my position."

Durand controlled himself with an effort, jammed his hands in his pockets and turned away, scowling darkly at the floor. "All right, Mr. Tracy," he muttered.

"And you won't let on, sir, that I told you?"

"No." Durand pulled on his mittens. Then to Tracy: "You say there is to be another party tonight?"

"Yes. But—"

"Good-day, Mr. Tracy."

Durand banged out of the office, stood for a moment considering matters, then headed for the center of the settlement. Ten minutes later he walked into Dr. Fraser's cabin.

"Why, hello, Durand!" hailed Fraser, a wiry wisp of a man.

"Hello, Fraser. Did you fix that fellow up?"

"Sure-thing. Tell the truth, Durand, it wasn't much. The poor beggar thought he was killed, though. Um. Haven't seen you in ages, old man. Where you been keeping yourself?"

"Working," clipped Durand. "My sub-camp is no playground. We *work* over that way."

"Eh—how's that?" piped Fraser.

"By the way, Doc, where is the man who was shot?"

"Here," said Fraser, going to the door. "Casey took him to his own shack for a while." He pointed the cabin out with a finger.

Durand left the doctor and soon was in the little shack with Casey and the wounded man.

"He's sleepin' now," Casey whispered. "Ah, the poor man was scared stiff."

"Too bad," replied Durand. Then: "Casey, I wish you'd come with me and show me that muskeg. They won't shoot if we just walk there."

"Sure, sir. Be right with you," agreed Casey, making for his coat.

The walk from Casey's shack to the beginning of the muskeg was about two miles on a beaten track, and they made it in half an hour. They climbed a short, steep bluff from the top of which Durand obtained something of a bird's-eye view of the contested section. He had a map in his hand, and he began figuring and making notes on it with his pencil.

After a while he motioned to Casey and they descended. Durand then led the way in the muskeg, studied the ground, wandered about making odd notes on the map. Casey followed, saying nothing, a thin puzzled frown on his forehead.

Finally Durand folded the map, stuffed it into his pocket and crammed a fresh load of tobacco into his pipe. "All right, Casey," he said. "I guess we'll go back now."

"You've got it all figured out, huh?" grinned Casey.

"Most of it."

They tramped on for five minutes in silence. Then Casey said: "You know, Mr. Durand, a lot of us fellers lost money on you."

"On me? I can't see how."

"Well, it was this way. When the Old Man got the gout an' had t' go home, a lot of us bet you'd be given his place. Yes, sir. An' I lost twenty dollars."

Durand laughed warmly and clapped the stocky gang boss on the back. "At any rate, Casey, I'm glad to hear you thought enough of me to bet on me."

"Yes, an' there's a lot more 'an me lost," added Casey.

Durand could not help feeling a little thrill of elation tingle in his veins. This confession of Casey's meant that a large number of men in Kimball's own camp had their own ideas as to who should be in charge. Even Casey's tone of voice when speaking of Kimball suggested that he did not think much of the man's capabilities. It was not that Durand was gloating over Kimball's low status among the men. He merely experienced a very human feeling of self-satisfaction at knowing that the men held *him* in some esteem. It was a vindication of his own belief in himself. He *did* believe in himself; not half-heartedly, but with a belief born of his own strong nature and indomitable will.

When they reached Casey's cabin Durand hung up his cap and opened his mackinaw. "If you don't mind, Casey," he ventured, "I'd like to stay here for the remainder of the day. I want to do some figuring."

"You know, Mr. Durand, you c'n hang around here's long as you want. O' course, you'll be goin' t' the boss's party t'night."

Durand chuckled, removed his mackinaw and hung it up. "I may, Casey," he replied, half to himself.

"I always useter wonder why you wasn't at the other ones."

"Busy," was the clipped rejoinder.

But the fact of the matter was that Durand had never received an invitation. Nor had he been invited to tonight's affair.

"That La Forge girl is t' be the guest o' honor, I hear," Casey said.

He did not see the bitter scowl on Durand's face.

CHAPTER V

DURAND IS FOULED

THE WILDERNESS plays strange tricks with the minds of men. While it is capable of molding a man into a tower of moral and physical strength, it is also capable of bringing him down just as it is capable of bringing down in one moment a tree that has stood for half a century. It gives and it takes away. It builds and it destroys. It is hated by one man and loved by another. In its austerity it is at once terrible and beautiful.

Kimball was a good engineer. Men said he was, anyway. He had, it is true, put over some big jobs; but never before in his life had he tackled a wilderness job. Intolerant, egotistic, he was used to adjusting conditions to his own individual taste. Prior to his present undertaking he had succeeded in this endeavor.

But now he was trying to batter his way through a stone wall. No man can adjust the northern wilds to his own desire. He must adjust himself to the rigid fabric of those high latitudes, and, if he is built of the right stuff, he will in time, perhaps, make the wilderness an ally instead of a stubborn enemy.

Kimball was out of his element. He was cracking under the stern test of the wilds, and the lamentable part of it was that he considered himself unbeatable. His thirst for excitement, for grand banquets, for the association of women, had increased over the past month. He neglected his work more and more, bawled out his men, bragged about his record and threatened to make the wilderness bend under his hand. His threats were many and huge. It was his way of trying to bolster up his nerve, for vaguely he realized that he, and not the wilderness, was bending, giving ground.

So another wilderness banquet was staged in the log hall. Fraser was there, wiry and alert; Dennison, in charge of what mail there was; Mike Talbot, the superintendent, with his distrustful eyes; Hugh Wayne, the Indian agent, and his wife; two traders and their wives, from an independent post ten miles to the northward; Slattery, the dynamite expert, who had been invited because he always was full of good jokes and knew how to tell them. Most important of all, Adrienne La Forge, the beautiful wilderness flower. Next to her sat Kimball, the man who put on a big front at the expense of a hundred men in a lonely sub-camp.

Adrienne was flushed, wide-eyed, sparkling with pure clean health. This indeed was an honor bestowed upon her. Kimball had toasted her and everyone at the table had cheered. She was bewildered, struck quite speechless in the thrill of her great happiness. She could only smile and speak with her midnight eyes, enveloping the other guests with the magic thankfulness of her gaze. Her skin was milk white, as though no northern blast had ever seared it. Her hair, dressed Madonna-wise, was black and lustrous. Small she was, and you did not have to see her walk to know that she was lithe and supple as the reeds that grow by those northern waterways.

Kimball himself beamed, and could not refrain from looking at her for longer than was polite. He was very attentive, and very often leaned close to her ear and spoke in low tones that brought to her face a rush of color or a bewildered smile.

Two waiters served and three cooks were in the kitchen. No more elaborate, extravagant meal was ever served in city or country. No expense was spared. There was much to choose from. The dinner got well under way and wine flowed freely. Slattery spun a yarn or two and the hilarity increased in tempo.

It was at this point that the door opened and Durand strolled in. He took off his cap, shoved his hands in his pockets and leaned back, regarding the revellers with moody eyes.

Slattery was in the middle of another yarn, but, sensing that something unpleasant was impending, he stopped and took a drink. Doc Fraser laid down his fork, wiped his mouth with his napkin and blinked rapidly. Kimball sat erect, pursed his thin lips and narrowed his pale, icy eyes.

"Durand," he snapped, "I thought you had gone back to your camp. *That* is where you belong."

"Oh, yes?" Durand took his pipe from his mouth.

"Yes!" rasped Kimball, rising. "I don't remember having invited you, and I think it is very impertinent of you to thrust your undesirable person upon us."

"Be that as it may, Kimball, I am here," was the low rejoinder.

"And you are making yourself more undesirable every second! Will you kindly relieve the unpleasant situation by quietly taking your departure and leave us to ourselves?"

Durand gave him a brittle chuckle heavy with scorn. "You are a much better actor than you are an engineer," he said. Kimball smothered an oath, kicked back his chair, and in his most military manner strode across the room and confronted Durand. With a rigid finger he pointed to the door. "Get out!" he cried.

"Don't make me laugh," muttered Durand, checking his hot temper with a vast effort.

"Get out, you insolent young boor!"

"Easy, friend! I was born in a lumber camp." His hand gripped his pipe so hard that the stem snapped.

Kimball turned to the table. "Slattery, Talbot, will you help me throw this fellow out?"

"Why don't you ask all of them?" Durand scoffed.

Slattery and Talbot looked at each other, nodded and rose. They left their seats, flexing their arms, clamping their jaws.

Durand threw away the remains of his pipe and jumped to one side, lowering his head and shoulders, spreading his legs and planting his feet solidly. Black fire surged up in his eyes and his jaw thews hardened.

"Think, Slattery and Talbot, before you get rash!" he flung at them. "I came here to say a few words, not to brawl. There are ladies present. If you're aching for a pair of broken necks, come outside. The moon's clear and I'll take on both of you." He shot a look at Kimball. "And you, too, if you're able."

Slattery and Talbot slowed down, seeming not so sure of themselves.

"Throw him out!" cut in Kimball, drawn to his full, lean height.

A chair at the table scraped. Adrienne had risen. Now she ran across the room and stood between the men. "Please—please do not fight!" she implored, raising her hands.

Kimball said: "Miss La Forge, this fellow—"

"Please—please—*please* do not fight!" she insisted. "It is not good to fight."

"You are right," put in Durand. "It is not good to fight. But if one of these men tries to put me out, I will fight! I didn't come here to brawl—not at all. I changed my mind about returning to my camp. Unintentionally, perhaps, all of you are conspiring against the welfare of that camp—against my men, who have worked faithfully for days and days on reduced rations."

He turned on Kimball, and all the guests leaned to hear him, caught up by the vigor and force of his deep voice.

"So this, Kimball," he pursued, "is the reason why you refused me rations for my men! I didn't think you were capable of it. I was blind. You didn't invite me because you knew I would be against it. And I am!"

"You are intruding on my personal rights!" flashed Kimball.

"And you have stamped on the personal rights of my men! These banquets would be all right under other circumstances. I'd enjoy them myself. But under present conditions they are traitorous. They are not vitally necessary. My men are necessary. Their grub is necessary. I will fight for the welfare of my men! I will fight you and every man-jack in your blasted camp! I am warning you, and these people are witness to the fact, that if you dare throw another party before the grub brigade arrives, I'll beat you to pulp and clean out every ounce of provisions in your storehouse!"

Kimball was like a man frozen stiff, and the pallor of a deadly wrath was on his face. No one moved. No one spoke. You could have heard a match drop, the silence was so great. Durand was putting on his cap.

"That's all," he said. "Expect me in the morning, Kimball, about that muskeg job. *That* is vital, too. Goodnight."

He turned and pulled open the door. As he was about to go out Kimball, up to this moment paralyzed by the awful rage within him, let fly with a knotted fist that landed with a terrific impact just behind Durand's left ear. It was a fierce, cruel blow of rage. Durand tottered, reeled back into the room, groping with his hands. Kimball, his breath hissing, struck again, and this time it was a direct, maniacal blow to the temple. Durand buckled, fell to his knees, toppled over sidewise, lay on the floor in a daze, muttering to himself. His great spirit working instinctively, he tried to push himself up with his hands, and succeeded in reaching only a sitting posture with his arms braced against the floor.

Then, like a bomb exploding from an unexpected source, Adrienne confronted Kimball and shook her little hands in his face. "It was a cruel blow!" she exclaimed. "It was very foul, that blow. I did not think, m'sieur, you would do such a thing."

Hugh Wayne, the Indian agent, was standing beside them. "Truth, Kimball," he observed tersely. "I never saw a dirtier blow in my life."

"I wish never to see you again!" was Adrienne's next shot. "You make a big show, make me guest of honor, while the poor men go without plenty food. That is not right. I do not want to be guest of honor when men go without food."

Kimball fell back a step, his body rigid, his eyes two pin-points of cold, glittering fire. "Fools! Fools! You are all fools!" he shouted, throwing up his hands.

Adrienne was now bending over Durand, bathing his head with a wet napkin. Wayne brought a tot of brandy, and Adrienne took it from him, pillowed Durand's head in the crook of her arm and poured the brandy between his lips.

Wayne went over and looked Kimball straight in the eye. "If I were you, Kimball, I'd drop out of sight before he gets on his feet," he advised in low tones.

"Is that so?"

"Quite. The inevitable slaughter would be an unpleasant sight for the ladies."

Kimball thought for a moment, tapping his chin. "Well, since you put it that way," he said, and went for his coat.

Wayne could not supress a sardonic smile. Apparently Kimball had misconstrued the intent of the agent's words.

On his way to the door Kimball hesitated, seeking a word or two with Adrienne. The glance she gave him was indeed withering. Kimball turned away with a savage gesture, yanked open the door and went out.

When Durand finally stood on his feet again, he looked around with quizzical eyes, and rubbed his head. He saw Adrienne before him, with the wet napkin in one hand and the empty glass in the other. He smiled slowly.

"Thanks," he said to her.

"It was nothing, m'sieur," she replied, and her warm, clean smile was like a benediction.

"Thanks, just the same. What hit me, anyhow?" He turned to Wayne. "Where is Kimball?"

"I made him go out, to avoid further complications."

"Oh, I see," muttered Durand. "Well, I guess I'll be getting along. Casey, the gang boss, said I could sleep in his shack."

"I'd better go along with you," ventured Wayne.

"No, thanks. Don't worry. I'll not bother Kimball. You see, I've got to talk business with him tomorrow." He turned back to Adrienne. "I want to thank you again for helping me. Good-night."

"Good-night, m'sieur."

She extended her hand. Durand took it and pressed it warmly in his own, looked for a brief moment into the depths of her dark, haunting eyes, then spun on his heel and swung out into the night.

He headed for Casey's cabin, trudging on a beaten path. A sharp, clear wind rushed against his face. The sky was a pale dome studded with a billion stars. The moon rode serenely above the hoary roof of the shadowy, murmuring wilderness. The scattered lights of the settlement shone with friendly warmth.

Deep in Durand's mind there was stamped indelibly a picture of a pale, beautiful face, with lips slightly parted against white teeth, and dark, mysterious eyes that stared searchingly into his own.

CHAPTER VI

DURAND COMES BACK—FAIR

IN THE morning Durand ate breakfast with Casey in the latter's cabin.

"How was the party?" asked the gang boss through a mouthful of egg.

"First rate," replied Durand. "Oh, fine!"

"Yeah? That's good. Pass the salt, will you? Slattery was there, I'll bet. They always invite him 'cause he's full of jokes. He's a good dynamite man, too. When's the next party?"

"I don't think there'll be any for a while."

"Uhuh. Course it's none o' my business, but that's a good idea. The storekeep seems worried sick over supplies. Hope that there grub brigade gets through safe. Well, I wonder what the boss is goin' t' say about that muskeg job. What do you think?"

"Don't tackle it yet, Casey," said Durand. "I'm going to have a little talk with Mr. Kimball on just that subject. Drop around at his office in a couple of hours."

"You got somethin' up your sleeve, ain't you?"

"Sure," chuckled Durand. "My arm."

Casey grinned from ear to ear.

Durand smoked a pipe before leaving for the senior's office, and went over his map and notes. Then he left Casey's shack, and a little later walked in on Tracy and wished him good-morning. Tracy was very nervous.

"Mr. Durand, I wouldn't disturb Mr. Kimball if I were you," he said.

"That's all right, Mr. Tracy. I've a very important matter to discuss with him. Ah—never mind announcing me. I'll walk right in." Durand strode resolutely across the outer office, shoved open the connecting door and entered the senior's sanctum.

Kimball looked up, sat erect and took a crack at his desk with a doubled fist. "By Godfrey, are you still around here?" he exploded.

"Sure thing. I told you last night that I would be over to see you about that muskeg affair. For the present we'll bury the hatchet, for there is something at stake more important than our personal scruples."

"The hatchet will never be buried between you and me! We are in a state of war. I am perfectly capable of handling that muskeg job. All you need to do is attend to affairs at your sub-camp. I'll take care of this camp."

"Well, what do you intend to do about that muskeg thing?"

"What do I intend to do? Why, run my line along the northern edge of it."

Durand came closer and leaned over the desk. "You can't do it, Kimball—not safely!"

"Can't I? Do you think I am going to be bulled out by those trappers that run their lines there? Not by a long shot!"

"It's not that. It will be unsafe to run as close as you intend along that muskeg. Your bed will be undermined. That muskeg gets the overflow of that river to the east. The ground there is nothing more than a shell—it's porous as hell. You have got to allow for expansion and contraction. The spring freshets, piling into the muskeg, will overflow your bed."

"That's a nice little speech, Durand, but you've exaggerated. Come out with it and say that you're afraid of the trappers."

"Oh, talk sense!" rasped Durand. "Why should I be afraid? I'm handling a camp seven miles away."

"Then get the hell over there and handle it!"

"You're getting nasty now, Kimball. One of your men was shot yesterday. More will be shot. I've gone over that land carefully, and there's no reason why the men should be killed off like that. If you lay your road on that line, just as sure as you're sitting there, your bed will crumble!"

Kimball shoved out his jaw. "Will it? Well, let me tell you something, you genius. I'll run my bed through there in spite of you and every damned trapper between here and Port Nelson!"

"For Lord's sake, Kimball, listen to reason! Forget for a few minutes that we hate each other. You will be the joke of the country if you pull a thing like that. There's only one thing to do: Blow that ridge apart. Instead of winding around the southern end of it and following the muskeg, blow through it in a straight line and you'll have a natural, solid bed from there on, at least a mile away from that porous, undermined land."

"What! Use seven thousand pounds of powder and two hundred of dynamite! You're off your head!"

"Listen, Kimball. I wish you'd come with me and look over the ground where you intend running that bed."

"I can't be bothered with your wild ideas. I know more about engineering than you'll ever learn. Don't try to run things, Durand. Go over to your camp and take life easy. I've declared war on you, and I mean it. I want no advice from you. You practically hanged yourself last night so far as I'm concerned. Get out."

"All right," Durand growled bitterly. "But I'll be on my toes. I think you are the one got hanged last night, pulling a dirty blow like you did. What's more, you'll cut your own head off if you try to buck natural conditions and run over that muskeg. It's not that you don't know better. But you just want to show the trappers you're boss. And now I suppose you'll do it even at the cost of your reputation merely because I'm against it and because you hate me."

"Yes, Durand, I hate you. You challenged me once; I challenged you. You've got eyes on that girl, too. Well, so have I… We'll see. Go back to your camp, and be your age, and don't bother me again about that muskeg."

Durand cut him with a dagger look, turned on his heel and made for the door. He paused with his hand on the knob. "That muskeg job will be the ruin of you," he said. "And remember, I'm still fighting, Kimball—on my toes!"

He swung out with that, and left Kimball muttering behind drawn lips. He threw a clipped good-bye to Tracy and banged the outer door violently after him. Swinging along on the trail that led back to his sub-camp, he tried to gather together his tumbling thoughts and regard things rationally.

He was not a cool man, this Steve Durand. He was a dynamo of energy, and turbulent blood flowed in his veins. At times he gave the impression of being cool, but this was the result of much internal struggle. He was essentially a driver, and when he considered himself in the right, he drove on and on with relentless force. He was cut out to handle big jobs, to handle men by the hundreds. He had the brains and the moral strength to give way when that was necessary and to slug relentlessly ahead when there was no other way out.

Leaving the valley, he entered a dense forest of balsam. The tang of the clean woods and crisp air in his nostrils was exhilarating. He was winding his slow way among the forest giants when a sudden commotion in the thickets on his left brought him to a standstill. There was a drumming sound that he recognized as the whirring wings of partridge routed out and trying to get away. A moment or so later the partridge zoomed by, and a split second later there appeared in hot pursuit a girl with a shotgun. She almost ran into Durand, who ducked back, whistling his surprise.

"Oh!" gasped the girl Adrienne, stopping short.

"Glad you didn't shoot!" laughed Durand.

"Twice already I have lost that partridge. Oh, well!" She jerked back her head and gave a care-free laugh.

"I'm on my way back to the sub-camp," he offered. "You live around here?"

"Yes. Not far away. You go back to your camp now, *oui?* Your head doesn't hurt no more?"

"Head's all right—fine. Wasn't much. Just made me dizzy."

"Oh, it was very wicked blow!" she exclaimed. "I was very sorry. I will never go again. I did not know your poor men were very hungry. Before you came there I was so happy—so happy it was pain. Then, when you spoke, I was very sad."

"Well, I—I didn't intend doing that."

"Oh, you did not mean to, I know very well, m'sieur. But I am glad I know now. I will not eat there when the poor men are hungry. I will never go near M'sieur Kimball again. He is very cruel, very wicked, to hit you from behind. I shall always fear him now."

"Oh, there's nothing to fear," he told her. "Well, you'd better try for that partridge again. I'll be moving on."

"Oh, I am so poor shot!" she laughed.

"But, m'sieur, sometime when you have more time, stop at our cabin on the edge of the balsam. You are very much welcome."

"I'll do that some time," he replied, and took her extended hand.

"Do, m'sieur. *Au revoir!*"

He left her standing there and tramped off. A little farther on he slowed down and looked back. She was still watching him. He saw her throw back her head and smile that delicious smile. Then she waved. He waved back, smiled to himself and continued on for his lonely sub-camp, now five miles distant.

CHAPTER VII

THE GOING OF WOLRAB

LANK ROPER, a gaunt, raw-boned figure of a man, was standing in the doorway of the cabin, discoloring the snow with meditative tobacco shots, when Durand came out of the poplars. They both caught sight of each other at the same time; Lank shifted his chew and made a very serious face.

"Well, Steve," he began, "I was just considerin' if I should plug over there an' see what happened. The Injuns got here with the grub all right. The men are singin' on their jobs again, some of them."

"Glad to hear it, Lank." Durand shook his friend's hand warmly.

"S'pose you had a little go-to, huh? One o' the Injuns told me 'bout the beginnin' o' the fracas. What you do?"

They entered the cabin and Durand shrugged out of his mackinaw. "Oh, I just tried to keep things peaceful until my boys were well on their way with the grub," he explained. "Then I hung around for a while, talking business with Kimball."

"Yeah?" droned Lank, cocking a dubious eye. "Sure! Bizness! I figured that's what was keepin' you. Yeah—oh, yeah!"

"Lank, you've got an evil mind," grinned Durand, sitting down.

"Mebbe so I have." He arched his eyebrows and pointed a bony finger at Durand. "Now, Steve, go ahead an' tell me that there little dark lump on your temple was got by bein' kissed wit' a canary bird. Go ahead, Steve, tell me that. Or tell me you bit yourself there."

"Falling branch, Lank," lied Durand, showing great interest in a batch of reports on the table.

"Fallin' branch me neck!" was the shot. "It ain't fair, Steve, you holdin' things back on your friend. If them bums over there are tryin' t' do you dirt, Steve, I wanter know. I c'n lick any six o' them wit' one hand tied behind me back. I tell you right now, young feller, it's you should be handlin' the whole shootin' match, an' that there knock-kneed son of a pie-eyed centipede, Kimball, should go back to his pink teas where he come from!"

"Whoa, Lank!" yelled Durand. "Take it easy, man! You're getting excited over nothing at all. Listen, old-timer. Go over and tell the cook to get me a meal ready. I'm hungry."

"Anyhow, Steve, I mean what I say, it ain't right—"

Durand stood up and laid his hand on Lank's shoulder, squeezing it good-naturedly. "Lank, if ever I need a man to help me, to stand by me in a pinch, you're the first man I'll call on. Shake on that, old boy!"

"You mean that?" Lank leaned closer, his eyes boring into Durand's.

"So help me, Lank!"

"Put her here!"

Two strong hands met with a crack, gripped like iron. Then Lank grabbed his hat and lunged out.

Durand sat back in his chair again. He knew that Lank was his true friend, and for that reason he did not want to tell him what had happened at the main camp. For if he did, Lank would lose his head and start trouble. It was Durand's innate sense of loyalty and honor that kept him from airing his own misgivings. He was aware that if he chose to circulate Kimball's recent actions, a whole camp of men would rise as one, and rank rebellion would be the result. Durand was big enough to bear his burden alone. Soon or later, though, Kimball would go too far, take a step too many, and chaos would envelop the camp.

Durand felt it in his bones that something was impending. He had a feeling that some dread issue was to arise, an issue that would test his own mettle to the utmost.

He was finishing the meal which the cook had brought him, when the door whipped open and Lank rocked in with a bloody bandage around his right hand. Durand laid down his fork and frowned concernedly. "What happened?" he asked.

"Ah-r-r, I opened me knuckles on Wolrab's jaw!"

"Wolrab!"

Lank was pouring warm water into a basin. "Yeah. Some fine day I'm goin' t' lay him out f'r good. He's a trouble maker, Steve. He's got a loud mouth, an' he's been tellin' th' men right along they ain't bein' treated right. He's been goadin' them t' ack nasty t' me. He talks too much, Steve. I set him on one job this mornin', an' then I find him doin' another. I tell him about it an' he says I'm dreamin'. I look him in th' eye an' tell him t' please repeat them words. He tells me t' go t' hell an' I lay him out prompt. Then I tell him he's fired an' we'll send him back t' Th' Pas wit' th' next brigade from th' main camp. O' course, if you want t' interfere an' hold him on, that's up t' you."

"Lank, I rely on your ability to handle the men," replied Durand. "Do you really think it's for the best that we let him go?"

"Speakin' frank, Steve, I do. I ain't told you all th' tricks he's pulled. Gen'rally I don't bother you 'bout them things. But he is a trouble maker. Lots o' nights I heard him speechin' in the barracks about the men bein' persecuted an' such. I been warnin' him right along t' cut it out."

"Well, Lank, you ought to know, being among the men more than I am. If you advise it, I'll give him his walking papers and an order for his pay. Go out and send him in to me."

Lank went out and came back half an hour later with Wolrab whose jaw was swollen and discolored. A black scowl clouded his broad, heavy face. He was a stocky man, built like an ox, with shrewd little eyes.

"We are dismissing you," Durand told him, "for disobeying rules and breeding ill feeling among the men. In a big venture like this we can't afford to employ men who work toward those ends. Here's your pay slip; you can collect from the paymaster at the main camp."

"This ain't a square deal at all," rumbled Wolrab, taking the slip.

"It's more than square," said Durand. "You've been trying to run this camp, and that doesn't go. You can go to The Pas with the next brigade in a week or so. The grub brigade is due soon, and when that arrives another will leave."

Wolrab moved toward the door, a malicious look in his eyes. "All right, boss," he growled. "You're goin' to regret this."

"Don't leave any threats behind," Durand gave him.

Wolrab chuckled harshly, pulled open the door and sagged out.

"And that's that, Lank," said Durand.

"Good riddance, Steve. With him gone things oughter work smoother. I'm puttin' a man named Galt in his place—a good man, quiet but steady. He used t' be a section foreman on the Soo."

"Use your own judgment, Lank," replied Durand. He fell to thinking for a few minutes. Then: "I didn't like that threat of his, Lank. I wonder what he's got up his sleeve."

"Aw, he just wanted t' have somethin' t' say, Steve."

"I—don't—know," demurred Durand.

"Aw, f'rget it, pardner!"

"For the present, all right. See here, Lank! Your hand—let me bandage it for you. Glory! You must have taken an awful clip at him!"

"Haw! Didn't you see his mug?"

Lank had not been made a labor boss by any trick of chance.

CHAPTER VIII

A WOMAN—AND TWO MEN

WOLRAB PULLED out of the sub-camp that same day, and Galt was given his job. In the mess-hall that evening, Durand talked to the men and impressed upon them his own interest in their welfare. He was well liked, and many of the men felt a little ashamed of having listened too intently to the insurgent talk of Wolrab. Durand's sincerity was in his eyes, in his voice, in his whole demeanor. Three rousing, lusty cheers boomed through the hall when he concluded and jumped down from the table.

Outside Lank poked him in the ribs. "Steve, they're all pullin' f'r you now!"

"It makes me glad, Lank, old boy. I like to pull with my men and have them pull with me. I like to play a square game all around."

Lank gripped Durand's arm and pressed it warmly. "Don't I know it, pardner! There never was a man more on the square than you are. Anybody says different I'll clout him! I'm all f'r you, Steve chum, an' when you're in a tight corner, remember, old Lank ain't never been backward 'bout comin' forward. Forty-eight I am, come May eighth, but I still got a wallop or two left."

"Wolrab ought to know!" grinned Durand.

They both had a great laugh over this, and clapped each other on the back. Then they linked arms and strode off for the cabin, while behind them in the mess-hall resounded the lusty voices of many singing men and the beating of tin plates.

Three days later Durand, feeling in good spirits because his men had responded so enthusiastically to his plea for co-operation, left for the main camp to be there at the arrival of the grub brigade, which was long overdue at the time.

The day was crisp and clear, with a sky almost cloudless and a sun that glittered dazzlingly on the snow—so much so, that Durand put on his dark glasses. He went alone, without his dogs, swinging along with great strides. The wilderness was never more beautiful. It tumbled away for countless miles like a green billowy ocean flecked with foam. It murmured and crooned in odd keys. There was something infinitely clean and wholesome about it all; something singularly inspiring in the vast bowl of the sky, in the crisp tang of the balsam-laden air.

It was a land that pumped rich red blood through a man's veins. It was a land that drove a man to his chosen star if that man had picked himself a star. It was a rough land, a stern land, but it could be gentle, too. In all its harsh fabric there was a strand of gentleness that could be found if one looked hard enough. It was a beckoning land, reaching out with great arms, trumpeting with the voice of the wilds, calling men to its white frontiers, to its lonely waterways and half-forgotten valleys.

Durand tramped on, drawing in great lungfuls of bracing air. And when he neared the main camp he paused for a while, looking about and rubbing his jaw thoughtfully. Then he smiled slowly behind his hand, turned off the trail and cut down through the balsam forest. Presently he came to a snug cabin deep in the woods, from the chimney of which rose a column of blue smoke. He crossed the small clearing, took off his mitten and knocked. A moment later the door opened slowly, then swung wide.

"Oh, come in, m'sieur!" It was Adrienne.

"On my way to the main camp. Just thought—"

"*Oui!* But do come in!"

Durand kicked off his rackets, removed his cap and entered the cozy sitting room where a small sheet-iron stove glowed cheerily. An old woman sat in a rocking chair, knitting.

"My mother," nodded Adrienne. "Mother, this M'sieur Durand, of the engineers."

"So!" exclaimed the old woman softly, and rose, extending her hand. "Adrienne she speak ver' mooch 'bout you, m'sieur. Eet is pleasure to meet you." She turned to Adrienne. "I weel mak' tea... Pardon, m'sieur."

When Madame La Forge went into the kitchen Adrienne and Durand sat down. Durand noticed that her right wrist was tightly bandaged and remarked it while he stuffed his pipe.

"Oh, that!" She caught her breath; then laughed suddenly. "I am so clumsy, m'sieur. Chasing partridge again, I fall on my wrist. Some day I will get that partridge! *Ma mére* poke much fun at me because I miss so many times the partridge."

Her bubbling good humor was at once engaging and contagious. Durand found himself quite unable to refrain from grinning or chuckling with her. Time sped by swiftly, however, while they chatted, each wrapped up in the other's personality, drawn closer to each other by some subtle, mysterious power. Neither Durand nor the girl was aware of the swift passage of time until Durand's gaze accidentally fell on the clock on the mantel.

"By George!" he exclaimed. "Why, say, it's past noon! Lordy, I've got to be moving."

"Oh, so soon?" she asked, inclining her pretty head.

"Yup. Sorry, though. Haven't enjoyed myself in I don' know when. Fact is, I'm coming back for more some time."

"That will be good. I enjoyed myself much, too."

Durand put on his mackinaw and Adrienne went with him outside, where he bent down to strap on his rackets. Then she walked with him to the edge of the clearing.

"Well, we'll have another chat soon," he offered.

She put her hand into his. "Very soon, I hope," she said softly.

Hand in hand, they stood looking into each other's eyes for a long minute, each sensing a peculiar sensation that forbade speech. Durand, with a lame little chuckle, finally released her hand and pulled on his mittens. He gave her a husky good-bye, waved his hand and swung off. When he had gone a hundred yards he looked over his shoulder and caught sight of her still watching him. He waved again, and she waved; they both smiled.

An hour later Durand strode into the main camp and made straight for headquarters. On the way he met Casey, the gang foreman, and they stopped. Casey was a little pale and limped badly.

"Accident?" asked Durand.

"If you c'n call gettin' scratched with a trapper's bullet an accident, why, yes."

"That muskeg job?" was Durand's quick question.

"Sure. I'm not hurt much, though. Bill Tyler, my best ax man, is laid up wit' a splintered arm. Gus Sholtz is got a shot hand. It happened yesterday. Dirty shame!"

"But you're off the job now?"

"Yeah, I am. Mike Cronin an' his gang has been sent on it. It ain't fair, Mr. Durand, t' put men on a job like that while them fellers are at target practise."

"Well, Casey, take care of your leg," said Durand. "I hope you'll be all right soon." He went on, and a few moments later walked into Kimball's office."

"Oh!" muttered Kimball disgustedly. "You over here again?"

"I see Casey's been shot up," replied Durand, sitting down.

"Unfortunate, to be sure," snapped Kimball, scanning a letter.

Here Durand noticed that the senior's right hand was bound with tape and gauze across the knuckles. "You got mixed up in it, too?" he asked.

Kimball shot him a fast look; then thought of his hand and pulled it from view. "No!" he rasped. "I—I fell on it in my cabin last night. Well, what do you want today?"

"Grub brigade in yet?"

"No! Damned laggards are nowhere in sight. I sent two scouts out yesterday as far as the river. They didn't see a sign... Well, is that all you came for?"

"That's all."

Kimball leaned forward. "Oh. Thought maybe you came over to see Mademoiselle La Forge."

"Well, that was on the side. I did stop to say hello, had tea and a bite to eat. H'm. Funny. You know, Kimball, she said she fell on her hand, too. Odd coincidence, don't you think?"

Kimball's jaw hardened. "Quite!" he spat out viciously. "I wish some people around here would fall on their heads and break them!"

Kimball was bitter as gall this afternoon. Something had gone wrong somewhere. He seemed harried, nervous, erratic. Someone had crossed him. "So you fired that fellow Wolrab?" he flung at Durand.

"You spoke to him before he left here?—Or is he still here?"

"No, I didn't speak to him. I wasn't here when he came. Tracy O.K.'d the slip and sent him to the paymaster. Since then he's dropped out of sight. See if you can't fire some more good men when you get back to your camp."

"He was an insurgent," came back Durand. "He crossed my man Lank Roper every chance he got. I know a good man when I see one, Kimball."

"Suppose you call that gangling idiot Roper a good man!"

"I do. You can't show me a man in your camp as good. He may not know the three R's, but he knows men and he knows how to handle them. I'd feel lost without him."

Kimball snorted impatiently and jammed a fresh cigar between his teeth. He was about to put a match to it when Tracy opened the door and shoved in his head.

"Mr. Kimball, sir, Cronin, the new boss of that muskeg job, has been shot through the side!"

"Dammit!" exploded Kimball, jumping to his feet. "Who brought the news? Send him in!"

Tracy called the messenger into the private office.

"Yes, guv'nor, Mike was shot, 'e was. Six shots was fired an' we up an' tykes Mike ter the doc's. One o' the bloomin' Polacks got 'is 'at shot off but he weren't hurt. Hit's a bloody shyme, y' know, the goin's on o' those. Now, guv'nor, if I was—"

"Never mind!" cut in Kimball. "Cronin is wounded. How badly?"

"Ow, the doc thinks 'e is 'urt pretty bad."

"No one else hurt?"

"No, sir. I was almost 'it, though, guv'nor. I was tykin' a breathin' spell, an' I says t' Polack Joe—"

"Enough!" barked Kimball. "Get out!"

The Cockney effaced himself and Tracy went out after him.

Durand, leaning back in his chair, was studying the senior intently. Kimball flung himself down into his chair, lit another match and connected with Durand's gaze, holding it while he puffed on his cigar. He snapped the match away with a savage gesture.

"Well, you confounded ass, what are you staring at?" he raged.

"Just thinking, Kimball. Thinking about all the trouble you're making just to run a line through a rotten stretch of country. The game is not worth the candle. If it was practical, I'd say fight; but, man, you're playing a losing game. It will be your funeral."

"Cut that stuff! And don't talk again about blowing through that ridge. I wish to hell you would stay at your camp! Every time you come here you get on my nerves." He jerked to his feet, shaking with wrath. "You are trying to break me, Durand! You are trying to make a fool of me! But you won't do it! You won't! I'll beat you in the end. I'll beat everybody! Do you hear? I'm a better man than you are, and I'll prove it! I'll—"

The door opened again, slowly, and Tracy stood there, his hands clasped together as if in prayer, his face pale, his lower lip quivering. He looked like a man who had seen a ghost. He was struggling for words.

Kimball moistened his thin lips, cleared his throat. "What now?" he cried. "Speak, you fool! *Speak!*"

Durand turned in his chair, regarding the clerk with a puzzled frown.

CHAPTER IX

THE GRUB BRIGADE IS LOST!

"**T**HE—THE GRUB brigade," began Tracy, "has been—been—"

"Yes—yes!" snapped Kimball, "Come on! Out with it!"

"The grub brigade has been—*held up—attacked!*"

"What!" choked Kimball, falling back a pace, kicking away his chair.

Durand was on his feet now, his fists clenched. "Who told you?" he asked Tracy.

"One of the guides just came in—man named Brown. Here." Tracy pointed through the door.

Durand went out with Kimball at his heels. The man called Brown was slumped in a chair, fagged out, half asleep. Durand shook him by the shoulder. "Tell us about it, Brown," he urged.

"Aw, don't bother me… tired 's hell," mumbled Brown. "Run all the way… tired."

"Just a few details," pressed Durand. "Where it happened, just what happened. Come on."

Brown opened his eyes and blinked. "Well, was this way. We makes a camp last night. Twenty sledges loaded down. There's forty Injuns wit' us an' five whites or 'breeds, I don't know jest which. Anyhow, we makes a camp. We was holed up f'r five days by thet blizzard. Hell of a time! Never saw so much dam' snow come down in all me borned days. Well, anyhow, as I was sayin', we makes a camp—"

"That's three times you've made camp!" snapped Kimball.

"No, sir, beg pardon, there was only once we made a camp, beggin' your pardon. You should ha' seen thet snow, though—"

"Oh, he's drunk!" rasped Kimball.

"No, he's dead tired," said Durand. "He's so tired his mind's wandering a bit... Listen, Brown! Tell us where you were held up, by whom, and what happened."

"Oh—yes," nodded Brown. "Well, we makes a camp. Everybuddy's kinder happy 'cause we was figurin' on reachin' here t'day. We gets t' singin' an' raisin' the merry hell, like a man will, o' course, when—*whoops*—a gang o' roughnecks comes rompin' outer the woods. I figure there was only about fifteen o' them, but they had the jump on us. They begins blazin' away prompt and meanful. Right away the Injuns turn tail an' run around yellin' like a lot o' stuck pigs. Me an' the other four whites tried t' put up a fight, but somehow or other we're licked t' a frazzle before we start. Then I notice some o' the raiders roundin' up the Injuns an' makin' them handle the dogs. I get a bootiful crack on me knob an' I pass out o' the play in act one, scene one. When I come to later the camp's cleaned out, except o' course them as is daid. A few Injuns, two o' my trail mates—white, them last, I mean."

"Where'd it happen?" Durand put to him.

"Two mile 'r so beyond the river, where there's a ridge looks f'r all the worl' like a horse shoe, wit' the open ends pointin' north. Well, we was camped just inside the eastern arm."

"I know the place," nodded Durand grimly.

"It—it's terrible!" ventured Tracy.

"It's tragic!" muttered Kimball, biting his lower lip. "Well, we'll have to get the police on the job. Imagine! Between two and three hundred men here, and the brigade held up! The police—of course, the police. Get a man away to the nearest post, Tracy."

"Wait a minute," said Durand. "To send a man for the police would mean a wait of at least two weeks and probably more. In the meantime what are your men going to do for grub?"

"They will have to wait. What else?" asked Kimball testily.

"But will they wait? They're a wild lot, and they get mighty nasty on empty stomachs. Out of the lot you'll get only about a dozen who will stick with you. I know. I've had it happen in my own camp, and it will happen again there."

"Well, my dear Durand, what is your particular bright idea?"

"This is no time to get sarcastic, Kimball. My plan is very simple: Take the law in our own hands, strike out and recover the brigade. I'll take charge of the expedition. You can stay here and keep the men in order. Lank Roper can handle my camp for the time being. I'll send a man there explaining things."

"Where do you propose getting the men?"

"Right here in this camp. Ten will be plenty. We ought to be able to scrape up enough guns to go around."

"A rather reckless plan, Durand."

"Better than waiting two or three weeks for the police. Better than having the camp rise up in mutiny, raze the buildings and cut loose generally. You've never faced a mutinous mob, have you? I have and I can think of pleasanter things."

"Well," sighed Kimball, "it's your suggestion. I'll have no hand in it, but I shan't oppose you. I am still following the usual procedure by sending for the police."

"Go ahead. I'll have it cleaned up long before they get here. You are trying your hardest to buck me now without hurting yourself. You will find, I'll wager, that the men behind this hold-up are none other than a delegation of trappers who are making life miserable for you on the muskeg."

"That's a lie! They knew nothing of the brigade."

"They found out somehow. And when I get back with the brigade, Kimball, you are going to talk sense and come to terms. You are going to do the practical and sane thing by blowing through the ridge!"

"I'm damned if I will!" snarled Kimball.

"I'm damned if you *won't!*" came back Durand hotly. Then he lowered his voice and leaned closer to the senior. "And, by the way, see that you don't fall on your hand again!"

"I don't get you, Durand!"

"Oh, yes, you do! And don't forget, either: There are other ways for a man to get his neck broken besides falling off a cliff. Do—you—get—that, Kimball?"

Before Kimball had a chance to reply Durand was on his way outside.

The young engineer first went direct to the cabin of Casey. Here he asked the gang foreman for a list of men whom he thought would be willing to fight to save the grub brigade. Briefly he explained the condition of things. Casey bewailed his own inability to join because of his wounded leg, but he named a dozen likely men.

"They're tough birds, Mr. Durand," he explained. "They'd rather fight than eat. A couple are ex-pugs an' I'd swear a couple more has seen time behind the bars. But if it's just scrappers you want, them is your men. They're rough, I says, an' you'd best not be too gentle wit' 'em yourself. But I guess you c'n handle 'em. Most o' them's in Cronin's gang, an' you'll find 'em hanging round the bunkhouses."

Durand thanked Casey and headed for the bunkhouses. He had the list of names on a piece of paper and one by one he gathered the men together. It was a hard-boiled, tobacco-spitting bunch that he faced, but he looked them all straight in the eyes with a challenging gaze that gave them to understand he was boss. They were tough, but Durand's moral fibre was just about as tough as any and tougher than most.

"I understand you boys are fighters," he told them. "Well, the grub brigade from The Pas has been held up and run off. I want ten men to go with me and get it back. Who's ready?"

There was a stir among the men. The news of the disaster brought curses from them, guttural snarls and black looks. They regarded one another quizzically. One man spoke up, saying he would go if he were promised a pound of tobacco.

"Sure," said Durand. "A pound to every man."

"Make it five pounds, mate," clipped one hardcase. "I uster to sail out o' Seattle on a tub where the only grub was 'baccy."

"Five pounds to every man that comes along, then," Durand agreed. "Bring what arms you have."

The ex-seaman took in a reef on his broad belt and spat on his hands. "Say, mate, this listens good. I ain't had a decent, honest-t'-Gawd brawl since I was second on a windbag poachin' seals in the Pribylofs back in ninety-six. The skipper was a dirty souse an' the mate got religion; hell broke loose an' you should ha' seen them decks run red! Now lead me t' this fight, mate… Come on, fellers, stir your stumps!" he roared to the others.

The men broke up, swinging away to get their rifles, revolvers, or whatever armament they possessed. The ex-seaman laughed from the depths of his bull throat and dragged a pearl-handled knife from his belt. The blade was long and slim, curved slightly at the point and sharpened to a razor edge.

"This is all I need," he rumbled, and pulled up his left sleeve, revealing a broad scar. "See that? A Chink in a dump in Fu-chau did that—with this knife. I kept the knife. Ho! Ho!"

Singly and in pairs the men returned to where Durand was waiting. There were ten in all, and every man-jack of them looked capable of holding his own. Durand looked them over critically, nodded with complete satisfaction, and gave the signal to start. He took the lead himself, and the little band swung through the camp with a fine reckless swagger, a pugnacious look on every bronzed, bearded face. And Durand looked every inch their leader. He was their leader. He was born to be a master of men, and destiny had always mapped his course where the going was roughest.

CHAPTER X

DURAND SHOWS HIS METTLE

THERE ARE times when a man can get himself out of a jamb by a clever stroke of mental strategy or by the clever handling of his tongue. There have been many such instances of tact. But on the other hand, you cannot deny that there are times when a man must fight. Yes, if a man stacks up against the big things of the world, big in the cosmic sense of raw men getting back to raw earth, he must be ready to fight.

Durand was ready. Upon his success depended the welfare not only of his own sub-camp but of the main camp as well. If he failed, there would be an uprising of the hordes of laborers against the pitifully few leaders of the enterprise. They would ransack the camp and there would be a carnival of destruction. They would demand food. There would be no food. They would vent their anger upon the leaders, destroy with childish, malicious intent the things they themselves had toiled in constructing.

"We've got to win," Durand muttered to himself as he strode at the head of his nondescript crew. "We—have—got—to—win!" he repeated more grimly.

The ex-seaman rocked along behind him, a devil-may-care tilt to his craggy chin. Behind the ex-seaman a huge, stoop-shouldered Swede trudged ponderously, his gorilla arms hanging limp at his sides. What a gang of two-fisted, hardbitten roughnecks! But they could fight! That much was necessary—no more.

Unlovely, bearded, dirty, they looked quite as dangerous as they really were.

Durand led the way through a grove of poplars and finally came out upon a frozen waterway; he paused for a few moments to get his bearings. Then he motioned to his men and struck out across the snow-crusted ice of the river. In the distance a shaggy ridge rose above the lower wilderness that swept down to the river bank.

Once across the waterway he plunged into the thick forest of spruce; his hard little band surged after him, one trying to beat the other. Durand had the "horseshoe" ridge in view now, and he lengthened his strides, beating his way through stubborn thickets and leaping over fallen trees. The spirit of the chase was pounding in his blood. His men caught up the spirit and pounded vigorously behind him.

At last they reached the spot where, it was evident, the grub brigade had camped the night before. There were half a dozen dead fires, scattered cooking utensils, dog tracks, and the bodies of those who had fallen. Durand stopped long enough to place these bodies in the lower branches of trees outside the reach of wolves. Later he would see that they received decent burial.

It did not take him long to pick up the trail made by the stolen brigade. A brigade of such size could not help leaving a track as broad and as plain as the course of a river. It led north, veering gradually to northeast. Soon it came upon a narrow, winding creek that finally brought Durand and his men back to the waterway they had crossed before, but a mile or so farther north. This river flowed northeast, and tracks on the crust showed that the brigade had traveled in that direction.

Dusk flung its bat-wings over the land before long, but Durand did not stop; nor did his men seem eager to stop. They still strode on in their reckless manner, cracking jokes among themselves, taking the whole affair as if it were a lark. Their idea of a rousing good time was a healthy brawl, plenty of flying fists and a few broken noses into the bargain. The ex-sailor recalled memories of hot nights in the turbulent streets of Singapore, and cracked the big Swede heartily on the shoulder.

The Swede grunted animal-like and grinned at the snow.

Far on the frigid polar rim the Aurora unfurled pale, ghostly ribbons that hissed sibilantly among the stars. The night wind caught up snow particles from the crust of the river and flung them at the men's faces. The men spat them away and laughed.

The hours wheeled by as the little band swung farther into the north. Marks of the brigade still showed on the crust, but a little later, when Durand led the way around a sharp bend, the tracks left the ice and entered a balsam forest. The outfit halted.

Durand said: "Ten to one they're camped in the valley beyond this. We'll go on in and then you boys had better take a rest before starting things."

"T' hell wit' the rest!" grumbled the ex-sailor. "When I was in Durban in ninety-four—"

"Aw, give us somepin' original!" rasped a hawk-nosed man.

"Give you a poke in the jaw, mister, if that's original," was the return shot.

"None of that, men," cut in Durand. "Argue when this is over. Just now we've got to hang together. Come on!"

The grumbling ceased and the men followed Durand into the balsam forest, where a path had been trampled through the scrub by the large brigade. The way led up a slight incline. The trees were bunched closely and towered to heaven like cathedral spires. Vagrant shafts of moonlight danced among the deep shadows. Presently they came to the edge of a shallow valley, and down in its black depths they saw the yellow glow of campfires.

"Ho! Ho!" rumbled the ex-seaman, flexing his arms.

"Let's go," said Durand, swinging off.

Satisfied grunts came from the throats of the men as they followed Durand down the slope. They jostled one another in rough good humor, impatient to get into the thick of the impending clash. They crashed noisily through the thickets, and Durand was forced to hold them in check, recommending a more cautious approach.

"Keep this racket up and they'll hear us before we're within rifle shot," he concluded.

"Yeah, boss," rumbled the ex-seaman. "It's this white hope wit' his elephant's feet."

"Sailor, Ay bane giff you vun crack on de yaw!" stated the Swede very slowly.

"Sh-h! Cut it out!" clipped Durand. "Now, let's go on. Everybody quiet. Follow me."

The men followed, though there was still a little friction between the ex-seaman and the Swede; the ex-seaman giving his pointblank opinion of one Swede in particular and all Swedes in general, and the Swede retaliating with his own opinion of a man who once had to poach seals for a living in the Pribylofs. However, they soon became separated, and the grumbling quieted down.

Durand was still in advance, picking his way carefully, while the lights of the camp grew closer with the swift passage of time. Finally he was able to make out the figures of men walking about or sitting by the fires. He could see, too, many dogs and sledges. The men that walked about, he now observed, carried rifles. He raised his hands, his men slowed down and gathered about him.

"We'll split," he explained, "and attack from two points at the same time. I'll take four men and work around to the side." He looked at the ex-seaman. "You take the remaining five and creep up right from here while we crawl around. Get close enough so you can charge as soon as we let loose, only allow a little while for us to draw their fire."

"Sure," nodded the ex-seaman, looking about at the men. "You gotta take the Swede, though. I ain't goin' have any lead-hoofed lummox spoilin' my parade."

"I've chosen him already," said Durand.

The Swede doubled his huge fist, worked his jaws slowly and squinted dismally at the sailor. The latter glared back and bared his teeth ferociously. Durand stepped between them, told the sailor to gather his men, and clapped the Swede on the back.

Finally he crawled off with four good men behind him, and soon was shut from sight of the other band. The smell of woodsmoke drifted to his nostrils. He heard the yelping of the dogs. Nearby an owl hooted three times. Night life was afield in the shadows of bush and tree.

Presently Durand and his men were so close that they could hear the fires crackling and the conversational voices of the outlaws. Durand saw, at this point, that a band of Indians were herded together about one huge fire, and that two men with convenient rifles loitered near them. Durand divined that these were the Indians who had fallen captives to the outlaws and been made to drive the dogs to this secluded valley. At another fire sat half a dozen rough-looking fellows whom, he guessed, were the leaders of the lot. Half a dozen others went about the camp on different duties. The sledges were all abreast of one another on the northern borders of the camp, and the mass of dogs lay in the lee of this barrier.

Durand took in all the details carefully, then turned and regarded his men. A question was in his gaze, and the answer was in theirs. They leaned forward, crouching, muscles tense, the light of battle now glinting in their eyes.

"Remember," warned Durand, shaking his finger at them, "the idea is not to see how many men you can kill just for the sake of killing. We want the grub. We'll overwhelm and try to prevent as much shooting as possible."

"I t'ought this was to be a real fight," whispered one hoarsely.

"So it is," was Durand's answer. "It's to be a real fight and not a slaughter. Now! All ready—on your toes!"

"Let her rip, pard!" spat one.

Durand waved his arm, half rose and broke into a run for the camp, his revolver gripped tight in his hand. Behind him, abreast of him, tore his hard-bitten little band. They all burst upon the camp like a cyclone. The first of the outlaws was knocked horizontal in less time than it takes to tell it.

Hoarse shouts of dismay, of anger, went up. Men tumbled to get their weapons in action. A shot spat viciously, went wild, rattling through the low branches. Two more outlaws went down under the sudden, devastating onslaught. The rest strove to bunch together; had almost succeeded, when, from another point, the ex-sailor and his men bolted from the thickets with express-train speed.

There was no long range work. The two sides met at close quarters and the camp went mad. The dogs yelped, howled, and began fighting among themselves. The Indians who had been under guard rose in mass and fell back, unable to understand what was going on, or why. The two guards left the Indians and galloped to join their companions.

Oaths, howls of pain, dire threats, sharp commands, rang out and commingled to form a horrible, blood-curdling din. A man crumpled under a murderously-driven rifle-butt. The steel of a broad hunting knife clanged across the steel of a long revolver. Muscles strained till they were like knotted cables. A man dodged a terrific knife thrust—dodged and stopped a flung rock with his jaw.

The ex-sailor, his left cheek bruised and bleeding, was plowing into the milling fighters with the steady persistence of a steam-roller. His arms moved with lightning swiftness, his craggy hands, like two lumps of pig-iron, struck with bone-crushing, demoralizing force. His shoulders formed a battering-ram that seemed capable of plowing through a stone wall—capable, at least, those shoulders were, of plowing through beef and bone and sinew.

The Swede fought hunched over, his chin on his chest, his feet lagging, but his long, powerful arms doing a world of damage. Three men were attacking him, yet he stood his ground resolutely like some shaggy ape at bay.

CHAPTER XI

HARD MEN FIGHT HARD

DURAND WAS in the middle of things, too. Already he carried marks of conflict: a swollen ear, a bruised cheek-bone, a cut over the left eye. But these did not slow him down, did not dampen his vigor and the whirlwind, dynamic speed of his fighting. He was an accomplished boxer, but he did not box now. Boxing was out of the question; a man had to drive and drive, and pound away continuously. He had to brawl, use his head, his hands, his shoulders. He had to take a solid blow on the button and shake it off while he bored in, half-blinded. There was no time to clinch and clear his brain while he tied the other fellow up. To go down meant to go out. He had to stay on his feet—stay on his feet and fight; and three out of six blows against him were foul. Or were they foul? Everything is fair in war. Well, this was war!

Durand twisted away from an upthrust knife and escaped being impaled by the breadth of a hair. The man who had delivered the thrust lost his balance and reeled past, crashing through one of the fires and scattering hot coals as he leaped frantically away. For a brief moment Durand stood idle and unmolested.

Then a struggling, heaving, contorting knot of men broke up and ran about aimlessly swinging their hands and yelling on general principles. Two of this number tore headlong into Durand, with heads lowered bull-like, and fists flailing. Durand stepped to one side, let one man have a short, solid jab to the mouth. It stopped him as effectively as if he had run into a tree.

The other man did run into a tree, cursing a blue streak as he reeled away on shaky legs.

Durand saw that three men were trying to bring down the hard-fighting ex-seaman, and he started to aid him. But before he could join that special little argument, a short, broad hulk of a man rocked into the scene, glaring about evilly. His gaze settled on Durand, and with a gorilla roar he charged.

Durand barely had time to brace himself for this new onslaught; in a flash he saw that the man held a broad knife in his hand. He stood tense, leaning forward, his eyes glued on the knife as it swung for his throat in a mighty arc. He caught the steel-thewed arm as a man catches a ball, and the point of the blade stopped within three inches of its mark. He lunged with a mighty effort to one side seeking to unbalance his foe. He only succeeded in lowering the knife arm, while the man stood rooted to the snow like a tree.

"You—can't—throw—me!" grunted the man.

The voice struck a chord of memory within Durand. He looked closer at the swarthy, brutish face, the shrewd, beady eyes, and gasped his astonishment.

"*Wolrab!*"

"S'prised, ain't you?" snarled Wolrab. "Told you you'd regret firin' me!"

"Damn you!" New strength surged into Durand's muscles. "*You* will regret this, Wolrab, you dirty skunk!"

Wolrab's knife hand swung up again with a mighty effort. The blade tore a button off Durand's mackinaw, and Wolrab bared his stained teeth in a fiendish snarl. Grim-lipped, Durand forced the outlaw's arm back slowly but surely, the veins on his own temples stood out with the tremendous exertion. This Wolrab was like a huge rock to move. He seemed imbedded in the earth.

But Durand persisted. Inch by inch he forced that stubborn arm back, until finally Wolrab, with a sudden deft shift, relaxed for a brief second. The result was that both men went crashing to the snow. The outlaw's plan failed, however, for he was not quick enough to get from under Durand as they fell. The engineer was top man when they hit the snow, and he still gripped the hand with the knife.

Now he began to twist that hand, pinning Wolrab down with one knee planted on the man's chest. Wolrab writhed and swore and snarled. He was helpless under Durand's double hold, and when the knife fell slowly from reluctant fingers, he spat in Durand's face. Quick as a flash Durand had him by the throat, while his knees formed a steel vice against Wolrab's loins that quite paralyzed him.

He gasped for breath, choking, groping with his own hands for Durand's throat. But he only groped. He was beaten—beaten to a standstill. His struggles became weaker.

"Leg—leggo!" he groaned. "Gawd's sake... leggo... I'm licked... tell you..."

Durand released his pressure slowly, got to one knee, then up to his feet, picking up the knife as he rose. Wolrab rolled his head from side to side, still struggling for breath. He certainly was a beaten man.

Nearby the ex-seaman was sitting on a stump and chewing a fresh wad of tobbaco. The Swede was placidly stuffing his pipe, squatted between two outlaws who were on the way back to consciousness. The Indians still watched from the shadows, muttering among themselves. The dogs had quieted down. The wild brawl was over.

Wolrab was sitting up now, massaging his neck and grimacing painfully.

"Satisfied, I hope?" Durand asked him. "I didn't think you would carry your grudge against me this far. If the grudge was personal, why didn't you have it out with me alone? I think it was a pretty bum idea, settling a grudge at the expense of the whole camp."

Wolrab grumbled disgustedly. "This wasn't against you so much," he said, looking around at his prostrate men with dismal eyes. "It was more against Kimball. O' course, don't think I'm holdin' any love f'r you—not a bit. But I done this t' get square with Kimball."

"Why Kimball?"

"Well, he run me out o' his damned camp because I knew too much about him. Guess he was scared I'd get sore an' spill the beans."

"Get down to facts, Wolrab. I think you're just stalling, trying to invent lies. Well, save your breath!"

"You think so, eh?" droned Wolrab. "If you want proof, go ask a gal that lives a mile or so from the main camp, just off the trail to the sub-camp. Go ask her about Kimball. She'll tell you what she thinks of him."

"What's her name?"

"I don't know—somethin' like Forge—I don't know."

Durand's blood began to throb in his veins. "This girl—Kimball—what about them?"

"Well, it was this way," said Wolrab, frowning. "When you gave me my walkin' papers I lit out f'r the main camp t' get my pay. I was nearin' the camp, though not in sight of it yet, when I hear a scream. I runs in what I think is the right direction, an' I run smack into Kimball an' this here gal.

"Well, Kimball was rough-housin' her, an' he had her one arm twisted behind her back. She was fightin' like a wildcat, too. The odds wasn't fair, though, so I up an' take a smack at Kimball. The gal faints away an' Kimball yanks his gun on me. I grab a hunk o' wood an' crack him on the hand before he's able t' draw, openin' his knuckles pretty. Then I fleece his gun, tell him t' slunk, an' trot the skirt t' her shack, where her old lady thanks me.

"But that ain't why I made this comeback at Kimball. Naw, I don't think enough o' women t' do that. Anyhow, I left the cabin an' went t' the main camp an' pops in t' see Kimball an' talk things over. I get my pay slip signed, an' then I ask Kimball how much is it worth t' keep quiet about him attackin' th' little gal.

"He tells me there's no money in camp o' his. I ask him why not tap the camp treasury. Oh, no! He couldn't think of that.

He tells me t' give him time t' consider. That night I gets drunk an' when I wake up I'm layin' way off in the woods, damn near freezin'. Two trappers find me, an' I'm taken to a camp near the muskeg. Them is the trappers are against that line bein' run through. We talk about it. I tell them there's a grub brigade on th' way an' offer t' lead a band t' capture it, so's there won't be any food in th' camp an' th' men 'll rise up. Y' see, Kimball hired them two guys t' get me drunk an' lose me some place. I was wonderin' how come so many free drinks. Kimball's a rat!"

Durand stood transfixed, staring at Wolrab, through him, beyond him, with glazed eyes. He remembered Adrienne's bandaged wrist. He remembered Kimball's bandaged hand. He had thought Kimball capable of many shady deeds, but not of this—attacking Adrienne! Why, the man must be mad! Was the north "getting" him? Was he breaking under the stern test of the wilderness?

"Wolrab, are you lying?" Durand put to the man somberly.

"If you think I am, ask this here gal if you run acrost her. But don't ask Kimball—that is, if you want the truth. Or maybe you don't give a hang what Kimball does t' gals hereabouts. I ain't worryin' much. I ain't no gentleman. Kimball's s'posed t' be one." He cackled ironically at this.

Durand turned away with a savage gesture, the tumult within him showing in his dark, tempestuous eyes. Adrienne—was she safe now? He found himself concerned more over Adrienne's welfare than anything else. But he must not forget his trust. He had come to bring the grub brigade to the camp. He had won his battle for his men. Now he would vindicate himself—and Adrienne. And he would settle that bitter bone of contention, the muskeg.

He turned to his men. "At dawn we start back for the camp," he said. "If you want to take a nap, go to it."

"Aw, I can't sleep," replied the ex-seaman. "Let the rest turn in." He jerked a thumb toward the silent Swede. "Better tell the white hope t' take a sleep, too. He needs more than a sleep, though. Ain't he a sight f'r sore eyes! Ho! Ho!"

"Sailor, Ay tank Ay vill giff you vun yolt on de yaw right now," stated the Swede in his matter-of-fact way, leaning forward.

Durand jumped between them. "Now cut this damned foolishness out!" he barked hotly. "We've got what we've come for. You two birds can fight all you want as soon as we get back to camp. Lay off now!"

The ex-sailor spat reflectively. "All right, mate, just as you say," he nodded; then leveled a finger at his friendly enemy. "Don't forget that, Swede. I'll see you when we get to camp."

"Yas, sailor. Ay vill see you, too."

Upon that understanding they subsided.

Durand now left his men and approached the Indians. One or two of them recognized him, and he called them forth and had a few words with them, explaining that everything was all right now and that in the morning the brigade would start for the camp. They nodded understanding and went back among their companions to spread the news.

Durand, his head too full of thoughts to sleep, sat down by one of the fires and stuffed his pipe moodily. One of the Indians with whom he had spoken shuffled over and without saying a word added fresh fuel to the red coals. The other Indians gathered around the various fires. The ex-seaman had fallen sound asleep; the Swede, too. Their fight was over. Tomorrow each man would receive five pounds of tobacco. They worried about nothing else.

But Durand felt that—for him—the fight was not yet over.

CHAPTER XII

VICTORY!

DUSK—GRAY DUSK of dawn, though it was hours past dawn. An ocean of snow was cascading from the sky, burying the wilderness in a new tomb of virgin white. The main camp lay vague and wraith-like in the lap of the broad valley, like an encampment seen in a mirage. Columns of smoke from many pipe-like chimneys rose and was smothered by the falling snow. Burly men in burly coats tramped in various directions, nodding or waving their hands as they passed one another.

Out of the mysterious whiteness that veiled the country of deep forests beyond, came the long-awaited grub brigade. Twenty heavily laden sledges strung out in single file, with shaggy, fur-swathed dogs hauling and straining in the traces. On either side of the train men trod on broad snowshoes; some pushed at the gee-bars of the sledges, while others, here and there, cracked thirty-foot caribou-gut whips in the air to keep the dogs plugging hard.

The long line of men and dogs and sledges moved steadily into the valley. Cabins began to loom in the white murk, and figures appeared from all directions, shouting cheers and clapping the men of the brigade on the shoulders. Word had spread long hours before of the lost brigade, and those in the valley had eagerly awaited fresh news.

Durand strode in the lead, ahead of the lead-dog of the first sledge. Everybody he passed cheered him. Everybody seemed happy. Durand was not. There was a grim, haggard look on his face; dark, restless fires burned in the depths of his eyes.

"Hur—r-ray f'r Boss Durand!... Three cheers f'r a fightin' man!... A man must fight t' boss this camp. That's Durand!... Who's all right? Boss Durand's all right! Wh-e-e-e!..."

Men came from everywhere. The shouts increased. It is was like the homecoming of a victorious army. The ex-sailor, not many paces behind Durand, threw out his chest and tried to look very military and heroic. The Swede plodded along as if nothing had happened, his body hunched forward from the waist, his eyes staring at the heels of the man ahead of him.

The brigade swung past the mess-halls and the cooks came out and beat pans together. Two men threw their arms about each other and danced. Another group started a good natured snow fight. The toiling dogs yelped and pulled harder.

Durand led the way up to the storehouse, where he stopped, turned and raised his hands. A moment later a gang of men were starting to unload the first of the sledges, while the other teams were drawing up to convenient positions. Everybody jumped in and helped in the unloading.

After a few words with the store-keeper, Durand left the milling men and tramped straight for headquarters. He had not joined in the festive spirit. His work, his fight, was not yet completed. Now or never he would bend Kimball to his will. He had saved the camp from a revolution, from mob rule. Now he would call a showdown with Kimball.

Reaching headquarters, he found Tracy reading a book. The old clerk upon seeing him immediately closed the book and hid it. "Ah, sir, thank God you are back!" he cried. "You succeeded?"

"About the grub? Yes. But there are other things. Where's your boss?"

"Mr. Kimball, I think, is at his cabin. Mademoiselle La Forge came here looking for you. She had heard about your going to recover the lost brigade, and she seemed very anxious. Mr. Kimball invited her to wait for you at his cabin."

"He did, eh?" rumbled Durand, scowling darkly. He swung out of the office, banging the door soundly behind him, and headed for Kimball's living quarters, a quarter of a mile away. He was dog-tired now, but the grand old spirit of his, the dynamo of driving force that burned in his heart, would not let him deviate from his purpose. Now or never he would show Kimball that *he* was the better man. He would show Kimball that he was a master of men.

He reached the cabin, leaned against the door a minute or so before knocking. He thought he heard excited voices, scuffling sounds inside, but he wasn't sure. He rapped on the door, listened again. He heard no sound now. He waited a little impatiently. He was tired. He ached to get the whole thing over with. Minutes passed; he knocked again—waited. Then he beat on the door with both fists. He was about to step back and then hurl his weight against the door when it opened, and Kimball faced him.

"Oh, it's you!" exclaimed the senior softly. "Come in."

"Thanks. About time you opened the door." Durand rocked in, pulling off his mittens and flinging them on the table. He threw an inquisitive eye about, looking for Adrienne. No sign of her. He dropped into a chair, extending his legs.

Kimball was smoking a fresh cigar. He was calm, collected, but there was a vague hint of uneasiness in his eyes.

Durand brought his fist down upon the table with a bang. "Well, Kimball, I've brought in the grub brigade, with the timely aid of ten good men and true. Before I left I threatened to come back with the brigade and then see you about that muskeg job. I'm here. The more I think of your plan the more I am convinced of its extreme foolishness. And I'm making it plain to you now that I'll come out in the open and block any attempt you make to run your line through that muskeg. We'll blast through that ridge if I have to steal the dynamite to do it. I will drag every official from the main office up here to this God-forsaken country before I'll let you go on with that muskeg venture. I've talked reason with you, bullied you and if necessary I will punch your head off to make you listen to reason."

"Er—speak to me about it tomorrow, Durand," clipped Kimball. "I am not feeling so well just now. Um—little cold, headache and all that. You know how it is."

"Yes, I know," said Durand, rising. "We'll settle right now. And another thing. Wolrab was at the head of that gang."

"Ha-ha! That comes of your firing him! I told you—"

"Guess again, Kimball. He did it to get square with you. You got him drunk because you were afraid he'd talk. You had him dumped off in the woods. He wanted money to keep quiet. He knew something about you. He told me everything. How is your hand?"

Kimball blanched, fell back a pace, fumbling with his cigar. At this moment there was a faint cry in the adjoining room—a faint cry for help, Kimball sucked in a breath and held it.

Durand shot a fast glance at the door to the room. "Who's in there?" he demanded.

"Er—I—"

"Damn you, Kimball, open that door!" roared Durand.

Before Kimball could move the door opened and Adrienne, flushed and disheveled, tottered in. She seemed in a daze, but she saw Durand, and reached out toward him, smiling weakly.

"Take—me—away," she murmured. "Oh!…" She reeled into Durand's arms, sobbing, and he held her to him with a strong, reassuring arm. A fierce, black wrath flamed in his eyes. His teeth crunched.

"Don't you dare move, Kimball!" he ripped out.

He turned to Adrienne and let her down gently into the big armchair near the stove. Her eyes opened slowly and smiled into his own. Her lips quivered. She clutched at his sleeve.

"Please—please, do not leave me. Take me away—home."

"Tell me, Adrienne," he urged. "What happened. Did he?—"

"Oh, he would not let me go. I come to see if you are safe. I hear you have gone to save the grub brigade. I come wait for you. I think maybe you will be hurt and I could help. M'sieur Kimball tell me it is all right if I wait here. Then he remain here, and I don't like the way he look at me. I want to go out again. He will not let me go. I run to the door. He catch me and hold me, but I break loose. He catch me again. We struggle. I become faint. Then I hear knock on the door. M'sieur Kimball pick me and throw me in other room. Then you... Oh, please stay very near me!" Durand pressed her hand in his own, and she put her lips to his rough knuckles.

Kimball was deathly pale, his back against the door, his hand on the latch-string.

"Don't move another inch!" warned Durand bitterly, advancing. "So that's the kind of a skunk you are. How I'd love to break your neck in two, Kimball. Pity you've got only one good hand just now. That saves you the beating of your life. But you are beaten now, you fool, and you alone are the cause of it."

Kimball relaxed. His shoulders drooped. His head sank. He dragged his feet to a chair by the table and sank down, burying his face in his arms.

"None of that," said Durand. "Take it like a man. The medicine is bitter, isn't it? Well, you'll swallow it all. You'll take worse than a physical beating. *That* would wear off. You'll take a professional beating! You'll sign an order which will start the men drilling on the ridge. Kimball, you are going to blow through that ridge and run your line a mile north of the muskeg. I am going to take this lady home now; when I return some time during the day, I want to see a gang beginning on the ridge.

"That hurts, doesn't it? I couldn't hurt you a tenth as much by bashing in your face. Well, I want it to hurt. Think it over. And don't forget to write that order."

Durand went to Adrienne, helped her on with her coat and took her out of the cabin. Arm in arm they walked away from the camp, striking the trail that wound through the balsam forest.

The snow still fell in great white clouds, clinging to their warm faces, hissing down through the branches.

"You shouldn't have come all the way to the camp for my sake," Durand ventured.

"Oh, but I wanted to so very much!" Adrienne cried.

"Well, anyhow, I'm glad you wanted to. From now on, though, you are going to have a steady caller at your little cabin. He's going to pester the life out of you."

"Oui! That will be very wonderful. I shall very much enjoy being pestered—oh!—every day!"

"Well," chuckled Durand, stopping and holding her at arms' length, "I'll have to work sometime."

They both laughed at this. Then Durand drew her closer to him, enveloping her in his great arms. Her dark eyes were two pools of happiness now. Her lips were slightly parted against white teeth, but closed when he bent down. Unmindful of the falling snow he gave her his first token of a great love born of the wilderness.

"No one shall ever dare hurt me, now," she murmured.

"No one," he told her softly.

IT WAS late that same day when Durand returned to the main camp. He went straight to Kimball's cabin. After a few knocks with no response forthcoming, he pushed open the door and entered.

The place was deserted. He searched both rooms. The stove was dead, the ashes cold. The bed-room was stripped of blankets and the senior's array of trail togs. Durand was a little puzzled. Finally, after a last look, he went out slowly, stood for a moment in perplexed indecision. Then he set off for the office.

Arrived there, he found Lank Roper parading up and down the private office, smoking a cigar like a lord. Lank stopped short when he saw Durand and jammed his hands against his hips.

"So there you are, Stevie, my man!" he exclaimed, rocking on his heels. "I hear that you went an' rescued the grub brigade. I was on the way here an' stopped t' see a fight over at the mess hall between a big Swede an' a big ex-sailor. There they was bangin' away at each other, until all of a sudden they both connects with each other's jaw at the same time an' both gets knocked out. Haw! Haw! I got speakin' t' Cronin, a gang-boss, after the fight an' he told me what you done. I'm kinder sore, though, Stevie, 'cause you didn't invite me. 'Tain't right, me bein' your friend an' all."

"I had to act quick, Lank," offered Durand. "What's more, I left you in charge of the sub-camp. By the way, have you seen Kimball?"

"I was comin' t' that," said Lank. "Funny. Him an' this here Tracy went somewhere. I came here as they was leavin'—them an' a dog-team… Here—this letter was on the desk, addressed t' you."

Durand took the letter slowly, tore it open bit by bit, spread the sheet before him and frowned.

My Dear Durand:

You win. I lose. I am a broken man, and confess it. I cannot bear this camp any longer, this wilderness—you, everybody. Hence I am taking Tracy with me and leaving for The Pas and then the city, where I belong.

I misjudged you. I misjudged the girl. I played my game and lost.

I hold no love or affection for you, Durand. If anything, it is hatred I bear you. But you have beaten me. That is that.

You are automatically placed in charge now, until further in-structions are sent you from the main office. No doubt you will remain in charge.

It is, therefore, left to you to blow through that damnable ridge!
Kimball

RETURN OF THE EXILE

FUR COUNTRY—"PLAY STRAIGHT WITH A PAL!" IS THE CREED OF THE NORTH—AND A MAN MUST BE STRONG TO MAINTAIN IT.

SPRUCE AND poplar walled the frozen water. The waterway itself was narrow and straggled willy-nilly through the silent wilderness beneath its covering of ice. Sometimes it toppled in a froth of cold foam over rugged rocky falls, and once below, disappeared again beneath the ice, rolling on its long journey northeastward to the winter-locked vastness of Hudson's Bay. Sturdy hills, some of them attaining the dignity of minor mountain ranges, billowed majestically into the clean, cold blue of the Arctic sky. Winter was full abroad in the land, and its white hand seemed to have throttled all signs of life, of human existence.

Yet life was afield; one solitary spot of life that moved slowly but steadily on the frozen river. A tall man who swung his broad rackets rhythmically, bent forward at the waist under the burden of a double rucksack. A young man, clean-shaven, grim-lipped, with a blue bandanna tied across his forehead and shielding his keen blue eyes from the sun-glare.

The Exile was returning to his native land. The river, the rugged hills, familiar land-marks that a month ago had been fond memories, were now realities; and the spell of it all tugged at his heart and at times brought a lump to his throat which he downed with some effort. A man's return to old haunts is sometimes more conducive to emotion than his going away. There is the thought of old friends, of hands to shake, tales to tell over drowsing pipes, of good times gone and better times to come.

But this was not so with the Exile. Though he was returning to a land he loved so well, a land that had reared him from birth, he did not expect the usual cheerfulness, the hearty handclasps, the warm welcome of old friends. There might be one or two, he reflected. He hoped, at least, for one.

Young though he was, scarce thirty, an unforgettable shadow clouded his soul. A weaker, more timid man would have stayed away, accepting the inevitable. But the Exile was neither weak nor timid, for he was returning to a town where once on a time he had been driven out and told not to return. Threats of death had accompanied that order.

When the red sun was settling behind the wall of the world and twilight shadows were creeping down through the valleys, he plodded into Fort Comfort, which nestles at the base of a low hogback far on the white frontier.

A man passed him coming from the opposite direction, squinted up as they drew abreast, then came to a dead stop and opened his mouth in amazement. The Exile, bending under his heavy pack, stared at the snow underfoot and plodded by silently. The other man gazed after him, then struck his thigh sharply, muttered to himself and continued on his way half running.

Soon the Exile drew up before a low, wide cabin which had a weatherbeaten sign over its entrance bearing the one word, STORE. He took off his rackets, stuck them in the snow beside several other pairs already there, and, after a moment's thoughtful hesitation, pushed open the door and rocked in.

He closed it with a slow kick from his heel and stood there staring levelly across the room at a short, stubby man who was sitting in a spacious, rough-hewn arm chair dozing with half-shuttered lids. The lids flickered open suddenly, and the pipe in the man's mouth wobbled. Then the old chair creaked as he shifted his bulk with much effort and heaved to his feet.

"Dave," he said in an awed whisper, "is it you?"

"The same," nodded the Exile.

The dumpy old man rolled across the room and stretched out a thick paw. The Exile's face relaxed, and a little laugh broke from his hitherto tense lips. He gripped the outstretched hand and pressed it tightly in his own.

"Matt, I didn't know—I didn't know if you'd be glad to see me," he jerked out haltingly.

"Aw, Dave, sure I am," came back Matt Shane, the trader. "But, f'r God's sake, man, Fort Comfort ain't no place f'r you. There ain't nobody got any use f'r you. There ain't nobody believes you didn't get rid of Hal Starin up north two years agone."

"You believe in me, old timer," the Exile said, smiling.

"I do that, Dave, s' help me, spite of all the rest."

"And, Matt, I thought there'd be somebody else here who'd believe in me a little, too."

"Um. You mean Colly?"

"Yes," nodded the Exile.

"Hal was her husband, y' know," reminded the trader.

"I know—I know, Matt. But at the time she sort of stood by me, in a way."

The trader tapped the Exile's chest.

"Dave, I'm an old man an' I got a habit o' using my eyes. 'Tween me an' you, Colly never married Hal Starin because she loved him. It was her stepmother hounded her to it 'cause Starin showed signs of havin' money."

"Oh"—The Exile stopped him with a raised hand—"forget that part of it, Matt. She liked him a lot.... Can I bunk with you for a few nights, old timer?" he asked abruptly.

"Sure you c'n, Dave. Better take off that pack. Only, m' boy, I'm afeared this town ain't none too healthy f'r you."

The Exile took the burden from his shoulders and carried it over behind the counter. Then he shrugged out of his white-fox capote, unbuttoned the gray wool sweater he wore and dropped relievedly into a chair by the big sheet-iron stove. He had his pipe out and was cramming it with tobacco when the door whipped open and half-a-dozen men rumbled in purposefully.

"So you've come back, Dave Paddison," barked the leader, biting the Exile with a bitter, black look.

"Yes, I've come back, friends," replied Paddison.

"Bah!" snarled the other, slashing a mittened hand through the air. "Don't you call us friends! We're no friends of yours. We're no friends of a man who goes into the woods with another man, comes back and says he's dead, and can't explain how he died. How about it, men?" he flung over his shoulder.

"You're right, Ches," said one, and the others nodded.

Ches went on: "There's no evidence to hang you accordin' to the law. You say he just died an' you buried him an' you can't find his grave now. You say it took you three days to dig that grave, the snow and earth was so froze up an' all. Now us men have always said any grave it takes three days to dig oughter be remembered. Sayin' that he just died from some sickness you don't know about, ain't satisfied us yet. You should ha' trucked him on home here."

"We were three hundred miles north," defended the Exile without heat, yet you saw he was controlling himself with an effort. "There were a lot of blizzards and little food, and Starin was a big man—weighed one-ninety. It was the best I could do."

"Listen!" dragged out Ches Bogart. "Everybody knows you an' Hal Starin didn't like each other. When he married Colly Dunne, the day afterward you an' him got in a hot argyment right here in this trade-room, and you took a crack at him."

"Wait, Ches," put in Matt Shane. "I was settin' right here that day an' Hal started it. He said, 'Well, Dave, I guess I'm a hell of a lot better 'an you are.' Dave said, 'The hell you are.' An' Hal said, 'The hell I *am!*' That started it, an' Hal got so loud-mouthed that Dave started f'r him, only I stepped in."

"You," Ches Bogart said, "better keep your mouth out o' this. Hal did win Colly 'cause he *was* the better man. An' wasn't it kinder strange for Paddison here to offer to travel with Hal to the fox grounds? Now wasn't it?"

"That was because Colly got us together and made us make up," the Exile offered. "I was bound for the Barrens, and so was Hal Starin. There was no reason why we couldn't go part of the way together. Colly asked it, because she knew I'd had more experience on those trails than Hal."

Bogart scoffed at this.

"There was nobody saw you bein' made up with Hal by Colly," he argued. "She said that afterward, but she's a woman an' was fool enough to try to make it easier for you. Anyhow, we all still got the same suspicions we had then, an' we come here to tell you to mush out by dawn tomorrer. If you ain't out o' here by tomorrer, there's plenty o' rope handy an' plenty o' limbs to hang it on." His teeth clicked sharply on the threat, and his black beard bristled over the outthrust jaw.

The Exile got to his feet, standing spread-legged, his keen blue eyes clashing with Bogart's like steel rapier points. A little lump of muscle appeared at either corner of his firm mouth. His voice, hitherto mild, now bore a snap of challenge. He said:

"Bogart, you never liked me, nor I you. You seem to be doing an awful lot of talking as the mouthpiece of Fort Comfort. Well, cut it! You're giving the impression that your interest in this affair is wholly unselfish. But is it? Aren't you still kind of sore against me for doing what I did four years ago to you?"

"Don't try to pull anything like that!" rumbled Bogart darkly.

"Ten to one nobody in Fort Comfort knows that I made you stay miles clear of my trapline over near Jackson's Knee."

One of the men, a man Paddison knew only slightly, put in: "If we do or don't, what right had you t' go doin' *that?*"

"Call it an unwritten law of the woods, if you like," the Exile told him slowly. "If I spend a whole year running a decent line of traps, I don't expect another man to run his so damned close that we meet each other every day. And I drove Bogart away by force."

"Damn you," growled Bogart, "you didn't! I found better grounds someplace else."

"Have it your way, then," was Paddison's reply. "Anyhow, you moved on, and from that day forward you nursed a solitary dislike for me."

Bogart got control of himself, though his fists were clenched hard.

"That has nothin' to do with this. We all agree that you got to move out of Fort Comfort tomorrer mornin' or take the consequences. Ain't that right, boys?"

"Yup, Ches, it is," grunted one, and the others agreed in like manner.

The Exile gave a brittle, hard little laugh. "The whole town against one man, eh? All right, go to it. Come for me, all of you, every damned one of you who once called me friend—come for me. I'll be here—right here—waiting!"

Bogart said, "Right-o! We'll come for you!" He turned sharply and, pulling open the door, lunged out. The men straggled after him, muttering among themselves.

Paddison, the Exile, stood for a long moment glaring at the closed door; then suddenly relaxed and dropped back into the chair. Old Matt, scratching his ear thoughtfully sighed heavily, took a chair opposite and settled back with his chin resting against his chest.

"Well, Dave, there y' are," he droned through his pipe.

The Exile said nothing. He was staring at Matt—staring through and beyond him, thinking.

Matt sighed, blinked his old eyes. A lazy man, the trader—lazy and lovable. Many's the time he had snoozed in his favorite chair while a light-footed Indian walked stealthily off with a side of bacon. Even now he was dropping away to sleep under the soothing warmth of the trade-room stove.

Paddison, regarding him, seeing the venerable old head drop lower and lower, smiled to himself. Only Matt had stuck to him when everybody else in Fort Comfort had looked askance at him, entertaining thoughts of suspicion when he had returned from the Far North without Hal Starin and told his story. Someone else, too, had in a futile way tried to help him. Alaric Dunne's daughter, Colly, whom Starin had married before the trip.

As he was turning these thoughts over, the trade-room door opened and a girl muffled in furs slipped in. Black hair, black as the raven night, enveloped her head and framed a face of rare loveliness whose cheeks now were touched with the rosy color which only clean breezes and good health can give.

"Colly!" the Exile exclaimed softly, rising to his feet.

"Oh, Dave, you—you came back!" she breathed.

They both started toward each other at the same time, and their hands met and held tightly. Wide brown eyes searched the man's face with mixed happiness and pain.

"Dave, you shouldn't have come back! You shouldn't have! They—they'll—"

"Are you glad to see me, Colly?" he asked simply, with a slow smile.

"Oh, Dave, am I glad? Of course—of course. But you don't understand."

"Then I'm happy, if you're glad," he said, as if nothing else in the world mattered.

"Dave, please don't speak and act as if this were paradise. It's not by any means. The whole town—everybody—is against you. Even my dad. He doesn't say much, nor join with the other men, but he is suspicious too."

"Bogart," chuckled the Exile, "and half a dozen others just dropped in to pay their respects."

"I know—I know, Dave. Bogart is at our house now. I heard him telling dad. He said he gave you until tomorrow morning to get out."

"And did he tell what I said?"

"That's what I came here about. Dave, you must get out. It's the only thing. Please don't let them—let them—"

"I understand, Colly," he murmured.

"But, you, Dave, you're going away before they harm you, aren't you, please?"

He smiled his slow smile at her, pressing her hands tighter in his own, and shook his head.

"Colly, this is one time when I'm prepared. Last time they caught me when I wasn't looking. Not this time, though."

"But there will be a dozen against you!" she insisted.

"Well, there will be a dozen, then. I've told them all I—I can tell them and—and that's that."

She came still closer to him. "Dave," she said softly, "I—wonder—if you have told them all you—can—tell them?"

He stepped back quickly, dropping his eyes and searching in his pockets for a match.

"Yes—of course—of course, I have."

Colly shook her head wearily and sighed. Then, pleadingly: "Please, Dave, go away. Please, for my sake. I don't want to see any harm come to you."

"I've decided to stick it out, Colly." There was no shaking him.

"Oh, if I hadn't married Hal all this wouldn't have happened. I tried to make the best of it—make the best of something I really wasn't prepared for, half against my own wishes."

"There, there, Colly," he told her. "Better go home now."

"But, Dave—" Her eyes were swimming.

He shook his head. "No, Colly, I'm calling their bluff," he said.

She swayed a bit toward him, her arms half-outstretched. Then she spun about, stifling a sob, and ran from the trade-room out into the moonlit night. Paddison started after, but stopped with one foot outside the door. He saw she was still running.

The Exile re-entered the cabin slowly, and stood with his back against the closed door. He lit his pipe and watched the match burn away in his fingers.

Matt was still snoring.

AT NINE o'clock that same night, when the Exile and the trader were playing checkers by the red-glowing stove, there drifted in to them the strains of a man's voice raised in song.

"Aw, that's a feller just come in from the Barrens this mornin'," explained Matt. "Headin' f'r the Outside. Claims he made a big fortune in blackies."

The door banged open and a cheery-faced, rugged little man stamped in. Just now, apparently, he was carrying considerable liquor.

"Hurray!" he chortled. "Hurray f'r me! I'm a-goin' clean down ter Winnipeg. I'm a-goin ter stay at the Garry, git all togged out on Portage Avenue, an' have one hell of a hair-raisin' time. Four years I been up in this God-f'r saken North. Four years o' frost-bite, o' runnin' lousy traplines in a lousy country, an' then chasin' foxes damn nigh ter Baker Lake. This, m' friend stranger, is the first time I been south o' Fifty-six in four years. An' feller ain't I glad t' be headin' f'r the Outside! Gawd made the world in five days an' spent the sixth pitchin' snowballs at the Nor'west. 'S truth! Four years...."

He lunged for a chair and sat down with such force it almost toppled.

The Exile was regarding him steadily, smiling faintly. Presently the old-timer's eyes met his, and Paddison looked away and studied the checkerboard. The old-timer wiped his mouth with the back of his hand and leaned forward.

"Say, m' friend stranger, seems like I seen you some place before, ain't I, huh?"

"I don't know," replied Paddison, jumping one of Matt's men. "I don't remember you, anyhow."

"H'm." The old-timer stroked his chin musingly. "H'm. Must ha' been somebody else, then." He leaned back, crossing one leg over the other, and went on squinting at Paddison with bleary eyes.

After a while he got up, took off his capote and moccasins, spread a thick blanket on the floor in one corner, and lay down.

"G'-night, gents," he yawned, and rolled over.

Paddison and the trader played for another hour.

"You c'n sleep in the spare bunk," Matt offered, stifling a yawn.

"Thanks, old timer," said the Exile. He went to bed a little later and lay awake for a long while. Tomorrow they would come for him, the men whom once on a time he had known for friends. Bogart would lead them. Once he had clashed with Bogart, over in the Jackson's Knee country. And Bogart had nursed a grudge from then on, telling no one of the incident of the traplines. Nor had Paddison told anyone, not until tonight.

He fell asleep presently, and when he awoke again the east was growing lighter. Dawn was beginning. The Exile rose and dressed quickly. He wandered into the trade-room, where darkness still prevailed. The door of the stove was open, throwing a pale rosy glow into the murk. He threw in a fresh log and lit one of the lamps.

There was a knock at the door, and the Exile gave a little start, then tensed. He did not move at first, but when a second knock came, more insistent this time, he flexed his lips and crossed the room slowly. Raising the heavy bar, he opened the door and stepped back.

It was Colly. She slipped in, all out of breath, and gripped one of his steel-thewed arms.

"Dave, you haven't gone yet!" she cried. "Oh, please Dave—please go. The men are getting together. I didn't sleep all night."

"Why?" he asked with that simplicity of his which was so disarming.

"Oh—I—why—"

He suddenly laid his hands on her shoulders.

"Colly, is it because you still care for me the way you used to a few years ago?"

"Why, Dave, you… Please, go, Davy!"

He shook her gently. "Answer me, Colly!"

Her face, her eyes, swam before him. Her red lips parted against gleaming teeth in a peculiar half-smile that was more a show of anguish than anything else.

"Oh… Davy!"

Instinctively his strong arms went about her and he buried his face in her dark cloud of raven hair. For a long moment she clung to him, sobbing silently. Then she looked up at him, her eyes moist.

"Dave, they'll be coming," she cried. "Go—go! I—I'll go with you—"

"Colly!"

"I will, Dave! Anywhere!"

He released her, falling back a step, a little stunned, with a wild joy surging through his heart. He had never dreamed that this would happen. Thoughts of Colly had really brought him back to Fort Comfort, to the white frontier that had made him an exile; thoughts of her and a vague hope that the men had mellowed toward him. But they had not. They were still bitter.

"Colly, they will follow us," he told her quickly.

"I don't care, Dave."

"Nor I—for my own part."

They would flee eastward and find a missioner in two days, at most. Then—well, anywhere.

"We must be quick!" he clipped. "Sit down, Colly."

Leaving her, he ran across the traderoom and broke into Matt's bed-chamber. The trader was a late sleeper, and was snoring peacefully. The Exile shook him awake.

"Matt, I'm leaving! Get up—quick! Colly and I. We'll need some grub."

He dragged the old trader out of bed, and Matt groped hastily for his pants, blinking weary eyes, though his spirit was full awake and eager to help. Half-dressed, his thin old hair tousled, he rolled into the trade-room puffing like a wheezy locomotive. Recklessly he pounced on the stores behind the counter.

"Dave," he called, "go line up them dogs o' mine."

"What? Dogs? Why, Matt—"

"Go git like I say. You'll need a sled an' dogs. You c'n fix it up later. I ain't worryin'." Just like the Matt of old.

"Bless you, Matt!" cried Colly.

" 'S all right, Colly. Um—here's couple sides o' bacon, some sacks o' beans, flour. Um."

Paddison ran outside and around to the kennel. Quickly he lined up the five dogs, all of them mongrels, but big, sturdy, hard-pulling brutes notwithstanding. He threw them some frozen fish, and then put a box of fish on the sled for use on the trail. Back in the trade-room, he found a stack of supplies on the counter.

The old timer from the higher North yawned awake.

"Hurray f'r me!" he exclaimed, and then, seeing such signs of activity, closed his mouth and got to his feet, mildly perplexed, muttering a ruminative "Umph!"

Matt was lunging about behind the counter, puffing and snorting, boring freely into his stock of provisions. Paddison grabbed what lay on the counter in his two arms and, dashing across the room, almost bowled over the old timer.

"Ugh!" grunted the latter, reeling back. When he got his balance again he mused, "Durn me, if I didn't have sech a bad mem'ry f'r faces I'd remember where I seen that chum."

Matt and Colly, taking the remainder of the provisions between them, hurried out and around to the kennel. Paddison was strapping on his snowshoes, and Colly had brought a pair from the store for her own use. Hastily all helped in packing the sled and tying down the moosehide cover.

"Now, git," said the old trader. "Git, an' may God bless you both! I'll see you again, I hope—some day."

"Good-bye, old Matt!" cried Colly.

The Exile thrust a crumpled roll of bills into the trader's hand.

"Aw, say, Dave, you didn't have to—"

"It's not all I owe you by any means," cut in the Exile, "but take it." He gripped the trader's hand hard. "Good-bye, Matt, old friend."

He turned, picked up the caribou-gut dog-whip and cracked it sharply over the dogs' head. The team straightened out, the harness crackled, and the big twelve-foot toboggan "broke" with a crunching sound from the frozen crust.

Paddison ran up ahead and Colly swung in behind, and the outfit moved off, breaking through a tangle of low thickets. Matt stood watching them until the gloom of early morning swallowed them up, then wiped a damp eye and, sighing, waddled back into the trade-room. Thus the Exile and the girl plunged into the maw of the trackless wilds. Paddison pushed through the graying dawn with long strides, grim determination in the set of his lean, clean jaw and in the steely glitter of his blue eyes.

When he looked over his shoulder now and then, he waved to Colly, and smiled encouragement through his grimness.

The sun reared itself up before them, shooting its white fire across the wilderness of snow and cathedral spruce. The last gray patches of dawn were driven from the roof of the world, and ridges of snow glittered like mammoth jewels under the beams of the climbing sun. The wind blew sharp from the north, fresh and exhilarating and laden with the sweet perfume of the forest.

They soon struck a wide field of hummocky muskeg where the going proved arduous, and the dogs stepped gingerly, as the sharp ice needles clawed at their legs. Once across this, Paddison plunged into a grove of poplars, and an hour later came out upon a narrow waterway. Here he stopped for a moment, went back and gripped Colly's hands.

"You did fine, Colly," he smiled. "Now you'd better ride on the sled for a while. I'm going to drive the dogs for all their worth while I can."

The girl did not argue. She realized the need for speed, and, pressing the man's hand warmly, she curled up on the toboggan.

Swiftly the outfit sped along on the snow-encrusted ice. The dogs pulled like prize racers, now warmed to their task. The leader particularly seemed a glutton for hard work, and would allow no slouching on the part of his mates.

At noon they stopped for a bite to eat and to spell the hard-pressed dogs. The Exile was impatient of delay, but common sense told him that the dogs must rest.

"Bogart and the rest are well on their way after us by now," he ventured, and downed hot tea.

"We'll outstrip them, Dave," Colly said, looking back. "No signs of them yet. Oh, pray to God we do!"

"To God—and Matt's old ruffians here," supplemented Paddison.

Ragtag ruffians they were indeed, those dogs, but they took up the trail again with the same old vigor, and the leader was still the hard taskmaster he had started out to be. The miles reeled off.

Luck stayed with them most of that day. It was about three in the afternoon when, after tugging with the dogs up a steep slope, they struck a narrow trail that ran along the edge of a high ridge whose side was a sheer drop of two hundred feet or more. Paddison was leading the way cautiously when misfortune struck them. Suddenly it came, without warning.

A stretch of false crust broke abruptly beneath the heavily-laden sledge. The sledge pitched sidewise. Colly called to Paddison even as she dived to stop it. The Exile spun around, saw the sledge plunging and leaped for it. But he was too late. It toppled over the edge of the trail, dragging the struggling dogs with it, and pitched plummet-like down the sheer drop in a cloud of snow.

Paddison had only time to catch Colly. Even then he slipped and would have plunged down with her had he not grasped a convenient bush and held on grimly.

"Crawl up, Colly!" he gasped. "Step on my shoulder—then up."

When they stood on safe ground again, they looked down below and saw a huddled mass among the rocks and thickets. One or two of the dogs were struggling, but the others lay motionless.

"Oh!" choked the girl.

The Exile patted her shoulder with a reassuring hand. "There, there, Colly. Misfortune will happen. Now we'll have to back-trail until we can find a place to go down and save some of the provisions."

Grimmer than ever, he turned and started off, with the girl close behind. It was dusk when they found a place where they could descend to the valley below, and a moon was shining when they finally reached the broken sledge and the dogs. Two dogs were dead, one had a broken leg, and only two were of any use. Grimmacing, Paddison shot the maimed dog.

Out of the caribou-hide sledge wrapper he fashioned two makeshift packs loaded with provisions and strapped them on the backs of the two remaining dogs. He stuffed as much as he could into his own ruck-sack and strapped it to his back.

"A good moon tonight, Colly," he said. "I guess we'll have to keep going."

"Yes, Dave," she nodded, though she was dead tired.

They pressed on through the thick forest. Midnight came and passed, and at three in the morning the two dogs, struggling under burdens strange to them, began to flounder. Colly, too, was dragging her webbs on with great effort, and finally she stumbled and could barely rise again.

"We'll stop," decided Paddison.

"No, Dave. I—I—"

"Colly, you've done wonderful. But you need rest. The dogs, too, are fagged."

He spread blankets for her on a bed of balsam and, wrapping himself in another blanket, sat propped against a spruce and drowsed off. The man, the girl, the ragtag dogs—all were exhausted from the long trek.

It was daylight before they made a fire and cooked a hasty breakfast. Refreshed, they took up the trail again, and soon were plodding through a lean, open country of willows and stunted jackpine and frozen swamps. The hills now were low and naked, and the bitter wind from the far frozen seas tore unobstructed over the ragged land, lacerating the travelers mercilessly.

An hour before noon, while they were taking a brief rest, their two dogs cocked up inquisitive ears and pointed their noses westward. Paddison listened, too, and heard the faint yelping of dogs in the distance. He sprang to his feet, and Colly followed him. His jaw set hard and for a brief moment he pressed her to him.

"They're coming, Colly!" he bit off. "Nearer than we think, because the wind's against them."

"Dave—Dave, they won't harm you!" she cried.

For answer he released her and snapped his whip at the dogs. They started off, and, taking the girl's hand, he followed them at a stiff trot. There was no place to hide. The land was too naked, too open, and it seemed even futile to run.

Nor was it long before, looking back, Paddison saw dark figures moving swiftly across the snow. Men and dogs—three swift teams. Shouts reached his ears, and he muttered deep in his throat. The two lumps of muscle again appeared at the corners of his mouth, and his eyes, became flinty hard. Suddenly he stopped, swinging the girl behind him, and stood tall and straight, with his hand resting on the revolver-butt in his belt.

"Damn them!" he clipped, his lips curling for an instant.

"Please, Dave, don't do any—killing!"

The pursuers swept into full view now, and in the lead were Bogart and Alaric Dunne, Colly's father. Ten men straggled behind them, all running, all armed with rifles.

The Exile stood spread-legged, rooted as solidly to the snow as a great tree.

"Ha!" roared Bogart exultantly. "We got you! Ha!"

With a silent oath Paddison whipped out his revolver, and in a flash Bogart ducked behind the broad bulk of Alaric Dunne. Paddison gritted his teeth and held his fire. He could have shot down Dunne easily, but the thought that, after all, Dunne was Colly's father, checked him.

But Bogart, seeing this, and still hiding behind Dunne, let fly with a shot that tore open the sleeves on Paddison's right fore-arm from wrist to elbow. With a dull groan he fell into a crouch, dropping his gun.

Colly leaped for it and jumped to the fore, her dark eyes blazing.

"Ches Bogart, you coward!" she screamed.

"Easy, Colly," counseled her father, stopping before her.

The Exile, holding his wounded arm close to his stomach, rushed suddenly at the grinning Bogart and crashed his knotted left fist terrifically against the bearded jaw. Bogart reeled and tumbled flat on his back. Paddison dived after him, but the other men pounced on him and tore him away by sheer force of numbers.

"Look out for his poor arm!" cried Colly.

Wildly she clawed her way through the men, striking out with her fists, until she reached the Exile and clung to him.

"Oh, my poor Davy!" she choked.

Alaric Dunne was regarding him with frigid eyes. "Mister, you did a wrong thing by runnin' off with my daughter," he ground out.

He laid a heavy hand on Colly's shoulder and, though she rebelled hotly, pulled her away from the Exile.

Bogart was struggling to his feet, fuming with red rage. He pointed a mittened hand at Paddison.

"We'll leave him here, that's what we'll do!" he shouted. "Leave him just like he left Hal Starin."

Paddison's breath hissed through clenched teeth. Colly cried: "Then you'll leave me with him! I won't leave him! I won't!"

"Easy, Colly," came her father's heavy voice.

"He—he's bewitched her!" fumed Bogart.

Dunne turned slowly on him. "He's wounded, Ches. We'll take him back to Fort Comfort, then drive him out."

"But—"

"We'll do that, Ches," repeated Dunne.

Bogart swallowed his rage, turning away with an oath.

One of the men shouted suddenly and pointed to a single team of dogs and two men that were plugging out of the West. Everybody looked, and as the newcomers drew nearer, Dunne said:

"It's Matt an' that trapper who's bound out. H'm. Wonder what *they want*."

The Exile stiffened and moistened his frost-bitten lips.

Puffing, snoring, rocking on his feet like an old bear, Matt Shane reached the gathering and promptly flopped down on a sled to catch his breath. The old timer, who had been at the gee-bar of his sled, went around and clapped the trader on the back.

"Durn me, m' friend, if there ain't some good old live steam left in you yet!" he chortled.

Matt flapped a hand wearily. "Ugh—um—tell 'em wh—what you—ugh—told me," he groaned.

The old timer straightened and squinted about at the frowning men, then clamped his eyes on the Exile.

"Durn me, m' friend stranger, I just *knowed* I seen you before some place!"

"You hold your tongue!" Paddison flung at him.

"Well, I would, if things wasn't like they are," went on the old timer, turning to the men. "Friends, Matt here told me a'ter you all left what the hull rumpus was about, an' that's how I come ter remember this young gent here. Seems like you folks believe he up an' played dirt by a man named Starin. Right?"

"Right," nodded Dunne heavily.

"Well, he didn't. That there Starin chum was shot dead like he durn well deserved ter be."

"An' who," asked Dunne, "shot him?"

The old timer's eyes narrowed. *"Why I shot him!"* he said.

Mutters rumbled through the crowd. The old timer jammed his hands against his hips and proceeded calmly:

"I shot him like any one o' you men would do if you ketched a man robbin' your grub cache. That's a law o' the woods, I figure. I ketched him at it and yelled ter him. He turned on me and pulled his gun, but I had mine out an' shot him clean, though he didn't die till later."

"Where," rumbled Bogart, "was this here Paddison at the time?"

"Gimme chance. I'm comin' ter that," replied the old timer. "This Starin, like I said, didn't die right off, an' there was me with a wounded man on me hands. By rights I should ha' left him, but anyhow I made up a lean-to. Seems like bad hearts speak a heap when they're dyin'. Well, Starin babbled crazy-like about him leavin' Paddison half snow-blind an' without grub. Mind, he had some grub in his sack when he robbed my cache. Me, I would ha' cashed in if that cache'd been empty when I got there. I was kinder fagged out myself with a bad cough an' all.

"It was next day I seen far off a man reelin' zigzag across the tundra. I yelled, but he was far off, like I said, an' didn't hear. So I plugged out ter head him off an' led him back ter my lean-to. He could see a li'l' bit, not much, an' he saw Starin layin' there. I mind he made a lunge f'r him, but I stepped in, sayin' Starin was bad shot. Then he turned on me, thinkin' I'd shot Starin just f'r a joke 'r somethin'. But I explained, an' then Starin started ter pass off.

"I still remember some o' his last words. Was this he said, 'F'r Gawd's men don't tell how I died! Bury me here. Say I— well—just died natural.' I mind he turned ter Paddison, sayin', 'Promise me that! Don't tell—don't tell *her*—anyone—why an' how I died.' Well, me an' Paddison swore solemn to him we'd tell nobody, an' then Starin died an' Paddison spent three days diggin' a grave. I see Paddison's kept his oath, an', gents, I would ha' kept mine, only I ain't seein' the livin' persecuted ter satisfy the unworthy dead."

All the men of Fort Comfort had fallen silent, and they stared at the ground or at one another with troubled eyes. It was Alaric Dunne who first broke the silence. He turned to the Exile, who was standing now with one arm about Colly.

"Dave, is there anything else you want to add?" he asked.

"That man has told everything," replied Paddison slowly. "It's too bad it had to be told. There's nothing I can add, except that what he says is true. Hal Starin tried to rob his grub cache and paid the penalty. He told me that before he died."

Dunne strode over and laid a heavy hand on Paddison's shoulder. "It is too bad it had to be told," he said. "We were all fools. It was us made it be told." Lowering his head, he passed on.

"My poor, dear Dave!" whispered Colly softly. "Now let me fix your arm a bit, till we get to Fort Comfort."

The man who once had been an exile brushed a kiss across the girl's rosy cheek.

Bogart, scowling under bushy brows, turned and busied himself over his dog-team.

Matt Shane, standing now, caught Paddison's eye and grinned meaningly, then looked away and took a satisfied tobacco shot, chuckling liquidly to himself.

The old timer said: "Well, gents, let's get goin'. I was aimin' ter be on my way south by this time. Let's mush. I'm headin' f'r the Outside with money ter burn. Winnipeg, the Garry, an' quarter cigars! Hurray f'r me!"

THE RAW WHITE EDGE

YUKON—WITH BLINDING SNOW AND FANGS OF FROST THE WHISPERING STORM GODS GUARD THEIR GOLD—AND MAN MUST KEEP HIS COURAGE AT THE RAW WHITE EDGE TO PLAY THE GAME AGAINST THEM.

THE FREEZE-UP was close at hand. The long, lean Arctic winter was throttling the primitive land in its talons of ice. The spirit thermometer was down to forty below and still dropping, and Dawson honkatonks were packed with bearded, boisterous and grimy men from the ends of the earth. Some there were who well knew the rigors of that bitter country; knew the stark loneliness of its unmapped, half-mythical trails; knew the nightmare of near starvation on the frigid polar rim under the weird death-dance of the ghostly northern lights. But many were cheechakos who tried to hide their rawness behind a chesty swagger and a reckless, devil-may-care manner of drinking and talking.

The stragglers were pouring in from the coast, weary and haggard, but with the gold fever burning in their eyes. The gruelling six-hundred mile trek from Dyea to Dawson was no pleasure jaunt, and some who had left Dyea with high and mighty hopes of gouging raw gold from the pitiless Dawson country, died by the way. Some had died of pure exhaustion on the staggering grind over Chilkoot. Others had gone down in the mad whirlpools of White Horse, or in the cruel slush-ice of lonely Lake Labarge.

But Dawson welcomed the stragglers. It welcomed them with the news that drinks were a dollar a throw, moosemeat two dollars a pound, with beans at one and a half, and flour at two. The Tivoli Saloon was in full blast. The bar was jammed. Faro, roulette, stud- and draw-poker were doing a thriving business.

The roof was the limit and frequently the roof was thrown off. Men swore with the grand carelessness of potential millionaires, and the room, heated by a big, red-hot stove, steamed with thawing furs and blanket-clothing.

"Bum-luck" Jackson, who stood six-feet-three in his siwash socks, weighed one-hundred-ninety pounds, and was probably the lankest man between Dyea Flats and the Yukon, took a crack with his bony fist at the bar and said:

"Yessir, gents, when good luck was handed out I must ha' been sleepin' or somethin'. 'S fact. Why, say, even when I was borned, I mind me old man told me later the roof was leakin' rain, the doc sprained an ankle gettin' there, me grandmother scalded herself, our cow was struck by lightnin'; an' t' wind it up, me folks, who had their hearts set on a li'l' baby gal, got me instead. If you c'n beat that, I'll be a wall-eyed son of a lop-side malemute. Have a drink!"

He flapped his hand in the air, boomed to the bar-tender, and the four cheechakos gathered about him, shook with laughter and named their poison. He shifted a chew the size of a golf-ball, spat next to the cuspidor, and drew a hand across his bewhiskered chin. He had a lantern jaw, a beak of a nose all out of true and shaggy eyebrows that were always bent in a serious, though not ill-tempered, frown.

"Why," he was continuing, "they's no man like me. 'S fact! Take the time I was prospectin' on Moosehide Creek, over near Circle City. Injuns swiped me grub. Me pardner got sick. I started f'r Circle with him on the sled. The lead-dog got sore and ripped open the wheeler's throat. Next day another dog broke a tendon and I had t' shoot him. Same afternoon we got caught in a snowslide, an' I busted me nose. Look at it! It's a disgrace t' any face. Then me pardner went crazy outta his head and shot part o' me ear off. See? Turrible! Come a blizzard that lambasted the livin' daylight outta us, and when I finally lugs me pardner into Circle he goes an' dies on me. He allus was a kind o' unthankful critter, Gawd rest his soul.

"An' that ain't all. Now I mind the time—'twas over at Cassiar Bar—"

"Bum-luck, it wasn't at Cassiar Bar. It was on the Porcupine, darn you!" a deep, good-humored voice rumbled at his elbow, and a broad hand thumped solidly on his shoulder.

Bum-luck twisted his head and looked into a pair of twinkling, keen blue eyes that were on a level with his own. The man behind the eyes was young, burly and good-looking in a rough-and-ready way. He had a stubble of black beard, and this was coated with pale frost that already was turning to silvery vapor. White teeth shone as the young man grinned, and a low, liquid chuckle rolled pleasantly in his throat.

Bum-luck threw up his long arms and brought them down on the man's shoulders. His frown disappeared, his pale eyes widened and shone with pure joy. His voice trumpeted—

"Dang your hide, Bart, so you got back! Lor' bless me heathen soul, you're a sight f'r sore eyes. Whatcha drinkin'? Come on, have a drink. Huh, whatcha drinkin'? Gents, me pardner, Bartholomew Dongan. Me *pardner*, gents!"

Dongan laughed, poked Bum-luck playfully in the ribs, and shoved up against the bar. Bum-luck draped his arms about his partner's neck, shifted his enormous chew, and hailed the bar-tender in his bull-voice.

Dongan gripped the lanky man's arm and said near his ear: "Listen, Bum. This is no party. I've just plugged in from Forty Mile and I've got something up my sleeve."

"Ho! Your arm, Bart? You can't fool me!"

"Now cut out the comedy, Bum. This is straight goods. Ditch these tin-horns and come on over to the cabin."

Bum-luck's face fell. He seemed disappointed. "Aw, shucks, Bart, let it hang f'r a while. I been entertainin' these gents an' enjoyin' meself. I loves t' talk, old husky, an' I don't get the chancet often."

"You love to talk and spend your dust on any tin-horn 'll listen," said Dongan. "Now forget it, Bum. Sink your rum and come on over the cabin. We need money, and I've got an idea how we can make enough to live till the next big strike."

"Aw, s' look here, Bart—"

"Come on, Bum," insisted the husky man, tugging at his arm.

He swept up his whisky, said, "Here's to you, pardner!" and flung it down neat, rasping his cavernous throat.

Bum-luck downed his, opened his mouth to protest further, but Dongan hauled him away from the bar with firm but gentle persistence and headed for the door. The lanky man flung over his shoulder:

"See you later, gents!"

"No you won't," chuckled Dongan, opening the door and dragging his partner outside, while the four cheechakos whispered among themselves.

They rocked down the street side by side, their moosehide moccasins crunching rhythmically on the snow. The wind cut sharp as a knife, and their breaths spumed forth into the frigid air like streamers of thin smoke. By the time they reached their moss-chinked logcabin, which was only a ten-minutes brisk walk from the Tivoli, their faces were red as two beets. Dongan lifted the latch and banged in, and Bum-luck, turning his head to take a tobacco shot, followed a split-second later, booted the door shut with his heel, and leaned back against it, a little disconsolate.

"Dang it, Bart," he complained, "you make me sick, you do. You can't let a critter enjoy hisself. You're allus chuck full o' energy, allus bangin' around some place, allus got ideas. Me, I reckon if I wanted t' lay down an' die peaceful, you'd be again' it or somethin'."

Dongan, a young mountain of sheer vigor, swung a muscled leg over the corner of the table and pulled off his mittens, leaving them to dangle at the end of the strings which ran up to his neck. The dynamic energy of youth sparkled in his eyes, rang in his deep-toned laugh, was apparent in the little lumps of hard muscle that forever shimmered at the corners of his mouth.

"Bum," he chided, "I think you're getting old."

"Old me eyebrow!" retaliated the lanky man, glaring suddenly. "I'll be forty-eight come May the tenth."

"Then shut up and—"

"An' don't tell me t' shut up!"

"All right, then be quiet. And peel your ears. Listen! We're going to shake Dawson's dust from our heels and plug for the mountains."

"S'pose you're startin' another Squaw Creek stampede," essayed Bum-luck. "S' look here, Bart. If it's gold you better leave me out. I'm the original bum luck guy, an' I'm contagious as hell."

"Forget it!" scoffed Dongan. "Now tell me. What's the latest price on moosemeat here?"

"Two or two-an'-a-quarter. But that don't mean nothin', 'cause they ain't no moosemeat t' be had. Darn me, I been eatin' so much bacon o' late I beginnin' t' look like it."

"All right," went on Dongan. "Say two dollars a pound. I've been poking around in the mountains, and I know where there's a herd of moose bottled up in a blind valley. Yes, sir, Bum. There's only one entrance to this valley, where they went in. Then by an act of providence to mankind and you and me in particular, a hunk of ice, of I don't know how many tons, slides down from the peak and jams in this entrance. There they are, eating moss and headed for starvation. It's our chance to make seven or eight thousand dollars and stay on easy street till there's another gold stampede. And we'll be warding off a meat famine in the bargain."

"Wait a minute," cut in Bum-luck. "How the devil we goin't' get this meat out if the valley's bottled up?"

"How? Why, wake up, pardner. This jam is only about thirty feet high. On the inside it's sheer—falls right away, which is why they can't climb out. On the outside we can climb up and make a rope ladder to go down the inside. Then we can haul up the meat bit by bit with a line and let it slide down the outside. We could use dynamite, but we're almost broke and 'll have t'use what dust we have got to buy a few sleds and some old mongrels. We don't need fast dogs; just ones that 'll pull. I can get 'em near Forty Mile, and we'll buy them *after* we've got the meat cached. It'll save dog-grub and, anyhow, we don't need 'em before."

"Well"—Bum-luck dragged off his cap and scratched his head—"well, I reckon I got t'go. Only I wisht you'd get less ideas in that head o' yourn."

"But we need the money, Bum," argued Dongan.

"Ten t'one, with me along, somethin' 'll happen. I'm allus only one jump ahead o' Bum-luck an' sometimes I slip an' get overtook."

The burly man laughed. "Oh, forget it, pardner. It's imagination. Go out and buy some ammunition and plenty of heavy rope. I'll pack the sled meanwhile and we'll get under way in an hour. And don't tell a soul!"

"Yeah—awright," grumbled the lanky man. "But s'pose I jest stop in t' the Tivoli an' finish the story I was tellin' them gents. Won't take long. An' they was interested."

"Bum," said Dongan, standing spreadlegged, "you stop in at the Tivoli and I'll re-break your nose."

"Ah-r-r, be your age. I'll—I'll—"

"Now, Bum, old pardner," chortled Dongan, as he crossed the room and took his friend's arm. "Cut out grumbling. Our bank's low and we want to get to that valley before somebody else accidentally gets there. Hop to it, old sour-face!"

"S' look here! Don't call me sour-face!"

Chuckling, Dongan thrust a couple of nuggets into Bum-luck's hand, pulled open the door and rough-housed him outside. Bum-luck stood glaring and grumbling and working his chew, while Dongan kept chuckling from the doorway. Then the old-timer spun on his heel and tramped off, trying hard to suppress a grin that would not be suppressed. Bum-luck was only happy when he could get a crowd around him, buy all the drinks, and relate his past misfortunes.

IT WAS a hard land in those days. It was a brutal land. It took a man and broke his back and spirit or made of him a better man than ever he was before. It gave no quarter and asked none. You had to stand up and fight back day in and day out, and if you were shaky on your pins you went down in less time than it takes to tell it, and nobody missed you. The Yukon trail was strewn with the bones of men who died in the name of gold. Some had the heart but not the strength, and others had the strength but not the heart.

Those who won through hung around the saloons as moths hang around a flame. They had come for gold, and they wanted nothing else. For gold they killed and lied and cursed God and the mothers that bore them. When a new stampede broke loose, the hordes tore out to stake their claims. The weak were trampled under foot, left to die of the bitter cold by the way; and men shot each other in the twinkling of an eye over a stake line that might have been a hair's breadth out of the way.

Bart Dongan, who was rounding thirty lusty years, had come to the Northland five years back, after having been kicked out of college and, subsequently, out of a soft home. The salmon fisheries claimed him for a while, and later the lumber business. Though he came to the Klondike for gold, he was not swept up in the madness. He turned his hand to anything in order to keep the proverbial wolf from the door, and the many things he could think of toward such an end, sometimes drove his partner to distraction. Bum-luck was a lazy, indifferent, good-natured soul, while Dongan was a dynamo of energy, with a brain that was forever planning new ventures.

And now they were trekking into the naked, glacial mountains, on the winter-locked rim of the universe. There were no strong woods to take the brunt of the ice-fanged wind. Trees grew in scattered clumps, and most of them were scrawny and naked. Black thickets straggled stark and skeleton-like across the glazed surface of the snow.

Six lean malemutes strained at ice-caked breast-bands and drew the heavily-laded ten-foot sled. A dozen feet ahead of the lead-dog Dongan strode on short, broad snowshoes. Bum-luck sagged along behind the sled at the gee-bar.

That part of his face below the nose was covered with a thin coating of frost, where his exhaled breath kept congealing. Even the faces of the dogs were sheeted with ice. Dongan's stubble was frosty, and little ridges of frozen rheum were under his eyes. Often he rubbed his nose vigorously with the palm of his mittened hand, and the returning blood circulation pricked like countless red-hot needles.

"Say," called Bum-luck, "reckon the bottom must be outta the thermometer."

Dongan stopped and looked around. The dogs stopped. Bum-luck stopped, discolored the virgin snow with a stream of tobacco that froze immediately.

"I'm spittin' brown icicles," he observed.

Dongan rocked back and stood beside him. "Mercury must be frozen stiff all right, Bum," he grinned.

"Doggone, if I didn't keep chewin' this 'baccy me jaws 'd freeze. I'm thinkin' how nice it'd be settin' back in the Tivoli next t' the big stove."

"And telling the tin-horns about your bum luck," added Dongan, with a mischievous wink.

"You keep naggin' me about that, old husky, an' I'll sure spread your nose all over your handsome young mug. Why, by cripes, I feel like warmin' up on you now!"

"I was feeling the same, Bum," retorted Dongan, flexing his arms. "Bet you a pound of tobacco, to be paid next time in Dawson, that I can put you on your back."

"Bet's on!" boomed Bum-luck, dropping his dog-whip.

"Let's go!" laughed the burly man, squaring off.

They both lunged for each other, locked and began rocking back and forth. They did not dally with each other. Dongan spun his lank, powerful partner around in a terrific attempt to whirl him off balance. But Bum-luck thwarted the attempt and bore Dongan back across the snow under a sweeping charge that for a moment threatened to topple the younger man. Dongan stopped it, however, and the little lumps of muscle at the corners of his mouth bulged with the almost superhuman strength he exerted to check Bum-luck. Then with a sudden movement he dropped back and down to his knees, bored up under his partner, lifted him clear and heaved him over his head. Spinning about, he dived for Bum-luck as the latter sprawled on his back, landed solidly and flattened his partner against the snow in a hold that was not to be broken.

"Ugh—ah—um—ugh—" choked Bum-luck, his eyes bulging, his jaws working.

"Down? Are you down, Bum?" laughed Dongan.

"Ugh—y—eah—I—ugh—"

Dongan jumped up, grasped his partner's hand and hauled him to his feet. Bum-luck ran around in circles, bent over at the waist, hacking and waving his hands. Finally he stopped, breathing hard, straightened up and rasped his throat, while his eyes watered. He put a hand to his mouth, and whipped away his wad of tobacco.

"Daggone, I—I almost choked t' death on that," he said. "I'll never wrastle you again with a chaw in me mouth."

"Ho-ho! You owe me a pound of tobacco, Bum."

"If it wasn't f'r me swallowin' that—"

"Grin, you old sour-face! Grin and bear it!"

"Darn you, don't call me sour-face!"

"Then grin. Show your teeth—"

"S' look here, Bart! You cut out makin' fun o' me. You know dang well I ain't got no teeth t' show. I—I—" The grin came much against his will, and flapping a hand at the burly man, he rolled back to the sled, sat down and gnawed off a fresh chew, trying to look very angry again after the involuntary grin.

"Well, old timer," said Dongan, dropping his bantering mood, "I guess we'd better mush."

Bum-luck got up and threw his gaze about the ragged, unlovely wastes.

"Reckon we better, Bart, old husky," he replied.

There was never any bitterness between these two. Although at times they cursed each other, threatened to beat the stuffings out of each other, in each heart there was deep respect, one for the other. Dongan's brittle banter, and Bum-luck's tirades, were just so much excess steam blowing off. Once on a time Bum-luck had carried his partner through a howling blizzard with the mercury at fifty-five below, and on another time Dongan had nursed the old timer through the scurvy. They never talked about it because they were not sentimental men, but between them there was an unbreakable bond of friendship which each tacitly understood and never mentioned.

As they were about to start off, Dongan raised his hand, stared keenly over the back trail.

"Look, Bum!"

Bum-luck looked, and both saw a string of men and dogs topping a bare ridge in the distance. The two partners glanced at each other, frowned perplexedly, and again turned to watch the moving train of men and dogs.

"Looks like another stampede," observed Bum-luck.

"Say, Bum, you didn't hint to anybody in Dawson where we were heading, did you?"

"Naw, o' couse not. I ain't no fool. But you mind they was no hint time o' the Squaw Creek rush. A bunch o' critters slipped outta town mysterious. Another bunch saw 'em, an' before long they was a stampede. You mind how you drug me away from the Tivoli? Well, I'll bet me red shirt, the only one I got, that some critters there smelt a rat."

"By George, Bum, you may be right!"

"Sure I may," declared Bum-luck. "Doggone, I never seen meself start on somethin' without Bum-luck trailin' me. Honest. I'm the bum-luckest critter— Why, dang me, I'll bet the other shirt I hope t' own some day that when I croak an' get buried it'll be just me stinkin' luck t' wake up when they's six feet o' sod on top o' me!"

"No, Bum. If that's what started it, old timer, it was my fault for—"

"Nope. It's me, old husky, the bum-luckest sourdough that ever had the bum luck t' get hisself borned. Why, even that was a mistake. Me folks wanted a gal an' got me. Me last pardner died in Circle City, an' the one before that drowned hisself in the Stewart. I'm a accident, Bart. I'm a accident, that's allus happenin' t' someone else. I'm six accidents all rolled in one, an' a dozen mistakes. I was with you when you busted your ankle in the Tanana Hills an' that awful blizzard come. I goes an' gets scurvy an' ties you down when you should ha' been in on that big stampede. I could kick meself in the slats f'r bein' the bum-luck critter I am. I'm a hell-bent jinx, old husky!"

"Now shut up, Bum," clipped Dongan. "This is serious. They must have been following us since yesterday, hanging back. Probably the small bunch that started has been increased by the way and have given up the idea of hanging back. Blast the luck!"

"It's me, old husky. It's yours lovin'ly, Bum-luck Jackson, hisself in person, pleased t' meetcha. Start thinkin', Bart. Get your think-machinery grindin', an' figger a way t' shake this gang. I warned you not t' take me along. I—"

"Dammit, close your jaw, Bum!" ripped out Dongan. "You talk so much about bad luck, it's no wonder we get it. Look at them come!"

The horde surged down the distant slope in what appeared to be an endless line. Some had sleds and dogs and led the race. Others ran, slid, stumbled under light packs. On they came, with new figures continuously topping the bald knob of the hill and tearing down the ice-hummocked trail. There were young men and old men, boys of eighteen and grandfathers of sixty-odd; white beards and black beards and faces that were yet too soft to grow even a downy stubble. The big men bowled over the little men, and nobody turned to lend a hand to those who fell and clawed at the snow and ice.

Gold was their god, and that god was the devil. It drove them to madness, to anger, to black hatred. Feet that once had known the feel of silk and patent leather and soft velvety rugs, now pounded the frozen trail in grimy socks and moccasins. Voices that once on a time had drawled philosophy and culture in the meditative atmosphere of library or drawing-room, were now coarse and brutish with the lust of gold and mythical millions.

"Let's mush a while," ventured Dongan.

"Let's, Bart," nodded his partner. "An' in the meantime keep thinkin' them thinks o' yourn."

Bum-luck took the lead and Dongan, taking up the whip, cracked it and helped the dogs "break" the sled from the frozen crust. The outfit moved forward, swinging down toward a stretch of muskeg, while the brittle Arctic air carried to their ears the maudlin yelping of harried dogs commingled with the shouts of men.

The leaders of the horde caught up with the two partners when they were working across the field of frozen, jagged muskeg. The first of the lot was "Chilkoot Charley" Hansen, a whale of a Swede who many times had lugged a one-hundred-and-fifty-pound pack over the muscle-tearing grade of Chilkoot Pass. Recklessly he drove his team of six big Hudson Bay dogs, and shouted:

"Ha-ha! Vee seen you sneakin' out o' Dawson last night. By yumpin' yimminy, yah! Keep mushin', Bum-luck. Show us vere is it de new diggin's. Ay bane make a million dis time, yah! Den Ay go home to Marstand by the Skagerrack an' marry her mine Brunhilde. By yumpin' yimminy, yah!"

"Charley, you're all wrong," said Dongan. "We're not after gold this time."

"Ha-ha, Bart! Ay t'ink you are, yah. Mush!"

Others came thundering up, raising clouds of fine snow, and milling around the two partners. Men snarled amongst themselves, just as the dogs snarled. With one team were two of the cheechakos to whom Bum-luck had been relating his misfortunes the day before.

"Hot on your trail, Bum-luck," called one of them. "Thought it damned funny the way your pardner pulled you away yesterday. Looks suspicious when a man comes in from the trail at forty-five below and then takes his pardner and goes right off again."

"Just as I thought," muttered Dongan near Bum-luck's ear. "Well, let's keep moving and see what happens. We'll steer clear of the valley for a while. Think of something, Bum, to shake them."

"That," replied Bum-luck, "is up t' you, Bart."

Dongan cracked his whip and Bum-luck ran up ahead of the team. They started off and the hungry horde crowded after them, singing and cursing with wild abandon. And while they sang and cursed one here, and another there, crumpled to the snow, clawed ahead on hands and knees, and finally collapsed. The others trooped by, their eyes, like their thoughts, fixed on the lanky man in the lead, who they thought was the key to their still unrealized and unreasonable hopes of fortune. Gold hunger gnawed at their brains even as food hunger gnaws at the stomach. In their immense singleness of purpose they swept away a thousand years of civilization from the book of time. The seed of their cave-dwelling forebears would not be downed. They were raw men on the raw white edge of the world, willing to sell their souls to the goddess of gold.

Dongan and Bum-luck plugged deeper into the crenelated mountains, each trying to think of some plan by which they could dissuade the horde from following them. At three in the afternoon the early twilight of the high latitudes began to fling out over the wilderness, and deeper darkness followed close upon its heels.

Dongan called his dogs to a halt, raised his hands and shouted:

"We'll stop and camp."

"No, by yimmy," argued Chilkoot Charley Hansen, rubbing ice particles from his bearded jaw. "Vee keep mushin', yah. De moon she kooms up dam' soon."

"That's the stuff," seconded a cheechako. "We'll mush till midnight."

"No. We'll camp now," was Dongan's idea, as he stood spread-legged.

The men milled about him, growling and waving their fists threateningly. Bum-luck elbowed his way to his partner and they stood back to back.

"We'll camp now," stated Bum-luck, frowning darkly.

Chilkoot Charley pulled his revolver and slammed the muzzle against Dongan's stomach, A dozen other guns sprang into view, and the growls of the horde became more ominous.

"Ay t'ink we mush now, yah," rumbled the Swede.

Dongan and Bum-luck turned to regard each other. The lank man spat lazily and drew a hand across his mouth, still eyeing his partner.

"I reckon it's mush, then, old husky," he said. "These bums ha' got the drop on us."

Dongan nodded and uncoiled his whip, brushed by Chilkoot Charley and grasped the gee-bar of his sled.

"All right, you blasted fools!" he flung at the horde, and cracked the whip with a savage gesture over the dogs.

They lined out and continued through an arduous muskeg, while overhead in the darkening sky pale stars began to wink and grow in number. The moon came up and flooded the naked land with its ghostly, silver radiance, and shadows paced the men and dogs as they swept onward through the Arctic night.

Dongan, taking the lead from Bum-luck, led the way up a steep hog-back, topped it and swung down into a valley where a narrow, frozen waterway meandered through scattered bunches of balsam. Some of the men faltered on the upgrade and finished on hands and knees, then let themselves slide down the other side, upsetting others and crashing into the dogs.

The burly young man reached the narrow creek and jogged along on its hard surface. Behind him men swore and dogs snarled viciously, but he did not turn his head. Presently he espied a dark blotch on the right-hand shore and toward this he steered. It proved to be the remains of a campfire.

"Bum," he called in a voice that most of the men could hear, "drive our center stakes here and I'll drive the corner stakes."

Bum-luck opened his mouth in frank amazement. Chilkoot Charley waved his arm and roared.

"Ha-ha! Dis is it. Say, Bart, how t' hell you find dis?"

"I picked up an old sourdough on the road to Forty Mile," explained Dongan. "He was dying and before he cashed in he told me about it." He put his hand in his pocket and drew forth a couple of nuggets. "This is a sample he gave me."

"By yumpin' yimminy!" exclaimed Chilkoot Charley, and dived off to cut his stakes.

The others left their dogs to curl up and followed his example. Axes rang and laughs boomed. Men crashed through the thickets, crashed into one another and lashed out with savage blows on general principles.

"Drive your center stakes, Bum," repeated Dongan to his still mystified partner.

"What—what the devil—" began Bum-luck.

But Dongan cut him short with—

"Don't stand there like a mummy. Get started!" And with that the burly man grabbed his axe and went off to cut and drive his corner stakes.

It was a night of pandemonium, of bitter arguments and sudden blows. Those who had driven their stakes flopped down exhausted near their dogs, rolled up in their robes and slept till the first thin streak of dawn. Some did not stop to sleep, but started right back for Dawson to register their claims and get supplies.

When the last of the horde had gone, Dongan yawned awake, sat up and found Bum-luck regarding him with a dubious frown. The burly young man rubbed his jaw and grinned slowly, winking a mischievous eye. Then he heaved to his feet.

"Well, Bum, let's get started for that valley before those moose die of starvation or somebody else spots them."

"But, you old husky, what about this?"

"Oh, this!" Dongan chuckled. "I had to get rid of those birds somehow. I was wondering if they'd fall for it. I camped here one night. This was my fire. Gold? Don't you believe it. I just staked here so as they'd follow me and then we could get rid of them."

"Well, you son of a gun!" howled Bum-luck, and for once he grinned, from ear to ear, without being urged.

A WEEK later Bum-luck sat atop the ice jam in the blind valley and watched four teams of dogs running toward him with empty sledges. He spat with satisfaction and looked down at the mound of moosemeat which soon would be sold in Dawson.

The two partners had hauled the meat up over the jam by means of a stout rope attached to the traces of their six-dog team. Bum-luck had worked on the inside, and Dongan, adding his strength to that of the dogs on the outside, had managed to haul over three-hundred pounds at a time. When all the meat was outside, Dongan had gone off to hire or buy as many teams as he could secure.

And now he was returning with three teams besides his own. Bum-luck climbed down from the top of the jam, and a little later Dongan arrived at the head of his team, with the three other teams, along with three Indian drivers, close behind.

"All fixed, Bum," called the burly man. "I didn't have to go far. Struck a camp I didn't expect to find and hired these teams."

Bum-luck rubbed his hands together and looked cheerful.

"Now, dang me, I c'n squat in Dawson f'r a while an' enjoy meself," he said. "An' s' look here, Bart. If you go thinkin' up any more ideas I'm goin' to smash you f'r sure."

Dongan grinned and wagged a finger at his partner.

"Remember, Bum, you owe me a pound of tobacco already."

"Ah-r-r, go away with you!" grumbled Bum-luck good-naturedly.

They set to work immediately loading the sleds, piling the meat high and solid and arranging to carry their personal equipage on their backs, to conserve space. At noon they were ready to start. They cooked a hearty meal for themselves and the Indian drivers, and broke trail custom by feeding the dogs in the middle of the day.

At one o'clock they started for Dawson under a dull, portentous sky that appeared pregnant with snow. The harness creaked, the heavily laden sleds crunched over the snow; and the two white men plodded under the weight of their packs. They were just an hour on the trail when snow began to fall.

"Looks dirty," observed Dongan, throwing an eye across the brooding heavens.

"Oh, we ain't in Dawson yet, old husky," replied Bum-luck, wagging his head. "Don't f'rget that Bum-luck Jackson is with you, an' he draws bum luck like a wet tree draws lightin'."

"Now my remark didn't call for an oration, Bum."

"Anyhow, I'm tellin' you what's what."

"Oh, shut up."

Bum-luck shifted his chew. "S' look here. I don't like bein' told t' shut up thataway."

"Well, then, be quiet," said Dongan.

"All right, but don't tell me t' shut up."

Following this brief exchange of words, the two partners busied themselves aiding the dogs over a series of bad hummocks. Later, crossing a frozen swamp, Bum-luck, who was in the lead, broke through an air hole and sank in water to his knees. Swearing a sizzling blue streak, he was hauled out by the two nearest Indians, while Dongan hastened to build a fire.

"Holy smokes, hell, dammit and doggone!" raved Bum-luck. "If we ever get this meat t' Dawson I'll drink myself deaf, dumb, an' blind, marry six squaws and grow a Chinese pig-tail!"

"Now, Bum," said Dongan, hacking at the old timer's already ice-caked footgear. "Take it easy, pardner."

The Indians tended the fire while Dongan removed Bum-luck's moccasins and socks and began rubbing the numb legs and feet with snow. When the prickling sensation of circulation was felt, Bum-luck squirmed and made a wry face, and little by little Dongan drew the feet toward the warmth of the flames.

Twilight was already lowering, and they made their camp there for the night. Next morning Bum-luck was in good shape again, and they started with the first faint color of dawn. The day passed with snow still falling and the dogs wallowing to their bellies. The men's parkas were sheeted with ice that crackled as they moved, and icicles hung from their hoods, while their beards were white with frost.

No misfortune occurred all day, so it was inevitable that over the campfire that night Bum-luck should tell of misfortunes that had befallen him in the full years behind. Dongan fell asleep listening, and Bum-luck then addressed the Indians. And when they fell asleep he grumbled his chagrin and rolled in his own blankets, while the dogs chewed ice lumps from their bruised feet.

Next morning the snow stopped falling while breakfast was making, and all the lonely wilderness lay entombed and beautifully silent. The vastness of it all was appalling, and made man feel finite and futile in the face of its lordly omnipotence.

The outfit moved with its burden, pushing slowly but doggedly through the fantastic drifts, down, steadily down, towards lower country.

That afternoon, when the cold, gray twilight was again sweeping over the land, they plodded into Dawson. Faces appeared at cabin windows, and then those faces came to the doors. Men stopped and looked and asked, and Bum-luck replied:

"Meat—moosemeat. Two dollars a pound. In God we trust; all others cash. Two dollars a pound—no bargains."

They stopped in front of the Tivoli, and the two partners, telling the Indians to remain by the sleds, strode into the saloon and on up to the bar. The place was crowded, and most of the men appeared to be in particularly high spirits.

"Moosemeat!" roared Bum-luck. "We got plenty of it t' sell, an' we're in the market at two dollars a pound—cash in gold!"

"Hurray!" the crowd yelled.

Out of the mob broke Chilkoot Charley Hansen, his huge face beaming. He smashed into the two partners and clapped his ponderous hands on their shoulders.

"By yumpin' yimminy!" he boomed. "Why t' hell ain't you on dat claim? Ay bane yust koom in f'r axtry grub. Averybody he bane get rich. Soon Ay go back to Marstand by de Skagerrack an' marry her mine Brunhilde."

"Huh?" gulped Bum-luck. "What's 'is, huh?"

Charley dug a hand into his pocket and thrust a nugget as large as a walnut under Bum-luck's nose.

"Yah, look! Vee all be rich like hell! De creek have no name, so vee call her Bum-luck Creek. Yah! You sell me some moosemeat—yah. Yompin' yimminy, Ay knowed you vass make a strike!"

Bum-luck spun on his partner.

"Bart, did—did you know—?"

"Not a thing, Bum," replied Dongan, quite as awe stricken as the lanky man. "So help me, Bum, I just did it to—"

"Then f'r Lord's sake, file our claim!" broke in Bum-luck. "I'll sell the meat to the trader. Oh, bless me heathen soul! If this ain't the limit!"

He gripped his partner's arm and lunged outside to the dog teams. He stopped there, took Dongan's hand and pumped it furiously. The burly man finally broke into a grin, pulled his hand loose and took a playful jab at the lanky man's jaw.

"Now, darn you, Bum," he said, his blue eyes sparkling, "if you ever mention hard luck again to me, I'll just naturally tear your old hide to ribbons.

"Ho! Ho!" roared Bum-luck. "The bad luck must ha' broke at last. Bart, I'll get me a new red shirt. I believe in Santa Claus, pink elephants, the Klondike an' Dawson likker! An' Bart, old husky, I'm goin' t' give you five pounds o' 'baccy an' t'-night I'm goin' t' squat in the Tivoli an' talk me head off."

"What, Bum, about your bum luck?"

"Shucks, no! About all the good luck I'm goin' t' have from now on. I'm a scraggly old wolf what's got religion, an' it's me night t' howl! An', old husky, how—I—am—goin'—t'—*howl!*"

IT TAKES A MAN

YUKON—TO HURL YOUR STRENGTH AGAINST THE SNOWS AND THE BLIZZARD'S ICE-CLAWED BREATH—TO BUCK A STACKED DECK AND A CROOKED DEAL WITH A WOMAN'S SMILE FOR STAKES—TO LOSE AND TO LAUGH AND TO KEEP ON FIGHTING—*THAT'S* WHAT TAKES A MAN!

CHAPTER I

YUKON

JEFF BARNES landed on the beach at Dyea with five hundred pounds of luggage and provisions, seventy-five dollars, and a firm conviction that he would drive his way into the maw of the Arctic wilds and wrest a fortune in gold from the stubborn earth.

Barnes was that kind of a man. Tall, lean, hard-bitten, dogged, with an unbounded faith in his own ability, he had recently rounded thirty-two years, with the last ten of them spent on the far, ragged edges of the world playing with the precarious dice of destiny. He had made and lost a couple of fortunes in his day, and now he was resolved to make another, hang onto it, settle down some place, and maybe find himself a wife. He was not a success yet, but he believed he had the makings; and a man's belief in himself is half of any game.

His financial condition was, of course, nothing to brag about. Not when you take into consideration that Indian packers were charging thirty-five cents a pound to freight goods over Chilkoot, and that you had to pay as much for a single mangy, half-winded dog as you might have paid a year ago for a whole team of hard-pulling, big-lunged malemutes. The outlook was not cheerful, but Barnes was used to black outlooks, and didn't worry himself to distraction on that count.

He stood on the beach by his heap of worldly goods, while the last of the arrivals poured from the Seattle steamer and added their luggage to the general confusion. Some laughed, challenging the gods of the wilderness. Others swore at the crisp wind and the newly fallen snow. Barnes neither laughed nor swore. He smoked his blackened briar and watched the old-timers, the cheechakos, the Indians and the dogs milling about like a vast army preparing to leave for some fighting front.

Near him a couple of men were building a fire in the lee of their packs and stamping their feet against the penetrating chill of onrushing twilight. Barnes took his pipe from his mouth and said:

"Will you boys keep an eye on my stuff? Want to get a drink."

"Sure thing," waved one of the men.

"Thanks," nodded Barnes, and swung up toward Dyea's main street.

Dog teams were on the prod, trotting off for the wilderness with heavily laden sledges, while bearded, fur-swathed men paced them and cracked long thirty-foot whips. Big-limbed Indians tramped by under huge, one-hundred-pound packs, their straps creaking, their necks held taut against the rigid head-bands. Everywhere there was movement, unrest. Everybody seemed to be going somewhere, or coming from somewhere.

Dawson represented the star by which all men steered. Dawson—almost six hundred lean, bitter miles to the northward. Not as the crow flies, but as a man must travel, winding his way through the raw, naked country by wind-torn passes and glacial valleys, across treacherous marshes and lonely, mountain-walled lakes where the frigid breath of King Winter was already turning the cold blue waters to sheets of ice. Fresh snow bonneted the tangled hills and lay in fantastic drifts in the yawning ravines, and the sun, rapidly going into declination, no longer took the lacerating bite from the howling polar winds.

Barnes was conscious of this restless, surging sea of humanity—these hundreds of men, thousands of men, going and coming. Some were totally unfitted for the gruelling test; others were only too well fitted. Men who not so long ago had worn

white collars, shaved and bathed every day, now went about in grimy woolens and tangled beards, and mingled with one another freely—the gentleman with the bum, the honest man with the cut-throat.

He found himself in a low-ceiled saloon throbbing with the movement and talk of a hundred men. He weaved his way to the bar amid the smells of a dozen kinds of tobacco and a dozen other smells that were not of tobacco. He called for a drink and had to raise his voice before the smooth-faced bartender caught his order.

Men departed and entered continually, banging the doors. Somewhere at the far end of the murky saloon a piano was being banged and a violin was screeching. A big stove glowed red. A roulette wheel whirred, and chips rattled. A man cursed his soul in a high-pitched, maudlin voice, and a woman laughed hysterically. A window smashed. There was a shot commingled with a scream.

Barnes leaned with his back to the bar, one heel hooked on the rail, and frowned perplexedly. Next to him stood a small, broad, chunky man with a red beard, a nose like a gnarled pine knot, and twinkling blue eyes.

"You wonderin' what's happened?" he ventured, jerking his head toward the crowd, and grinning slowly.

"Kind of," said Barnes.

"Well, m' friend, don't let it worry you. Just in, ain't you? Hum. Thought so.… Don't let it worry you, I says. Just some feller gettin' throwed out f'r sayin' too much. It happens reg'lar. Oh, yeah. I know. Ain't I been throwed outa places already f'r sayin' the wrong thing at the wrong time. Say, I bet I been throwed outta more places between Dyea an' the Nordenscold than any sourdough in the hull damn North."

"I can appreciate your pride in such a record," said Barnes. "I suppose you're going to add that each time you were pitched out you got a bullet in the slats—and liked it."

"Well, naw"— He paused to chuckle and take a tobacco shot—"naw, I reckon I ain't been shot at much. Thet would kinder make me sore. But I tell you, m' friend, this is a hard country now. Half o' these critters 'll never get over Chilkoot, and half o' them thet gets over 'll wish t' hell they never did. You goin' t' Dawson?"

"I am," nodded Barnes, as though it were the easiest thing in the world.

"It takes a man," said the old-timer, "t' buck the Yukon cold these days."

"Exactly," agreed Barnes. "Maybe you take me for a pink-cheeked Boy Scout just out of grammar school and still kind of damp behind the ears."

"Wal, no, not a-tall."

"All right, then. There's no country can beat a man who's set on beating it. I've hunted gold in Australia and in the wilds of New Guinea. I've gone on several lost treasure hunts and sweat blood with the thermometer at a hundred and twenty-five. I'm in perfect trim physically and the Yukon is my meat. I've come to make my pile and I'm going to make it."

"M' friend, you sure have got faith in yourself," grinned the man with the red beard.

"And why not?" demanded Barnes. "I've beaten the New Guinea jungles, the Australian bush, the walloping heat of the plagued Malay States, and I can beat the Yukon. Who ever got

anywhere by being a shrinking violet? Who ever won to suprem-
acy by doubting his own ability, wondering if the other fellow
was the better man? In this hardshell old world of chance you've
got to have a big opinion of yourself. You've got to consider yourself the equal of the best man that was ever born and the equal
of the two best men on your birthday and all national holidays."

"M' friend, if you didn't look so gol-darned capable I'd say you
got thet learnin' from books."

"Books hell! Raw experience is the meat of life and books are
only the dessert."

"Hurray! M' name's 'Brick' Jordon. Have a drink!"

"Call me Barnes. And about the drink, wait a while. I feel
lucky just now, and luck is the soup that comes before the meat.
I've got a measly seventy-five dollars to my name, but before
the day's out I'm going to be one of the richest men heading
for Dawson."

Brick Jordon wagged his head. "M' friend, you got altogether
too much confidence."

"Watch me!" clipped Barnes.

He shouldered his way from the bar to the roulette wheel
and stood watching the players. Brick Jordon drifted after him,
throwing away his old chew and taking a fresh one. Barnes stood
there for a quarter of an hour without playing, and then as a man
slipped away with a mournful countenance, he placed five one
dollar chips on number twenty-five. The ball whirred, and when
it came to a stop Barnes won a hundred and seventy-five dollars.

Following this he placed some scattered bets and managed to
win seventy-five dollars. Then he took a chance again on number
twenty-five, placing ten chips, and cleared up three hundred and
fifty dollars. The next five bets he lost, and then three times in a
row he won, adding a thousand dollars to his pile.

By this time he had drawn the attention of the other players
and the onlookers, and the game-keeper began to throw him
sidelong distasteful looks. But Barnes went on smoking his pipe
and giving his attention to no one, and his luck stayed with him.

Brick Jordon, forgetting to grind his chew, looked on with an amused and rather pleased half-smile twitching at his mouth.

Barnes continued to win, and when he had cleared up thirty-five hundred dollars the keeper said: "You sure are ridin' a hunch, ain't you, stranger?"

"I sure am, keeper," replied Barnes.

"Well, how about try in' your luck at another table?"

"This one suits me, all right."

"I know, but it don't suit me."

Barnes took his pipe from his mouth and bit the man with a level, hard stare. "Tin-horn, eh?" he queried.

"I ain't just runnin' a charity table, that's all."

"Dam' right you're not. Never knew roulette to be a charitable game. It's my night, and I'm playing my luck."

"Well, play it somewhere else."

A tall, dark man, standing near the keeper, raised his finger and said to Barnes: "How's your luck at cards, stranger?"

"Good tonight," replied Barnes. "How's yours?"

"Tolerable."

"All right, let's go. This tin-horn keeper is looking for suckers."

Brick Jordon plucked at his sleeve. "Better go easy, m' friend."

"This is my night," Barnes chuckled.

It was his night. Good cards came his way from the very start, and every time he opened he made the ante so stiff that some of the players squirmed. One of these was a slim, sallow young man who appeared very much out of place in that rough, raw company. Ted Hillyer was his name, and his chips dwindled rapidly under the hard, seasoned playing of the others. He kept wetting his lips and fidgeting with his cards, and his dark eyes were feverish with the hope of winning and the dread of losing.

When he lost on three jacks against Barnes's three queens, he flung his cards in the air and beat with his fists on the table.

"Dammit," he flung at Barnes, "can't you hold small cards?"

"Not tonight," replied Barnes, stacking his chips. "If the game's too stiff, why don't you drop out?"

"Drop out my eye!"

"Well, then stop crabbing. This is not penny ante."

Hillyer slumped back in his chair and glowered at the next five cards that were dealt him.

Barnes went on winning, sweeping aside all opposition and taking it all as a matter of course. Watchers milled about the table, and he became the object of admiration and not a little envy.

He had increased his seventy-five dollars to five thousand, and was well on the way to another thousand when Hillyer ran out of money.

"Here," said the young man huskily. "How much will you give me for this?" He held up a diamond ring, while his feverish eyes darted hungrily about the table.

Barnes said: "Better keep it for a rainy day. This is my night, and I can see it's not yours. You'll lose your shirt."

"Never mind about that," snapped Hillyer. "What are you—afraid I'll stage a come-back?"

"Not a bit of it," laughed Barnes shortly. "All right. Let's see the trinket."

He picked up the ring, regarded it closely, held it up to the light and remarked: "This is a lady's ring."

"Well, what about it?" asked Hillyer.

"Nothing. Give you a hundred dollars in chips."

Hillyer agreed, and the game went on. But, indeed, it was not his night. His chips dribbled into the pot, and his last chip went in a stiff betting tilt with Barnes. He lost, and with that he leaped to his feet, shaking with passion.

"Damn you," he hurled at Barnes, "you're one of these lousy, crooked card sharps! You can't lose! You—"

"Easy there!" someone warned.

But Hillyer kicked back his chair, flung off a restraining arm and shook his knotted fists at Barnes.

"You—you're crooked!" he screamed, half sobbing.

Barnes laid down his blackened pipe and stood up, and there was a bad light in his keen, hard eyes. Calmly he walked around the table, to face the palsied stranger. Hillyer backed away, his lower lip quivering, his eyes blazing with a rage wild and impotent. With a sudden, frantic movement he dived for the gun at his hip.

CHAPTER II

THE WOMAN IN THE CASE

BARNES LEAPED swiftly, surely, like a great charging cat. He caught Hillyer's hand on the draw, and a shot went wild through the ceiling.

"Drop that gun!" he barked.

"You—you—"

"Drop it or I'll break your arm!"

Hillyer writhed and squirmed, trying to tear himself loose. His gun went off again and a shot smashed one of the lamps hanging from the ceiling. Barnes rushed him against the wall, bending his arm behind his back and twisting his wrist in a hold that made the young man cry out with pain. He dropped the gun, and then Barnes sent him tumbling across the room. He sprawled over the faro table, crashed down to the floor with a couple of chairs on top of him, and a number of outraged players swore and kicked him on general principles.

Then the door banged open and a woman stood on the threshold, flinging inquisitive eyes about the smoke-filled, boisterous saloon. Her gaze settled on Hillyer as he was rising on wobbly legs, his face bruised and bleeding. With a little cry she ran to him and put her arms about him, aiding him to his feet.

She somehow threw a spell over the rough-clad, rough-mannered men. The din died, and the men edged away and backward. She was a young woman, very young, very pretty, clad in a tan mackinaw and moosehide moccasins. Her toque was many-hued, and that part of her hair which showed beneath it was like spun gold and shimmered. Her eyes, now, were two dark pools of anger and indignation as she swept them back and forth over the men.

"Who did this?" she cried. "Who did this?"

The men scuffled about uneasily. A bar-tender breathed into a glass and polished it with a great show of industry while he gazed at the ceiling and whistled noiselessly. Brick Jordon shifted his chew, cleared his throat and ventured:

"Miss, he brung it on himself, he did. He was playin' cards an' he lost right along, an' when he was cleaned out he called a man crooked."

"Well, I shouldn't be surprised if you were crooked," she gave Brick hotly. "You look like a crooked man, anyhow. You are all wolves—all of you! Look at his poor face. You—you must have kicked him!"

"Miss, it wasn't me—"

"I'm the man you want to talk to, miss," cut in Barnes, coming forward and standing spread-legged, with his hands jammed into the pockets of his mackinaw.

"Then you—you kicked him, you brute!" she accused.

"No. I beat him at cards," corrected Barnes evenly. "I cleaned him out and he accused me of playing crooked. He pulled his gun and I took it away from him and flung him off. He fell over a table and in the mix-up he got kicked. It was madness to pull the gun, and I realized he didn't know what he was doing. He was crazed for the moment at his loss, and my only desire was to get the gun away from him."

"Oh, you are just a smooth-tongued gambler," she told him. "I know your type. The Yukon will be swamped with them. You wait and sit in the warm dives and fleece the men who hunt for gold. You haven't the courage to tackle the Arctic trails. It takes a man to do that. But you— Oh, all of you are hounds, wolves!"

With that she dragged Hillyer toward the door. A man opened it and the two disappeared.

In the saloon the tension relaxed. Men began to move about. Glasses clinked at the bar. The roulette wheel whirred. The din grew again, and a moment later the piano and violin broke into action.

"Well," said Brick Jordon to Barnes, "that's that."

"A mighty pretty girl," mused Barnes, gathering up his money. "Wonder what she's doing in Dyea."

"Dunno. Anyhow, let's have that drink I spoke about before."

"Wonder what relation she is to the young chum."

"Dunno. Maybe his wife. Anyhow, you—um—smooth tongued gambler"—he grinned over this—"let's have that drink."

Half an hour later they were out under the low, clear stars of the evening, moving side by side down the beach, where many campfires glowed. Neither had sworn partnership to the other, yet they kept together, and it seemed that as yet they had no intention of parting.

"Well, you sure had a lucky evenin'," Brick remarked as they reached Barnes' luggage.

"Just as I told you," replied Barnes. "I felt it in my bones. Only it was rotten to have it end up that way."

"Well, women is women," philosophized Brick. "They act first an' think afterwards. They c'n call a man all kinds o' names an' he's jest gotta stand f'r it. Women with me is tabu. Some men says women is a necessary evil, like hootch, African dominoes an' castor oil. I c'n do without all o' them."

"Brick," chuckled Barnes, lighting a fresh pipe, "you get interesting. I don't agree with you, but you're interesting. What do you say to hooking up with me and beating the Yukon to a frazzle?"

"Who, me? Huh! M' friend, I'm almost dead broke."

"But you know the Yukon."

"Yeah, I reckon I oughter."

"All right. I don't. What I lack in knowledge of the country and what you lack in funds and equipment make things about even. We need each other, I think."

"Lookin' at it that way, maybe you're right," nodded Brick. "I'd sure like t' hook up with you. You got brains. You got guts. You're the best damn cheechako I ever seen."

"Then it's done!" clipped Barnes, slapping his knee. "Go get what stuff you have got and bring it over here. We'll hire some Indians to pack our dunnage over the Pass. We're going to beat the Yukon, Brick—beat it to a frazzle!"

"Yeah, but don't be so danged sure," advised Brick Jordon.

"Ho! Ho! I was never so sure of anything in my life!"

So the compact was made, and the two men, vastly different, became partners. Such high-sounding confidence from another man might have fallen flat on the wind-bitten ears of Brick Jordon, but coming from Barnes, it was a different matter. It was different because there was something about Barnes that breathed of command and capability. You sensed it the moment you laid eyes on him. He had the courage of his own convictions and the aggressiveness to carry them out. He was a hard-eyed, hard-headed bulldog of a man, and already the crowd in the saloon where he had played were talking about him.

Brick, having lugged over his own equipage, departed again to hire some Indians for the pull over Chilkoot. Barnes was lying on his blankets by the campfire he had built, smoking his pipe and meditating, when a mackinawed figure detached itself from the horde on the beach and came toward him. In a moment he saw it was Hillyer, and nodded curtly with no friendly overtures.

"Listen, Barnes," said Hillyer, kneeling down, "I'd like to buy that ring back."

"Why?" asked Barnes.

"Well, I'd just like to. I've got the hundred dollars with me."

"What makes you think I'll take a hundred dollars?"

Hillyer's eyes clouded and he bit his lip for a moment. "Well, I thought you'd take a hundred, seeing as—"

"Seeing as I paid you a hundred for it. Who was the lady came and took you away from the saloon?"

"Why—why, my sister."

Barnes frowned over his pipe and regarded for a moment the toe of his moccasin. Then he said suddenly:

"Tell you what, Hillyer. I don't like the opinion the lady must have of me. I'll return the ring to her personally and try to square myself. You'll come with me and tell her what a damned fool you were."

"No—no," Hillyer hastened to object. "I—I'll give you the money here."

"To hell with your money! I want myself squared with the lady. And, by the way, where did you get the hundred dollars?"

"I—I— Well, I don't see—"

"As it's any of my business." He sat up abruptly, took the pipe from his mouth and pointed the stem at Hillyer. "I'm curious about something. When I was a kid in college—I did only two years—I sold diamonds to help pay my way, and I got to know quite a bit about them. Now I'm curious to know why you're willing to pay me a hundred dollars for an imitation diamond that's worth about ten dollars, if that much."

Hillyer opened his mouth to say something, but closed it again sharply and ground one mittened hand in the palm of the other, while his eyes darted about evasively.

"Come, Hillyer, and tell me why," persued Barnes.

"I—I well, I always thought it was genuine."

"I don't mind telling you that I think you're lying. At any rate, you'll take me to your sister. I paid you the hundred dollars for a whim, and to give you a last chance for a come-back. Now it's my whim to have myself squared."

"Dammit, Barnes, you're hard—hard as nails."

"So I am. Hard as hell."

"But I won't take you to her!"

"All right," nodded Barnes. "Then you'll not get the ring."

Hillyer stood up, his hands clenched, his lower lip quivering under the whiplash of chagrin. Then he pivoted on his heel and tramped off.

"See you in Dawson," Barnes called after him.

Hillyer threw an oath over his shoulder.

CHAPTER III

THE ATTACK AT CRATER LAKE

THERE WERE no dogs or sleds to be had in Dyea for love of money. Hence, on the following day, Barnes and Brick pulled out of town with twelve hundred pounds of freight and a string of Indians that had promised to see them over Chilkoot. As they trudged past the many groups preparing to start also, Barnes saw Hillyer standing some distance off, in company with another man, and regarding him intently. He slowed down a trifle, and Brick, who was bent way over under his one-hundred-pound pack, bumped into him.

"Darn it, Jeff, don't stop sudden like that," he complained.

"Sorry, Brick, old brick. Just caught Hillyer looking at me, and he doesn't seem pleasant. Know the bird with him?"

Brick craned his neck with an effort, grunted and discolored the snow with a stream of tobacco juice.

"Sure. They call him 'Duke' Wandel. Owns a saloon in Dawson an' makes money. A big-timer, smooth as glass an' hard as ir'n."

Barnes murmured, "H'm," and moved on, wondered vaguely what Hillyer and Duke Wandel had in common.

But soon the task at hand made him give it all his attention. He began to know what real work meant as he toiled along under his mountainous pack, with every muscle in his lean, strong body taxed to its utmost. Directly ahead of him he saw the legs of one of his Indians moving rhythmically, the calves straining, the feet scarce leaving the ground.

He felt the jab of the Arctic cold probing his skin, coursing into his lungs, numbing his nose. He felt the frost forming around his mouth where his breath fell back to freeze. He was on the long, hard trail to Dawson, along with thousands of other men, and he was out to make a fortune.

He knew he had no soft snap ahead of him. He knew that days and weeks of toil, of snow and ice and low temperatures, lay ahead. Yet he believed that he could overcome every grim obstacle the Northland had to offer. He had stood up against other hard lands. He would stand up against this.

The days that followed tested his mettle. At first his halts were frequent, for although his muscles were in good trim they had to be tuned to this particular kind of work. Once or twice the Indians evidenced a desire to desert them and return, but Barnes bribed them with more money and kept them on.

On the way up Chilkoot he thought his back would break or his head would snap from his shoulders. Although a raw wind whooped down from the icy heights, he sweat under his burden. Yet he saw Brick sweating and straining, too, and he saw many others collapse on the awful grind, and this heartened him.

At the top of the pass, a thousand feet above timberline, the Indians dropped their packs, were paid off, and returned. From then on the two partners were forced, like many others, to move their freight forward in relays.

When they made a twilight camp at Crater Lake not a breath of a breeze stirred, but the air was bitter cold and a mitten removed for too long meant a frozen hand.

"Well, she's some tourist country, ain't she, Jeff?" bantered Brick.

"She's my meat, Brick," replied Barnes.

"Jeff," said Brick, grinning, "you're sure the real goods. For a time in Dyea I was thinkin' kinder you were maybe just a little full o' hot air. But you ain't, damme."

"Maybe I've got just a little more hot air than most men, Brick," retorted Barnes. "I make tall statements sometimes, but

I try my best to keep up to them." He waved a mittened hand toward the North. "I said Dawson was my destination, and I'll get there come hell or high water."

"That's a mighty tall statement, Jeff," said Brick.

"Watch me keep up to it," was the brief rejoiner.

IT WAS a raw, bitter night, with the passionless vault of the Arctic sky coldly aflame with millions of low-hanging stars. The two partners faced each other across their small campfire, hunched in their thick winter robes, smoking after-supper pipes. Here and there in the windless gloom other campfires glowed, with men and packs in black silhouette, and snatches of conversation drifting vaguely about.

Brick was the first to crawl into their small tent, and Barnes, finishing his pipe a little later, followed him. He was tired with the tiredness of lusty health, and dropped off to sleep almost immediately.

Some time later he awoke to find several dim, fur-swathed figures bending over him. He started to heave up, to say something, but a long revolver barrel rapped soundly against his forehead, and he slumped back, gritting his teeth, while his brain spun crazily and his muscles seemed suddenly sapped of even enough strength to raise a finger.

Vaguely he sensed that rough, strong hands were dragging him from the tent. Then he was being held on his feet and half-dragged, half-carried away from the tent. The still cold bit through his clothing and gnawed into his very marrow. But it revived his dazed senses in some measure, and soon he was able to see that he was being taken through a stretch of dwarfed trees. He saw no campfires, no camps.

"Hey, let me go!" he ripped out suddenly, heaving from left to right.

But a pair of powerful hands were gripping his left arm, and another pair no less powerful were gripping his right. The owners of these hands were Indians—big fellows, grim and silent. Another Indian was trudging behind him, and he felt something hard jammed against the small of his back.

Presently his captors stopped in the lee of a spruce grove, still holding him securely. The one who had brought up the rear swung ahead and disappeared. A few moments later he returned with another man. This man was tall and well-built and strode with something of a swagger. His parka hood was drawn close about his face, concealing his features.

"Where's that ring?" he asked in a muffled voice.

"Find it," clipped Barnes.

"Sure."

The man, bending his head so that Barnes could not by any chance catch a fleeting glimpse of his face, began a quick, systematic search. Soon he gave a satisfied grunt, stepped back and thrust the ring into his pocket. Briefly, then, he spoke to the Indians:

"You got your orders. Go to it. Meet us at Linderman." With that he spun on his heel and trudged off.

Barnes felt the Indians' hands tighten on his arms, while the third man got behind him and poked him in the back with a revolver. He was shoved along through a mass of low thickets that clawed at his legs. He had not, it is true, seen the mysterious man's face, but, using snap judgment, he reasoned that man was Duke Wandel, whom he had seen in company with Hillyer as he and Brick were pulling out of Dyea. The man was too big for Hillyer, and, reflected Barnes, his build was mighty like that of the man whom Brick had pointed out as Duke Wandel.

But why so much ado over one solitary ring, and especially a ring that was worth no more than ten dollars?

The Indians were still forcing him along, and the one who brought up the rear was continually reminding Barnes of his presence by jabbing him with the muzzle of the revolver. For a while he had thought that they might be taking him back to his camp, but now he realized that they were not.

There was no sign of the camps. They left the dwarfed trees and plodded across a bald, bleak ridge, then swung down an ice-hummocked ravine. For an hour—and still another hour—they trudged on, winding through clumps of wind-blown willows and dwarf oaks, or across stretches of muskeg where the slush ice crackled under their feet.

Improperly clothed, Barnes was numb all over. Occasionally an involuntary shiver convulsed his body, and his teeth chattered. It was the still, bitter cold that clawed at a man's marrow like talons of ice.

It must have been an hour later when the Indians stopped, conversed briefly in undertones; after which one of them marched off into the cold, pale gloom, while the remaining two still gripped Barnes tightly.

Fifteen minutes passed, and the Indian reappeared, muttered in dialect, and they all continued onward, jerking Barnes along with them. They wound up along a twisted, ice-caked ridge of solid rock. Dimly Barnes could see below into a dark ravine, walled on all sides by sheer walls of rock coated with ice, and he thought they were traveling perilously close to the edge.

It was while he was meditating over this that doom swept down upon him. The Indians, who had been plodding along doggedly, suddenly whirled to life. Barnes was swung around sharply, while the Indian who had been dogging his footsteps, bent down, wrapped arms about Barnes' legs and threw him. The other two hurled him away savagely at the same instant, and a split-second later Barnes was hurtling down the steep wall of the ravine.

Wind rushed by him, ice-particles spun about his face. He skid, bounced, rolled in swift descent, clawing wildly and futilely. On down to the maw of the dark, deep chasm, battered, bruised, buffeted left and right by the cruel, harsh surface. He landed, finally, in a drift of snow, feet first, and sank almost to his chest. He was dazed, choking for breath, his head spinning and his blood pounding dully through his veins.

For a while he relaxed, and then shook himself and gazed about. Presently he began to claw himself free, and when he was able to stand erect he looked up and saw three forms leaning motionless over the rim of the ridge. He shook his fists at them. In a moment they were gone.

After a while he moved about, scanning the sheer, unscalable walls. The pocket was not large, and it took him less than an hour to explore it and to come to the conclusion that he was imprisoned. For a brief moment he wanted to lie down and sleep, but he reasoned that this would bring nothing short of death by freezing.

And it was not time to die yet. Bulldogs do not give in easily. Barnes was a bull-dog of a man and cherished life dearly. Not as a coward cherishes life, but as a man full to brimming with the red-blooded love of life and chance and ambition for greater things. He had made a boast that he would reach Dawson come hell or high water. Was this to be his end—a hopeless prisoner of the North in a blind ravine? He shook a fist at the raw, wild country.

"Not yet, you haven't got me!" he muttered.

And with that he started trudging back and forth, swinging his arms vigorously, determined to stay on his feet and keep moving until the last spark of life was snuffed out. Fate had dealt him a rotten blow, but he was not the man to whimper over spilt milk. So he kept on trudging, back and forth, back and forth, determined to stick it out to whatever end, bitter or otherwise, Fate chose to deal him.

CHAPTER IV

VENGEANCE IS BORN

WHEN BRICK Jordon won back to consciousness he realized that he had been dealt a savage blow on the head. He remembered vaguely dark figures bending over him and then the crushing impact of a revolver butt. Now he stared about a little dazedly, saw that Barnes was missing from the tent, and groped to his feet.

He struggled into his trail togs, took a gun and shuffled out into the starlit gloom. He found a trail leading away from the tent and followed it. After a little while he reasoned that the trail was made by four pairs of feet—one pair Barnes'; the others, he didn't know. But he followed, setting his rocky old jaw a little harder, squinting with grim, vengeful eyes.

The trail led away from the camps and through clumps of thickets and dwarfed trees. He wound after it, bent over to see the tracks, trudging doggedly. Later he dragged to a stop in a small spruce grove and scratched his beard perplexedly.

He saw two diverging trails. One was made by a single pair of feet; the other by the four pairs of footprints he had followed from the camp. He wondered what significance lay in the single pair of tracks. For a while he was undetermined which trail to follow. Finally, however, he chose the one made by the four men, reasoning that whatever might have taken place in the grove, Barnes was still with the three who apparently had made him prisoner.

So he plodded north, while the Aurora flung its pale, fantastic ribbons of cold fire across the night sky and the ragged wilderness. The stars were temporarily dimmed. The wind blew with an edge, sighing plaintively. From far away came the mournful, lost-soul call of a wolf.

On the crest of a ridge studded with wind-blown, ravaged scrub Brick stopped to spell his lungs and to scan the pale, nebulous gloom that lay over the hushed land like a frosted mist. He saw no signs of life, and muttered in his beard.

"I'd sure like t' know what them bums are up to," he mused bitterly. "Poor Jeff, so chock full o' grit an' ambition an' then goin' an' gettin' kidnapped before we reach even Linderman or White Horse. It ain't the crack on the dome I got that makes me sore. It's seein' a real, honest t' goodness he-man like Jeff gettin' such a dirty break. Jumpin' Jerusalem, the country sure is gettin' its quota o' muck these days."

He rasped his throat, spat distastefully, and plodded on. Well, he was Jeff Barnes' partner and so long as there was a trail visible he would follow it to hell and beyond. And if a storm should howl down out of the Polar wastes he would still bang around the country until Jeff was either located or avenged.

Brick did not look at their partnership from a purely commercial standpoint. Such a point of view is reserved for white-collared men who sit at polished desks, dictate to perfumed secretaries, and worry about nothing except the bank account. According to Brick's code, when you took a partner you shared in his failings, his virtues, his battles and his victories. It is a code which rugged, reckless pioneering men have carried as their banner since the beginning of time.

Hence Brick wound his way into the maw of the wilderness seeking his partner. All night he traveled, doggedly, tirelessly, losing the trail for a while and then stumbling about until he found it again.

The Aurora faded and the low, cold stars again glittered in the Arctic vault. The pale, frigid winter moon sailed his course across the desolate, beshrouded wilds and steered for other, gentler worlds that lay back of beyond.

IT WAS near noon of the following day that Brick Jordon looked over the edge of the blind pocket and exclaimed:

"Hell!"

He saw Barnes staggering about in circles, shoulders sagging, legs bent at the knees, chin pressed to chest. He was fascinated, and remained quiet for a long moment. He was fascinated at the spectacle of his young partner tottering, swaying, weaving about with a vast, heroic effort, struggling doggedly to stay on his feet, to stave off the cold, sinister clutch of the Arctic. And suddenly Jordon, hard soul though he was, felt pity and at the same time unbounded admiration for the man. It was that picture of heroic effort, of dauntless spirit and high endeavor, that, so far as Jordon was concerned, welded a friendship more enduring than gold.

"Hey, Jeff!" he called down.

Barnes sloshed to a standstill and looked up through blurred, red-rimmed eyes. He flung up an arm in greeting, and the arm flopped back to his side limply, heavily. He swayed on his spread feet like a great tree in the grip of a storm.

" 'Lo, Brick!" he sent up dully.

"Listen!" shouted Jordon. "I see you're bottled up. Now look here. I'll drop down some wood and matches an' you go make a fire n' kinder thaw out. Meanwhile I'll hoof it off t' the nearest camp an' see if I c'n get some rope t' haul you up. Get me?"

Barnes nodded.

"All right, then," went on Brick. "Now I'll gather some wood."

He left the ridge, and within an hour was back with an armful of dead branches, which he threw down into the pocket along with a bunch of matches wrapped in a bandanna weighted with a chunk of ice.

"I'll get back quick as I c'n," called down Brick. "Then we'll talk things over."

Barnes waved wearily, stumbled to pile the wood in a heap, and in a little while had a fire going. He chuckled grimly, ironically. Now more than ever was he resolved to bludgeon his way through the remorseless North to Dawson. Vengeance was burning deep in his soul—vengeance against the men who had tried to bury him in a tomb of ice.

Indeed, they had played with the wrong man. Barnes was not a man given to easy forgiveness. His life had been too hard for that, his knowledge of men too vast. He was not of the type who, when slapped on one cheek, blissfully turns the other. He always was ready to strike back and strike hard.

He sat by his little fire, warming himself, resting, and vitality steadily pumped through his system again. Brick appeared on the ridge again as the early twilight of the high latitudes was spreading its eagle wings over the vast sweep of desolation.

Brick had a generous coil of heavy rope with him, and he snaked it down into the pocket. Barnes made a loop at his end and wedged it under his arms. Brick shouted:

"Kinder walk up the side as I keep haulin', Jeff. All right now. Let's go."

Brick began pulling, and slowly but surely Barnes was drawn up from the grim pocket that not so long ago had impressed him as a living tomb, terrible in its serene silence. When he reached the ridge he crawled to safety and dropped down, relaxing his aching muscles.

"Well, Brick, old brick," he said, almost jocularly, "I owe you one life."

Brick spat out of the corner of his mouth. His broad, rugged face was grave. "Cripes, Jeff, you got a dirty deal, all right!"

"How'd you come to find me, Brick?"

"Well, mostly by dumb luck—nothin' else. I mind I woke up t' see some Injuns bendin' over us in the camp. Before I could move I got a crack on the poor old bean an' went f'r a trip among a lot o' stars. When I come back t' earth again, which is when I woke up, I see you're gone. Then I started trailin'. An' how about you?"

Briefly Barnes told what had happened, and added: "I'm sure it was Duke Wandel in the clump of trees. He took the ring, walked off, and the Indians brought me here and pitched me over."

"An' now what's on your mind, Jeff?"

Barnes got to his feet slowly, flexing his tired muscles.

"Dawson's still on my mind, Brick— Dawson or bust—and"—he paused, his eyes narrowing, his lips flattening against his teeth—"Dawson and Duke Wandel and that limp-kneed Hillyer."

"Jeff, remember Wandel's a big guy in Dawson—big an' powerful," observed Brick.

"When I get through with him, pardner, he'll be smaller than a louse. If you want to break with me now, all right. I'm not asking you to put your foot in my personal pot of trouble."

Brick's jaw went up, and his hands knotted. "Jeff, we started from Dyea pardners. We're pardners now. I ain't the kind pulls my freight alone when trouble's around the corner. I'm a hunk o' glue, Jeff, old boy, an' I stick like hell."

Barnes grinned and laid his hand on the stocky man's shoulder.

"Brick, you sure are a brick. I'm almighty glad I met you in Dyea. From now on we're two hunks of glue—iron glue, pardner—and we'll stick."

Their hands met, gripped hard. Then Barnes said:

"All right, Brick. Let's get back to camp."

CHAPTER V

DUKE WANDEL OF DAWSON

DAWSON, THE goal of thousands, the bright star by which men steered a trail of hope from the far reaches of the world, was beginning to shiver under the first bites of the probing fangs of winter. Snow had fallen weeks before, and short spells of cold had snapped out over the land, but only now was the real, grim North boring in and starting to stifle the wilderness rivers with ice.

Duke Wandel was in from the south. He had barely escaped the freeze-up, but he was in, satisfied with himself, with his arduous trek, and with other things which he kept to himself. He did not arrive as other men arrived—bearded, haggard, red-eyed, grimy from the toil of the trail. He arrived with the swagger which was part of him, his head up, challenge in his hard, pale eyes, a slow, crooked smile on his lips. He was clean-shaven, and his trail togs showed no signs of wear and tear. He always traveled with two dozen men at his beck and call. Even so he arrived in Dawson.

He left his two companions—Ted and Ruth Hillyer—in a snug cabin within the town limits, and strolled over to his saloon. He strode in through the main entrance chewing on a fresh cigar. For a moment he stood in the doorway, letting in cold drafts of Arctic air, so that the attention of the crowd would be drawn in that direction. Then when the murmur of greeting rose to a din, he chuckled through his smile-twisted lips, kicked the door shut with his heel, and with a self-satisfied, slightly pompous air headed for the bar while the milling men fell back and made way for him.

"Everybody drinks on me—on the Pot of Gold, biggest and best saloon in the Yukon," he boomed as he reached the bar. "Pile up, you sourdoughs and trail-pounders and cheechakos. Rinse your throats with rum, you hard hides!"

He flung his smooth, powerful hand aloft with a grand gesture. It pleased him to make a grand gesture.

Cheers surged from lusty throats to drum and thunder through the vast board structure, and moccasined and booted feet thumped and rasped against the floor as the men stormed the bar. Women in spangled, gaudy dresses squirmed and clawed one another like vicious cats, to get a look at Duke Wandel. Bearded, sweaty men who had been their escorts but a short time back, swore bitterly in undertone, and envied the owner of the Pot of Gold.

One of these women, whom Dawson knew as Dolly Bodine, managed to weave her way to Wandel's side. She was pretty in a hard, glassy way, with a mop of jet, gleaming hair piled high, and a black, tight-fitting dress with a big, artificial gardenia on her right hip.

"Hello, Duke," she greeted, smiling tentatively, while a worried, hopeful light shimmered in her midnight eyes.

"Why, hello there, Dolly, old girl!" replied Wandel, clapping her on the back. "Have a drink."

"Sure." She laughed jerkily. "How—how you been, Duke?"

"Fine. Always fine." He shouted to one of the bar-tenders: "Drink for Dolly, Mike."

She leaned her elbow on the bar, threw sidelong, troubled looks at the big, debonair man, whose blond, slicked-down hair gleamed under the hanging oil-lamps. A vague tracery of pain flickered across her painted features.

Having ordered the drink, Wandel seemed to have forgotten her very existence. Several men on his right were complimenting him, making conversation, roaring with laughter at any slight witticism he flipped from his lips. Liquor slopped in glasses as half-a-dozen bartenders jumped to keep half-a-hundred palates moist and tingling.

Presently Wandel turned to pour himself another drink, and saw the expression of anguish on Dolly's face. He swung his eyes away quickly, however, pretending not to have seen, and sank his drink at one throw. Then he turned his back to the bar, and, still avoiding the woman's gaze, clapped her on the back.

"See you later, old girl," he said and started through the crowd.

She caught at his arm, swallowing hard. "Duke, can't you—let's sit in one of the booths and—well, talk a little?"

"Now, Dolly, run along like a good girl. I'm in from a hard trail and I want to be alone."

She followed him through the crowd, her lips trembling, but released his arm and stopped as he shrugged clear near one of the poker tables and waved to "Silver" Sam Hess. Silver Sam nodded briefly, his lean, dark face emotionless, his black eyes steady.

"Hello, Duke," he droned in a low, flat voice.

He had been watching Dolly and Wandel, and perhaps his thin lips were a little tighter than usual under his black, rapier-like mustache. His eyes shifted swiftly, almost imperceptibly, from Wandel to Dolly, and then dropped to a stack of chips on the table. He sat down quietly, shuffled a pack of cards, and placed them down for the cut. His thin, passionless face was shadowed by the broad brim of his steel-gray Stetson, but his eyes glowed like two living coals.

The three-piece orchestra—piano, violin and banjo—clashed into action. Dancers began to wheel about. Dolly was lost in the crowd, but presently she was seen in the heavy arms of a huge Swede who knew no more about dancing than a grizzly. Her eyes, however, followed the broad, straight back of Duke Wandel as he wound his way toward the rear. Nor were her's the only woman's eyes that followed him. There were exactly a dozen other pairs.

Wandel climbed a short flight of stairs, crossed a balcony that overlooked the broad, crowded hall, and entered a hallway that led to his private rooms in the rear left wing. Moy Pock, the shriveled, charred clinker of a Chinese who saw to his creature comforts and took care of his rooms, clapped his bony hands and chuckled dryly.

"Ah, the Master is come!"

"In a little while," said Wandel, eying his servant stonily, "a man will come to see me. Show him in. He is a—um—friend of mine."

The Chinese bowed, spreading his hands palmwise, and then helped Wandel off with his trail togs.

It was half-an-hour later that young Hillyer showed up. His pale face was drawn, and his eyes were shifty. Wandel was reclining in an easy-chair, wrapped in a snug bath-robe, his slippered feet resting on a foot-stool, a tall glass of liquor on the table at his elbow, Moy Pock hovering near to attend his every desire.

"Sit down," he flung at Hillyer, stifling a yawn. "Bury a drink under your belt, boy. Hell, you look like a bad case of nerves." Subtle mockery clung to his words.

Hillyer flopped down, poured himself a stiff shot of rum and choked as he sent it coursing it down his throat.

"I—my nerves are jumpy," he agreed. "But—I guess I'll be all right. Ever since that job at Crater Lake—"

"Bah!" scoffed Wandel. "I pulled the trick, didn't I?"

"You're—sure he'll never turn up?"

"Don't see how he can. My three boys dropped him into a blind ravine, way off the trail. If anybody ever finds him—well, he'll be dead by that time, and—the answer? He slipped, fell down there."

"I know—I know—"

"Then cut out your blasted yammering!" Wandel's pale, hard eyes flashed. He leaned forward. "You sure bungled things in Dyea, you young fool! Why didn't you let this guy Barnes give the ring to Ruth in the first place?"

"How could I? He might have passed a remark about its real value, and Ruth doesn't know anything about the rings. You know I had them shipped on to Dyea ahead of me."

"Well, anyway, you shouldn't have gambled with that hunk of glass in the first place. I thought you had more brains. Personally, the outfit of fake jewelry means nothing to me. I passed the hint to you in my letter that a little lump could be made up here by a man who was keen enough to set up a little store and sell fake jewels to these boneheads who don't know a diamond from a hunk of ice.

"I knew you were only a jeweler's clerk, and the idea'd hit you. With that outfit you've got you can clean up damn near forty thousand dollars. I'm your backer—apparently. I'll put you up in the little store down the street. My price to you, as we've made plain before, is that you do everything in your power to make Ruth like me—and accept me."

"Yes—yes, you wrote all about that in the letter," nodded Hillyer nervously. "But you know why Ruth came. She call's it for humanity's sake. About the hospital you said you were fixing up, and wanted a good nurse to take charge of it."

"It's near the end of the town," replied Wandel. "Used to be a saloon, but I bought the guy out. She'll have full swing there. She never cared much for me back in Denver. But I've always wanted her, boy, and I'll get her eventually."

"When she sees all you're doing to help humanity, she'll change gradually," mused Hillyer.

"Yes, but she's not shown it much on the way in from Dyea. Now you get busy, boy, and see that she treats me right."

"I—I'll try my hardest," mumbled Hillyer, shifty-eyed.

"You'd better," said Wandel.

He held Hillyer in the hollow of his hand, and he knew it, serene in his knowledge. His passion for Ruth Hillyer dated back five years when he had been in Denver. And when he saw, in Dyea, that Barnes might prove a stumbling-block in his well laid plans, he simply got Barnes out of the way—or so he thought.

He had gone to great expense in getting Hillyer and the fake jewelry to the North country, and in fixing up a sort of hospital, and offering Ruth Hillyer to take charge. Wandel had little or no compassion for suffering humanity, but he made this move to impress Ruth, to stir her adventurous spirit and get her North. He knew she loved her brother, weakling though Hillyer was, and he reasoned that, if things did not develop as he had planned, he could, by bending her brother, also bend Ruth.

He was saying, "Well, Ted, you'd better run along. I've some thinking to do. Begin tomorrow getting that store ready, and Ruth can start fixing the little hospital as she sees fit. And, remember, boy, your debt to me—remember!" His voice carried an edge.

"I—I'll try," gulped young Hillyer, and left, nervous and troubled.

A little later Moy Pock wafted in. "Miss Dolly—" he announced.

Wandel frowned impatiently. "Tell her I'm busy," he snapped. "Can't see her."

CHAPTER VI

THE COMING OF BARNES

TWO WEEKS passed. Dawson crouched under the hard lash of the full-grown winter. The spirit thermometer bowled down to fifty below. A blizzard, born on the Polar rim, grew to Gargantuan proportions and drove its devastating legions across the hard-bitten land. In its wake it left death and starvation and shattered hopes. Men were buried alive in tombs of virgin snow, side by side with the animals of the wilds, on lonely, half-mythical trails and in vast, unmapped valleys.

But Dawson honkatonks bleated and blared with the unrestrained, glamorous merrymaking of a frontier camp. Sunken-eyed men plugged in from their diggings and poured dust and nuggets over the rum soaked bars, and into the clutching, powdered hands of dance-hall women. The roulette wheels whirred a direful tune, and poker chips rattled a death-knell for more than one reckless, devil-may-care fool drunk with the weight of gold.

Jeff Barnes and Brick Jordon plugged into Dawson at the fag-end of the blizzard. Most of the way from Linderman they had been forced to move their dunnage forward in back-breaking relays. Toward the end they had hired packers to freight their stuff into Dawson, and when they made their camp among the flock of other camps surrounding the town, their joint finances were down to seven hundred dollars They had been caught in the freeze-up, but Barnes had insisted on pushing through to Dawson if it was the last thing he accomplished, and Brick had fallen into the habit of taking his word as law.

They stacked their dunnage in big mounds and set up their tent. They gathered a stack of firewood and made a fire in the sheet-iron stove within their tent. Night had closed down upon them, and they cooked a meal. They were dog-tired, and following their after-supper pipes, they turned in instead of making the rounds of the town's saloons.

"Well, Jeff, we're here," said Brick, yawning.

"Right," replied Barnes. "The beginning of the end, Brick."

"Better go easy, Jeff."

"Watch me!" chuckled Barnes, grimly.

Barnes did not start off for the center of Dawson until near noon of the following day. He spent the morning with clipper and razor and changed into fresh clothing. He had lost a little weight on the gruelling mush from Dyea, but he felt fine and looked as brown and as straight and as capable as ever.

He walked down Dawson's main street alone, and here and there men turned to gaze after him, and some remarked, "Ain't that the guy scared the tin-horn gamekeeper in Dyea?"

"Yeah… Barnes, I think."

"Now there's somethin' about that feller I like…."

Barnes continued on his way, puffing his blackened briar pipe, elbowing his way among the bearded, grimy men that were in endless motion. And again he was impressed by that air of unrest which had pervaded Dyea and which was more pronounced in Dawson; that vast surge and sweep of humanity, of men on the prod, going and coming, of great things soon to happen. No other country had impressed him so much.

A sign hanging from a small, roughboard shack drew his attention and he slowed down. On the sign was a legend:

THE DAWSON JEWELER

The sign was new, and as he stood under it he saw groups of men bang out, chuckling and clapping one another on the back. He heard snatches of conversation:

"… got a swell ring f'r Mazie, Bill—real diamond."

"Me, I got two f'r Ruby an' two f'r meself. I ain't no cheap skate, I ain't."

After a few moments of indecision, Barnes pushed open the door and entered the shop. Two miners brushed out past him and he saw that no others were present. Behind a short counter was young Hillyer, bent over and figuring on a pad of paper.

Barnes leaned back against the door and shot home the bolt with a sharp bang that was intended to draw Hillyer's attention. It did.

"Greetings," said Barnes simply.

Hillyer straightened, and every bit of color drained from his face. His eyes grew wide with awe and fear, and he clapped a hand across his mouth to stifle an involuntary cry.

Barnes crossed slowly to the counter and stood spread-legged with his hands thrust deep into the pockets of his fur coat. His keen blue eyes cut into Hillyer like points of steel, and the muscle lumps at either corner of his wide, firm mouth were hard as rocks.

"I want to buy a ring," came Barnes' steady, metallic voice. "A good one, Hillyer—say, about two hundred dollars."

There was a glass case on the counter, filled with rings and pendants and bracelets.

"Show me your prize collection," pursued Barnes ominously.

Hillyer trembled like a leaf in the wind. His lips fluttered against clenched teeth, and beads of perspiration stood out on his pale forehead. With palsied hands he reached into the case and set a tray of sparkling rings on the counter.

"Give me your glass," demanded Barnes.

"I—I haven't got one."

"Haven't you?" Barnes' hand came out of his pocket. In the hand was a revolver.

Hillyer fumbled on a shelf back of the counter and passed across a small eye glass. Quickly Barnes examined a few rings, then flipped the glass back to Hillyer and chuckled bitterly.

"So that's your game, eh?" he rapped out. "Fooling the public. In short, robbing these poor boobs who don't know what to do with their gold."

Customers were pounding at the door, demanding to be let in.

"Hillyer," went on Barnes, "when I landed on the beach at Dyea I was a man with a single purpose. I was headed for Dawson and I wanted gold. When I left Crater Lake, I had another purpose. It's this; to square accounts with you and Wandel. And so help me, I'm going to break both of you!" He paused, glancing sidewise at the door. "To begin with, don't you dare sell another piece of jewelry. Lock up and stay locked. Do you get me?"

"Y—yes," choked Hillyer, swaying against the counter.

"Now where does this Duke Wandel hang his hat?"

"He—he owns the Pot of Gold."

Barnes nodded. "Mind, now, you've closed up shop. If I spit what I know, which I'm apt to at any moment, ten to one you'll swing at a rope's end." He turned, walked to the door, unbolted it and strode out through the crowd of men.

A LITTLE farther on he entered the Pot of Gold Saloon, with his hand gripping the gun in his pocket. The place was only half-full, and only one of the roulette tables was in action. His eyes swept the place in a quick, thorough survey, but he saw no sign of Wandel.

He crossed to the bar and ordered a drink. A woman was standing next to him. It was Dolly Bodine, and she looked sad and meditative. Looking at Barnes, her face relaxed and she heaved a sigh.

"Hello, stranger," she gave him, with a half-smile.

"Hello," replied Barnes. "Have a drink."

"Sure thing."

They drank to each other's health and then Barnes turned half around and hooked his foot on the rail, again scanning the big hall.

"Just in?" asked Dolly, trying to make conversation.

"Just in," returned Barnes, seeming inclined otherwise.

Dolly looked him over with something akin to approval. He was, indeed, not bad to look at. Perhaps not as debonair as Wandel, but he possessed that unconscious poise, that lean, clean, springsteel ruggedness, that attracts attention.

"You seem to be looking for someone," she ventured.

"Yes. I thought Duke might be hanging around."

"You want to see Duke?"

"Oh, there's no hurry."

"Well, he's upstairs in his rooms—rear left."

Barnes took his foot from the rail and rubbed his jaw.

"Guess I'll go up and chin with him," he said casually.

He left Dolly, mounted the stairway and walked back to the door leading into Wandel's quarters. He tried the door, eased it open, and strode in. His hand was firm in his right pocket.

Moy Pock appeared phantom-like, rubbing his hands together, bowing, grinning his dry, cracked grin.

"Duke," clipped Barnes.

"Wait," said Moy Pock.

Barnes brushed the Chinese aside and walked on into the next room.

Duke Wandel looked up from a mass of papers and sucked in a sharp breath through teeth that clicked shut.

"Don't budge!" warned Barnes, darting a glance toward his right pocket. "Send out your Chink. Get rid of him."

Wandel's face was expressionless now. The first flash of surprise had disappeared. He leaned back in his chair, knocked the ash from his cigar and said to the Chinese:

"Pock, chase over to Miss Hillyer's and ask her if she'll take dinner with me?"

Moy Pock bowed, glanced at Barnes quizzically, and putting on a heavy coat, went out.

Barnes pulled his revolver from his pocket and held it steady.

"Get up, Wandel," he said crisply. "Walk into the other room and lock the outer door."

Wandel rose promptly and under threat of Barnes' gun crossed into the other room and turned the key in the lock.

"Now put up your hands," ordered Barnes.

Deftly he searched Wandel for weapons, and finding none, told him to back into the other room. Wandel stood at full height, rolling his cigar back and forth between his lips, appearing unperturbed and a little amused.

"Wandel," said Barnes, "you're a cool head, but you're surprised to find me alive. Your three Indians almost did a good job, but they didn't. I'm here to settle. I played my first card a little while ago. I made Hillyer close his shop and quit selling fake diamonds."

Wandel's eyes narrowed and his cigar remained motionless in one corner of his mouth.

"Now," continued Barnes, unbuttoning his coat, "I'm going to start on you. You're going to get the beating of your life. Shed as much as you want."

Wandel put aside his cigar, showing his teeth in a slow, crooked smile, and pulled off the sweater he was wearing. Barnes laid his gun on the mantel and stripped down to his blue woolen shirt. Together they shoved the table from the center of the room.

CHAPTER VII

THE GOLDEN GIRL

IN HEIGHT they were the same—six feet. Wandel, apparently, had the edge in weight. There was plenty of beef in his shoulders, and there was no doubting the fact that he knew how to handle himself. Barnes was leaner, and looked tougher in his leanness, and you somehow sensed that his muscular mechanism ran smoothly, like a wheel on ball-bearings.

He took the offensive, up on his toes. Wandel stood flat-footed, his chin in the air, his long arms stretched for long-range work. He blocked Barnes' first rush deftly and smacked the lean man a glancing blow above the left ear.

Barnes recovered, lowered his head and weaved in to break through Wandel's guard and drive six blows to the stomach, bringing up the attack and finally snapping back Wandel's head with a short, terrific crash under the jaw. Wandel staggered and clinched and for a moment they toiled about the room locked in each other's arms.

Then Wandel, his head clear, broke of his own accord and snapped a shot to Barnes' cheek as he fell out of the clinch. Barnes shook off the effects and waded in with a dazzling array of lefts and rights that drove Wandel up against the wall. When they broke clear Wandel's left eye was swollen and his lips were puffed up and bleeding. A hard, sullen stare was in his eyes.

He lunged at Barnes and they exchanged hard, smashing blows at close quarters. Barnes took a crack on the point of the jaw and went toppling to the floor. He was on his feet in a flash, however, and again they went to it at close quarters, driving blow after blow, breathing hard, laying each other's skin open with hard-knuckled fists that were slippery with blood.

The tempo of the brawl grew with the minutes, until finally they were slamming lefts and rights in furious counter attacks. Wandel went down and came up with one eye completely closed, and his whole face a bruised and swollen mess. Barnes hit the floor twice in a row, and came up again to knock Wandel sprawling.

There was a crowd outside the door, pounding the panels and demanding to know what the trouble was. Neither of the men paid any attention to this. They were in mid-career now, bloody and ragged and doing a world of damage, each to the other, with their flying fists. The table was overturned, chairs were smashed, the room in general was wrecked while one strove to beat the other down.

A sweeping blow landed flush on Barnes' jaw and he went careening over an upturned chair and smashed to the floor on his back. For a moment he lay still, while Wandel reeled about the room half-blinded, groping with his hands, choking for breath.

Barnes rolled over on his stomach, clawed dazedly to his knees, sagged a bit, then heaved to a crouch with a great effort and squinted as Wandel lunged for him. The two big men met with a thundering impact, each driving home a terrific, paralyzing blow. They fell into a clinch and staggered about the floor aimlessly.

Then they broke, fell back, and stood six feet apart, spread-legged, breathing hard, challenge still strong within them. Barnes grinned through all his numb, aching pain, and the muscles at either corner of his mouth hardened. Wandel snarled through clenched teeth and threw his hulk of a body forward. His face was beaten to a pulp, one eye was completely closed, and his feet dragged as he lunged. He had taken brutal punishment, even as he had given it, but the effects were more apparent on his face than on Barnes', though Barnes was by no means a sight pleasing to the eye.

Again they met at close quarters, grunting with the effort as they drove in their blows. Barnes came through with a clean, hard-driven shot that sizzled right through Wandel's high guard and stopped with a jarring impact between his eyes. Wandel's remaining good eye began to swell and color, and when another blow came on the heels of the former that eye was almost closed, and at any rate would be closed before very many minutes.

A new savage fury surged within him, and he bored into Barnes with every ounce of energy he could muster. Barnes, himself dazed, closed his guard and gave ground. He was driven smashing against the wall, and his head smacked soundly against the hard surface. His senses reeled, and he saw Wandel through a haze. He let fly with a terrific right that missed its mark, and Wandel, tottering for a moment, threw his whole weight behind a blow that connected with Barnes' jaw and snapped his head back against the wall with another brain-numbing thud.

Wandel sagged back, groping for his balance. Barnes, unable to see clearly, reeled sidewise and toppled to the floor. He groaned and rolled over. Pain stabbed through his head. Spots danced before his eyes, blinding him. All strength seemed to have deserted him for the time being.

Wandel, dripping blood, steered a crooked course for the door, turned the key and fell back as the crowd surged in. He leaned against the wall, trying to draw his shoulders erect, trying to lift up his chin. He said huskily:

"Drag—that—guy—out."

DOLLY BODINE clawed her way to his side, her eyes wide with horror, her lips quivering.

"Oh, Duke!" she cried. "What—what— Oh, my poor Duke!" She began sobbing hysterically.

Of the men who pushed into the rooms Silver Sam was the first to reach Barnes. Barnes by this time was working to his knees. Silver Sam bent to pick him up, and two sourdoughs jumped to assist him. They got Barnes to his feet and promptly rushed him toward the door. Another sourdough brought along his trail togs.

"Everybody—get—out!" choked Wandel. "Get out!" he repeated in what was almost a panicky voice.

Muttering among themselves, throwing sidelong glances at Wandel's battered face, the men stumbled from his rooms. Then Wandel flung at Dolly:

"Close—that—"

Words failed him, but Dolly understood and ran to close and lock the door. When she turned back it was just in time to see Wandel sinking to the floor and groaning deep in his throat.

Below, in the saloon, Barnes had regained his senses sufficiently to put up an argument with six men who were trying to make him sit down and take a drink.

"Damn you birds, lay off!" he ripped out. "Who said this was over? I tell you—"

"Hold on, Barnes," said Silver Sam in his low, soft voice. "Take it easy. You can just about stand on your feet. We found you on the floor and Duke standing up. It sure looks as if you were licked." There was a vague note of sadness in Silver Sam's voice, as though he wished the outcome had been otherwise.

"Yeah, mister," put in one of Wandel's friends, "you was licked all right. You was down and out. Why don't you take your beatin' like a man? You was down. Why don't you admit you was licked? It takes a man, I reckon, t' admit a thing like that."

Barnes turned on the man, clamping his jaw. For a long moment he just stared, and that man kind of wilted and moved back a few steps.

"Does it?" snapped Barnes. "All right, then, if you look at it that way, I was licked! Drink to Wandel! I'll pay for the drinks, and I'll drink to himself! A toast to the winner—to Duke Wandel. Pour 'em out, barkeep!"

He swerved to the bar, and a tall, gaunt man edged in beside him and tapped him on the shoulder.

"Barnes," he said, "you sure are a gentleman. I like your sand. If this here is defeat in one way, I reckon it's vict'ry in another. I'm drinkin' to you, friend."

"You're not!" clipped Barnes. "The drinks are on me, and we're drinking to Duke Wandel. Some day soon, stranger, you're going to have your way and, if you're still inclined that way then, you can drink to me. This thing between Wandel and me has just begun. Well—drink! To Duke Wandel, owner of the Pot of Gold and the man who beat Jeff Barnes to the floor!"

A moment later he was plunging through the door and out into the street. The gaunt stranger was at his heels, and caught at his arm.

"Barnes, can I take you to your camp?" he ventured. "My name's Sedlock—"

"No thanks. Let go."

Barnes shrugged away and lunged on.

He brought up short then, as he almost bowled over Ruth Hillyer. She looked up with a start, gasped, and then laid a hand on his arm.

"Come with me," she said. "Goodness, if you walk around in the cold with those cuts— Come, I say."

He somehow didn't feel like arguing any more, so he permitted her to steer him down the street and into her cabin, where she placed him in an easychair. She bathed his bruised face with warm water and then applied an antiseptic, and this revived in some measure his senses.

"Listen," he put to her. "Tell me, what the devil are you doing in a wild town like this?"

She was applying adhesive tape to his cuts. For a moment she did not reply. Then:

"I'm in charge of the little hospital here which Mr. Wandel has financed. Mr. Wandel also put my brother Ted in business. They are old friends from Denver days."

Barnes was silent for a while. He felt that this girl was entirely ignorant of the underhand work that was going on between her brother and Wandel.

"Miss Hillyer," he said finally, "do you hold anything against me for that affair in Dyea?"

"Why, no," she replied. "I later heard remarks among the men that it was Ted's fault, and that you merely took the gun away from him. Somebody else kicked him. I ought to apologize."

"Never mind that. But see here. I've a hunch you're going to find Dawson troublesome in the near future. And you're going to hear a lot about me that's unfavorable. I'll leave now. In a short while you'll hear a lot from other folks. You won't understand much of it. My pardner and I are pulling out to stake a claim, but I'm not through with Dawson yet and certain men in it. I'll be back first chance I get and ten to one you'll shoot me a look of scorn when I do. But, listen. If you're ever in a bad way and need a man to see you through, look me up. Well, thanks for patching me up. I'll get along."

"But wait," she interrupted, even while Barnes was buttoning his coat. "This is all mystery. Why don't you explain?—"

"I'm not in the habit," cut in Barnes, "of trying to prejudice neutrals against those whom I consider enemies."

"But—"

"I bid you good-day. Thanks for everything."

He banged out of the cabin and trudged back up Dawson's main street. His face still felt numb. It was lumpy with bruises. A mob of men were gathered in front of the Pot of Gold. Barnes did not pass unnoticed. Some of the men, hiding safely in the crowd, raised their voices and jeered. One remarked:

"Ha! There's the cheechako thought he could trim good old Duke. Ha! Don't it give me a horse laugh!"

Another voice cut in on the speaker: "Tighten your jaw, you long-eared animal!"

There were grumbling and mumblings, but Barnes did not stop to argue. He gritted his teeth and strode on, and a moment later he saw Brick Jordon making a bee-line for him. Brick was grave-faced and a little out of breath.

"Hell, Jeff, where you been?" he rumbled. "I been lookin' high up and low down f'r you."

Barnes explained where he had been, as they headed for their camp. Then Brick said:

"Man alive, you two guys sure must ha' sailed into each other! When I dropped into the saloon lookin' f'r you before, there was a few fellers stickin' up f'r you—Luke Sedlock among 'em. Sedlock says Duke's mug is in awful shape an' bets we don't see him f'r a couple weeks. Duke's sensitive that way. He don't like t' parade around with his mug patched up."

"Well, he can fight," replied Barnes. "He's no slouch. I've got no alibi, Brick. I was lying on the floor when the crowd broke in, and Duke was still standing. Act one is over. When Duke and I clash again dust will fly. But we've come for gold, too, Brick remember. Tomorrow we pull our freight for Forty Mile."

"That's talkin', Jeff!" was Brick's hearty agreement.

CHAPTER VIII

WANDEL SHOWS HIS COLOR

THREE WEEKS later Duke Wandel made his first public appearance since that fateful day. His eyes were still hard and pale. He still walked with a swagger, and still held his chin high. His face was almost healed. After a drink at the bar he crossed to one of the booths and sat down alone, lighting a fresh cigar.

Five minutes later Dolly Bodine joined him. She had nursed him to recovery, watched over him night and day.

"How are you feeling, Duke?" she asked now.

"All right," he grumbled, staring into his empty glass.

Her forehead puckered. "Duke, you—you're not—not like you used to be to me," she faltered.

He shrugged, made an impatient gesture.

"Duke," she went on softly, "I've played square by you. You know that, don't you? I ain't like the rest of the skirts here. I'm always lonesome when you ain't around. I—"

"For Lord's sake, forget it!" he snapped testily. "Cut out your moping!"

He heaved to his feet and left the booth frowning darkly. Directly opposite, Silver Sam, who sat at a card table toying with a stack of chips, tightened his lips and let his dark, fathomless eyes follow the owner of the Pot of Gold to the door. Then he looked across to the booth, saw Dolly with her face buried in her hands. He started to get up, but changed his mind and settled back with a slight shrug and a faint sigh. A strange manner of a man was this Silver Sam.

Duke Wandel walked down the street bundled in his furs. Men nodded and spoke to him, but he gave them no notice. He seemed buried in thought. The Dyea mail was just pulling out, the whips snapping, the dogs straining in their traces. Some men were shouting God-speed to the drivers. They had reason to. Letters were bound out—letters for home, telling of high hopes—letters from the raw, bald top of the world, some written in cramped, stiff style on bits of wrapping paper. Also, there were tragic letters, written by the partners of men who had passed out on the merciless white frontier. There were many of these.

Wandel reached the Hillyers' cabin, knocked and was told to come in. Ruth was just putting on her furs.

"Oh, hello, Mr. Wandel," she greeted amiably. "I see you're up and around. Good!"

Wandel closed the door and leaned against it, eying her speculatively. "You didn't seem to worry much about my condition," he said. "Haven't been around for three days."

"Well, I knew you were perfectly all right," she countered. "I've been pretty busy looking after some babies with the whooping cough, and those two partners who came in last week with pneumonia. And besides, I knew Miss Bodine was taking care of you."

"Listen," he clipped in a tone that made her look up. "I don't care a rap about that woman. I care about you. I want you, Ruth. I want you to marry me."

"Oh, that is absurd," she replied. "You see, I don't care enough for you. And I'm so busy! If you'll pardon me, I'll run along and look after some of my patients."

"Wait!" He blocked the door. "Listen to me. I'm sick and tired of being put off like this, and this 'mister' business gets on my nerves. I started this hospital stuff particularly for you. I supplied your brother with money to come up here, and that money also brought you up here. I'm still paying you—."

"For taking care of your hospital!" she flashed at him.

"Dam' the hospital! I started it so that I'd be near you."

"I thought it was for the sake of humanity!"

He bit his lip. "Well, what if it was? But it was for you too. I put your brother in business too."

"And why," she asked, "did the business suddenly close down? Ted won't tell me. You won't. I noticed, though, that it closed down the day that man named Barnes came in from Dyea. As soon as he turns up again I'll get it straight from him."

"Don't believe him!" warned Wandel. "He's a trouble maker. I'm not through with that bird yet."

"You've already said as much against him as you possibly could. Of course, he's not here to defend himself."

"He skint out to save his hide!" snapped Wandel.

"I don't believe it!"

"You're sticking up for him, eh?"

"No. I'm sticking up for nobody. I'm only playing fair. And another thing. I'm no longer working for you. I'll start a drive for funds to keep the hospital going, buy it from you, and pay you back whatever debts I unknowingly contracted. Now please excuse me. I must see my patients."

Her clear blue eyes met his own levelly and unafraid. In them was the challenge of a courageous woman. Wandel stepped aside in perplexed indecision. Ruth pulled open the door, gave him a last biting look, and went out.

Wandel glared at the closed door, crossed to a chair and sank into it with a low growl. He was still sitting there, nursing bitter thoughts, when young Hillyer rocked in carrying more liquor under his belt than he could manage.

"Heh—hello, Duke," he hiccoughed, and reeled over to another chair.

Wandel's brows bent in a malignant scowl. "Say, you," he grounded out. "Get down to brass tacks. Your sister has turned me down flat. A hell of a lot you tried to put me in right with her, you yellow swine!"

"'S the honest truth, Duke, I talked my—hic—head off—"

"Shut up! Get me straight, boy! She'll marry me or I'll spill to the sourdoughs how you sold 'em glass for diamonds and gold-dipped brass for solid gold."

Hillyer sobered a trifle. "Whuh—what about yourself?" he demanded. "You was in on it."

"Can you prove it? No! Me in on it? Hell, d' you think I'd bother with small change like that? But it looked big to you, a lousy thirty-dollar a week clerk! And a chance to see the world. I did it so you could bring your sister up, same as I started the stinking hospital. You can't prove I was in with you. I can say I backed you thinking the jewels were the real stuff. Who'll take your word against mine? Who? Why, you poor white-livered rat, I'm a big man in the Yukon!"

Hillyer shed his drunkenness like a cloak. His mouth gaped. Fear welled in his wide eyes, and the color flew from his face.

"Duke, you—you wouldn't do that?" he gasped.

"Wouldn't I?" snarled Wandel, showing his teeth. "Try me! I'll spill everything, and turn the mob on you. It doesn't take much to swing a man in this country. Guys have swung for swiping a pork chop. Don't forget it! And talk to your sister. If she doesn't change her fool mind, watch what happens!"

He got to his feet and moved toward the door, pulling on his mittens.

"Don't forget it, kid," was his parting shot.

Hillyer writhed in his chair, wringing his hands.

CHAPTER IX

CODE OF THE WILDS

THE STRIKES on El Dorado and Bonanza creeks were heard 'round the world. Jeff Barnes and Brick Jordon had stood on a wind-swept hill and gazed at El Dorado, down its valley spotted with camps and fires and reechoing with the ring of axes. It was, indeed, a town in itself, restless and surging with energy. Men tore nuggets from its frozen clay, and millionaires were made over night. Bonanza gave its precious yellow dust to calloused hands, to the good and bad alike, for Fate does not recognize values.

The two partners had moved on, day after day, winding their way through the trackless wilderness, hunting doggedly for signs of gold. Stakes were everywhere. Claims had been filed and staked off wherever they went—claims that doubtless would never be worked, yet which could not be violated.

A month after Barnes' fight in Dawson found them camped near Forty Mile, waiting for a blizzard to blow itself out. Their tent stood in the lee of some spruce scrub near a narrow creek, with drifted snow piled high about it. The storm had been in violent action for forty hours, pounding its way across glacial mountains and through valleys of strong woods—ranting, bellowing, striving with a maniacal persistence to annihilate all life that crawled or crouched on the raw, rugged fringe of the universe.

The two partners were lounging in their tent near the warmth of their portable stove. They had acquired a sledge and a team, and their four dogs huddled in the lee of the tent, half buried under the mounds of snow.

"Well, Jeff, here's a month gone, our provisions goin' down, an' nothin' t' show f'r it," said Brick, sucking moodily on his pipe.

"Don't weaken," chuckled Barnes. "We've only started. Luck will come our way some day, and we'll grab it."

"You believe a lot in luck, don't you, Jeff?"

"Brick, old brick, I do. Many a man who's won success will tell you, if he's honest, that he would not be where he is if he hadn't got the breaks. These birds who claim they've won to success by hard plodding and ideals and all that stuff are a lot of noise. You've got to take long chances, recognize luck when you see it, and be the first to grab. Misfortune's good for the system too. It's good to get knocked down and come up again. It toughens you."

"Jeff, I reckon you got a lot o' bum breaks in your time, huh?"

"Yes, sir, Brick," nodded Barnes.

"An' you still got faith in your ideas, huh?"

"Absolutely! It's taken me a long while to form them, and I'm sticking by them. They've been knocked cock-eyed more than once, but they're still whole. I— What's that?" he asked suddenly raising an ear.

Brick looked toward the closed tentflap, listened too. A moment later a mittened hand pulled aside the flap and then a figure swathed in fur and snow shoved in and plunged head-long at Brick's feet.

Barnes heaved up and bent over, frowning concernedly. He grabbed the stranger by the shoulders and with some effort turned him over on his back. The stranger's face was almost hidden in his parka hood, and it was covered with frost. Brick pulled back the hood and icicles crackled in his hands.

"Why, say," exclaimed Barnes softly, "it's young Hillyer!"

"Huh? The guy you—"

"The same," clipped Barnes. "Pull off his duds. He's winded and pretty far gone. What the devil is he doing over this way?"

"Darned if I know," grumbled Brick.

Between them they drew off Hillyer's parka. When Brick tried to remove the mittens, he grimaced and shook his head.

"Here, Jeff, we gotta thaw him some before we take off his mitts. They're froze to his hands…. H'm. We sure got a messy job ahead of us."

Barnes shrugged into his furs and went out to gather some snow. When he came back Brick had removed most of Hillyer's clothes, and the two partners worked hard to stir the blood back into Hillyer's darkened face. His socks, like his gloves, were frozen to the skin, and getting them off was a slow and painstaking task.

He was pretty far gone, and the partners realized it. They made hot tea and poured it between his frosted lips. When he was partly revived he began coughing, and the lines of pain that contorted his face made it plain that the cough was racking his lungs.

"I reckon he's a goner, Jeff," gritted Brick.

"It looks that way, Brick. If we could get him to Forty Mile, there might be a chance."

Brick rubbed his jaw and eyed his partner bluntly. "D' you f'rget, Jeff, he's the guy caused you a lot a trouble?" he asked.

"Not a bit of it," shot back Barnes. "But he can't fight back now, and I'm not going to leave the kid flat. He's yellow and hasn't got the guts he was born with. But I'd get no kick out of leaving him in a lurch like this."

Brick clamped his jaw and nodded understandingly.

Hillyer's eyes flickered open, darted about the tent and finally settled on Barnes. He was in pain and his eyes were dull, yet he recognized the man who had cleaned him out in Dyea and forced him out of business in Dawson.

"Well, Hillyer," said Barnes crisply, "what are you banging around this neck of the country for?"

"I—I'm dying!" whispered Hillyer hoarsely.

"Maybe," nodded Barnes. "Your arms and legs are in bad shape, and I can tell that your lungs are hard hit. We may be able to get you to Forty Mile if the blizzard lets up."

Hillyer coughed, tossing on his blankets. When he subsided he looked at Barnes and ventured:

"You're no—no friend of mine, are you, Barnes?"

"Friend of yours? I should say not!"

"But—but you're a friend of my sister—Ruth—aren't you?"

Barnes bit him with a keen eye. "If you think you're going to get pity by dragging in your sister you're way off, Hillyer. I once told her I'd help her if she ever needed any help, but that doesn't include you."

"Barnes, you're hard!" groaned Hillyer.

"You told me that in Dyea, and I didn't deny it. I don't deny it now."

"But listen," urged Hillyer. "Try to help Ruth. She'll need help. Barnes. Wandel—hell, he's liable to do anything to her. He wants her but she won't have him. He'll get her—if not fair, then foul."

"If she's in danger," cut in Barnes, "why aren't you with her?"

Hillyer writhed in agony, both mental and physical. "I—I couldn't buck Wandel," he choked. "I—ain't got the nerve. I'm weak, Barnes. Wandel's been goading me to get Ruth to marry him. I've tried my hardest, but she won't have him. Now he's threatened to expose me about the fake jewels and turn the mob on me if Ruth doesn't give in to him. I told her about it—she never knew about the crooked deal until then. She's a fighter, Barnes. I knew she wouldn't give in. She made me feel cheap. Then she said the best thing I could do was drop out of sight and hide for a while. Said she'd take care of herself."

"And you let her?" snapped Barnes derisively.

"Y-yes. I—I— Oh-o… He flung an arm across his face.

"Cripes!" muttered Brick Jordon distastefully.

Barnes pursed his lips and smacked fist into palm. There was no pity, no compassion, in the hard stare he bent on Hillyer. He was, indeed, a hard man, and while he could forgive weakness, realizing that he himself was not totally perfect, he was of that stiff-backed company of men who cannot tolerate cowardice.

"What'll we do, Jeff?" came Brick's voice.

"I know what we *ought* to do," rapped out Barnes, almost savagely.

"Yeah, me too," nodded Brick.

"But we can't!" was Barnes' next shot. "We've got to get this bird to Forty Mile and into a warm cabin where somebody can take care of him. He doesn't deserve it, but—well, it kind of goes against the grain to drop him in a drift and leave him there."

"Yeah, I understand, Jeff,"

"All right. You'll take the sled and team and drive him there, Brick, I'll take a light pack and mush for Dawson."

"When the blow's over," put in Brick.

"I'm not going to wait that long," replied Barnes. "I'm starting now. She'll blow over soon. I wanted to make a strike and have something to stand on next time I crossed Wandel. But that's off just now. I'm going to go at him again like I am."

"I'll wait for you in Forty Mile, Jeff."

"Good, Brick!"

"An', Jeff, old boy, go easy."

Barnes chuckled grimly. "Watch me!"

CHAPTER X

STAMPEDE!

IF JEFF Barnes was a hard man, his was the hardness of mettle—of courage. He was not a mild, retiring soul. He gave free voice to his ideas, his likes, his dislikes. At times he was inclined to be loud, but he always drove his points home with conviction, and was never hollow. He lived according to his own peculiar code, and cared not one whit whether you agreed with him or disagreed. He was the type of man you could admire immensely or hate vastly.

He pressed along on broad snowshoes, his parka hood close about his head his pack heaving with the motion of his shoulders. All about him cathedral spruces reared into the white cloud of the billowing, wind-harried snow. It was only a little past midday, yet the wilderness was a world of pale gloom, with the bowl of the sky invisible and remote. The wind was like a thing possessed. It fought frantically with the spruce tops, whistling shrilly. It bore deep down among the sturdy trunks, booming and crashing like thunder, wrestling mightily with the stalwart giants of the forest. It drove before it a stranded wolf, and knocked over a brace of bewildered ptarmigan. It was a mad, hungry, demolishing wind—a brute of the brutish wilds—a killer.

Barnes toiled on, weaving his way through the matted forest, clawing his way across twisted windfalls, fighting grimly for every foot of ground he gained. And presently he came out upon a narrow watercourse, where the wind bowled along at a mad pace and slammed the hard snow against his back and drummed and roared by his ears.

But he trudged on resolutely, following the winding stream, putting the miles behind him slowly but persistently. It was about three in the afternoon that he saw, dimly, the figure of a man looming through the white clouds, head bent against the wind, shoulders sagging under a mountainous pack. He saw, too, that other men were following. Barnes slowed down and the leader, almost bumping into him, shuffled to a stop and braved the drive of the wind and snow to look up.

"Oh, hello there, Barnes!" he greeted.

Barnes squinted and saw it was Sedlock, the man who wanted to drink with him in Dawson after he had fought Duke Wandel.

"Oh, hello," replied Barnes. "Tough going, eh?"

"Yeah—some. S' look here. Where you headin', friend?"

"Dawson."

Sedlock swayed closer, turning his face from the wind.

"Shucks!" he scoffed. "T' hell with Dawson. Listen! There's a creek rotten rich with dust ten miles outa Forty Mile. I got it straight from a feller useter be my pardner. He's on his way to file his claim now. We're wisin' up only them we call friends, an' gettin' a head-start on the rush that's bound t' foller. I'm tellin' you this, Barnes, because I liked the way you went an' stood up against Duke Wandel. About face, friend, an' come with us. It's the real goods, an' before long there'll be a stampede. Come on! Get first choice!"

Barnes was suddenly thoughtful. His chance had come. Luck had walked into him and was inviting him to share a secret and beat the horde of stampeders. He watched the string of fur-swathed, frost-bearded men swing by, bending under their packs. The blood tingled in his veins. He saw himself weighted with virgin gold, his fortune made, his boast that he would beat the Yukon, come true.

And then he thought of a girl alone, a golden-haired, clear-eyed girl who had led him from Front Street to her cabin, bathed and bandaged his bruises and cuts. Her weakling, cowardly brother had said she was in danger. Barnes' muscles tensed. He had promised to help her if ever she were in danger.

"Come on, get started!" urged Sedlock.

Barnes gritted his teeth, looked over the back-trail, watched the men tramp by and disappear, one by one, into the whirling, smothering clouds of snow. Gold! And he had come to get it! Why shouldn't he go and get it, then? Lady Luck had smiled on him by throwing Sedlock across his trail. Gold….

And a golden-haired girl in Dawson—a girl in danger!

He turned to Sedlock. "Sorry, old timer. I've got to get to Dawson," he said.

"Shucks! Let it wait! This is the chance of a lifetime!"

"I know," agreed Barnes. "And thanks for letting me in on the secret. But I've *got* to reach Dawson. S' long. Good luck."

"But, say—"

Barnes waved his hand and rocked off, and a few minutes later was alone with the storm. So luck had come and gone. A bitter, ironical situation. He chuckled in his grim, hard way. He cursed the storm and the country, and a mood of recklessness began to flow through his veins. He quickened his pace. His stubble of beard was coated with ice, and his breath spouted like sheets of pale smoke.

He traveled a few hours into the night, and later found shelter in a tumble-down trapping shack. He built a fire on the frozen floor, boiled tea and chewed on warmed-over bannocks. Fully dressed, he rolled in his blanket and slept till five in the morning.

It was pitch-dark when he took up the trail. He was on it two hours when sleds and dog-teams began to pass him going in the other direction. The men drove their dogs savagely. Then groups of men with packs on their backs hurtled by, stumbling in their haste.

Barnes understood their haste. The new strike was already known, and the hordes were on the stampede. He saw some stumble and crawl along on hands, on knees, while others rushed over them, cursing with impatience. With the first gray color of dawn the wind died and the falling snow thinned out and finally stopped. And still an endless line of shaggy, grimy men moved through the timber and over the naked ridges.

At a little past noon Barnes topped a rise and saw Dawson in the distance. He stopped and leaned against a dwarfed tree, staring at the city of mushroom shacks, rough-board halls and the legion of tents—the mad, rough, raw city in the wilderness. Men with packs still trudged by him, swinging up from the valley with a purposeful tread.

Barnes swore under his breath and plunged down on the last lap to Dawson. He wanted action now. He had thrown his one big chance to the winds, and the vengeance he held for Wandel was now strong within him.

He remembered Ruth Hillyer's cabin and reasoned that he ought to stop there first. When he reached it he rapped soundly on the door. He received no answer, and listened intently. He thought he heard a muffled voice. Impatient, he knocked again.

This time he heard a cry—a woman's cry, half-stifled, he thought. He pulled his revolver and moved across to the window. It was covered with ice and he could not see inside. He heard a dull thump, and a man's voice.

"Well!" he bit off, and suddenly smashed the window with his gun.

Quickly he thrust in his head, with his revolver raised. He saw Ruth Hillyer just break away from Wandel. Her hair was disheveled, her eyes were burning with indignation, and one shoulder of her dress had been ripped away.

"As you are, Wandel!" clipped Barnes, his gun steady.

Wandel was in a crouch, his face flushed, a cold fury in his pale, hard eyes.

Ruth ran to the door and unbolted it. She looked at Wandel and pointed to the door.

"Get out!" she ordered.

"First get rid of your gun," added Barnes. "Quick, mister!"

Wandel drew his revolver and threw it on the table. Then he strode across the room and outside. Barnes left the window and met him as he came out. Wandel's eyes were hard as agate.

"Still butting in my affairs, eh?" he droned, his chin in the air.

"I'll see you later, Wandel," said Barnes crisply. "Pretty soon one of us is going to pull out of Dawson."

"Not me," returned Wandel. "I've got business here."

"You won't have when I get through with you. Drift!"

Wandel squared his shoulders, jammed his hands into his pockets, bit Barnes with a stare of challenge, and walked off.

Barnes turned to see Ruth at the doorway with a shawl covering her shoulders.

"Come in, please," she invited, still a little white-faced.

He entered and heaved off his pack. The girl was rearranging her hair and saying:

"Get off your parka, won't you? You're just in, and I'll make you something to eat. And I must thank you. Oh, that man! I don't know what I'm going to do."

"I'll get a bite down the street," Barnes told her. "I heard you were in trouble and I mushed in to see what I could do."

"You heard? Who—"

"Your brother." Briefly Barnes explained how Hillyer had wandered into their camp and told them everything, and how Brick Jordon had taken him on to Forty Mile.

"And—and you did all this for us, after all the bother we've caused you?"

"For your brother, no. I'll be frank and say I can't bear the lad. But you fixed me up after that row with Wandel and I promised my help if ever the occasion arose."

"I can't blame you for your attitude toward Ted," she said. "He let himself become entangled by Wandel and wasn't strong enough to fight clear. Oh, that Duke Wandel is a monster! Somehow I must get out of Dawson. I can't bear it here any more. He won't agree to sell the little hospital. He just wants to drive me to the wall, make me helpless. It's terrible!"

"Listen," put in Barnes quietly. "The only way you could escape Wandel is by getting out of the North entirely. You can't do that until Spring. I've come to Dawson to square things with him. I've gambled all my life and I'm going to gamble now. If anything should happen to me, beat it to Forty Mile and look up my partner Brick Jordon. Tell him I sent you and he'll see no one harms you."

"Oh, I—I don't know what to say, really."

"Just say you trust me, and let it go at that."

"I do trust you," she hastened. "And do you remember that night in Dyea? Do you remember I said it takes a man—?"

"Yes, I remember," he nodded.

"Well, it does take a man, and you've proved it. I'm mighty proud to shake your hand. Will you let me?"

They shook, and five minutes later Barnes was striding down Front Street to get a room at the hotel.

CHAPTER XI
THE BITTER CONTEST

AFTER SUPPER he shaved and sat for a while in his room counting his money. He was down to three hundred dollars, and it was all the money he had. He sat back and smoked his pipe thoughtfully. It took him five minutes to come to a decision.

Ten minutes later he walked into the Rivoli, bought a brace of cigars and stuck one in his mouth, leaving it unlit. He sank a drink of whisky neat, threw open his furs and crossed to the gambling room and the faro layout. The lookout eyed him with a bored stare.

The dealer was breaking a new deck of cards. He was skinny and pale, and his face looked ghastly under the green eye-shade he wore. But his hands were deft, and he shuffled the cards swiftly and nonchalantly, and slipped them into the box.

Barnes took chips and tried his luck gingerly. He missed on four tries and hit on the fifth. He played rapidly, without hesitation, and after a few more failures began to win steadily. He won so consistently, in fact, that he began to draw interest. Some men remembered him from Dyea. The dealer eyed him speculatively, and the lookout didn't seem so bored.

Someone remarked: "That chum's a gambler; still this is the first time he's done any gamblin' in Dawson. Funny."

Barnes heard the remark but paid no attention. He was absorbed in his game. His winnings piled up steadily, and the bank squirmed. He said nothing, looked at nobody, but stood motionless. Then he sprang a surprise by gathering up his pile and withdrawing.

"You're crazy, stranger," muttered a miner in his ear. "This here is your night."

Barnes chuckled. "You bet it's my night, old timer."

He lit his cigar, buttoned his coat and strode out of the Rivoli, much to the satisfaction of the bank and to the dumb amazement of the men who had watched him win. He walked down the street, nodded to some men who greeted him by name, and swung into the Pot of Gold carrying five thousand dollars.

The big place was packed and murky with tobacco smoke. On the way to the bar he met Dolly Bodine.

"Made a strike yet?" she asked.

"No, but I am tonight"

"How?"

"Just hang around," he gave her; then: "Dry?"

"All right."

She ordered creme de menthe and Barnes took his whisky straight.

"Duke around?" he inquired, offhand.

"What d' you want him for?"

Barnes shrugged.

"Listen, mister," she told him, "you cut picking on Duke. He's a friend of mine. I just know you're here to start another brawl. Lay off him."

"Girlie, I'm not brawling tonight—not a bit of it. I'm out for bigger game."

"What d' you mean?"

"Hang around," he replied shortly, and strolled off.

Dolly mused to herself: "There's something in the wind. Something big's going to happen tonight or I miss my bet."

A LITTLE later Wandel came down from his rooms above. He was freshly shaven and his slicked-down hair gleamed. He wore a blue jacket, a checkered vest and a white silk shirt. The old swagger was still part of him, and his chin stood high. He favored a couple of women with his slow, crooked smile but refused to dance or drink with them. He stood at the foot of the stairway, drawing on a large cigar, running his gaze slowly over the crowd. Then his eyes remained fixed and his teeth closed hard on his cigar.

Barnes was approaching. He elbowed his way through the gathering and in a moment stood facing the owner of the Pot of Gold.

"Well, here you are again," dragged out Wandel, displeased.

"Said I'd see you later," was Barnes' steady reply.

For a moment they regarded each other evenly.

"Well?" drawled Wandel.

Barnes said: "Well, it's this. You've beaten me with your hands once"— He smiled.

Wandel tensed, and his eyes clouded at the memory of that bitter fight in the room.

"And," pursued Barnes, "I've come to beat *you* in another way, if you've got the guts to buck me."

Wandel crossed his arms and rocked on his heels. "Yes? And what's on your mind?"

"Cards," said Barnes. "It's my night."

"Sure of that?"

"Try me."

Wandel unfolded his arms. He bared his teeth in a self-satisfied smirk and threw back his shoulders.

"It's your funeral, guy. Come on," he ground out. "What's your game?"

"Stud or draw."

"Draw's my game, then."

They took a table, got a fresh deck, stacked their chips and cut for the deal. The game began, and little by little watchers drifted over. Nearly everybody knew that these two men were

not friends, and the news that a game between them was under
way spread rapidly, and before very long their table was hemmed
in by a circle of men and women.

For the first few hands the betting was mild, with each
man feeling out the other. But the cards warmed, and the bets
mounted steadily. The first really stiff tilt was a hand dealt by
Barnes, and he lost a thousand dollars on three jacks against
Wandel's three queens. As the game was two-handed, these
were considered mighty high cards.

Five minutes later Barnes raked in two thousand dollars on a
pair of kings, and murmurs of approval rose from the watchful
gathering. He followed this up with a five-hundred dollar pot
which he bluffed on a pair of tens. For a while the honors were
even, each man holding his own.

Then Barnes went off on one of his spectacular streaks, and
more than one of the onlookers remembered the night in Dyea
and spoke about it.

"Them were small stakes, then," was one remark. "If he repeats
the way I seen him in Dyea he'll clean up."

Wandel tightened down to his play, his cigar dead between his
lips, his hard eyes narrowed. His chips dwindled with amazing
rapidity. He broke two pair to try for three of a kind, holding
aces. He missed on the draw, and Barnes came through to smash
him with eights over deuces. He played sharply, he bluffed, he
tried every legitimate ruse he knew, but it seemed that Barnes
was always one jump ahead of him.

At the end of the first hour Barnes was twenty thousand
dollars to the good and tearing along on the wildest streak of
luck he had ever known. A few men in the saloon had drifted
out and spread the news along the street, and newcomers kept
piling in. Other games stopped, and the bar was deserted.

Dolly Bodine stood behind Wandel, her hands knotted, her
body rigid, her face a little pale. Near her stood Silver Sam, his
hat tilted over his eyes, his gaze never leaving the play.

Wandel's face was taking on color. The muscles at either side of his mouth were hard as rocks. He had called for three different decks during the first hour, and now he called for another. But new decks didn't seem to matter. When a man has a winning streak and knows how to play it, you can't stop him with fresh cards.

Barnes lost three hands in a row, but he came back strong and won six straight, and his capital climbed up steadily, while he never had to buy chips. At times the crowd was quiet and tense, watching eagerly as the men bet against each other.

At the end of the second hour Wandel was perspiring and his eyes were glassy. Steadily his wealth was flowing across the table into his opponent's hands. Then Dolly leaned over and whispered:

"Give it up, Duke. You'll be wiped out."

"Mind your damned business!" he snapped.

She was not the only one who sensed his disaster. Silver Sam sensed it and pursed his lips against his even teeth. Possibly every man in the big hall sensed it.

Barnes never let up on him. He made the sky the limit, beat him at every turn, watched him hunch over and gnaw his cigar to shreds. He knew that Wandel was crumpling, and he gave no quarter. Dolly Bodine bit her rouged lips and wrung her hands. Silver Sam was as impassive as ever, and his jet eyes never flickered once.

When, at last, Wandel sat back and wiped the perspiration from his haggard face, the onlookers moved and whispered and watched him like so many hawks. Wandel stared at Barnes with narrowed eyes. He jerked his frayed cigar from his mouth and flung it away.

"Broke, eh?" inquired Barnes, clicking his chips.

Wandel's fists knotted and his mouth hardened. "You think you're game, don't you?" he growled dully. "You think you're sitting high and pretty, eh?"

"I'm not in the humor to carry on small talk, Wandel," replied Barnes simply. "Chips talk right now."

Wandel drew in a slow breath. He leaned forward. "Get this, Barnes," he droned. "See my establishment? Look it over. All right. The Pot of Gold, and everything in it—rum, cigars, employees—everything against your pile."

"Duke!" choked Dolly.

"Shut your trap!" he snarled. Then to Barnes: "Everything, mister, on the turn of a card. A stranger'll shuffle the deck, slap it on the table, and we'll each turn a card—you first. High card wins."

Dolly Bodine clasped her hands together and stifled a sob. A low murmur of awe trickled through the onlookers. Men stared at each other with gaping eyes. Silver Sam closed his eyes for a brief moment, as if weighing something thoughtfully.

Barnes let a bunch of chips dribble through his fingers. He said: "You can't frighten me, Wandel. Your idea is all right by me. Just a suggestion, though. You can take this bet or leave it. I'll stack my pile against the Pot of Gold to the tune that I can beat you senseless. I can pound your head off. You hold the record around here of having beaten me once. I say you can't do it again. Wandel, I'm a better man than you are in any way you care to mention. I can beat you at cards, and I can lick you to a frazzle! My pile here says I can do it!"

There was a chorus of "Ah's" among the gathering. Men rubbed their hands together in gleeful anticipation. None had seen that last brawl. All were eager to see these two big men clear the bar for action and sail into each other.

Wandel colored. He sat back, eyeing Barnes narrowly. He remembered only too well that last struggle. His face still bore scars that would never fade. He thought quickly, and no man knew what scheme was formulating in his brain. He drew himself together and leaned forward.

"Afraid to bank all you've got on the turn of a card?" he sneered.

"Rats!" snapped Barnes. "Not a bit of it. I'm just making it plain that I can knock the daylights out of you. Afraid to bank on the turn of a card? Hell, you're on the wrong track, Wandel. You can't bluff me. The cards, then! Let 'em ride!"

Some men in the crowd seemed disgruntled. They had hoped for a fight, a raw, brutal fight. But Wandel had the right to stick to his choice, and as a fortune now rested on the turn of a card, interest did not by any means lag.

An old sourdough volunteered to shuffle the cards, and the two players leaned back. A fresh deck was broken for the occasion, and more newcomers crowded and shoved to get a look. The cards were well shuffled and then placed in the center of the table, and the sourdough stepped back and flung up a hand.

"Go to it," he drawled.

Barnes chuckled in his grim, hard way, reached out and flipped up the top card. It was a five of clubs, More than one in the audience groaned. Barnes sat back again, his lips firm, his eyes resting steadily on Wandel.

Then Wandel leaned forward and met that stare for a long moment. Try as he would, however, he could not see the slightest hint of fear or anxiety in those keen, unflinching blue eyes. His own gaze wavered, bent to the fateful deck. The hand he put out to turn his victory or defeat, was moist and clammy.

The place was so quiet that a sigh would have been audible. Dolly Bodine was leaning over Wandel's shoulder, her face drained of all color, her body shaking. Her hands opened and closed nervously, and it seemed that she ached to thrust out a hand and close it over Wandel's, to prevent him from turning his card.

But Wandel turned the card.

"Oh… God!" shrieked Dolly.

Silver Sam's dark eyes glittered.

It was the *trey of hearts!*

Barnes never moved. He did not smile. He sat absolutely still and watched Wandel heave up out of his chair, his eyes shut, his mouth twisted in a hard grimace.

"Duke!" Dolly was crying, as she threw her arms about him. "Don't care, Duke! I love you, Duke! It doesn't matter! I—"

He spun on her and flung her away with an oath. "Damn you, get away!" he roared. "Go pick up some greasy sourdough! Whoever said I loved you? Get with the rest of the dancehall skirts, where you belong!"

She shrank back, wilted, her mouth wide with horror and anguish, her hands clapped to her cheeks.

Silver Sam went for his gun, his lips tight, but somebody ripped it from his hands. Then he saw Dolly toppling and jumped to catch her. His face was terribly grim as he lifted her in his arms and carried her out of the mob.

Barnes stood up. "Wandel," he said smoothly, "here's a bet. Since I own the Pot of Gold now, I'll bet it against one of your cigars that I can wipe up the floor with you!"

"Hurray!" shouted an old-timer. "There's odds f'r you!"

Wandel stood swaying on his feet, baffled anger surging in his eyes. He pursed his lips and ground his teeth. With a muttered curse he turned away. Growls rumbled through the mob. Barnes took a solid crack at the table with a doubled fist.

"I *can* trim you, Wandel!" he rapped out. I'll raise the odds. My pile and the saloon against one of your choice cigars!"

"Holy smokes!" exclaimed a sourdough. "The man's gone crazy!"

Wandel turned to face Barnes. "For reasons of my own," he said thickly, "I refuse the bet."

"All right," Barnes laughed scornfully. "Then sign over the place to me while there are plenty of witnesses."

Perspiring, Wandel had the papers drawn up and signed over the building and the business to Barnes. Then he fled to the rooms upstairs to get his belongings.

Barnes was carried to the bar with the surging crowd. There was no getting out of it. The band started, and in short time the Pot of Gold was a-throb with the booming voices of the men who had seen the dramatic spectacle of the rise of Barnes and the fall of Wandel. They were to speak of it in days and months to come, on lonely trails and far waterways, where men are measured by their courage.

CHAPTER XII

THE BRUTE WITHIN

WANDEL MIGHT have passed out of the picture as a martyr to the gods of chance. He might have made his exit with his chin up and his shoulders squared. But he didn't. He was beaten, broken, and the savage animal within him, which for so long had been carefully guarded behind a pose, asserted itself.

When he left the Pot of Gold, he cursed Barnes and every man in the place. He banged out through the doors with a pack which he had gathered together in his former rooms, and went to the kennel where he kept his dogs. He lined up a ten-dog team to a big toboggan, and piled on his light equipage. The Indians that had been his drivers prepared to accompany him, but he cursed them back.

He drove his team through a series of dark, unfrequented lanes, and presently halted behind Ruth Hillyer's cabin. He saw a light in the window, and chuckled harshly in the depths of his throat. In one hand he carried a coil of rope. Cautiously he worked around to the front and rapped on the door.

After a moment he heard Ruth's voice—

"Who is there?"

"Barnes," he replied in a guarded tone.

There was a pause, and the door opened on a crack.

He drove against it with his big shoulders and sent Ruth sprawling backward across the floor. He lunged in, kicked the door shut, and grabbed her around the waist as she tried to scramble up and reach for the rifle hanging on the wall.

"You—you leave me go!" she stormed twisting and squirming.

"Not a bit of it, kid!" he snarled raucously. "You're going to do as I say. I'm boss now, and I'm not playing gentleman, either. I'm through with that—"

"You never were a gentleman!" she bit at him. "You have always played the part, and fooled many people."

"Ho! What if I did!" he snarled. "It's got nothing to do with now. I'm taking you north, sweetheart—"

"Oh... don't!" she shuddered at the name, gritting her teeth.

"Yes, sweetheart," he repeated cackling at her discomfiture. "North, you and me—'way north. Don't like it, eh? Thought you wouldn't. Well, I don't care! I'm making you mine, and mine you're going to be. Got a big team outside and a nice comfortable sled. You'll get a nice joy ride. Ho! D'you get me?—*joy ride!*"

For a moment she did not struggle. She stood rigid in his embrace, her forehead gleaming, her eyes wide, her lips pursed. She was a woman—beautiful and adorable, with all her slim, pure beauty crowned by that wealth of rare golden hair. She was a woman for whom many a man would die fighting—and gladly.

Wandel's eyes gleamed as he gazed down upon her hurt loveliness. His arms tightened about her. She knew that look in his eyes—she knew well what it forebode. She tried a woman's ruse.

"Please—please, let me go. You're mad tonight, Mr. Wandel. Think. You can't win. You'll have every man in Dawson on you. Please. And I still have some sick children to look after. I can help them because I know—"

"To hell with that!" he snapped. "You can't stall me off, my pretty. I don't fall for a line like that. I'm not green when it comes to women. I've made a blamed fool of myself long enough because of you. But that's all over. I want what I want. I want you! You're coming with me, see? You wouldn't have me one way, so you'll have me another!"

"Let—go! I—"

He crushed her in his big arms and smothered her with kisses. She kicked and clawed and bit at his face. He laughed brutishly, even while blood trickled down his cheek. Her eyes were wild with fury, her lips curled in disdain and fierce contempt.

"You—dirty—rat!" she hurled at him. "There'll be somebody to make you pay for this!"

"Who—Barnes? Will he make me pay? Ho! When I get through with you—

"Stop! Stop! Oh, I'll kill you!"

He exerted greater force, setting his jaw. He twisted her arms behind her back till she cried with the pain. He wound the rope about her wrists. She fought on, and he found her difficult to handle.

"Damn you!" he snarled. "You're wasting my time! This will quiet you!" He struck her a blow flush on the jaw and she groaned and went limp.

Quickly, then, he tied her hands and feet and wound a bandanna around her mouth. He took a bearskin robe from a cot and wrapped it about her. Then he blew out the light, gathered her in his arms and slipped outside and around to his waiting team.

He placed her on the toboggan and covered her entirely with blankets, so that no part of her was visible. He cracked his whip, snarled a command to the shaggy lead-dog, and drove off. He had no definite plans. He knew of a lonely valley to the northward where there might be an old trapping shack. He laid a course for that valley, but beyond that his plans were vague.

He drove his dogs at a mad, unreasonable gait. He gave no thought to consequences. His financial downfall had shattered his reason, smashed his poise. Dawson had seen him slide from a debonair, arrogant magnate, to a brutal, savage, hard-losing roughneck.

He lunged on, using his whip again and again. He cleared Dawson and bored his way into the tangled hills. The night sky was aglow with the pale, nebulous fire of the low-hung stars.

There was no wind. The trees stood tall and white and silent, cloaked with snow. The valleys were wrapped in dark shadows.

Wandel traveled all night, while Ruth heaved and tossed on the toboggan so that finally he was forced to lash her down. He cursed and belabored his straining dogs, plowing through drifts, chopping away matted windfalls, setting a pace that would have killed most men.

At an hour past dawn he halted to spell his dogs and snatch a cold meal. It was only then that he removed the gag from Ruth's mouth, and forced kisses against her lips. She was helpless, bound hand and foot, and almost fainted with disgust at his brutish coarse attacks.

"Oh-o, you vile hound!" she screamed. "You cur—you—you—"

"Go ahead, babe!" he laughed. "Call me what you please. It won't do any good. I've got you and we're going North to a nice quiet valley. Ho! Ho!"

"I always feared you were this kind," she told him hotly. "Some inner sense always warned me against you. I was a fool to believe you a gentleman. You are absolutely the vilest piece of humanity in the North—the vilest, I tell you!"

"Nothing like Barnes, eh?"

"Oh!" she shuddered. "Don't mention his name. He's a man. He'll beat the life out of you. God, I wish I could have known him better in Dyea!"

"Ho! It'd do you no good now, kid!"

Soon he was on the prod again, lashing his dogs, weaving through a wild, desolate country. A new wind was working out of the north, with an edge like steel. It froze the breath against Wandel's face. All day he pressed on and at nightfall, staggering with weariness, he made a camp in the lee of a spruce clump.

He made a spare meal, and Ruth ate a little in the name of common sense. She must keep her strength. She felt she would need it. For a while after the supper Wandel sat looking at her and taunting her, laughing at her discomfiture, making coarse jests.

Then he became weary and, seeing that she was securely bound, he rolled in his robes on a bed of balsam and went to sleep. Hours later he was awakened by the sound of Ruth crying:

"Help! Help!"

He sat up with a start. "Shut up, you fool!" he roared.

He looked around and noticed that one of his dogs was standing and sniffing the wind, which was now puffing out of the southeast. He got to his feet, his hand on his revolver. He listened, and faintly he heard the yelp of a dog come down the wind. His jaw hardened and his hand tightened over the butt of his gun. He thought he heard a sound in the thickets to his left and swivelled sharply. Then he heard the distant dog yelp again.

"Damn it!" he growled, and fell into the crouch of the hunted.

"Don't move, Duke," came a low, portentous voice from somewhere in the dark thickets.

Wandel spun around, a startled cry on his lips. A chill convulsed his body and he felt his scalp contract.

"Stay there, Duke," came the voice again. "I've got my gun on you. Drop yours. Drop it, I say, or I'll riddle you!"

Wandel's gun fell to the snow. "Silver Sam!" he bit off breathlessly.

"Yes, Duke, the same. Silver Sam. Dolly committed suicide after the insult you handed her t' other night. You're rotten, Duke. She loved you, she did. She was a good girl until you got hold of her. Me, I always loved her, and I still love the mem'ry of her. Makes no difference if she never loved me. But you're getting yours now, pretty soon. Keep your hands high and move three paces away from that gun. You'll get yours, Duke, you lowdown son of a sidewinder."

For a moment the voice was silent, but presently it continued: "Lady, will you yell for help? It'll kind of give the posse something to steer by."

Ruth shouted at the top of her lungs.

"That's the stuff, lady. Don't move, Duke!"

Wandel writhed on his feet. That slow, low voice was so calm, so quiet, so deadly. It sent shivers up his spine, coming as it did from the darkness of the bush. He ached to reach down and regain his revolver, but he knew Silver Sam, and he knew Silver would not hesitate to shoot.

The yelps of the dogs grew nearer, and then Wandel's own huskies began to raise their voices. Soon the shouts of men could be heard and the crack of whips.

Suddenly the leaders loomed out of the pale gloom. A big, fur-swathed man caught sight of the camp, yelled to the others, and came on in great bounds. In a moment he was upon Wandel, gripping his arms. The man was Jeff Barnes, and his face was deadly with grimness.

"Well, Wandel, there's two dozen men behind me and they're after blood," he bit off.

Neither of them noticed an arm slip out of the nearby thickets, and a hand close over the revolver which Wandel had dropped. In a moment, hand and revolver disappeared.

Then there was a deafening roar and a spurt of livid flame, and Wandel choked, ground his teeth, swayed for a moment and then crumpled to the snow.

Barnes swung back, bringing up his own gun, every muscle tense.

Silver Sam sagged out of the thickets, his revolver smoking.

"It's all right, Barnes," he said in his low voice. "He's played dirty all his life, and posses in these parts are getting so law-abiding of late that Duke would have got off easy. He handed Dolly Bodine a raw deal, and I just paid him back. I trailed him ahead of you fellers. I lost my gun falling with a drift, but I kept trailing him. I laid in that bush telling him I had a gun on him. I bluffed him into believing it, and kept him here till you come. Then I reached out for the gun I'd made him drop. Now I'm satisfied."

While the rest of the posse surged up Barnes crossed to Ruth and bent down.

"Oh, I hoped—I knew you'd come," she cried.

"I'm glad you did," he replied, cutting away her bonds. "I hired Ole Svensen's crack team, and the other boys fell in. I didn't know until the next morning that you were gone. I'd had a streak of luck and cleaned Wandel out of every cent including his saloon. I didn't want to tell you about it that night because it was late and I thought you'd be sleeping."

"So that was your vengeance against him? Oh, he was terrible! I shiver when I think of it."

"Well, don't think of it. Think of the future. As soon as the dogs have rested we'll head back for Dawson."

CHAPTER XIII

THE REWARD OF THE STRONG

TWO WEEKS later Barnes was drinking at his bar in the Pot of Gold when the door banged open and a short, broad, red-bearded man rocked in.

"Well, hello, Brick!" greeted Barnes.

"Howdy, Jeff," grunted Brick, clumping up the bar. "Boy, lets drink t' our health. Here. Lookit this." He pulled his hand from his pocket and dropped a nugget on the bar.

"Where'd you get it, Brick?"

"On our claim. I filed one for you an' me. After I packed Hillyer into Forty Mile I met Sedlock and he said he'd seen you headin' f'r Dawson but you wouldn't take the tip he give you. So I took the tip, and him and me were the first ones to stake on the creek. I just was to the Gold Commissioner's office."

"Brick, old brick, we sure have beaten the Yukon!" chuckled Barnes. "Come on. The drinks are on the house."

"What you mean—house?"

"Why, say, Brick, don't you know I own this saloon?"

"You what!"

Barnes explained briefly while the drinks were served.

"Sonofagun!" exploded Brick. "An' I had t' miss all them fireworks! You sure got some business here, Jeff."

"But I'm going to sell it, Brick," said Barnes. "It's not my game. I've got loads of money now, and I've got a buyer. The life's too soft, Brick. I want to get out on a claim and toughen up and get the thrill of yanking virgin gold from the earth. In the spring I'm going south, I expect. By the way, how did young Hillyer make out?"

"Still in Forty Mile, pullin' around." Brick raised his glass. "Here's t' you, Jeff."

"Thanks, pardner."

They downed their drinks and then Barnes said:

"Don't forget that anything here is yours as well as mine until the buyer takes it over. We're still pardners, Brick, and split two ways in everything. Have a cigar."

"Sure, Jeff. But look here. It's near dinner time. Let's go over t' the rest'rant an' put on the nose-bag."

Barnes chuckled and clapped his partner on the shoulder. "Got a better idea, Brick. You stick with me and you'll get a home-cooked dinner that you'll rave about for months to come."

"I don't get you, Jeff."

"Come on." Barnes linked arms with Brick and steered him out of the Pot of Gold.

And arm in arm they strode down Front Street. Men spoke to Barnes, hailed him heartily. He was the man of the hour in Dawson, and on all trails leading out of Dawson.

"Darn it, Jeff," complained Brick, "you make me feel small."

"Don't forget, Brick, old brick, that you're my pardner," said Barnes warmly.

Soon they reached a small, snug cabin, and Barnes, pushing open the door, waved Brick in and followed. A table was neatly set in the center of the room, and the appetizing odor of cooking food drifted in from another room.

Barnes threw off his mackinaw and Brick followed suit. A moment later Ruth came in from the kitchen, her face radiant, her blue eyes sparkling.

Brick, always uncomfortable in the company of women, shifted from one foot to the other and glanced obliquely at the ceiling. When he saw Barnes cross the room, take hold of Ruth's hands and plant a kiss on her raised lips, he gulped, blushed, and looked for the nearest exit.

Barnes half-turned and grinned.

"Brick," he said, "I want you to meet the wife." Brick's jaw fell. He perspired. He scratched his red beard and struggled for breath. This was too much—too many surprises for one day.

"I said I want you to meet Mrs. Barnes," repeated Barnes, amused.

"Ugh—yeah. Hello—glad t' know you—Mrs. Barnes."

"Why, Brick," she laughed, "Jeff has told me all about you."

That made it easier. And by the time they sat down to dinner Brick had shaken off his shyness and did considerably more talking than anybody else.

When, later, Ruth and Barnes were alone, the lean man said:

"Sweetheart, I'm going to be away for a while on the claims Brick has staked. I'm going to get rid of the saloon. I don't want it. It's not my game. I want to dig for gold, pardner. I came up here for gold. I swore I'd get it. Certain things blocked me and made me travel other trails for a while; but the gold's still to be dug. In the summer we'll strike south, you and I. How about it, eh, pardner?"

Ruth was close to him, her arms up about his neck, her face resting on his chest.

"I'll miss you, Jeff," she told him, "but I'm awfully glad you're getting rid of the saloon and I'm proud to see you going off into the wilds when you could just as well take it easy here in Dawson. I'll wait for you, Jeff. I'll pray for you every night. I know you'll come through. There's no beating you, Jeff. Oh, I'm so proud of you! And—and I'm so happy—so happy, Jeff!"

"I'm glad, pardner," he whispered in her golden hair. "I'm mighty glad you're happy. I'm happy, too. I know a place in California, way back up in the hills, where it's always sunshiny and breezy. There's a ranch I want to buy—for us. And we'll need a kind of foreman about too, you know."

"Brick!" she whispered.

"Good old Brick!" chuckled Barnes.

IT WAS a week later that Barnes sold his saloon to a man from Circle City. Men called Barnes a fool for selling the Pot of Gold. Some of the bolder ones tried to dissuade him, pointing out what a fortune could be made over its bar and gaming tables. But Barnes was deaf to all this well-meant counsel. He had ideas of his own and the courage to stick by them.

On the next day a crowd saw him mushing out of Dawson behind a ten-dog team of hard-pulling malemutes. Brick Jordon paced him. The sled was heavily-laden, and the runners sang over the hard-packed snow. Barnes had his capote hood thrown back, and the tassel of his dark red toque bobbed jauntily as he trotted near the gee-pole. He smiled and waved to those who shouted lusty fare-ye-wells.

"Holy smokes!" exclaimed one sourdough to his partner. "C'n you figure a critter like that? I mean he's flushed with coin and yet he goes an' bangs off t' work a claim. Holy smokes!"

"Henry," returned the other heavily, "they is men—an' men. Most critters as flushed as him would, I reckon, squat in Dawson an' lead a soft life till the break-up. I know danged well you would. Me too. Henry, it takes a man t' do whut he's doin'."

Ruth stood in the doorway of her cabin and watched her husband swinging along the trail that led to the maw of the white wilderness. Her face was radiant. She was both happy and sweetly sad. *She* knew he was no fool. She understood. And she was proud of him. In the summer they would go south—to the California hills, where it was always breezy and sunshiny....

She waved her hand, blew a kiss from her fingers, as she saw Barnes turn to fling up an arm just before a bend in the trail hid him from view.

"Dang it, Jeff," complained the redoubtable Brick Jordon as they pushed forward, "even I think you're a big idjit f'r doin' this—f'r pluggin' into the blasted wilds when you don't have t'."

Barnes chuckled and deftly snapped his thirty-foot caribou-gut whip in the crisp Arctic air. He said:

"So do I, Brick, old brick. So do I."

IT TAKES A MAN

We asked Fred Nebel what was percolating in his brain when
he wrote his complete novel in this issue and Fred says:

In "It Takes a Man," I merely gave Jeff Barnes a code, a
purpose, and a philosophy of life. I just let him roll, and he
worked out the story for me. As a character he interested me
more than the plot, but with him crashing his way through the
Yukon cold, a plot was inevitable. When you start a man of his
type on a big adventure, big things are bound to happen. Above
all I tried to make him human, and gave him his faults and his
virtues.

Vengeance, of course, grew to be the keynote, and while it
burned strong within him, it never dimmed the purposeful
spark that sent him Yukonwards for gold. Somewhere we've
heard of vengeance being for the Lord alone. This may be all
well and good in milder climates, where the gigantic struggle
for life and fortune are tempered by the balm of an existence
far from elemental. But in raw lands—in any raw, rugged
land—the ghosts of cavemen stalk the pilgrim, and Time turns
backwards, and all talk must be man talk.

This may sound ancient in these days of ultramodernism.
But rough men, elemental men, men who could hold a grudge
until doomsday—they are the men that built empires and
tramped a broad road 'round the world.

Frederick L. Nebel.

www.ingramcontent.com/pod-product-compliance
Lightning Source LLC
Chambersburg PA
CBHW020637030726
47498CB00002B/249